PENGUIN BOOKS

THE ADVENTURES OF FELUDA

Satyajit Ray was born on 2 May 1921 in Calcutta. After graduating from Presidency College, Calcutta, in 1940, he studied art at Rabindranath Tagore's university, Shantiniketan. By 1943, Ray was back in Calcutta and had joined an advertising firm as a visualizer. He also started designing covers and illustrating the books brought out by the Signet Press. A deep interest in film led to his establishing the Calcutta Film Society in 1947. During a six-month trip to Europe, in 1950, Ray became a member of the London Film Club and managed to see ninety-nine films in only four-and-a-half months.

In 1955, after innumerable difficulties had been overcome, Satyajit Ray completed his first film, *Pather Panchali*, with financial assistance from the West Bengal Government. The film was an award-winner at the Cannes Film Festival and established Ray as a director of international stature. Together with *Aparajito* (The Unvanquished, 1956) and *Apur Sansar* (The World of Apu, 1959), it forms the Apu trilogy — perhaps Ray's finest work to date. Ray's other films include *Jalsaghar* (The Music Room, 1958), *Charulata* (1964), *Aranyer Din Ratri*(Days and Nights in the Forest, 1970) *Shatranj Ke Khilari* (The Chess Players, 1977) and *Ghare Baire* (The Home and the World, 1984). Ray has also made several documentaries, including one on Tagore. In 1987, he made the documentary *Sukumar Ray*, to commemorate the birth centenary of his father, perhaps Bengali's most famous writer of nonsense verse and children's books. Satyajit Ray has won numerous awards for his films. The British Federation of Film Societies and the Moscow Film festival Committee have both named him one of the greatest directors of the second half of the twentieth century.

Apart from being a film-maker, Satyajit Ray has also been a writer for the last twenty-five years. In 1961, he revived the children's magazine, *Sandesh*, which his grandfather Upendrakishore Ray had started and to which his father used to contribute frequently. Satyajit Ray has written numerous poems, stories, essays and novels in *Sandesh*, and has also published several novels in Bengali, most of which have become bestsellers.

In 1978, Oxford University awarded him its D.Litt degree.

Satyajit Ray lives in Calcutta. He is married, with one son who is also a film-maker.

*

Chitrita Banerji was born in 1947 and was educated at Presidency College, Calcutta and Harvard University, USA. She has worked for various development agencies as well as a publishing firm in America. She has translated Bengali short stories into English for literary magazines and the BBC. She has also translated the Bengali novel, *Arjun* by Sunil Gangopadhyay, into English for Penguin.

She is presently the Assistant Editor of *Sunday* magazine, Calcutta.

SATYAJIT RAY

THE ADVENTURES
OF FELUDA

**Translated from the Bengali by
Chitrita Banerji**

PENGUIN BOOKS

Penguin Books India (P) Ltd., 210 Chiranjiv Towers, 43 Nehru Place, New Delhi-110019, India
Penguin Books Ltd., 27 Wrights Lane, London W8 5TZ, UK
Penguin Books USA Inc., 375 Hudson Street, New York, N.Y. 10014, USA
Penguin Books Australia Ltd., Ringwood, Victoria, Australia
Penguin Books Canada Ltd., 10 Alcorn Avenue, Suite 300, Toronto, Ontario M4V 3B2, Canada.
Penguin Books (NZ) Ltd., 182-190 Wairau Road, Auckland 10, New Zealand.

The Golden Fortress was first published in Bengali by Ananda Publishers 1971.
The Buccaneer of Bombay was first published in Bengali by Ananda Publishers 1977.
Mystery at Golok Lodge was first published in Bengali by Ananda Publishers 1981.
Trouble in the Graveyard was first published in Bengali by Ananda Publishers 1979.
Copyright © Satyajit Ray, 1971, 1977, 1979, 1981, 1988.
All rights reserved.

All four novellas published together in English as *The Adventures of Feluda* by
Penguin Books India Ltd. 1988.

10 9 8 7 6 5

This translation copyright © Penguin Books India Ltd. 1988.
Made and printed in India by Ananda Offset Private Ltd. Calcutta.
All rights reserved.
Typeset in Baskerville

To Bijaya

Translator's Acknowledgements

Though translation is almost as lonely an endeavour as writing, this book owes a lot to the support extended to me in various ways by several people.

First and foremost, of course, is Satyajit Ray, who gave generously his time and attention. Despite his numerous other commitments, he went through the entire manuscript with exemplary patience, and gave me suggestions that made significant improvements in the text. Being a translator of renown himself, he encouraged me to take liberties with the original Bengali text that a more possessive author might have found difficult.

At home my parents patiently put up with a fractious and moody daughter who constantly worried about deadlines and performance. At work, chief editor, Aveek Sarkar and editor, Vir Sanghvi, were kind enough to make allowances for me, and even to arrange time off for me to complete this project. Gautam Banerjee went out of his way (literally) to do some vital liaison work when I was on leave, helping me reach an ever-receding deadline. Sanjit Dutta helped me enormously by making arrangements for the entire manuscript to be typed. And last but not the least, I wish to thank my editor, David Davidar, for putting up gracefully with all the frustrating delays and uncertainties.

Chitrita Banerji   Calcutta,
                                                    February 1988

Contents

Foreword

I have been an avid reader of crime fiction for a very long time. I read all the Sherlock Holmes stories while still at school. When I revived the children's magazine *Sandesh* which my grandfather launched seventy–five years ago, I started writing stories for it. The first Feluda story — a long-short — appeared in 1965. Felu is the nickname of Prodosh Mitter, private investigator. The story was told in the first person by Felu's Watson — his fourteen-year-old cousin Tapesh. The suffix 'da' (short for 'dada') means an elder brother.

Although the Feluda stories were written for the largely teenaged readers of *Sandesh*, I found they were being read by their parents as well. Soon longer stories followed — novelettes — taking place in a variety of picturesque settings. A third character was introduced early on: Lalmohan Ganguly, writer of cheap, popular thrillers. He serves as a foil to Felu and provides dollops of humour.

When I wrote my first Feluda story, I scarcely imagined he would prove so popular that I would be forced to write a Feluda novel every year. To write a whodunit while keeping in mind a young readership is not an easy task, because the stories have to be kept 'clean'. No illicit love, no crime passionel, and only a modicum of violence. I hope adult readers will bear this in mind when reading these stories.

Satyajit Ray

Calcutta
February 1988

THE GOLDEN FORTRESS

Feluda noisily slammed together the covers of his book. Two hard clicks, produced by the snapping of his fingers, accompanied a cavernous yawn. 'Geometry,' he pronounced.

'Don't tell me you've been reading a book on geometry all this time!' I said.

The book was loosely covered with newspaper — which was why I had not been able to make out the title. All I knew was that it had been borrowed from Uncle Sidhu, who has a passion for buying books, and is most particular about taking care of them. Not too many people are allowed to borrow his precious books, but Feluda is an exception. And every time he brings home one of Uncle Sidhu's books, the first thing he does is to put on a wrapper.

Feluda lit a Charminar and blew two smoke rings before replying. 'Of course not, there's no such thing as a book on geometry. Any book can be a geometry book simply because all of life is geometry. You must have noticed — that smoke ring, when it left my mouth, was a perfect circle. Now think of how the circle pervades the whole universe. Look at you own body. The pupil of your eye is a circle. With the help of this circle you can see the sun, the moon and the stars. In reality, they are spheres rather than circles — each one a solid bubble — i.e., geometry. The planets in the solar system orbit the sun in an elliptic curve — more geometry. When you spit out of the window, as you did just now — though you shouldn't, it's most unhygienic, next time I catch you doing it, I'll box your ears — the spittle descends in a parabolic curve. Again geometry. Have you ever observed a spider's web carefully? Do you know what complex geometry is involved in that creation? The formation of a square is the first step in the weaving of the web. Two diagonals are then added to form four triangles. From the intersection of those two diagonals begins the spiral web, which gradually expands to fill the whole of the original square. It's such a fantastic phenomenon that you can wonder about it for ever . . .'

It was a Sunday morning. The two of us were sitting in the ground-floor living room of our house. My father had gone off to visit his childhood friend, Uncle Subimal, for their regular Sunday rap session. Feluda was sitting on the sofa with his legs propped on the low table in front. I sat on the divan, leaning on the bolster which I had pushed against the wall. In my hands I held a plastic puzzle with three little iron balls. For the last half-an-hour I had been making vain attempts to bring all three balls into the centre of the puzzle. It was sinking into my head — this too was a matter of intricate geometry.

Close by, from the puja enclosure in Nihar and Pintu's house, came the strains of a popular song from some Hindi film. Fine spiral lines on a round music disc. Geometry.

'It is not only things which are visible to the naked eye,' Feluda was carrying on with his lecture. 'Even the workings of the human mind can be understood with the help of geometry. For instance, an ordinary person's mind will follow a straight line. A complicated person's thoughts will zig zag like a snake. And as for a madman, who knows which direction his mind will choose to follow — the most complex kind of geometry.' Thanks to Feluda, I have already had to encounter all kinds of people — straight and zig zag, sane and loony. I began to wonder what geometric pattern would fit Feluda. When I finally asked him, he said 'I suppose you can call me a many-pointed star or luminary.'

'And what about me — am I a satellite of that star?'

'You are a point, something which the dictionary defines as having a position but no magnitude.'

Actually, I quite enjoy thinking of myself as Feluda's satellite. My only regret is that often it is not possible to be a satellite. I had managed to tag along with him during the Gangtok imbroglio simply because school was closed then. But I had been left out of both the cases that followed — the murder in Dhalbhoomgarh, and the fake will in Patna. Right now we were enjoying our puja holidays. And I had been thinking for the last few days what fun it would be if some problem turned up. But that my wistful thinking would suddenly take solid shape was entirely unexpected. Feluda of course says that often a thing will happen if you want it intensely enough. Whether that is so or not, I am only too happy to take the credit for having willed the events of this particular day.

The loudspeaker in Pintu's house had just started blaring out a second popular Hindi song, Feluda had just tapped ash into the ash-tray and picked up the *Hindusthan Standard*, and I had just begun to think of going out — when the knocker on the front door was rattled loudly. My father was not supposed to get back before mid-day. So it had to be an outsider. I opened the door to find a mild-mannered gentleman wearing a blue shirt over this *dhoti.*

'Does someone called Prodosh Mitter live here?'

The gentleman almost had to shout, to make himself heard above the din of the loudspeaker.

Feluda left the sofa and came forward on hearing his name.

'Where are you coming from?'

'All the way from Shyambazar.'

'Come in.'

The gentleman entered.

'Please, have a seat. I am Prodosh Mitter.'

'Oh! You are so young that I . . .'

The gentleman looked rather sheepish as he sat down on the chair next to the sofa. But his smile vanished almost immediately.

'What is it?' asked Feluda.

Our visitor cleared his throat. 'I've heard so much about you from Mr. Kailash Choudhury. He, er, happens to be a client of mine. My name is Sudhir Dhar. I have a bookstore on College Street — Dhar & Co. — you may have seen it.'

Feluda nodded briefly. Then he spoke to me. 'Topshe, please close the window.'

Shutting the street-side window lessened the volume of the song, and our visitor started speaking in a more normal voice.

'About a week back, the newspapers carried an item about my son. Did you . . .?'

'Can you tell me what exactly it said?'

'It was about a boy who could recall his past life.'

'Oh yes, a boy called Mukul, right?'

'Yes.'

'So the news was correct?'

'Well, you see, the kinds of things he's been saying makes us think . . .'

I knew all about this recalling of past lives. There really were people like that — suddenly they would start remembering their past existence. Of course, even Feluda says he does not know for sure whether there is such a thing as a past life or reincarnation.

Feluda opened his packet of Charminar and held it out towards our visitor. But the gentleman shook his head with a slight smile, thus informing us that he was a non-smoker. Then he started talking.

'Perhaps you will remember — my son who is only eight, has been describing a place he is supposed to have visited. And yet, it is such a place that not even our ancestors have set foot there, not to speak of the boy. We are very ordinary people, I'm sure you can see that. I have to look after my bookstore, but the market these days . . .'

'Doesn't your son talk about some fort?' Feluda almost deliberately interrupted the gentleman.

'Yes, indeed. He calls it the Golden Fortress. A cannon stands on the roof of the fortress and the boy says he's seen a battle being fought and people dying. He says he used to wear a turban on his head, and ride over the sands on the back of a camel. He often talks about sand. About elephants and horses and other things. Yes, he also talks a lot about peacocks. He has a mark near his elbow — it's been there since he was born. We used to think of it as a birthmark. But he says that a peacock once bit him — and apparently that's the mark from the bite.'

'Does he say clearly where exactly he used to live?'

'No — but the Golden Fortress was visible from his home. Sometimes he sits and scribbles on paper with a pencil. And he says — look, this is my house. Mind you, it does look like a house.'

'Couldn't he have seen the picture of such a house in some book? After all, you do have a book store.'

'Yes, that's quite possible. But other boys look at picture books too. Does that mean they have to babble like this during their waking hours? You haven't yet met my son, mister. Otherwise you'd see, his whole being seems to be somewhere else. His own home, his brothers and sisters, his parents and relatives — he seems to identify with none of them. The boy hardly ever looks at us when he speaks.'

'How long has he been like this?' asked Feluda.

'Well, almost a couple of months now. You know something, it all started with those drawings. It had been raining heavily that day. I'd just got home from the shop — and he was showing me his drawings. At first I didn't take any notice of them. One does so many crazy things during childhood! He would go on and on, and I wouldn't even listen to him. It was my wife who first noticed something odd. For the next few days I listened to him, and observed him carefully. Then I thought of another one of my customers — have you heard of him — Dr. Hemanga Hajra . . .'

'Yes, yes. The parapsychologist. Of course, I've heard of him. In fact, the newspaper said he's supposed to take your son on some trip.'

'No longer supposed to. They've gone already. He visited us three times. Then he said — this sounds like Rajasthan. Quite likely — I said. Finally he declared — your son is the kind of person who remembers his past life, I've done a lot of research on people like that. I'll take your son to Rajasthan. If we can turn up at the right place, I'm sure your son will remember many more things. And that will be of great help to me. I'll pay for all his expenses, and I'll look after him most carefully — you don't have to worry about a thing.'

'And then?' Feluda's voice and the manner in which he sat forward showed me clearly that he was beginning to feel quite interested. 'Then — by then he took Mukul with him and left.'

'Didn't the boy object?'

Our visitor gave a sad smile. 'What do you think? As soon as he heard the words, Golden Fortress, he was ready to leave! You haven't yet met my son. He's not quite like other boys. In fact, not at all like them. He would wake up at three o'clock in the morning and start humming some tune. Not any popular film tune, mind you — definitely a folk song. But I know for sure it didn't come from any village in Bengal. I myself have an interest in music — I play the harmonium a little — so you see . . .'

The gentleman had been talking for quite some time. But he still had not told us why he had come to Feluda, why he needed the services of a criminal investigator. But suddenly, one question from Feluda lent a different colour to the whole story.

'Your son has also been talking about some hidden treasure, hasn't he?'

Our visitor seemed to collapse suddenly. With a huge sigh, he said, 'Yes, my dear Sir, that's the whole trouble. It was all right to tell me about the treasure. But to disclose it to newspaper reporters has been a disaster.'

'Why a disaster?' asked Feluda. The next moment, he called our servant, Srinath, and asked for some tea.

'You'll see why,' said our visitor. 'Hemanga Babu left yesterday for Rajasthan with my son in the morning by the Toofan Express, and. . .'

'Do you know where in Rajasthan,' broke in Feluda.

'I think he mentioned Jodhpur ', replied Sudhir Babu. 'He said, since the boy has been talking about sand, we'll start with the north-west. Anyway — the main problem is that last evening a boy who is Mukul's age was kidnapped from our neighbourhood by some person or persons.'

'You think they mistook him for your son?'

'I have no doubts about that. There's even some resemblance between the two. Shibratan Mukherjee, the solicitor, lives in our neighbourhood. This boy, Nilu, happens to be his grandson. As you may well imagine, everybody in that household gave up the boy for lost. The police were called in — it was one hell of a mess. Now that they've got him back, of course things have calmed down.'

'That was really quick, to return the boy so soon.'

'Yes, early this morning. But what good is that! I feel I'm going crazy. Obviously, the kidnappers realized that they'd got hold of the wrong boy. But this boy has told them that Mukul has gone off to Jodhpur. Now suppose these ruffians go chasing after him to find the hidden treasure — can you imagine . . .'

Feluda was silent, thinking hard. Four wavy lines had appeared on his forehead. My heart was beating fast. Not for any other reason — just the hope that all of this might result in a Rajasthan trip during this puja vacation. Jodhpur, Chitor, Udaipur — all these were only names I had heard or read about in history. And also in Abani Tagore's *Rajkahini* which Uncle Naresh had given me for my birthday.

Srinath brought the tea in and set it out on the table. Feluda extended a cup towards Sudhir Babu. The gentleman spoke with some hesitation this time.

'From what Kailash Babu said about you, it seems you are most — so I was wondering — if only you could go to Rajasthan just once! Of course, if you go and find that they are safe, then there's nothing more to be done. But in case you find there's been some trouble — well, you know, I've also heard a lot about your courage. Of course, I am only a man of limited means. I realize it's almost an act of presumption on my part to come to you. But if you do agree to go, then, well, I can manage to pay your return fare.'

Feluda must have sat unmoving for at least one whole minute, while the frown lingered on his forehead.

'I'll let you know my decision by tomorrow,' he said finally. 'You must have a photograph of your son at home? The picture in the newspaper was not very clear.'

Sudhir Babu took a sip of tea from his cup. 'I have a cousin who is a camera buff — he once took a picture of Mukul. My wife has it.'

'Fine.'

Our visitor finished his tea, put down his cup and got up.

'I have a phone in my shop — 34-5116. You'll find me there from ten in the morning.'

'Where's your home?'

'Mechhobazar. Number 7, Mechhobazar Street. It's right on the main road.'

Having seen our visitor out and shut the door, I turned to Feluda.

'You know, there was one word I couldn't understand.'

'Parapsychologist!'

'Yes,' I said.

'Those who study the more obscure aspects of the human mind are called parapsychologists. Take, for instance, telepathy. One person gets to know what is in the mind of another. Or he can influence the thoughts of another person by the sheer power of his will. It sometimes happens that you are sitting in a room, when you suddenly think of an old friend. And right at that moment, that same friend rings you up. Parapsychologists will say this is no coincidence. It's telepathy that is behind all this. There are other things too. For instance, extrasensory perception— ESP for short. Which means, being able to know future events in advance. Or this business about remembering one's past life. All of these constitute the field of parapsychological research.'

'Is this Hemanga Hajra an eminent parapsychologist then?'

'Of the few we do have in our country, he's supposed to be a big name. I think he's travelled abroad, given lectures at various places, has probably even formed some kind of society.'

'Do you believe in such things?'

'What I believe is that it is foolish to believe or disbelieve anything without adequate proof. History is full of examples of how a closed mind can make fools of us. Do you know that at one time people used to think the earth was flat? They also believed that the earth ended at a particular point, beyond which you couldn't go. But when Magellan, the world traveller, started on his travels from one point, went round the whole world and returned to the same point — well, that was when the flat theorists had to think again. People have also believed that the earth is motionless, that the sun, the planets and the stars orbit the earth. At one time there was a group that used to think that the sky was a huge inverted bowl inlaid with stars, like so many jewels! Copernicus proved that it's the sun that is motionless, that the whole solar system including the earth, moves round the sun. But Copernicus had thought of this movement as circular. Kepler came and proved that the movement followed an elliptic curve. After that there was Galileo. . . anyway, what's the use of telling you all this? That underdeveloped puerile brain of yours can't even begin to grasp any of it.'

Feluda may be a great sleuth, but even he could not guess

that it was impossible to ruin my pleasure with little digs like this. For I knew already that we were going to spend the holidays in Rajasthan. And what is more, travelling in a new place would go hand in hand with the unravelling of a mystery. Let's see how good my telepathy is!

Though Feluda had asked for a day to make up his mind, he decided upon the Rajasthan trip within an hour of Sudhir Babu's departure. When he told me, I said, 'I hope I'm going along too?'

'If you can mention five fortress towns in one minute, you have a chance,' said Feluda.

'Jodhpur, Jaipur, Chitor, Bikaner and . . . and . . . the Bundhi Fort!'

Feluda glanced at his wrist watch, jumped up from the sofa, and changed from *panjabi* and pyjamas to shirt and trousers in three–and–a–half minutes flat.

'It's Sunday today,' he said. 'Fairlie Place will be open till two o'clock. I'll run along and make our reservations.'

He had done the job and was back home by one. The first thing he did was to get the phone number from the directory and ring up Dr. Hemanga Hajra's home. When I asked him why on earth he was ringing up a man who was known to be away, Feluda said, 'I needed proof that our Sudhir Babu had been telling the truth.'

'Did you get your proof?'

'Yes.'

He spent the whole afternoon stretched out on the bed with a pillow under his chest, rummaging through five books. Two of them were Pelicans — on parapsychology. He said he had borrowed them from his old college buddy Anutosh Batabyal. Of the other three, one was Todd's book on Rajasthan, another was *A Guide to India, Pakistan, Burma and Ceylon*, and the third was a history of India — though I can't remember the name of the author.

Later in the afternoon, after we had our tea, Feluda said, 'Get ready. We must go and visit Sudhir Babu once.'

I might as well tell you, my father was very pleased when he heard about our Rajasthan expedition. As a child, he himself had visited Rajasthan twice with Grandfather. 'Don't miss Chitor,' he told us. 'The fort at Chitor makes your spine tingle. You can easily make out what brave warriors the Rajputs were simply by looking at their forts.'

We turned up at Number 7, Mechhobazar Street at about six–thirty in the evening. When he heard that Feluda had decided to make the trip, Sudhir Babu's face once again wore that expression of embarrassed gratification.

'I don't know how to express my gratitude,' he said.

'There's no need for gratitude yet, Sudhir Babu,' said Feluda. 'Why don't you just assume that we are going on a pleasure trip and not because of you?'

'Anyway, I hope you'll have some tea?'

'There's very little time. We're leaving tomorrow, and we have to do two things before we start. One — we must have a photograph of your son. And second — if possible, I'd like to meet that boy Nilu — the one who was kidnapped.'

'Normally, that boy wouldn't be home at this time of day,' said Sudhir Babu. 'As it is, the pujas are going on. But his family will probably not let him go out today. Wait a minute, let me first get you the photograph.'

Solicitor Shibratan Mukherjee's house was three houses down from Sudhir Babu's on the same sidewalk. The gentleman was at home. He was sitting in the living room in front of the house and having tea with a gentleman whose face was marked by leucoderma. On being told by Sudhir Babu about our visit, he said, 'My grandson's becoming quite a well–known character, I see, thanks to your son. Please do sit down. Manohar!'

When the servant appeared, Shibratan Babu said 'Bring tea for these gentlemen. And see if Nilu is around. Tell him I want to see him.'

The three of us were sitting in three chairs around a large table. The walls on both sides had ceiling–high book cases stuffed with fat volumes. Feluda says no other profession requires as many books as law does.

I took this opportunity to take a quick look at Mukul's photograph. It had been taken on the roof of his house. The boy was staring straight into the camera, eyebrows drawn together in a frown because of the glare of the sun.

'We too have asked Nilu all sorts of things', said Shibratan Babu. 'At first he wouldn't speak at all. Nervous shock had reduced him to silence. Since the afternoon, he seems to be becoming normal again.'

'Didn't you call the police?' asked Feluda.

'We did, once we discovered his absence. But the boy came back before the police could do anything.'

At this point, the boy Nilu came in with the servant. Sure enough, there was a lot of resemblance between him and the boy in the photograph. It was quite obvious that Nilu had not yet been able to shake off his terror. He stared at us with distrust.

'Have you hurt your arm, Nilu?' Feluda asked suddenly.

Shibratan was about to say something, but Feluda signalled him to keep quiet. Nilu himself answered the question.

'When they pulled me by the arm, it felt like it was burning.'

The mark of a cut above the wrist was clearly visible.

'You said 'they',' said Feluda. 'Does that mean there was more than one person?'

'One man clamped his hand over my eyes and mouth before he picked me up and got into the car. The other was driving. I was scared.'

'I would have been scared too,' said Feluda. 'Much more than you. You are very brave. Well, what were you doing when they grabbed you?'

'I was going off to see the puja figures. Mati's family celebrates the pujas at their house. Mati is in my class at school.'

'But weren't there people on the streets then?'

'There's been some trouble here, day before yesterday', explained Shibratan Babu. 'A couple of explosions. I think the streets were comparatively deserted because of that.'

Feluda nodded and said 'H'm,' before turning to Nilu again.

'Where did they take you?'

'I don't know. They'd blindfolded me. But we drove for a long time.'

'Then?'

'Then they made me sit on a chair. One of them said, "Which

school do you go to?" I told them the name of my school. Then he said, "If you give correct answers to all the questions I ask, we'll drop you off in front of your school. You can make your way home from there, can't you?" I said, 'Yes'. Then I said, 'Hurry up with your questions. If I'm late going home, my mother will shout at me. Then the man said, "Where is the Golden Fortress?" I said, 'I don't know, neither does Mukul. He only talks about it.' Then the two of them spoke in English for a while — "Mistake", they said. Finally they asked me, 'What's your name? I told them that Mukul was my friend, but he'd gone off to Rajasthan. Then they said, "Do you know the name of the place he's visiting?" I said "Jaipur"

'You said Jaipur?' asked Feluda.

'No, no, Jodhpur. Yes, I said Jodhpur.'

Nilu paused. All of us were silent too. The servant had brought in tea and sweets, but no one paid any attention to those.

'Do you remember anything else?' said Feluda.

Nilu thought for a while before answering. 'I think one of them was smoking a cigarette. No, a cheroot.'

'You know what a cheroot smells like?'

'Yes, my uncle smokes them.'

'Where did you sleep that night?' asked Feluda.

'I don't know,' replied Nilu.

'Don't know? What do you mean, you don't know?'

'They said to me — "Drink this milk." And they gave me some milk in a heavy glass. I finished it. After that I fell asleep, still sitting where I was.'

'What happened then? When did you wake up?'

Nilu looked at Shibratan Babu with a rather woebegone expression. 'He woke up only after he had been brought back home,' said Shibratan Babu with a smile. 'They'd left him in front of his school. He was fast asleep then. It was probably very early in the morning. Our newspaper boy happened to see him as he did his morning rounds on his bike. He is the person who came to us with news of Nilu. Then I went out with my son, and brought Nilu home. The doctor said they must have dosed him heavily with some barbiturate.'

Feluda looked rather grim. He picked up his tea cup and just said, 'Scoundrels,' between his teeth. Then he patted Nilu on the back and said, 'Thank you, Nilu Babu. You can go now.'

Once we had taken leave of Shibratan Babu and come out on the street, Sudhir Babu asked Feluda, 'Do you think there's cause for worry?'

'Well, it's obvious that some extremely greedy and desperate men have become much too interested in your son. But it's hard to say whether they'll go all the way to Rajasthan. One thing though — you'd better give me a letter. After all, Dr. Hajra doesn't know me. It will certainly help if you do the introductions.'

After he'd written the letter, Sudhir Babu repeated his offer of paying our fares to Rajasthan. But Feluda would have none of it. Our friend accompanied us to the bus stop and said, 'Please, Sir, do at least let me know once you've reached Rajasthan. I'll be terribly worried. Of course Dr. Hajra has also promised to write. But even if he doesn't, I hope you at least . . .'

When we got home, Feluda sat on the bed and opened up his famous Blue Notebook Vol.VI, before packing his things.

'Tell me some of the important dates, I want to make a note of them' he said. 'When did Dr. Hajra start for Rajasthan with Mukul?'

'Yesterday, 9th October.'

'When was Nilu kidnapped?'

'Also yesterday, in the evening.'

'They returned him this morning, that is, the 10th. We are starting tomorrow, the morning of the 11th. We reach Agra on the 12th. The same afternoon, we take the train and reach Bandikui at night. Our train will leave Bandikui at midnight — we reach Marwar on the afternoon of the 13th. We change trains there and reach Jodhpur the same evening, that is the 13th . . .'

Feluda went on muttering to himself like this for some time and made God knows what calculations. Then he said, 'Geometry. Here also we have geometry. A single point — with several lines converging on that point. Geometry . . .'

It's been half–an–hour since we took the train for Bandikui from Agra fort station. We had three hours in hand at Agra. So we utilized the time by visiting the Taj Mahal once again after ten years. Feluda also took that opportunity to give me a short lecture on the geometry of the Taj.

Oh yes — I should mention one important thing we managed to take care of yesterday before we left Calcutta. The Toofan Express leaves at nine–thirty in the morning. So we had got up very early in the morning. At about six o'clock, once we had had our tea, Feluda said, 'We must pop in and see your Uncle Sidhu once. It will be very helpful if we can get some information out of him.'

Uncle Sidhu lives on Sardar Shankar Road. It takes us five minutes to walk over there from Tara Road. Uncle Sidhu, I should tell you, has gone into numerous business ventures throughout his life — he's made a lot of money and lost a lot too. These days he doesn't do any work. He has a passion for books, so he buys large numbers of them. Some of his time is spent reading. The rest of the time he plays chess all by himself with the help of chess books, and experiments with food. The experiments mostly consist of mixing different foods together and eating them. For instance, he says omelette mixed with yoghurt, tastes heavenly. He is not really related to us in any way. He just happens to come from the same ancestral village (which I've never seen) as we do. His family lived right next door to ours. That's why my father calls him brother, and I call him Uncle.

When we reached his house, we found Uncle Sidhu sitting on a stool right in front of the door, while the barber gave him a haircut. Not that he has any hair, barring a fringe at the back of the head. He moved his stool sideways when he saw us and said, 'Sit down. Yell for Narayan, he will bring you tea.'

The room contained nothing beyond one divan, a couple of chairs, and three huge bookcases. Half the divan was occupied by books. We knew that the empty space on the divan was where Uncle Sidhu liked to sit, so we sat on the two chairs. Feluda had brought the book he had borrowed — still with its improvised cover — and he shoved it into a gap in one of the shelves of a bookcase.

The haircut was still going on when Uncle Sidhu said, 'Felu, I know you are doing a lot of sleuthing. Have you read up on the history of criminal investigation? Whatever work you may specialize in — you'll find that a knowledge of its history always increases both your pleasure and your confidence.'

'Yes, of course,' said Feluda gently.

'Take, for instance, the method of identifying criminals by their fingerprints. Do you know who really discovered it?'

Feluda winked at me and said 'No, I can't exactly remember the name. Though, I must have read it somewhere.'

I realized that Feluda remembered the name perfectly. But he was pretending forgetfulness just to please Uncle Sidhu.

'Huh! Well, if you ask around, many people will promptly mention the name of Alphonse Bertillon. But that's wrong. The correct answer is Juan Vucetich. Remember that. He was an Argentinian. He's the one who first laid stress on the imprint of the thumbs. And he was the first person to have divided that imprint into four categories. Of course, the Englishman Henry developed this system even further several years later.'

Feluda looked at his watch and decided not to waste any more time. 'You must have heard of Dr. Hemanga Hajra? The one who's working in parapsychology?'

'Of course, I have,' said Uncle Sidhu, 'Why, it was just the other day that I saw his name in the papers. What do you want with him? Has he been making trouble? He's not that kind of person though. On the contrary, he's exposed many frauds.'

'Is that so?' Feluda knew he was about to hear an interesting story.

'Don't you know about it? It happened about four years ago. I think a Bengali gentleman in Chicago — though one can hardly call him a gentleman, the worst kind of sleazy character — had opened a spiritual clinic. Right in the heart of Chicago, mind you. Naturally, Americans by the score became his clients. They are a whimsical race, and they have money to burn. The man claimed to be able to cure the most incurable diseases by the use of hypnotism. Exactly what Anton Mesmer did in eighteenth–century Europe. Our Bengali crook also had a few accidental successes, as is often the case with such people. That was when Hajra went to Chicago to deliver some lecture. Having heard about this clinic, he went to see it with his own eyes — and sure enough, he exposed the fraud. It was a huge scandal. In the end, the American Government threw the crook out of the country. Yes, yes, I remember now — the man used to call himself Bhabananda. This Hajra, however, is a solid character. At least, so it seems from his writings. Two of his pieces are in my collection. Look inside the bookcase on the left, bottom shelf, right–hand corner. You'll find three journals of the Parapsychological society . . .'

Feluda had borrowed all three journals. Right now, in the train, he was going through them carefully. I was watching the view outside. We had left Uttar Pradesh and entered Rajasthan a short while back.

'The sunlight seems very strong here! No wonder the people are so strong!'

The words came from the bench in front of us. It was a four berth compartment, and there were also four of us passengers. The man who spoke appeared to be a most inoffensive creature. He was quite thin, and in height he must have been at least a couple of inches shorter than myself. I was only fifteen, so I still had hopes of growing. This gentleman was thirty–five at the very least — so he was likely to remain just as he was. Until now, I had no idea that he was a Bengali. An outfit consisting of a half shirt and trousers was hardly any indication. The gentleman looked at Feluda and gave him a little smile.

'I have been listening to you two for quite some time. It's really a great piece of luck, to encounter people of one's own kind so far from home. I had taken it for granted that for one month I would be forced to abandon my mother tongue!'

'How far are you going?' asked Feluda, perhaps more out of

politeness than anything else.

'Let's get to Jodhpur first. I'll decide after that. How about you?'

'We too are thinking of Jodhpur for the moment.'

'Wonderful — splendid! Do you also write by any chance?'

'No,' smiled Feluda. 'I only read. Why, are you a writer?'

'Does the name Jatayu ring a bell?'

Jatayu? The man who writes those thrilling adventures? I've even read a couple of his novels — *The Sahara Shivers* and *The Fearful Foe* — from our school library.

'Are you Jatayu?' Feluda asked.

'Yes, my dear Sir,' the gentleman bared his teeth and bent his neck—'This humble fellow carries the pseudonym of Jatayu. Namaskar.'

'Namaskar. My name is Prodosh Mitter. This is Master Tapeshranjan.'

How could Feluda manage not to laugh? As for me, I felt the laughter bubbling up inside me, right up to my throat, just like the contents of a soda water bottle. This was the great Jatayu! And I used to think, from the stories he wrote, that he'd beat James Bond hollow!

'My real name is Lalmohan Ganguly. But, please, don't ever tell anyone. The pseudonym is like a disguise — once uncovered it loses all charm.'

We had bought some sweets from Agra. Feluda extended the packet towards our new acquaintance and said, 'You seem to have been travelling for quite some time.'

'Well, yes,' said the gentleman as he picked up one of the sweets. Immediately, however, he looked rather flustered. He stared with amazement at Feluda and said, 'How did you know?'

'I can see your real complexion, before you got sunburnt, peeping out from under your watch strap,' replied Feluda with a smile.

'Good God!' said the gentleman with rounded eyes. 'You seem to be frightfully observant! Yes, you're quite right. Delhi, Agra, Fatehpur Sikri — I've managed to see a little off all these places. I've been travelling for about ten days. Previously, I'd just been sitting at home and writing my stories. I live in Bhadreswar. Finally this year, I decided to travel a little. I thought it would help my writing. And adventure stories seem to take off only in places like these. Just take a look outside — what harsh mountains, swelling up like biceps and triceps. Bengal, if I may say so, has no muscle — other than the Himalayas, of course. How can you have a roaring adventure in plain country?'

The three of us went on eating the sweets. I noticed Jatayu casting sidelong looks at Feluda. Finally he said, 'How tall are you? Please don't mind my asking.'

'Nearly six,' answered Feluda.

'Oh, magnificent height. I've made my hero a six–footer too. You must know about him — Prakhar Rudra. A Russian name — Prokhor — but suits a Bengali perfectly, you must admit! To tell you the truth, I am making my hero do everything that I have wanted to do but couldn't. Not that I didn't try myself. Way back, when I was in college, I remember seeing Charles Atlas's advertisement in the papers. There he would be, standing with his chest forward, muscles swelling, hands on his hips. What arms, what a chest — and his waist, exactly like a lion's ! Not an ounce of fat on his whole body. Only rippling muscles from head to foot. The ad said — just follow my system, and you'll have a body like mine within a month! Well, maybe in their country. In Bengal it's impossible! My father had money — I wasted some of it. I sent for the lessons, followed the instructions religiously — but what good was it? I remained the same as ever. My uncle said to me — swing from the curtain rods everyday, and you'll be tall in a month's time. I don't know how many months I spent swinging from the rod, until the day the rod came down, bringing me with it. My knee cap was dislocated from the fall, but I remained the same five three–and –a–half. I had to accept that I simply would not grow any more; no, not even if I was used for a rope during a tug–of–war! Finally, I said to myself–What the hell, I won't think about muscles in my body. Instead, I'll think of the muscles of my brain. And mental height. So I started writing my thrillers. Lalmohan Ganguly seemed a most unsuitable name. That's why I decided to use pseudonym — Jatayu. The fighter. Just think of the fight he gave Ravana!'

Even though our train was supposed to be a fast passenger

train, there were so many stations to be stopped at, that the
train could hardly move for more than fifteen or twenty minutes
at a stretch. Feluda had abandoned parapsychology and had
started on a book about Rajasthan. There were pictures in it of
all the forts of Rajasthan. He was examining them carefully, and
reading up on them with the deepest attention. There was a
fourth gentleman occupying the upper berth facing us. His
moustache and dress were enough to tell us that he was not a
Bengali. He went on devouring one orange after another — the
peel and fibre he collected on an Urdu newspaper spread out
in front of him.

Feluda had started marking his book with a blue pencil he
had taken out from his pocket, when Lalmohan Babu said, 'Please
— don't be offended — but are you, by any chance, some kind
of a sleuth?'

'Why?'

'Well, er, I mean, the way you hit upon the truth about me
was . . .'

'I'm interested in little things like that.'

'Great! You did say you were going to Jodhpur, didn't you?'

'For the moment.'

'Is there a mystery? If there is, then I'm latching on to you
— if you don't mind. Such an opportunity will never come again.'

'I hope you have no objections to riding on a camel's back?'

'Good heavens! Camels!' Our friend's eyes gleamed with excitement. 'The ship of the desert! My dear Sir, it's always been
my dream! I even wrote about the Bedouins in my *Blood–red Rose
of Arabia*. And also in *The Sahara Shivers:*

'Amazing creatures — camels. There they go in a line through the
sea of sand, carrying their own water supply in their stomachs. How
absolutely romantic — Ohh!'

'Did you mention the stomach in one of your novels?' asked Feluda.

'Why, is that a mistake?' said Lalmohan Babu with some discomfiture.

Feluda shook his head. 'The water comes from the camel's hump,'
he said. 'The hump is actually accumulated fat. The camel oxidizes
the fat and makes its own water. It can go without water for ten or fifteen days at a stretch, just on the strength of that fat. Of course, I've

also heard that once they do come across water, they can drink twenty–five gallons in ten minutes.'

'Thank god, you've told me,' said Lalmohan Babu. 'I'll correct the mistake in the next edition.'

Though the trains in these parts seemed determined to move at a snail's pace we were only too thankful that they were not running much behind schedule. That would have been a disaster, since we had to make so many connections.

We saw our first peacocks at Bharatpur station. There were three of them happily stepping over the train tracks opposite the platform. Feluda said, 'You'll see peacocks and parrots all over the place here, just as you see crows and sparrows everywhere in Calcutta.'

As for the people, they seemed to be sporting turbans and sideburns of ever-increasing dimensions! They were all Rajasthanis. They wore short *dhotis* reaching down to the knees, and shirts with buttons on one side. On their feet were heavy *nagra* shoes, and many of them carried sticks.

We were sitting in the refreshment room at Bandikui station eating mutton curry and *chappatis*. Lalmohan Babu said, 'I think its highly probable that there are one or two dacoits among all the people you see here. Did you know — the Araballi mountains are supposed to be a stronghold for dacoits. And surely you don't need me to tell you how powerful these dacoits can be. They have been known to escape from their prison cells by bending the bars of the windows just with their bare hands!'

'I know,' said Feluda. 'And do you know how a bandit punishes somebody who offends him?'

'Bump him off, surely?'

'Oh no. That's the funniest part of it. He hunts him down, no matter where he may be hiding, and then chops off his nose with his sword.'

The piece of meat did not seem to be able to make its way from Lalmohan Babu's hand to his mouth.

'Chop off his nose!'

'That's what I've heard.'

'My dear sir, this sounds something straight out of mythology. How barbarous!'

Though we managed to get on the midnight train to Marwar only after a frantic scramble in the dark, we had no trouble finding seats. We even slept well. On waking up the next morning, we saw an old fort on top of a mountain, through the windows of the moving train. In another minute, the train stopped at Kishangarh station.

'If a place had — garh at the end of its name, then you can safely assume that somewhere in the neighbourhood there is a fortress like this on top of a hill,' said Feluda.

We got off at Kishangarh, and had some tea standing on the platform. I noticed that the clay teacups here were bigger and stronger than the ones we have in Bengal. The tea also tasted different. Feluda said that was because of the camel's milk in the tea. Perhaps that was why Lalmohan Babu drank two cups of tea in succession!

By the time we had had our tea, brushed our teeth and splashed our faces with water from the platform tap, and got back into our compartment — we found a Rajasthani man occupying one end of Lalmohan Babu's bench. He had a huge turban on his head, was wrapped up to his nose in a shawl and sat with his legs raised, his chin resting on one knee. Through the fold of his shawl, I could see the bright red of his shirt.

As soon as Lalmohan Babu laid eyes on this character, he lost no time in moving away from his bench and occupying one corner of ours. 'Why don't you two make yourselves comfortable,' said Feluda and promptly sat down right next to the Rajasthani passenger.

I was sitting and contemplating the man's turban. Just the thought of how many times the cloth had been wound to form the turban, bemused me totally. Suddenly I heard Lalmohan Babu addressing Feluda in whisper.

'Highly suspicious! He's dressed like a real peasant, and yet he is travelling in a first class compartment, Who knows what quantities of diamonds and precious stones are hidden in that bundle of his!'

There actually was a bundle beside the man. Feluda smiled a little, but did not answer.

The train started moving. Feluda took out the guide book on Rajasthan from his bag. I opened Newman's Bradshaw time–table and made out the names of all the stations that would fall on our route. What extraordinary names they had — Galota, Tilonia, Makrera,

Bhesana, Sendra. Who knows where these names came from. Feluda says place names often have a history behind them. But who's to find out what history?

The train was rattling along, I was immersed in day dreams about Shiladitya, Bappaditya and the other kings in *Rajkahani,* when I felt a tug at the corner of my shirt. I turned around to find that all the colour had drained from Lalmohan Babu's face. As our eyes met, he gulped and hissed one word, 'Blood.'

Blood? Was the man crazy?

But his eyes swivelled around immediately towards the Rajasthani in front of us. The man was fast asleep, his head bent back, his mouth open. Then I noticed his feet, as they rested on the bench.

There was an abrasion of the skin beside his big toe, and some dried blood. That was when I realized that what had appeared to be mudstains on his clothes was actually dried, reddish blood.

I looked at Feluda — he was absorbed in his book.

Lalmohan Babu must have found Feluda's unperturbed air quite unbearable. He spoke up abruptly in that anxious, parched voice, 'Mr. Mitter, suspicious blood stains on our new co-passenger.'

Feluda raised his eyes once from his book, inspected the sleeping man and said, 'Probably caused by bugs.'

Such a mundane explanation seemed to depress poor Jatayu infinitely. But it was easy to see that his fears had not been laid to rest, from his shrinking manner, and the way he cast covert frowning looks at the sleeping man.

Our train got into Marwar at two–thirty in the afternoon. We had lunch at the station refreshment room and walked up and down the platform for about an hour. By the time we boarded the three–thirty train for Jodhpur, the suspicious character in a red shirt was nowhere to be seen.

This time, our journey lasted only two–and–a–half hours. But repeated sights of packs of camels roused Lalmohan Babu to heights of excitement. We reached Jodhpur at ten past six. The train was late by twenty minutes. In Calcutta, the sun would have set by now. But since this was further west, there was quite a bit of sunlight left.

We had booked our rooms at the Circuit House. Lalmohan Babu told us that he would be staying at the New Bombay Lodge.

'I'll come over early tomorrow morning,' he said. 'We can visit the fort together.' With that, he made his way to the line of waiting *tongas*.

We took a taxi and left the station. We'd been told that the Circuit House was fairly near. As we drove along, I could catch glimpses of a very high wall through the gaps between the houses. The wall must have been as high as a double — storey building! Feluda said that, at one time, the entire city of Jodhpur had been surrounded by that wall. There are seven gates at seven different points in the wall. Whenever there was news of enemy troops marching to attack, the gates would be closed.

As we took one more turn, Feluda suddenly said, 'Look! There, on your left.'

I looked, and saw a massive, brooding fort visible above the level of houses in the city. I realized that that must be the famous Jodhpur Fort. I also remembered that the kings of Jodhpur had fought for the Moghuls.

We reached the Circuit House while I was still speculating when I would have my first chance to have a close look at the fort. Our taxi entered through the gate, drove past a garden and stopped under a portico. We got off, took out our luggage, paid the fare, and went inside. A gentleman came forward, and enquired in English if we had come from Calcutta, and if Feluda was Mr.Mitter. When Feluda said yes, the gentleman said, 'A double room has been reserved for you on the ground floor.' As we signed the register, I noticed two names written several lines above ours — Dr. H.B. Hajra, and Master M. Dhar.

The Circuit House had a very simple plan. There was a large open area as you entered, to the left were the reception counter and the manager's room. The stairs going up to the first floor faced the visitor. A series of rooms lined the long verandahs to the left and the right. There were cane chairs on the verandahs. A bearer came and picked up our luggage, and we followed him down the right hand verandah, towards Room Number Three. A middle*- Naged gentleman with a military moustache was sitting on one of the cane chairs and talking to a gentleman wearing a Marwari cap. As we went past, he said in perfect Bengali, 'You must be Bengalis too?' Feluda smiled and said, 'Yes.' We entered Room Number Three.

It was quite a large room. There were twin beds side by side, with mosquito nets. On one side there were one double and two single sofas, and an ashtray on a round table. Apart from these, the room contained a dressing table, a wardrobe, and two bedside tables with water flasks, glasses and bedside lamps. The door to the attached bathroom was to the left.

Feluda asked the bearer for some tea, switched on the fan, and sat down on the sofa saying, 'Did you notice the names in the register?' 'Yes,' I said, 'But I do hope that the gentleman with that turned–up moustache is not Dr. Hajra.'

'Why not? What's wrong with him being the man?'

I could not easily come up with an explanation of what was wrong. Feluda noticed my hesitation and said, 'Actually, you didn't like the look of the man you just saw. You really want Dr. Hajra to be a nice, quiet man with a smiling, friendly face — isn't that so?'

Feluda was quite right. This man seemed too shrewd. Besides, he was much too tall and formidable looking. Not at all what we think of when we say 'Dr.'

The tea came when Feluda had barely finished his first cigarette. And hardly had the bearer left the room, than there was a tap on the door. Feluda called out,'Come in,' with his best British accent. The curtains parted, and the military moustache made his entrance.

'Hope I'm not disturbing you?'

'Not at all. Do sit down. Would you like some tea?'

'No, thank you. I've just had some. And frankly speaking, the tea here is not the best. Why blame this place only — India is supposed to be the home of the best tea, and yet how many hotels or government guest houses or bungalows serve you good tea? Just think of it! But go abroad, and — do you know that I've had wonderful tea in a place like Albania? First rate Darjeeling tea. Not to speak of other cities in Europe. The only thing I have disliked abroad is their practice of putting tea leaves in a cloth bag — what they call tea bags. You have hot water in a cup, and the tea leaves will be in a bag with a piece of string tied to it. You have to soak the bag in the water to make your brew. Then you can add milk or squeeze lemon into it, according to your taste. I myself prefer lemon tea. But that needs brew of good quality. The tea here is most ordinary.'

'You must have been to lots of places then?' said Feluda.

'That's what I've done most of my life,' answered the gentleman. 'I am what you might call a globe–trotter. I've also got a passion for hunting. That's something I acquired in Africa. By the way, my name is Mandar Bose.'

I had heard of globe–trotter Umesh Bhattacharya. But this name was quite unknown to me. The gentleman seemed to have read my mind.

'But, of course, I can't expect you to have heard of me. When I first set out on my travels, the papers carried stories about me. It's been thirty–six years since then. I've only been back for the last three months.'

'In that case, I have to say your command of Bengali is quite remarkable.'

'Look here, Sir, I believe that is something which depends entirely on yourself. If you want to go abroad and forget your Bengali, then you can do so within three months. And if you don't want to, then even thirty years is not time enough to make you forget. But I have to admit that I've had a lot of contact with other Bengalis. I once set myself up as an ivory dealer in Kenya. My partner there was a Bengali. We were together for seven years.'

'Are there any other Bengalis staying in this Circuit House besides yourself?'

I had noticed many times before, Feluda was never one to waste time on useless conversation.

'Yes indeed,' replied the gentleman. 'That's what strikes me as so strange. Now I have to believe that Bengalis are no longer happy in Calcutta. That's why they are dashing around here and there at the drop of a hat. Though I must say, this other gentleman has come with a purpose. He's a psychologist. But there's something odd about him. He's got this eight–year–old boy with him — who's supposed to remember his past lives. Apparently, the boy had been born near some fortress in Rajasthan in a previous birth. So this gentleman has brought the boy along and is searching for that fortress. It's hard to make out whether the doctor is a fraud, or whether the boy's been spinning this absurd story. Certainly, there's something suspicious about this boy. He doesn't speak properly to anybody. Refuses to answer all questions. Very fishy. You know, I've seen a lot of fraud and hypocrisy in the last thirty years. But I never thought I'd have to see such things here again.'

'Have you come to do some trotting here too?'

The gentleman laughed as he got up from his sofa.

'To tell you the truth, I haven't had a chance to see my own country properly yet. By the way — you haven't yet told me about yourself.' Feluda introduced himself and me. 'I have never set foot outside my country,' he said.

'I see. Well — if you come to the dining room around eight - thirty, then we'll meet again. For me it's early to bed and early to rise.'

The two of us accompanied the gentleman out on to the verandah. As we emerged, we saw a taxi entering through the gate. It pulled up under the parties. A gentleman of middle height, fortyish, got out, followed by a thin, fair skinned boy. Evidently, these two were Dr. Hemanga Hajra and Master Mukul Dhar who remembered his previous birth so well.

Mr. Bose said, 'Good evening' to Dr. Hajra, before going towards his own room. The latter came along the verandah, holding the little boy by the hand until the unexpected sight of two unknown Bengalis made him stop short and look rather flustered. Feluda smiled at him and folded his hands in greeting.

'You must be Dr. Hajra?' he said.

'Yes . . . but you . . .'

Feluda produced his card from his pocket and handed it to Dr. Hajra, saying, 'I want to discuss something with you. To tell you the truth, we are here to look for you. At the request of Sudhir Babu. He's also given me a letter for you.'

'Oh, I see. Mukul, why don't you run along to our room. I'll be there as soon as I've finished talking to these gentlemen.'

'I want to go to the garden.' The voice was sweet as a bell, though curiously monotonous.

'All right, you can go to the garden,' said Dr. Hajra, 'but be a good boy. Don't go outside the gate, all right?'

The boy did not answer. He hopped down to the gravelled path. Then he jumped over a flower bed and stood still on the grass. Dr. Hajra turned to us with a somewhat embarrassed smile and said, 'Where shall we sit?'

'Why don't you come to our room?'

The hair around Dr. Hajra's ears had turned gray. The eyes indicated a sharp intelligence. Close up, he seemed nearer fifty than forty. The three of us sat on the sofas. Feluda gave Sudhir Babu's letter to Dr. Hajra, and offered him a Charminar. The gentleman smiled saying 'Sorry, I'm not a smoker,' and glanced at the letter.

When he had finished, Dr. Hajra folded the letter and put it back in the envelope.

Feluda then told him the whole story of Nilu's kidnapping.

'Sudhir Babu was afraid that those men had perhaps come all the way to Jodhpur in search of Mukul,' he explained. 'That was what made him anxious enough to come to me. You may say, my presence here is mostly at his insistence. But even if there are no problems for me, to take care of this trip will not have been in vain. I've always felt a yearning to visit Rajasthan.'

Dr. Hajra thought for a while before replying.

'I must say, nothing has occurred so far which can be a cause for anxiety. You know something — I wish those newspaper reporters hadn't got hold of so many details. I told Sudhir Babu — please, let me finish my investigations, then you can talk to as many reporters as you wish. Particularly that story about the hidden treasure. I may know there's no truth in the story. But there are always some people who are easily tempted.'

'What do you feel about this business of remembering past lives?'

'What I think is no better than throwing stones in the dark. And yet, what else can I do? It's not as if one or two such cases have not occurred before. And some of their stories have been found to be totally accurate. That was why I decided, when I heard about this boy Mukul, that this time I'd do a really thorough investigation. If I found that his stories also proved true in every detail, then I'd take this as a landmark incident and conduct my research on that basis.'

'Have you made any progress?' asked Feluda.

'One thing I have been able to conclude — it was no mistake coming to Rajasthan. Mukul's whole air has changed ever since he set foot on this soil. I mean, just think about it. Here's this boy who's left his parents and brothers and sisters to come away with a total stranger, and in all these days he hasn't mentioned his family even once.'

'What kind of a relationship does he have with you?'

'No problems. As you can see, I'm the one who's taking him to the land of his dreams. And his whole being is there, in the land of the Golden Fortress. Every time he sees a castle here, he jumps with excitement.'

'But has he seen the Golden Fortress yet?'

Dr. Hajra shook his head. 'No, that he hasn't. I showed him Kishangarh on the way. Last evening, he saw the fort here from outside. Today, we went to see Barmer. But each time he says — 'no, not this one — let's go and see another one.' It certainly requires patience. I know, however, that it's quite useless to go to Chitor and Udaipur — there's no sand in those parts. Sand is what he talks about, over and over again. All the sand is in this area — and that's how it used to be in the past. I think I'll take him to see Bikaner tomorrow.'

'I hope you won't mind if we come along with you.'

'Certainly not. Far from minding, I'd feel a bit more secure if you were with us. There was this one incident . . .'

The gentleman stopped. Feluda had taken his pack of cigarettes from his pocket, but didn't open it.

'There was a phone call last evening,' said Dr. Hajra.

'Where?' asked Feluda . . .

'Here, in Circuit House. I was away at the fort then. Someone apparently called up to enquire if a gentleman and a little boy had come here from Calcutta. Naturally, the manager said, yes.'

'But it is quite possible that someone here has read about you in the Calcutta newspapers,' said Feluda. 'Maybe they called here to verify that. There are plenty of Bengalis in Jodhpur. Wouldn't it be natural for them to be curious about something like this?'

'All right, I accept that. But in that case having found out we had arrived, why didn't the caller try contacting us again? Why didn't they come looking for us again?

'Hm,' Feluda nodded grimly. 'I think it's best for me to accompany you. And please, don't let Mukul wander off by himself too often.'

'Of course not!'

Dr. Hajra got up.

'I have arranged for a taxi to come and pick us up tomorrow. There's only two of you — so I think we'll manage with one cab.'

As he made his way to the door, Feluda abruptly asked, 'By the way — were you connected with an incident in Chicago, say about four years back?'

Dr. Hajra frowned.

'Incident? I have been to Chicago, but . . .'

'Something to do with a spiritual clinic?'

Dr. Hajra burst out laughing. 'Oh yes — that affair of the great Swami Bhavananda? Whom the Americans called Bhabhananda? Yes, something did happen. But the papers exaggerated it. The man was a fraud all right. But you'll find lots of frauds and quacks like that among unorthodox practitioners. Nothing more than that. It was actually his patients who caught him out. And, of course, the news spread. I was requested by the press to give them my opinion. And I tried to be as charitable as I could. But the papers made a mountain out of a molehill. Later, I even met the man. In fact, I myself decided to go and see him so that I could clear up the whole mess — and we parted as friends.'

'Thank you. I had a totally different impression from reading the newspaper reports.'

We followed Dr. Hajra out of the room. It was evening already. The western horizon was still red, but the street lights had been lit. Where was Mukul? We had last seen him in the garden, but he was not there anymore. Dr. Hajra took a quick look inside his room and came out again looking worried.

'Where on earth has that boy got to now,' he said, as he went down from the verandah. We followed him into the garden. But it was quite certain that the boy was no longer there.

'Mukul!' called out Dr. Hajra, 'Mukul!'

'He's heard you,' said Feluda. 'Look, he's coming.'

In the dim twilight, we saw Mukul come in from the street through the gate. At the same time we saw a man walk rapidly along the opposite footpath towards the new palace in the east. I could not see his face, but there was no mistaking the bright red colour of his shirt, even in that dim light. Had Feluda seen him too?

'Mukul, you really shouldn't go out like that you know.'

'Why?' asked Mukul in his unemotional voice.

'Because it's a strange place — there are so many wicked people here.'

'But I know him.'

Mukul stretched out his arm, and pointed in the direction of the street. 'That man, who was there just now.'

Hemanga Babu put his hand on Mukul's shoulder and looked

at Feluda. 'That's the trouble,' he said. 'It's impossible to make out which people he really knows and which people he is supposed to have known in his earlier birth.'

I noticed there was something in Mukul's hand — a piece of paper which gleamed in the light. Feluda had also noticed it, for he asked, 'Will you show me that piece of paper in your hand?'

Mukul gave it to him. A piece of golden tinsel, two inches long, half-an-inch wide.

'Where did you find this?'

'Here,' said Mukul pointing to the grass with his finger.

'Can I keep it?' asked Feluda.

'No. I found it.' That same flat tone, the same cold voice. Feluda had to return the piece of paper.

'Come Mukul,' said Dr. Hajra. 'Let's go inside. We'll wash up and then have dinner. See you, Mr. Mitter. We are leaving tomorrow at seven–thirty, after an early breakfast.'

Before we went to dinner, Feluda wrote a postcard to Sudhir Babu, informing him of our arrival and giving him news of Mukul. By the time we had had our baths and got to the dining room, Dr. Hajra and Mukul had already gone. I saw Mandar Babu, however, sitting in the corner opposite ours (with the non–Bengali gentleman) and eating his pudding. By the time our soup came, the two of them had got up. On his way towards the door, Mandar Bose raised his hand and said goodnight.

Two days of travelling by train had left me quite exhausted. I had planned on going to bed immediately after dinner. But I had to stay up a little because of Feluda. He lit a cigarette and sat on the sofa holding his blue notebook. I lay down on the bed. We had not put up the mosquito nets as we were equipped with anti–mosquito ointment.

Feluda pressed the back of his ball point pen, pushed out the point, and said, 'Tell me — who are the people we have met.'

'Since when?'

'Since the time of Sudhir Babu's visit.'

'Obviously, the first is Sudhir Babu himself. Then Shibratan. Then Nilu. After that Shibratan Babu's servant.'

'What was his name?'

'Can't remember.'

'Monohar. Then?'

'Then Jatayu.'

'What's his real name?'

'Lalmohan.'

'Surname?'

'Surname . . . surname . . . Ganguly.'

'Good.'

Feluda went on writing. I went on with my list.

'Then there was that man in the red shirt.'

'We met him — but did we get to know him?'

'No — we didn't.'

'All right — next?'

'Mandar Bose. And the man who was with him.'

'And Mukul Dhar, Dr . . .'

'Feluda!'

My scream silenced Feluda. My eyes were on his bed. Some horrible creature was trying to get out from beneath his pillow. I pointed my finger at it.

Feluda was up in a flash. As soon as he moved the pillow, we saw the scorpion. Feluda yanked the bedsheet off the bed in one sharp movement, and shook the scorpion on to the floor. Three solid whacks with his sandal took care of it. Then he tore off a piece of newspaper, picked up the crushed scorpion with it, and went into the bathroom where he opened the back door to throw out the balled–up paper. He came back to our room saying, 'That door had been left open for the sweeper to come in. That's how this fellow managed to get in. You'd better get some sleep now. We have to be up early tomorrow.'

But I couldn't be so relaxed about the whole thing. I kept on thinking of — No, I should stop. If my telepathy was any good, then maybe just the thought of danger would bring danger in its wake. It was much better to try and sleep.

CHAPTER 6

Next morning, as soon as I stepped out of our room, after brushing my teeth and washing up, I heard a familiar voice saying, 'Good morning!' I realized that Jatayu had arrived. Feluda had already come out and was sitting on a cane chair in the verandah, waiting for me. Lalmohan Babu continued with rounded eyes, 'My dear Sir, what a thrilling place this is! Full of powerfully suspicious characters.'

'I hope you are all right still?' said Feluda.

'All right! I feel marvellously fit. I even challenged the manager of our lodge to a wrist contest. But the gentleman refused.'

Then he came closer and whispered: 'I have a weapon in my suitcase.'

'A catapult, I suppose?' said Feluda.

'No Sir! A Nepalese dagger. Straight from Kathmandu. If anyone comes to attack, I'll just plunge it into his stomach. We'll see what happens after that. You know, I've always wanted to build up a weapon collection.'

Once again, I nearly laughed. But self–restraint was becoming a habit — so I managed not to. Lalmohan Babu sat down in the chair next to Feluda's.

'What is our plan today? Aren't you going to see the fort?'

'Yes we are,' said Feluda, 'but not the one here. It's going to be Bikaner.'

'Why Bikaner before anything else? What's going on?'

'We have company. They have a car.'

Another 'Good morning' came from the western side of the verandah. Our globe–trotter was coming.

'Sleep well?'

I noticed that Lalmohan Babu was taking in Mandar Bose's military moustache and impressive physique, with much admiration. Feluda introduced the two of them.

'Good heavens! A globe–trotter!' Lalmohan Babu's eyes goggled. 'I'll definitely have to cultivate you then! You must have had a host of thrilling experiences.'

'What kind do you want?' smiled Mandar Bose. 'Short of being boiled alive by cannibals, I've gone through everything under the sun.'

Unnoticed by any of us, Mukul had come out on the verandah. Now we saw him, standing quietly by himself, staring at the garden.

Soon, Dr. Hajra also emerged, equipped for the trip. He had a thermos slung over one shoulder and a pair of binoculars over other. A camera hung from his neck.

'It will take us nearly four–and–a–half hours,' he said. 'If you have thermoses, fill them up and take them with you. I've no idea what we can find on the road. I've instructed the management here — they'll give us four packed lunches.'

'Where are you all off to?' asked Mandar Bose.

The mention of Bikaner got him all worked up.

'If you really are going there, then why don't we all go together?'

'Just the idea!' exclaimed Jatayu.

'How many of us will be going then?' asked Dr. Hajra with marked lack of enthusiasm.

'It's out of the question for all of us to travel in the same car,' declared Mandar Bose. 'I will arrange for another taxi. I think Mr. Maheswari would also want to come with me.'

'Do you want to come?' Dr. Hajra asked Lalmohan Babu.

'If I do, I want to pay my share. I'm not here to sponge on anyone else. Why don't the four of you go together. I'll come with Mr. Globe–trotter here.'

I realized our new friend was hoping to increase his repertoire of plots by listening to Mandar Babu's adventures. Already he had written at least twenty–five adventure stories. The arrangement suited us fine. Five people in one car would have been a bit of a crowd. Mandar Babu talked to the manager and lined up a second taxi. Lalmohan Babu went back to his New Bombay Lodge to get ready.

'Please pick me up on your way out,' he said as he left. 'I'll be ready in half–an–hour.'

Let me say straightaway, that the fort at Bikaner was a write–

off, as soon as Mukul saw it. But that was not the most important event of this day. That happened at Devikunda — and it made us realize that we were dealing with a most dangerous criminal.

No adventures took place on the way to Bikaner. The only unusual thing was encountering. a group of gypsies after we had travelled about sixty miles. The gypsies had set up camp right by the roadside. Mukul asked us to stop the car, and went and wandered about among the gypsies. Then he came back and reported that he knew them.

I should also mention here a conversation that took place between Feluda and Dr. Hajra regarding Mukul. I have no idea whether Mukul, sitting beside the driver, heard any of it. Even if he did, his manner gave nothing away.

'Dr. Hajra,' said Feluda, 'will you tell me what exactly are the events or objects that Mukul says he remembers from his past life?'

'Well, the one thing that he mentions over and over again is the Golden Fortress. His house, apparently, was close to that fortress. And gold and jewels were buried under the floor of that house. The way he says it, one would think that the act of burying all this treasure happened in front of him. Apart from this, he also talks a lot about a battle. He mentions elephants and horses, soldiers and cannons, tremendous noise, terrible screams. Then he also talks about camels. He claims to have ridden on them. Peacocks too. Once a peacock is supposed to have bit him on the arm, and drawn blood. He also talks about sand. Haven't you noticed how excited he gets whenever he sees any sand?'

We reached Bikaner at a quarter-to-twelve. A little way before we reached the city, the road had started climbing upwards. The walled city of Bikaner stood on top of this incline. And the most noticeable thing in the city was the huge fort made of reddish stone.

Our car drove straight up to the fort. And I noticed, the closer we got, the larger the fort seemed. My father was right. The fact that the Rajputs were a most powerful breed is quite evident from the look of their forts.

As soon as our taxi came to a halt in front of the gates, Mukul piped up, 'Why are you stopping here?'

'Do you recognize the fort, Mukul?' said Dr. Hajra.

'No,' declared Mukul gloomily. 'This one is ugly. This is not the Golden Fortress.'

All of us had got out of the taxi and were standing on the road. As soon as Mukul finished speaking, a harsh sound came from somewhere. Immediately, Mukul ran to Dr. Hajra and put both arms around him. The sound had come from the park on the other side.

'Peacocks,' said Feluda, 'Has this happened before?'

Dr. Hajra was stroking Mukul on the head as he answered.

'Yesterday, in Jodhpur too. He can't stand peacocks.'

I saw that Mukul had become very pale. Again in that same grave, though sweet, voice he said, 'I don't want to stay here.'

'Why don't I get the car and wait at the Circuit House,' Dr. Hajra suggested to Feluda. 'You all have come all this way — I think you should have a good look around. I'll send the car back for you. When you are done with the sightseeing, you can come back to the Circuit House. But don't be later than two o'clock, or we'll be very late going back.'

For Dr. Hajra this trip had been a failure. Nevertheless, I could not feel too sorry. I was filled with a tingling anticipation at the thought of being able to see the inside of a Rajput fort for the first time.

As we went towards the gates, Feluda suddenly stopped short, and pressed my shoulder.

'See that?' he said.

'What?' I said.

'That man.'

I realized Feluda meant the man in the red shirt. But I could see no signs of a red shirt in the direction Feluda was staring. True, there were lots of people there — a small market had grown up outside the gates.

'Well, where is he?' I said.

'Idiot. Are you still looking for that red shirt?'

'What other man do you mean?'

'You must be the world's prize idiot. All you've noticed is a red shirt and nothing else. It was the same man, wrapped up to his nose in a shawl. Only, today he happens to be wearing a blue shirt. Remember, when we stopped to see the gypsies — that's when I saw a taxi going towards Bikaner. And there was a man in a blue shirt inside that taxi.'

'But what's he doing here?'

'If we knew that, kid, half the game would be over!'

The man had disappeared. I entered through the huge gates of the fort with a feeling of excitement. A spacious courtyard faced us as we entered. To the right of this stood the fort in all its glory. Pigeons nested in the crevices on the walls. About a thousand years ago, Bikaner was a prosperous city — but the sand has swallowed it up long since. Feluda said Raja Rai Singh had started building the fort about four hundred years ago. He was a famous general under the Emperor Akbar.

For some time one question had been pricking my thoughts. Why had Lalmohan Babu's party not shown up yet? Had they been late in starting? Never mind. I was determined not to spoil my pleasure in visiting these amazing historical relics by thinking too much about them.

The most remarkable thing inside the fort was the armoury. Not only were there plenty of weapons, but also a marvellously beautiful silver throne called Alam Ambali. Apparently, a present from the Moghul Emperor. There were also armour, helmets, shields, swords, spears, knives and God knows what else! Some of the swords were so huge and powerful that it seemed incredible to think of human beings using them. The swords had made me think once again of Jatayu, when I saw that my telepathy had brought the gentleman there. In front of the huge doors of the huge rooms of that huge castle, he seemed even more puny and ridiculous.

As soon as he saw us, Lalmohan Babu beamed, looked around and said, 'Do you think those Rajputs were giants or what? None of these seem meant for human hands.'

It was exactly as I had feared. After seventy kilometres, their taxi had had a flat tyre.

'Where are your fellow travellers?' asked Feluda.

'They've gone off to do some shopping. I couldn't resist coming inside.'

Having seen the Phul Mahal, Gaja Mandir, Shish Mahal and

Ganga Nibas, we had just reached the Chini Boorj, when we encountered Mandar Bose and Mr. Maheswari. The packages wrapped in paper that they carried in their hands showed they had been shopping.

'The weapons I have seen in the medieval castles or Europe and all that I've seen here proves one thing only; the human race is gradually becoming weaker, and I believe progressively smaller in size,' pronounced Mandar Bose.

'Just like me, eh?' said Lalmohan Babu with a smile.

'Yes, just like you,' replied Mandar Bose. 'It's my belief that there was not a single person of your dimensions in 16th century Rajasthan.' 'Oh by the way,' — Mandar Bose turned towards Feluda, 'This had been left for you at the Circuit House reception desk.'

The gentleman took an envelope out of his pocket and gave it to Feluda. There was no stamp on the envelope. Obviously, a local person had delivered it.

'Bagri, the young man who sits at the desk, gave this to us just as we were about to leave. He said he had no idea who had come and left it.'

Feluda said 'Excuse me,' read the letter and put it back in his pocket. I couldn't make out what was in it, nor could I ask him.

After wandering about for another half–an–hour, Feluda looked at his watch and said, 'Time to go back to the Circuit House.' I didn't feel like leaving the fort, but there was no other way.

Both the taxis stood outside. It was decided that this time we would travel back together. Just as we were getting in, the driver said that Dr. Hajra and Mukul had not gone to the Circuit House. Apparently, 'that boy' had refused to go there.

'Then where have they gone?' asked Feluda.

The driver said they had gone off to Devikunda. What was that? Feluda said there were mausoleums there commemorating the Rajput warriors.

A distance of five miles — it took us ten minutes to reach there. The place was really beautiful, and so were the mausoleums. Stone pillars on stone bases, with a stone roof overhead. From top to bottom they were covered with beautiful engravings. At least fifty such structures were scattered all around. The whole area was full of trees with flocks of parrots in them. They flew from one tree to another and called out raucously. I had never seen so many parrots together.

But where was Dr. Hajra? And where was Mukul?

I looked at Lalmohan Babu, and saw that he saw twitching with anxiety.

'Very suspicious and mysterious,' he said.

'Dr. Hajra!' Mandar Bose suddenly roared. His booming voice frightened off a flock of parrtos, but there was no other response to the call.

We started searching. What with all those mausoleums the place was like a labyrinth. As we wandered in and out, I noticed Feluda picking up a matchbox from the grass, and putting it in his pocket.

Ultimately, it was Lalmohan Babu who discovered Dr. Hajra. We heard him screaming, and ran up to him to find Dr. Hajra lying on the ground in the shade of a mango tree, in front of one of the stone bases covered with moss. He had been gagged and his hands were tied behind his back.

A strange helpless groaning came from his lips.

Feluda immediately kneeled down, unbound his hands and removed the gag. The cloth used for this seemed to have been torn off a turban.

'What's going on, Sir? How did this happen?' said Mandar Bose. Fortunately, Dr. Hajra had not been injured. He sat on the grass panting for a while. Then he spoke. 'Mukul said he didn't want to go to the Circuit House. So we just drove around for a while. As soon as we got here, he liked the place.' He said, 'These are *chhatris*. I know these — I want to get down and look at them.' We got down. He was wandering around by himself a little, while I waited in the shade of a tree, when suddenly I was attacked from behind. Someone clamped his hand over my mouth, threw me on the ground, held my head down with his knee, and bound my hands. Then came the gag.'

'Where's Mukul?' asked Feluda, his voice tense and anxious.

'I don't know. Though, I did hear the sound of a car after I had been left trussed up.'

'Didn't you see the man?' asked Feluda.

Dr. Hajra shook his head. 'All I know is the glimpse I caught of my attacker's clothes during the struggle. He was dressed like one of the locals. Not shirt and trousers.'

'There he is!' Mandar Bose shouted out suddenly.

Amazed, we all watched Mukul as he came out from behind one of the mausoleums, absently chewing a blade of grass. Dr. Hajra let out a breath, saying 'Thank God!', and went towards Mukul.

'Where were you, Mukul?'

No answer.

'Where have you been all this time?'

'Behind that,' Mukul pointed towards one of the mausoleums. 'I've seen things like that before.'

'Did you see the man who came here,' asked Feluda.

'What man?'

'He couldn't have seen anyone,' said Dr. Hajra. 'As soon as we got here, he ran off to explore. I had never even dreamt that anything like this could happen in Bikaner — so I wasn't particularly worried about him.'

In spite of this statement Feluda asked once more, 'You really didn't see the man — the one who bound up Dr. Hajra and gagged him.'

'I want to see the Golden Fortress.'

We realized it was useless asking Mukul any more questions. 'There's no point in wasting time any longer, 'Feluda said abruptly. 'In one way it's been fortunate that· Mukul was not with you or near you. If he had been, the man might have kidnapped him. If the man has gone back to Jodhpur, then we can still catch him if we drive fast enough.'

Within a couple of minutes, we were on our way back. This time Lalmohan Babu came in our cab.

'Those people drink too much,' he said. 'I can't stand the smell of alcohol.'

Harmit Singh, our Punjabi driver, raised our speed to sixty miles. Once, a dove which had been sitting in the middle of the road, crashed into our windscreen as it tried to fly away, and died. Mukul and I were sitting in front. I looked back at one point, and saw Lalmohan Babu sitting hunched up between

Feluda and Dr. Hajra, his eyes closed. His face was rather pale but the smile that touched the corner of his mouth made me realize that he had scented adventure with a capital A. Who knows, maybe he had already found the plot for his next thriller.

After a hundred miles or so, we realized there was no possibility of catching up with the villain's car. We could not go on assuming that his car too was not new, and could not drive as fast as ours!

By the time we entered Jodhpur, the city lights were glowing.

'Lalmohan Babu, shall we drop you off at New Bombay Lodge then?' asked Feluda.

'Yes, of course,' said that gentleman in a thin voice, 'But I was wondering whether after dinner, I could, er . . .'

'Certainly,' said Feluda. 'I will make enquiries whether there is an empty room at the Circuit House. Why don't you give us a call around nine, and find out.'

I was thinking of the events of the day. Obviously, we were dealing with a real tough adversary. Was he the man in the red shirt, who had gone to Bikaner today wearing a blue shirt? Who knows! Upto now, I could not figure out anything. And, I felt, neither could Feluda. Had it been otherwise, his face would have had a totally different expression. That was one thing I could sense very well, after all this time in his company, and after observing his methods of investigation.

Back at the Circuit House we all made for our rooms. Just before entering Room Number Three, Feluda spoke to Dr. Hajra.

'Please don't mind, but I'm going to keep this piece of cloth with me.'

Feluda had brought with him the cloth which had been used to tie up Dr. Hajra.

'No problem,' said Dr. Hajra. He then came closer and dropped his voice a little. 'Obviously, you realize Prodosh Babu, things are serious. Whatever we had anticipated seems to be happening. But I never guessed it would be so dangerous.'

'Don't worry,' said Feluda. 'After all, I'm here. You go ahead with your own work and leave the worrying to me. It's my belief that if you had gone straight back to the Circuit House, instead of making a detour at Devikunda, you wouldn't have had to suffer like this. Anyway, fortunately for us, the fellow could not get his hands on Mukul. From now on, you must stay close to us — then there will be less scope for misadventure.'

But the anxiety did not disappear from Dr. Hajra's face. 'I'm not worrying about myself,' he said. 'Scientists have to take a lot of risks in the course of their research. I'm much more worried about the two of you. Both of you are outsiders, so to speak.'

'Why don't you assume that I too am a scientist,' answered Feluda with a smile. 'I too am doing research — and for that reason, I too am taking risks.'

All this while, Mukul had been pacing up and down the verandah. Dr. Hajra called him, said goodnight to us, and went to his room looking preoccupied. We too entered our room. Feluda called the room boy, ordered cold Coca Cola, sat down on the sofa, extracted his pack of cigarettes and the lighter from his pocket and put them on the table with a worried look on his face. Then, from his other pocket, he took out a box of matches, the one he had picked up at Devikunda. An Ace brand matchbox. Empty. Feluda stared at it for a while before saying, 'In the course of our train journey, you saw all those *paan* and cigarette vendors at all those stations. Did you notice if any one of them was selling Ace brand matches?'

I spoke the truth. 'No, Feluda, I didn't notice anything.'

'No shop in the western region of India will have Ace brand matches. They are not sold in Rajasthan. This box of matches has been brought from outside.'

'Does that mean that it doesn't belong to the man in the red shirt?'

'That is a very silly question. First of all, wearing Rajasthani dress does not make one a Rajasthani. Anybody can wear it. Secondly, there were many other people, apart from that man, who went to Devikunda and therefore had the opportunity to commit crime.'

'Naturally! But we don't know any of them — so what's the use of worrying about them?'

'Now you're being silly again. Haven't learnt to exercise your grey cells yet, have you? Just think of how long after ourselves Lalmohan, Mandar Bose and Maheswari reached the fort today. And then consider −'

'I get it, I get it!'

Of course! This had not occurred to me at all. They had been forty–five minutes late in arriving. Lalmohan Babu had said that they had had a punctured tyre. But what if that had not been so? Suppose he had been lying? Or even if that story was correct, and Lalmohan Babu was not guilty, Mandar Bose and Maheswari could have gone to Devikunda instead of on a shopping expedition.

Feluda sighed and took out something else from his pocket. My heart missed a beat as soon as I saw what it was. I had forgotten all about it. This was the letter delivered by Mandar Bose.

'Who is it from, Feluda?' I asked with a tremor in my voice. 'I don't know,' said he, handing the letter over to me. As I took it, I saw it was in English. Just one line — written in capital letters with a ball point pen.

'If you value your life — go back to Calcutta immediately.' The letter was trembling in my hands. I quickly put it on the table and folded my hands in my lap in an effort to keep myself steady.

'What are you going to do Feluda?'

Feluda did not remove his eyes from the ceiling fan spinning overhead as he spoke, almost to himself, 'The spider's web . . . geometry . . . darkness now . . . can't see anything . . . when the sun rises, the light will fall on the web — it will gleam — . . . that's when the pattern of the web will become visible ! . . . right now, it's just a matter of waiting for light . . .'

CHAPTER 7

I had woken up once in the middle of last night — don't know what time it was — to see Feluda writing something in his blue notebook by the light of his bedside lamp. It is anybody's guess how late he had stayed up scribbling. But when I woke up at six-thirty this morning, he had already shaved and dressed and was ready. He has this theory: that when a man's brain works overtime, the amount of sleep needed is automatically reduced. And that does not affect one's health. As far as I can recall, Feluda has not been ill even once in the last ten years. I knew quite well that even here in Jodhpur, he had not stopped doing yoga. This morning too, I knew that he had finished that part of his daily ritual before I had woken up.

We met everybody in the dining room for breakfast. Lalmohan Babu had moved last night to the Circuit House. He was staying two rooms down from Mandar Bose, on the western side of the verandah. In between mouthfuls of omelette, he told us that a marvellous plot had come into his head. Dr Hajra looked quite worn out; apparently he had not been able to sleep well. Only Mukul seemed totally unaffected.

Mandar Bose spoke directly to Dr. Hajra for the first time today.

'I hope you won't take offence, Sir, but if you persist in carrying out research in such a weird area, you are bound to run into this kind of trouble. In a country like this, where superstition is so common, it's much better not to meddle with certain things. One fine day you'll see little boys all over the place claiming to remember their past lives. And the truth behind that will be their fathers' desire to get a little bit of publicity. How on earth will you deal with such a situation? How many little boys can you have trailing after you in strange, unfamiliar places?'

Dr. Hajra made no comment. Lalmohan Babu stared from one

to another, since he was still unaware of this business of the past life.

Feluda had already told me that he was planning go to the market for a while after breakfast. I knew very well that sightseeing was not going to be the primary motive behind this. We set out at about quarter–to–eight. Not two, but three of us. Lalmohan Babu was also coming along. Once or twice before this, I had tried to imagine the gentleman in the role of a villain.

But it was so utterly hilarious, that I had to banish such a possibility from my mind.

Though the neighbourhood of the Circuit House was quiet and not overpopulated, the rest of the town seemed quite crowded and busy. The old city wall was visible practically from every point. Along that wall were rows of shops, *tongas* waiting in line, houses, and God knows what else. Relics of the city of five hundred years ago had mingled and become one with the city of today.

We walked along, casually looking into a shop from time to time. I was aware that Feluda was looking for something — but I had no idea what. Suddenly Lalmohan Babu broke out, 'This Hajra — what kind of a doctor is he? This morning at the dining table Mr. Trotter was saying all those things . . .'

'Hajra is a parapsychologist,' Feluda answered. 'Parapsychologist?' Lalmohan Babu's brows drew together in a frown. 'I did not know you could have a 'para' sitting before psychology! Though I know it does before typhoid. Does that make it half–psychology — just as paratyphoid means half- typhoid?'

'Not half' said Feluda, 'Para means abnormal. The field of psychology is pretty vague at best. The part which is the most undefinable comes under parapsychology.'

'And what was all that about remembering past lives?'

'Mukul is one of those who can. Or so he claims.'

Lalmohan Babu's mouth fell open.

'This will be a goldmine for you, plotwise,' said Feluda. 'This boy keeps on referring to some Golden Fortress which he is supposed to have seen in his past life. He also claims to have lived in a house which had hidden treasure buried underneath.'

'My dear Sir, are we indeed going in search of those?' Lalmohan Babu's voice was hoarse with excitement.

'I don't know if you are, but we certainly are.'

Right there in the middle of the street, Lalmohan Babu suddenly clasped Feluda's hand.

'The chance of a lifetime! Please, please don't go off anywhere without telling me about it first. That's my only request.'

'We haven't yet decided where we are going next.'

Lalmohan Babu thought for a while and asked, 'Is Mr. Trotter also going with you?'

'Why? D'you have any objection?'

'I think that man is powerfully suspicious!'

A shoemaker was sitting on one side of the road. *Nagra* shoes were heaped around him. The people here mostly wore this kind of *nagras*. Feluda went and stood in front of the heap of shoes.

'Powerful — hm, you can say that again. But why suspicious?' he asked.

'Yesterday in the car, he was bragging like nobody's business. Said he'd shot a wolf in Tanganyika. But I know that in the whole of Africa you won't find a single wolf. I've read Martin Johnson's book — and this fellow thinks he can fool me!'

'What did you tell him?'

'What could I say? Couldn't possibly call the man a liar to his face! I was sitting sandwiched between the two of them. And have you noticed the man's chest? Must be forty–five inches at the very least. Plus, the whole road was lined with huge clumps of thorny cacti. Suppose I contradicted this fellow, all he would have had to do was pick me up and dump me behind one of those clumps. That would be it — a squadron of vultures would come down for a feast.'

'How many vultures do you think your body can feed?'

'Ha, ha, ha . . .'

By this time, Feluda had removed his sandals, put on a pair of *nagras* and started pacing about.

'Very sturdy shoes — you want to buy them?' asked Lalmohan Babu.

'Why don't you try a pair yourself?' answered Feluda.

There was nothing in that shoe stall small enough to fit Lalmohan Babu. But as he tried on the smallest available pair, he nearly had a fit.

'Rhino hide, my dear Sir — this isn't fit for anybody except a rhino!'

'In that case you can assume that ninety per cent of Rajasthanis are in truth rhinoceroses.'

Both of them exchanged their *nagras* for their regular shoes. The shoestall owner was grinning away. He too had realized the gentlemen had been trying out these poor men's shoes just to have some fun.

We strolled on. A radio in a *paan* shop was blaring out some Hindi film song. It brought to mind the puja festivals in Calcutta. They don't celebrate the pujas here — instead, they have the dusserah. But there was still a while to go before that.

After we had progressed some more, Feluda suddenly halted in front of a shop selling stone objects. It looked quite respectable, the name was Solanki Stores. Beautiful bowls, glasses, vases and other vessels made of stone were on display behind glass windows on the outside. Feluda was staring fixedly at them. The storekeeper advanced to the doorway and invited us to come in.

Feluda pointed at the window and said, 'Can I have a look at that bowl?'

The storekeeper did not disturb the window display but took out a similar bowl from the cabinet inside. A bowl made of beautiful yellow stone. I could not remember having seen anything like that before.

'Is this a local product?' Feluda asked.

'It is made in Rajasthan all right, but not in Jodhpur,' answered the storekeeper.

'Where then?'

'Jaisalmer. This yellow stone is only found there.'

'I see . . .'

I could vaguely recollect having heard that name, Jaisalmer. I did not know where exactly in Rajasthan it was located. Feluda bought the bowl. We returned to the Circuit House around nine–thirty, having digested our breakfast of egg and toast during the bumpy *tonga* ride back.

Mandar Bose was sitting in the verandah, reading a newspaper. He noticed the packet and said, 'What did you buy?'

'Just a bowl,' said Feluda. 'After all, one has to have a memento of Rajasthan.'

'Do you know, your friend has gone out?'

'Who, Dr. Hajra?'

'Saw him leave around nine, in a taxi.'

'And Mukul?'

'Went with him. He probably went off to report to the police. After yesterday's incident, he must be quite shaken.'

'The plot has to be modified,' remarked Lalmohan Babu, and went off to his room.

Once inside our own room, I asked Feluda, 'Why did you suddenly buy that bowl?'

Feluda sat down on the sofa, unwrapped the bowl and set it down on the table.

'There's something special about this,' he said.

'What?'

'For the first time in my life I've seen a bowl which deserves the paradoxical epithet of a stone bowl made of Gold.'

He did not say anything further but started flipping through the pages of the Bradshaw. I was left to my own devices. It was evident that at least for an hour I wouldn't get one word out of Feluda. Even asking questions would be of no use. Perforce, I had to go out.

The whole length of the verandah was free of people now. Mandar Babu had left. A foreign lady sitting at the other end had also disappeared. The distant sound of a drum came to my ears. Soon someone started singing to that beat. I turned towards the gate and saw a couple of beggars — a man and a woman — entering through the gate and coming towards the verandah. The man was beating on the drum while the woman sang. I went forward along the verandah.

When I got to the open space in the middle I suddenly felt like going upstairs. I had seen the staircase from the day we had arrived, and I knew there was a roof up there. I started climbing the stairs.

In the central portion of the first floor were four rooms side by side. On both sides, to the east and the west, were open roofs. The rooms appeared to be empty — or perhaps the occupants were out.

I went across to the western roof and had a grand view of Jodhpur Fort.

The beggars continued their music below. The tune sounded familiar. Where could I have heard it? Then I remembered — it was quite similar to the tune that Mukul usually hummed. It was the same tune being sung over and over — and yet it did not sound monotonous. I went closer to the low wall of the roof. This was the back of the Circuit House.

And I made a discovery! There was a garden in the back too. All we could see through the window in our room was a tamarisk tree. But it was impossible to guess that there was so much space here with so many different kinds of trees.

What was that bright blue thing moving behind the plants? Oh, a peacock. Part of its body was hidden behind the trees, which is why I was so surprised. Now I could see all of it. The bird was picking things from the ground and eating them. Very likely worms; I knew peacocks ate insects.

Suddenly I remembered something — it is very difficult to find a peacock's nest. Peacocks manage to find the most secret, tucked away corners to build their nests.

The peacock was advancing slowly, taking careful steps. From time to time it would swivel its long neck in all directions to have a good look around. Every time it turned its body, the tail moved with it.

Suddenly, the peacock stopped. The neck turned right. What had it seen? Or had it heard something?

The peacock retreated. It had seen something which had made it move away.

It was a man. Just below where I was standing. I could see parts of him through the gaps between the trees. He wore a turban. Not too big — a medium–sized one. A white shawl was wrapped around him. Since I was looking down vertically, it was impossible to see his face. Only the turban and his shoulders were visible. The hands were concealed under the shawl.

The man was advancing stealthily, step by step, from the west to the east. I was on the western portion of the roof. To the east, on the ground floor, was our room.

I had a sudden desire to find out where the man was going.

I ran through the rooms in the middle until I reached the opposite portion of the roof and bent over the parapet at the back.

The man was now exactly below me. He was getting closer to the window of our room. He took his hand from under the shawl. What was that gleaming on his wrist?

He had stopped. My throat had gone dry. One more step forward — A horrible shriek.

The man started and stepped back. It was the peacock calling out harshly. Simultaneously, I too screamed, 'Feluda!'

The turbanned figure ran at top speed and disappeared in the direction from which it had come. I also ran at breakneck speed down the stairs and along the verandah until I reached our door, totally out of breath, where I collided with Feluda and was reduced to a stunned silence.

Feluda pulled me into the room and said, 'What's going on?'

'From the roof — I saw this man in a turban . . . coming towards your window . . .'

'What did he look like? Was he tall?'

'I don't know . . . I was watching him from above. On his wrist . . .'

'What?'

'A watch . . .'

I had been afraid that Feluda would laugh the whole thing away, or make fun of me for being a fool and a coward. But he did neither. Instead, he went to the window without a smile, craned his head outside and took a good look around.

A knock on the door.

'Come in.'

The room boy came in with coffee.

'Salam Sahib,' he said. Having deposited the tray on the table, he pulled a folded sheet of paper from his pocket and gave it to Feluda.

'The manager asked me to give this to you.'

The room boy left. Feluda read the note, looked profoundly disappointed and dropped down on the sofa.

'Whose letter is it, Feluda?'

'Read it for yourself.'

It was from Dr. Hajra. On a sheet of notepaper bearing his

letterhead, there were four brief lines in English — 'I am convinced it is no longer safe for us to be at Jodhpur. I am going off to another place where I may have some chances of success. Why should you involve yourself and your brother unnecessarily in danger? That's why I've decided to leave without saying goodbye. I wish you good luck. Yours — H.M. Hazra.'

'He's been much too hasty,' said Feluda through clenched teeth.

Without bothering to drink his coffee he went straight to the reception desk. A new person was sitting there today.

'Did Dr. Hajra say he was coming back today?' he asked him.

'No. He's paid his bill and checked out. Didn't say anything about coming back.'

'Do you know where he's gone?'

'All I know is that he left for the station.'

Feluda thought for a few minutes before asking, 'Tell me, isn't it possible to get to Jaisalmer from here by train?'

'Yes, indeed. We've had a direct route for the last couple of years.'

'What time does the train leave?'

'Ten o'clock at night.'

'Isn't there a train in the morning?'

'Yes, but that only goes up to Pokran, which is halfway between here and Jaisalmer. And it left about half-an-hour-ago. Of course, if you can organize a car from Pokran then you can take this train for Jaisalmer.'

'What is the distance from Pokran?'

'Seventy miles.'

'What other trains leave Jodhpur in the morning?'

The gentleman looked through the pages of a book and said, 'There's a passenger train at eight which goes to Barmer. The Rewari Passenger leaves at nine. That's all.'

Feluda tapped impatiently on the counter several time with his fingers. 'Jaisalmer must be about two hundred miles from here, isn't it?' he asked.

'Yes Sir.'

'Will you be kind enough to arrange for a taxi? We want to leave by about eleven–thirty.'

The receptionist nodded and picked up the phone.

'Where are you all off to now?'

It was Mandar Bose. He had had a shower and looked impeccable as he stepped out of his room carrying a suitcase.

'We want to go and see the Thar desert,' said Feluda.

'Oh, that means the north–west. I myself am going east.'

'Oh, so you're leaving too?'

'Yes, My taxi should be here any minute now. Can't stay put in one place for long. And if you people leave, there will be nobody left at the Circuit House anyway.'

The gentleman at the desk had finished his conversation and put the phone down.

'It's arranged,' he said.

Feluda turned to me and said, 'Go and see if you can find Lalmohan Babu. Tell him we are leaving for Jaisalmer by eleven. If he wants to come along, he should get ready immediately.'

I ran towards Room No. 10. I had no idea why we were off to Jaisalmer now. What made Feluda choose this place over any other? Perhaps because it was near the desert. Had Dr. Hajra also gone off to Jaisalmer? Would this be the end of our troubles? Or just the beginning?

CHAPTER 8

It is nearly a hundred and twenty miles from Jodhpur to Pokran. From there to Jaisalmer is another seventy miles. It would take about six or seven hours to cover this distance of nearly two hundred miles. At least that was what our driver Gurubachan Singh told us. I noticed that this chubby, cheerful Sikh driver had the habit of periodically taking his hands off the steering wheel, putting them behind his head, and leaning back to rest his body. Not that the car had to stop — the necessary bit of steering would be done by Gurubachan's belly. It was not as much of a feat as I'm making it sound. For one thing, there was hardly any traffic on this road. For another, the road tended to run absolutely straight for five or six miles at a stretch. Barring any unforeseen accidents, it seemed likely that we would reach Jaisalmer by six in the evening.

Ten miles out of Jodhpur, and the landscape had begun to take such extraordinary shapes and colours as I had never seen before. In the immediate vicinity of Jodhpur, there were lots of mountains. The reddish stone quarried from those mountains had been used to build Jodhpur Fort. But for some time now, the mountains seemed to have vanished. Instead, undulating land stretched out to the horizon. This land was partly grass and partly reddish earth, part sand and part gravel. The familiar trees too seemed to have been replaced by acacias and unknown varieties of thorny cacti and bushes.

The other thing to notice were the wild camels. A number of them were grazing around just like cows and sheep. Some of them were the colour of tea with milk in it, some resembled black coffee. I noticed one of them happily munching away at one of those thorny plants. Feluda said that the insides of their mouths would often become raw and bleed from eating cacti, but since this was the only food available to them in these parts, they had learned to ignore the pain.

Feluda had also been telling us about Jaisalmer. Built in the 12th century, this town used to be the capital of the Bhati Rajputs. The Pakistan border lay only 64 miles away. Even ten years ago, it was very difficult to travel to Jaisalmer. There were no trains. Whatever road there was tended to disappear often under the sands. The place was so dry that even one day of rainfall in a whole year was counted as a piece of good fortune. When I asked him about important battles, Feluda said that Alauddin Khilji had once attacked Jaisalmer.

Ninety kilometres or about fifty-six miles along the way, our taxi suddenly punctured a tyre, emitted an ugly groan and came to a lopsided halt by the roadside. I felt quite annoyed with Gurbachan Singh. He had assured us that he had checked his tyres, gauged the air pressure and what not. And one had to admit, the car looked quite new.

All of us followed the Sardarji out of his car. Changing a tyre meant some hassle and a matter of fifteen minutes at the very least.

But as soon as we looked at the flattened tyre, the cause of the puncture became evident.

Along a biggish stretch of the road were strewn numerous nails. It was easy to see they had been newly bought.

We exchanged glances. Mr. Singh let out an unprintable expletive from between his teeth. Feluda, of course, said nothing. He put his hands on his waist and went on staring at the road, his brow furrowed. Lalmohan Babu took out a diary–like green notebook from a worn Japan Air Lines carrier bag, and scribbled something in it with a pencil.

By the time we had changed the tyre and removed the nails from the road, following Feluda's advice, and were ready to start again, it was a quarter–to–two. Feluda said to our driver — 'Please Sardarji, keep an eye on the road as you drive. As you can see, the enemy is after us.'

But driving really slowly would mean not reaching our destination till late at night. So Gurubachan Singh decided to reduce speed from 60 to 40 miles per hour. And let's face it — if one really had to keep an eye on the road, it would be impossible to go beyond 10 to 15 miles per hour.

We were about 160 km, or nearly a 100 miles into our trip, when disaster finally overtook us.

It was not nails this time, but board pins. At a guess, there were about ten thousand pins scattered over a patch 20 to 25 feet wide. Clearly, the tyre puncture expert was not taking any chances.

We also knew quite well that Gurubachan Singh had no other spare tyres in his boot.

The four of us got out once more. From the expression on Mr. Singh's face, I felt he would have been scratching his head, had he not been wearing a turban.

'Is Pokran a town or a village?' Feluda enquired in Hindi.

'It's a town, Sir.'

'How far from here?'

'About twenty–five miles.'

'Good God! . . . What shall we do then?'

Gurubachan Singh explained that any taxi going on this route was bound to be driven by someone he knew. It we could wait here until we got hold of such a taxi, he could borrow a. spare tyre from them, and then have his own punctured tyres mended once we were in Pokran. But who could tell whether such a taxi would indeed show up, and if it did, when! How long would we have to wait in the middle of this deserted expanse?

A group of three men with five camels went by us in the direction of Jodhpur. Each of those three was pitch black in complexion. One of them had a snow–white beard and sideburns! Perhaps it was the way they stared at us as they went past that made Lalmohan Babu shrink closer to Feluda.

'What's the nearest train station?' Feluda asked, continuing to pick up board pins. The possible plight of other cars had made all of us join him in this charitable action.

'Oh about seven or eight miles — Ramdeora.'

'Ramdeora...'

Once all the pins had been removed, Feluda took the Bradshaw timetable out of his bag. Opening it on a particular page which had been folded, he glanced over it, and said, 'No use. The morning train from Jodhpur was supposed to reach Ramdeora at three forty–five. Which means the train must have left us way behind.'

'But isn't there another train at night that goes to Jaisalmer?'

'Hm, yes. But that won't reach Ramdeora before three fifty - three in the morning. Even if we started walking right now, it will take us a solid two hours to get to Ramdeora. If I thought there was any hope of catching the morning train, then I'd say, let's walk. At least we could have reached Pokran. Now, in the middle of nowhere . . .'

Even in a situation as grim as this, Lalmohan Babu smiled as he spoke in a slightly shaky voice, 'Whatever you may say, this is a situation straight out of a novel. Who would have thought that even in real life . . .'

Feluda suddenly stretched his hand out, gesturing our friend to stop. Not a sound could be heard anywhere, as if the earth had suddenly become dumb. And in the middle of this silence we clearly heard a faint sound chug–chug, chug–chug, chug - chug. It was a train — the Pokran train was coming. But where were the tracks?

As we started in the direction of the sound, we suddenly caught sight of smoke in the distance. Immediately after that, we made out the telegraph post. The slope of the land had hidden it from our view. The red post had blended with the red earth behind to become almost invisible. Had it reached its head high into the sky we would have noticed it before.

'Run!'

Almost simultaneously with that shouted command, Feluda started running towards that smoke. I followed, with Jatayu behind me. Amazing! I could never have guessed the speed that frail body of his could produce. He outstripped me and nearly caught up with Feluda.

There was grass beneath our running feet. But not green, it was completely white, like cotton wool. We ran over that grass at breakneck speed and by the time we had reached the tracks below the slope, the train was within a hundred yards of us.

Without hesitating even for a moment, Feluda jumped right into the middle of the tracks, raised both arms overhead and started waving furiously. The train started to whistle, but above the sound of the whistle Jatayu's voice could be heard hollering,

'Halt, halt, halt . . .'

But obviously no one was listening. The train was a small one, but not one of the toy trains from Martin & Co., which you could flag down in the middle of the road like a bus. Whistling at top volume, and without reducing speed even by a second, the train came right up to us. Feluda was forced to move away from the tracks and the train went by, clashing and clanking, its thick, dark smoke obscuring the sunlight for a few minutes until it finally disappeared in the distance. Even at a moment as dark as this, I could not help thinking that a train like this seemed to belong only to a Hollywood western; that it should be running in this country seemed utterly unbelievable.

'Just think of the gall of that caterpillar!' commented Lalmohan Ganguly.

'Bad luck,' said Feluda. 'That train was running late. And still we couldn't take advantage of it. We might have been lucky enough to get a taxi at Pokran.'

Gurubachan Singh had been smart enough to come after us carrying our luggage. But we would not be needing it now. All we could see down the tracks was smoke.

'But what about camels?' suddenly burst out Jatayu in English, shrill with excitement.

'Camels?' asked Feluda.

'There they are, look!'

And sure enough, a band of camels was coming from the direction of Jodhpur.

'Good idea! Let's go!'

And we started running again.

'If they get really carried away, camels are supposed to raise their speed to twenty miles an hour!' declared Lalmohan Babu as he ran.

We managed to stop the camels. This time, the group consisted of two men and seven camels.

Three camels to take us to Remdeora proposed Feluda — how much? These men did not speak Hindi, they used some kind of local patois. But they understood some Hindi, and could speak a few words. Gurubachan Singh came up and helped in the negotiations. The men agreed to let us hire their camels for ten rupees.

'Will your camels be able to run?' demanded Lalmohan Babu. 'We need to catch a train.'

'Why don't you get up first,' said Feluda with a smile. 'The running will come later.'

'Get up?'

This was probably the first time that the implications of getting up on the back of a camel sank into Lalmohan Babu's mind as he stood confronting the beasts. I too had been observing the animals carefully. Their appearances was nothing less than grotesque — and yet their owners had decked them out in all their finery. On their backs were tasselled cushions, just like the ones I had seen in pictures on elephants' backs. There was a wooden platform to serve as a seat, and the cushion lay underneath. Geometrical patterns in red, blue, yellow and green decorated the cushions. The animals' necks too were draped with red shawls decorated with cowries. I realised these people really loved their animals, however ugly the brutes might be.

Three of the camels were already kneeling on the ground, waiting for us. Gurubachan Singh had collected all our belongings — two suitcases, two hold–alls and a few other small pieces — and brought them there. He asked us to wait in Pokran in case we managed to get the night train, he himself was quite confident about reaching there tonight. The luggage was strapped on to the backs of two of the camels.

Feluda turned to Lalmohan Babu. 'Did you notice how the camel sits down? First he folds his front legs and lowers the front portion of his body to the ground. Then the back. And it's going to be just the opposite when he gets up. The back will be raised first, and then the front. If you adjust your body keeping this in mind, there's no chance of a disaster.'

'Disaster?' croaked Jatayu.

'Watch,' said Feluda. 'I'll get up first.'

Feluda got on the back of one of the camels. As soon as one of the drivers let out a particular sound, the camel promptly raised himself with the most ungainly, lurching motion, just as Feluda had warned us. There was no disaster as far as Feluda was concerned.

'Get up Topshe. Both of you are lightweights. You'll have much less trouble.'

The camel drivers were grinning broadly at the antics of the gentlemen. I too braved the unknown; and as soon as I perched on the camel's back, the animal raised himself. I then realised where the problem lay — when the hind legs are raised, the rider is suddenly jerked forwards. I made a mental resolve to lean back far enough if ever I had to ride a camel again. That would help me keep my balance.

'Save me Maa—'

Instead of 'Mother', all that came out of Lalmohan Babu's mouth was a bleating 'Maa' for the simple reason that the camel raised its behind in one swift movement just as he was about to utter the word. As a result, our friend tumbled forward in a most inglorious heap. Immediately afterwards, the reverse motion elicited a fearful hiccup from him before leaving him absolutely perpendicular.

Having taken leave of Gurubachan Singh, we three Bedouins started on our journey to Ramdeora station.

'Got to cover eight miles in half-an-hour, there's a train to catch,' said Feluda, addressing the camel drivers in stentorian tones. On hearing this, one of the camel drivers climbed on the back of one of the animals and crisply rode ahead. Then the other man made several encouraging noises, and the camels started running.

As it is, they are ungainly animals — when they run, their bodies lurch and sway considerably. Even so, I did not find it a disagreeable experience. Underfoot lay sand and bleached white grass, the place was Rajasthan — how could you not feel the romance of it all?

Feluda had outstripped me. Lalmohan Babu was behind. Once Feluda turned around and called out, 'How do you find the ship of the desert, Mr. Ganguly?'

I too turned my head to see what Lalmohan Babu doing. He looked like someone suffering from the bitterest cold — the lower lip hanging loose to reveal tightly clenched teeth, the veins swollen on his neck.

'Well, how about it? Why don't you say something?' Feluda

shouted again.

From behind me came five words in English spoken in five painful instalments, 'Ship . . . all . . . right . . . talking . . . impossible.'

With much difficulty I suppressed laughter and concentrated on the ride. We were travelling along the side of the railroad tracks. Once I thought I could make out a plume of smoke in the distance before it disappeared again. The sun was going down. The landscape too was changing. Far in the distance I could make out a dim line of mountains. A huge sand dune flashed by to my right. I could see that it was untouched by human feet. Wavy lines marked the surface of the dune.

The camels were probably unused to running like this for too long at a stretch. Periodically they would reduce speed. But the appropriate noises from behind would urge them forward again.

It was about a quarter–past–four when we saw a square room–like structure in the distance, close to the tracks. What else could it be but a station?

As we got closer I could see we had guessed correctly. We could even make out the signal. This was obviously a railway station, and most probably Ramdeora.

The camels had slowed down again. But there was no need to prod them any more, for the train had come and gone. We did not know by what margin we had missed the train, but missed it we had, beyond the shadow of a doubt.

That meant, from now till three in the morning, we would have to sit on the platform of a station hardly worth the name, in an unknown place in the middle of a God–forsaken wilderness.

The station consisted of a platform and a tiny booking office, hardly big enough to serve its purpose. The station was still being built and it seemed quite uncertain when it would be completed. We chose a spot near the booking office, spread out our hold-alls and suitcases, and sat down. The reason for sitting there was a wooden post with a kerosene lamp suspended from it. In the darkness we could at least see each other's faces by that light.

There was a smallish village near the station. Feluda had already gone and surveyed the place. He reported that there was nothing remotely like an eating place there. So all we had with us by way of food was a box of Lalmohan Babu's — containing sweet, flaky pastries. We would have to survive the night on those pastries. The sun had set about ten minutes ago. Very soon, it would be really dark. There was little reason to hope that Gurubachan Singh would turn up. During the three hours we had been here, not a single car had driven past, either in the direction of Jodhpur or of Jaisalmer. So it did not look like we had any other option but to sit on this platform till three in the morning.

Feluda was sitting on his suitcase, staring at the tracks. Already I had seen him cracking his knuckles. It was easy to see that there was a lot of suppressed excitement within him — and that was why he spoke so little.

Lalmohan Babu opened his box, took out a pastry and bit into it before saying, 'Just think how one thing leads to another. If we had not had seats in the same train compartment from Agra, my holiday would have been totally different.'

'Do you regret what has happened?'

'Good heavens! No!' exclaimed Lalmohan Babu. 'But I must say, I would enjoy all this much more if only I had a better idea of what's going on.'

'What do you mean — going on?'

'Well, I don't know a thing. All I seem to be doing is being slapped back and forth like a shuttlecock. Not only that — I still can't make out who you are — the hero or the villain. Ha, ha, ha.'

'It's not likely to do you much good, is it?' said Feluda with a mischievous smile. 'After all, when you yourself are writing a novel, do you tell your readers everything in advance? Why don't you take this Rajasthan saga as a novel? When you come to the end, you'll see that the whole mystery has been solved.'

'Yes, but will I still be around when the story ends? Still alive and kicking?'

'Well, we've all seen for ourselves that when the need arises you can outrun the hare. Surely, that should give you a lot of confidence.'

During this, somebody had come by and lit the kerosene lamp. In that light we saw two turbanned men in local costume advancing towards us, tapping their sticks on the ground as they walked.

They came and squatted down on the platform, four or five feet from us, and started talking to each other in some incomprehensible language. One thing about these men made me gape. Both of them sported moustaches that had been coiled at least four times and looked like watch springs on both sides of their faces. I almost felt sure that if one pulled the moustaches straight, they would each be a foot long! Lalmohan Babu too seemed to be absolutely mesmerized.

'Bandits,' said Feluda.

'Surely not?' said Lalmohan Babu as he poured some water out of the flask and gulped it down.

'Absolutely.'

At this, Lalmohan Babu dropped the cover of his pastry box with a nasty, tinny noise, and became even more nervous.

The men's complexion resembled shiny new shoes which had just been polished with shoe blacking. One of them now took out a cigarette, put it between his lips, slapped his pockets several times, fished out a box of matches, and finding it empty, threw it towards the rail tracks. I heard a click and saw that Feluda had lit his lighter and was holding it out to the man. After the initial surprise, the man leaned forward, lit his cigarette and having borrowed the lighter from Feluda, he fiddled around with it until he managed to light it. Lalmohan Babu attempted to say something — but seemed unable to find his voice. The man tried out the lighter three or four times and gave it back to Feluda. This time Lalmohan Babu, attempting to put the box of pastries its lid shut tight now — into his suitcase, dropped the whole box, making a racket much worse than the last time. Feluda, however, did not take the least notice of this. He took out his blue notebook again, and started looking through it in the dim light.

Suddenly I noticed some kind of a light falling on a clump of bushes behind the booking office.

The light grew stronger. Then I heard the sound of a car. It was coming from Jaisalmer. Thank God! Perhaps Gurubachan would be lucky enough to solve his problems.

The car whizzed straight past us towards Jodhpur. I looked at my watch — it was seven–thirty.

Feluda raised his eyes from the notebook and looked at Lalmohan Babu.

'Tell me Lalmohan Babu,' he said, 'You are always writing all these novels. . . Have you any idea what a blister is, and what causes a blister?'

'Blister?. . . blister ?' Lalmohan Babu was totally at a loss. 'What causes it. . . well, er, for instance, scorching your hand when lighting a cigarette.'

'Yes, yes, but why should a blister appear on that spot?'

'Why? Oh, I see — why. . .'

'Never mind, tell me something else. Why does a man appear shorter than he is when viewed from above?'

Lalmohan Babu gaped at him in silence. In that dim light, I could see him rubbing his hands together. The two men beside us carried on their conversation in the same tone. Feluda continued to look at Lalmohan Babu.

Finally, Lalmohan Babu licked his lips and said, 'Why ask me such — I mean questions like —'

'I have yet another question for you. Surely you know the answer to this one.'

Lalmohan Babu sat dumb. Feluda seemed to have hypnotised him.

'What were you doing this morning near my window in the garden behind the Circuit House?'

For one instant Lalmohan Babu remained frozen. The next moment he burst out into voluble explanation, almost thrashing his limbs in excitement.

'My dear Sir — it was you I was going to see! Only you! But suddenly that peacock shrieked — and then I heard a shout — and I don't know, I felt terribly nervous. . .'

'But wasn't there a simpler route to my room? And did you have to put on a turban and a shawl to visit me?'

'My dear Sir, the shawl was only the bedsheet, and the turban nothing more than one of the Circuit House towels. How could I spy on that fellow without some kind of a disguise?'

'Which fellow?'

'Mr. Trotter, of course. Very suspicious! Lucky that I had gone along. Just look at what I found on the grass outside his window. Nothing less than a secret code! This is what I was going to give you when that dreadful peacock screeched and ruined my plans.'

I was observing Lalmohan Babu's watch. Yes, definitely this was the watch I had seen from the roof. Lalmohan Babu opened his suitcase, took out a wrinkled piece of paper from one flap, and handed it to Feluda. I guessed the paper had been balled up, and then flattened out again.

Looking over Feluda's shoulder, I saw by the light of the kerosene lamp what was written on it

IP 1625 + U

U–M

Feluda frowned as he stared at the piece of paper. I could not make head or tail of this algebraic message, though Lalmohan Babu whispered a couple of time, 'highly suspicious.' Feluda was thinking hard, and at the same time muttering to himself. '1625. . .1625. . . Now, where have I seen this number recently?'

'Could it be the number of taxi?' I suggested.

'No. 1625. . .1625. . .'

Before he had finished speaking, Feluda had suddenly whipped out the Bradshaw time table from his bag. He opened it at the marked page and started running his finger down from top to bottom until he stopped at one place.

'Yes. Arrival time is 1625.'

'Where?' I asked.

'In Pokran.'

'In that case P could stand for Pokran. 16.25 to Pokran. And the rest?'

'The rest. . .IP — and then + U.'

'I don't know, somehow that M in the second line is making me uneasy,' declared Lalmohan Babu. 'M suggests only one thing Murder?

'Wait a minute. let's first make out the first line.'

But Lalmohan Babu went on muttering, 'Murder. . . mystery. . . Massacre. . . Monster. . .'

Feluda kept the piece of paper on his lap and went on thinking. Lalmohan Babu took out his tin of pastries and offered them to us again. When I had helped myself to one, he held it out to Feluda and said, 'By the way, how did you figure out it was me near your window? Did you actually see me?'

Feluda picked out a pastry before he answered.

'You probably forgot to comb your hair after you took off that turban of yours. When I met you shortly after the incident, the state of your hair made me suspicious.'

Our friend smiled and said, 'Please Sir — I hope you don't mind my saying so, but you do seem like a cent per cent sleuth.'

Feluda took out one of his visiting cards and handed it to Lalmohan Babu. That gentleman was absolutely radiant. 'Oh! Prodosh C. Mitter! Is this your real name?'

'Of course. Why, do you have any reason to doubt it?'

'No, no — I was only thinking, what a strange name!'

'Strange?'

'Well isn't it, somewhat? Just look at the aptness of it. Prodosh. Pro stands for a professional. *Dosh* in Bengali means crime. C is to see — i.e., investigate. Therefore, Prodosh is equal to Professional Crimes Investigator.'

'Bravo! bravo! And what about Mitter?'

'That one I have to think about,' confessed **Lalmohan Babu** scratching his head.

'No you don't. I'll tell you what it is. You know the metres that taxis have. It's the same kind of metre — an indicator. Which means, it is not only investigation, but also indication. Find the criminal and indicate him by pointing a finger. How about that?'

It was Lalmohan Babu's turn to exclaim 'Bravo!' and clap his hands. But Feluda had become serious again. He took another look at the piece of paper in his hands, tucked it into the pocket of his shirt and took out a cigarette.

'I and U could have very simple explanations,' he said.

'They could just mean I and you. But that plus sign is a problem. And the second line is quite hopeless. . . Topshe, why don't you open out your hold–all and lie down for a while. You too, Lalmohan Babu. There's still seven–and–a–half hours to go before the train comes. I'll wake you up in time.'

It was not a bad idea. We unstrapped the hold–alls, spread them out on the platform and lay down. As soon as I was on my back I saw the mighty sky spread out above me, and immediately I realized that I had never before seen so many stars. Was that because the desert sky was particularly clear? Perhaps.

I fell asleep watching the sky. Once I heard a comment from Lalmohan Babu, 'Riding on a camel is really hard on your joints.' Later, it sounded like he was saying, 'M is murder.' After that I remember nothing.

I woke up to find Feluda shaking me. 'Get up Topshe, the train is coming.'

As we jumped up and re–strapped our hold–alls, the headlights of the train came in sight.

A passenger train running on the metre gauge. So the compartments were very small. As there were very few passengers, we were not too surprised to find an unoccupied first–class compartment.

It was dark inside; I groped for the switch and pressed it several times, but it was no use.

'Bulbs in trains get stolen even in civilized countries,' said Lalmohan Babu. 'It's useless to expect them in this dacoit country.'

'Why don't the two of you stretch out on these two berths for the night. I'll spread a rug on the floor and manage,' said Feluda. 'We still have a clear six hours to go — time to stretch out and relax a bit.'

Lalmohan Babu protested half–heartedly — 'Why should you be on the floor, let me . . .' But when Feluda firmly said 'Certainly not,' our friend happily opened his hold–all and spread it out on the berth. Perhaps he had his aching joints in mind.

Within barely a minute of the train moving away from the platform, someone jumped on to the footboard of our compartment. Lalmohan Babu said, 'Look here, this car is reserved. Ladies compartment.' At this, the door was wrenched open from outside. The bright light flashing from a torch blinded me for a few seconds. In the same light I saw a hand advancing towards us, and in that hand gleamed something with a metal barrel.

All three of us raised our arms over our heads.

'All right now gentlemen, just get up. The door is open, get off one by one.'

The voice belonged to Mandar Bose!

'But the train's moving!' said Lalmohan Babu, his voice trembling.

'Shut up!' roared Mandar Bose and came a couple of steps closer. The light from the torch kept moving from face to face.

'Don't try any of your sob stories on me mister! Haven't you ever got on and off moving buses and trams in Calcutta? Get up, get up . . .'

But before he could finish speaking, something happened which I will never forget. Feluda's right arm came down like a streak of lightning, caught hold of one corner of his rug, and yanked it violently. As a result, Mandar Bose's feet rose up in the air, while his body flattened back in a swift motion and thudded against the wall of our compartment.

Simultaneously, the revolver spun out of his right hand, and dropped on Lalmohan Babu's berth. The lighted torch slipped out of his left hand and fell on the floor. Even before Mandar Bose's body had fully hit the ground, Feluda was on his feet — in his hand was his own revolver which he had taken out of his coat pocket. 'Get up!' It was Feluda who was now roaring the command at Mandar Bose.

The metre gauge train was running through the desert, swaying on its tracks and making an ungodly racket. Lalmohan Babu had already hidden Mandar Bose's revolver in his own Japan Air Lines bag.

'Didn't you hear me? Get up!' Feluda roared again. The torch was rolling about on the floor. I could see that it was necessary to aim the light on Mandar Bose — otherwise he could take advantage of the darkness and do further mischief. But as soon as I tried to pick up the torch, I got into trouble. And what trouble — even now, the very thought of it chills my bones. The upper half of Mandar Bose's body was close to my berth. As I bent forward to pick up the torch, he made a sudden lunge, grabbed me in his arms and got up, still holding me. As a result, I happened to be between him and Feluda. Even at the height of danger I could not help appreciating the man's fiendish cleverness. I realised that though Feluda had won the first round in an astounding manner, he was in a tight spot in the second. And I also realised that the only person responsible for this was myself.

Mandar Bose continued to hold me from behind as he backed away towards the open door. Something was pricking me in the shoulder. It was a nail on one of his fingers. I remembered how Nilu had mentioned the burning sensation in his arm.

Gradually, I realised, we had come very close to the door. The freezing wind from outside was biting into my left shoulder.

Mandar Bose took one more step backwards. Feluda had his revolver trained on him — but could do nothing. The lighted torch was still rolling on the floor from one side to another with each swaying motion of the train.

Suddenly, a violent shove from behind made me fall almost on top of Feluda. And right after that I heard a sound which told me that Mandar Bose had jumped down from the running train. There was no way of telling whether he was alive or dead.

Feluda peered outside from the doorway for some time before coming back. Then, having replaced his revolver in its usual place, he sat down and said,

'I'll be really sorry if the villain does not at least break a bone or two.'

Lalmohan Babu laughed, perhaps a shade too loudly.

'Didn't I tell you, that man was a suspicious character!' By now I had drunk quite a lot of water from our flask. The thumping in my heart was slowing down, my breathing was becoming normal. I could hardly believe what a terrible thing had happened in the space of a few seconds.

'That man got away this time,' said Feluda, 'Only because of master Tapesh here. Otherwise, I would have put my gun to his head and extracted every bit of information from him. Of course . . .'

He stopped, then continued. 'I've noticed that every time I am in real danger, my brain functions with extra clarity. Now I can unravel that code perfectly.'

'You don't say!' said Lalmohan Babu.

'Yes, it's really quite easy,' said Feluda. 'I, is of course I, P stands for Pokran, U means you, and M is Mitter — Prodosh Mitter.'

'What about the plus — minus?'

'I P 1625 + U. That is, I am reaching Pokran, at 16.25, you must come and join me.'

'And U — M!'

'Easy. Get rid of Mitter.'

'Get rid of!' echoed Lalmohan Babu huskily. 'That means the

minus sign meant murder?'

'Why think of murder? If he had thrown us out of a moving train in the middle of the night, it was highly likely that we would have been badly injured. On top of that, we'd have had to wait another twenty–four hours for the next train. By then, they would have accomplished their purpose. All they needed to do was to keep us away from Jaisalmer. That was why there were all those nails on the road. When it became evident that the nails had not stopped us, there was this attempt to get us off the train.'

It was at this moment that I became aware of something.

'I can smell a cheroot, Feluda,' I said.

'I smelt it as soon as the man entered our compartment,' said Feluda. 'I had also realised before that one of the guests at the Circuit House also smoked cheroots. That bit of tinsel Mukul had in his hand is the kind that is usually wrapped round a cheroot.'

'That man also has one really long nail. I think my shoulder must be as badly scratched as Nilu's arm.'

'Yes, but who's the 'I' who's giving all these instructions?' queried Lalmohan Babu.

Feluda sounded very grave when he answered.

'If you compare the writing on that threatening note we found in the Circuit House with the writing of this code, then only one man comes to mind.'

'Who?' we both asked at the same time.

'Dr. Hemangamohan Hajra.'

That night I managed to get only three hours of sleep. When I woke up, the sun had already risen. I saw that Feluda had got up from the floor and was sitting on one corner of my berth, looking out of the window. On his lap lay the blue notebook, in his hands were two letters — one, the threatening note in English, the other the letter written by Dr. Hajra I looked at my watch, it was a quarter–to–seven. Lalmohan Babu was still fast asleep. I was absolutely famished, but did not feel like eating any more pastry. It would be nine before we reached Jaisalmer. Clearly, I would have to forget about food during these two hours.

The landscape outside was quite extraordinary. Slightly undulating stretches of land for miles on end — not a house, not a human being, not even a tree could be seen. And yet you could not call it a desert. Though there was sand in some areas, most of the land was covered either with dry bleached grass, or reddish earth and red and black chips of stone. Somehow, it seemed hard to believe that there could be a city beyond this.

We came to a station — it was Jetha Chandan. I opened the Bradshaw and found that the station after this was Thaiyat Hamira. Right after that came Jaisalmer. There were no shops, no people, no porters, not even any vendors at this station. Altogether, one felt this train had somehow reached an undiscovered corner of the earth. Much as a rocket might land on the moon.

Almost as soon as the train started moving out of the station, Lalmohan Babu woke up, yawned hugely, and said, 'I had a most fantastic dream. There was this group of dacoits. Their moustaches were coiled like sheep horns. I had hypnotised them all and was leading them through a fort. Inside the fort was an underground passage. We went along that passage to a chamber. I knew the room was supposed to contain hidden treasure. But when I went there all I saw was a camel sitting on the floor eating pastries.'

'How do you know it was eating pastries?' asked Feluda. 'Did he open his mouth to show you?'

'Didn't have to. There was my pastry box, clear as can be, lying open in front of the camel.'

Shortly after leaving Thaiyat Hamira, I noticed the misty outline of a mountain in the distance. This too was one of those flat table mountains of Rajasthan. Our train seemed to be heading in the direction of that mountain.

By eight o'clock, there appeared to be something on top of the mountain. Slowly I could make out a fort. It occupied the entire mountain top and was perched there like a crown. The bright sunshine of a beautifully clean morning fell straight on the fort. Involuntarily, three words came out of my mouth, 'The Golden Fortress!'

'Right you are,' said Feluda. 'This is the one and only golden fortress in Rajasthan. I had some inkling as soon as I saw that bowl. Then my ideas were confirmed by the guidebook. The fort is made of the same stone as the bowl— yellow sandstone. If

Mukul can recall his past life, if there is indeed any such thing
as a past life, then it is likely that he was born here.'

'But does Dr. Hajra know about this?' I asked.

Feluda did not answer my question. He gazed steadily at the
fort and said, 'You know something, Topshe, this is amazing,
this golden light. I can see every detail of the spider's web in
this light.'

The first thing we did on getting off at Jaisalmer was to find a teashop. We discovered a new kind of dessert to have with our tea, and took care of our empty stomachs. We needed to have something sweet, said Feluda, because of the glucose it contained. There was a lot of work ahead of us — the glucose would give us energy.

Later, when we came out of the station, we discovered there were no cars to be had for love or for money. One solitary jeep was there — but it was obviously not for hire. Apart from this, there were no other vehicles — *tongas, ekkas,* cycle–rickshaws, taxis or anything else. I seemed to recall having seen a black Ambassador, just as I had been getting off the train — but even that had vanished.

'You can see what a small town this is,' said Feluda. 'So every place must be certain walking distance. The guide book mentioned a tourist bungalow. Let's try to find that first.'

We picked up our luggage and started walking. There was a gas station nearby — we asked a man there for directions, and he showed us the way. We found we would not have to go up the hill to reach the bungalow. It was situated to the right of the hill on level ground. Observing tyre marks on the sand as we walked, Feluda remarked, 'That Ambassador also seems to have gone in this direction.'

After about fifteen minutes of walking, we came to a single–storey building which had a wooden placard telling us that this was the tourist bungalow. The black Ambassador was parked right in front.

An old man wearing a khaki shirt, *dhoti* and coiled turban on his head emerged from the neighbouring outhouse — probably because he had seen us. Feluda asked him in Hindi if he was the *chowkidar*. The man nodded assent. His expression made it quite clear that he found our arrival entirely unexpected and also that he was quite suspicious about us. I knew very well that you cannot stay in these tourist bungalows without prior permission.

Feluda said he just wanted to leave our luggage there for the moment, and see if he could get permission to stay somehow. The old man said we would have to see the king's secretary to get permission. He even indicated the direction of the palace. In the distance, part of the yellow stone palace was visible above the top of trees.

The old man raised no objection to our leaving the luggage there. Of course, one reason could be the crisp new two–rupee note that Feluda pressed into his hand.

We left our suitcases and bedding in one room, refilled our flasks with water, slung them over our shoulders, and asked the *chowkidar* for precise directions to get to the fort.

'You want to go to the fort?'

The question, in English, came from the far end of the verandah. A gentleman had just emerged from one of the rooms in that portion of the bungalow. He had a fair complexion, was certainly not more than forty, and sported a thin, carefully trimmed moustache under a very sharp nose. Another, older, man now emerged from the room and stood beside the first gentleman. This man carried a stick, one of the kind we had seen in the market at Jodhpur. He was dressed in a rather ill–fitting black suit. I could not make out what part of India the two of them came from. But I did notice that the second gentleman had a slight limp. That was why he needed the stick.

'Yes,' said Feluda. 'It wouldn't be a bad idea.'

'Come along with us, we are going that way.'

Feluda took a few seconds to answer.

'Thank you very much. That is very kind of you.'

As we were walking towards the car, Lalmohan Babu whispered, 'I hope they won't try to throw us out of the moving car.' The car started on its journey towards Jaisalmer fort. The gentleman with the stick enquired, 'Are you from Calcutta?'

'Yes,' said Feluda.

Far away to the left, on the sandy surface, I saw some

mausoleums like the ones at Devikunda. Feluda told me that almost every city in Rajasthan had some of those.

Slowly, the car started climbing up the steep mountain road. After about a minute, we heard another car behind us. It was repeatedly honking at us. And yet, it was not as if we were driving particularly slowly. So why on earth was that fellow so impatient?

Feluda had been sitting in the back seat with the two gentlemen. Suddenly he turned around, looked outside through the back window and asked our driver to stop the car.

As the car came to a halt on one side of the road, a taxi stopped on our right. At the wheel, smiling in greeting, was Gurubachan Singh.

The three of us got out. Feluda thanked the two gentlemen in English.

'Our taxi had broken down midway along the road. It's here now,' he explained.

Gurubachan said he had managed to get a spare tyre from a taxi-driver he knew who was returning from Jaisalmer at six–thirty in the morning. And he had covered ninety miles in the last two hours. He had been waiting at the petrol station in Jaisalmer when he suddenly saw the black Ambassador.

A bit further along the road, we entered a market. There were lots of shops huddled almost on top of one another, a loudspeaker was blaring out some Hindi film song and there was even a tiny movie theatre displaying a Hindi film poster.

'Do you want to see the fort?' asked Gurubachan Singh. When Feluda said 'yes,' he stopped the taxi. 'This is the entrance,' he told us.

I looked to the right and saw an enormous gateway beyond which was a steep stone road leading uphill to another pair of gates. I realised we were standing in front of the outer doors. Inside was the real entrance to the fortress. Right behind the second gateway, rose the golden fortress of Jaisalmer.

There was a man standing outside the gates. You could see he was a guard. Feluda went up to him and asked if a Bengali gentleman and a little boy had come to see the fort this morning. Feluda even indicated Mukul's height with his hand.

'Yes they did. But they've left.'

'When?'

'Oh, about half—an—hour ago.'

'Did they come in a car?'

'Yes — they had a taxi.'

'Can you tell us which way they've gone?'

The guard pointed to the road going west. We took that road and made our way through narrow alleyways and crowded shops. Lalmohan Babu sat in front beside Gurubachan Singh, Feluda and I were in the back. After we had gone some distance, Feluda suddenly asked,

'I don't suppose you've brought that weapon of yours?'

Lalmohan Babu, disturbed in his meditations by this unexpected question, nearly jumped.

'The *Bhopali* — I mean — the Nepalese knife?'

'Yes, your *bhopali* from Nepal.'

'But, Sir, that's in my suitcase.'

'In that case, take out Mandar Bose's revolver from that Japan Air Lines bag next to you, and thrust it into your belt under the jacket. Make sure that no one can see it from outside.'

Lalmohan Babu's movements indicated he was complying with Feluda's instructions. I would have given a lot to have seen his face at this point.

'It's nothing to worry about,' said Feluda. 'If there's any trouble, just take it out, and simply point it ahead.'

'Yes, but what if there's something going on b—b—behind?'

'In that case, just turn around, and the back will become the front.'

'And what about you? Are you going to be non—violent today?'

'That depends on the circumstances.'

The taxi had left the market behind and come to an open area. During the drive, we had managed to ask a few other people which way the other taxi had gone. Besides, tyre tracks would appear in the sand on the road from time to time, to show us that we were still following Hemanga Hajra.

'This is the road to Mohangarh,' said Gurubachan Singh. 'It will be all right for another mile or so. But then the road is really bad. Nothing but a jeep can go over that road.'

But we did not have to go even that one mile. A little further on we saw a taxi waiting by the roadside. To the right, some distance away, there stood lots of abandoned single–storey stone houses — they had no roof, and looked more like cubby holes than houses. We realised this must have been an ancient village, the kind we had seen once or twice before. The residents had left these villages many decades ago. Only the walls still stood, because they were made of stone.

We instructed Gurubachan Singh to wait, and advanced towards the houses. Our Sardarji, I noticed, left the car and went along to the other taxi —probably to have a cosy chat with a compatriot.

It was oppressively still. If you looked back you could see in the distance Jaisalmer fort sitting atop the mountain. In front, opposite the road, also rose another mountain.

At its feet was a huge open space with a series of yellow stone bars that resembles gigantic pestles, planted in the ground.

'The graves of warriors,' whispered Feluda.

'My blood pressure tends to be on the low side,' announced Lalmohan Babu in thin, sepulchral tones.

'Don't you worry,' said Feluda. 'Before you know what's happening, it will be raised to its normal height.'

We were close to the houses now. Through the rows of houses ran a straight road. I could see very well that this was nothing like a Bengali village. There was a simple, geometric pattern here.

But where were the passengers of the other car? Where was Mukul? Where was Dr. Hajra?

Had anything happened to Mukul?

Suddenly, I became aware of a sound — very low; but one could hear it if one tried to listen. Tap — tap — tap.

Very carefully, without making a sound, we advanced a few steps and found overselves at a crossing. We stood exactly in the middle of the intersection of two roads, and the sound was coming from the right. On both sides the road was lined by ten or twelve houses which consisted only of walls and empty doorways.

We took the right hand road, and stealthily stepped forward.

Feluda said 'Revolver' through his teeth, so softly that we could hardly hear him. At the same time, his own hand went inside his jacket. Through the corner of my eye, I saw that

Lalmohan Babu's revolver had appeared in his hand, and it was trembling violently.

A sudden rustling sound made us stop dead in our tracks. The next moment we saw Mukul running out of the doorway of a house at the far end of the left side or the road. As soon as he caught sight of us, his speed doubled, and he came and threw himself in Feluda's arms. He was panting, his face bloodless, pale.

I was about to ask him what had hapened, but Feluda put his finger on my lips and stopped me.

With a whispered 'Look after him,' Feluda handed Mukul over to Lalmohan Babu, and silently went along in the direction that Mukul had come from. I followed him.

As we went forward, the sound too grew louder. It sounded like someone was moving stones — tap — clank — click — tap . . .

When he reached the house, Feluda moved close to the wall. Three more steps, and I too could see Dr. Hemanga Hajra through the yawning gap of the doorway. He stood in one corner of the room with his back towards us, and like a madman in a frenzy, he was lifting pieces of stone from a heap of rubble and flinging them aside, one by one. He was utterly oblivious of our presence in the doorway.

Feluda took one more step forward, the revolver in his hand raised in the direction of Dr. Hajra.

Suddenly, a violent flapping sound rose from above.

A peacock — leaping down from the top of the wall.

As soon as it landed, the peacock made a furious dash towards Dr. Hajra as he bent forward, and pecked him viciously under the left ear. As Dr. Hajra screamed in agony and pressed his hand over the wound, his white shirt–sleeve turned red.

The peacock, meanwhile, was still pecking at him. Frantically making his escape, Dr. Hajra suddenly confronted us and did a double take as if he was facing the dead. We backed away from the door, and the peacock chased him out of the house.

'I bet you'd never thought of this — that the place of the hidden treasure would also have peacock's nest with eggs inside, eh?'

Feluda's voice was steely, his revolver aimed straight at Dr. Hajra. I had finally understood that Dr. Hajra was the villain of piece, and his punishment had been entirely appropriate. But there were still so many unexplained mysteries that my head was spinning at the very thought of them.

We heard the sound of a car. Dr. Hajra was lying face down on the ground. Slowly he turned his neck towards Feluda, the left hand still pressing a bloodied handkerchief over the wound.

'You realise, there's no hope for you anymore,' said Feluda. 'All your exits are closed now.'

Before Feluda had finished, Dr. Hajra suddenly leaped up and made a mad dash in the opposite direction. Feluda lowered his revolver — for really there was no escape that way. From the opposite direction came the two gentlemen we had met recently. The one who did not have the stick caught hold of Dr. Hajra exactly as if he was catching a cricket ball, and held him fast.

The gentleman with the stick now came up to Feluda. Feluda transferred his revolver to his left hand, held his right out to the gentleman and said, 'Welcome Dr. Hajra.'

Great heavens! This was Dr. Hajra!

The gentleman shook hands with Feluda and said 'You must be Prodosh Mitter?'

'Yes, Sir. I think that blister on your foot, caused by those *nagra* shoes, is still giving you trouble . . .'

The real Dr. Hajra smiled.

'I called Sudhir Babu day before yesterday,' he said. 'He's the one who told me about your being here. I had no trouble recognising you from the description he gave me. Let me introduce you — this is Inspector Rathore.'

'And what about him?' Feluda pointed to the handcuffed man with bowed head, still bleeding from the peacock's attack, 'Is he the great Bhabananda?'

'Yes,' replied Dr. Hajra. 'Alias, Amiyanath Barman, alias the Great Barman — Wizard of the East.'

Bhabananda is now in the custody of the Rajasthan police. The charges against him — attempted murder of Dr. Hemanga Hajra, absconding with Dr. Hajra's possessions, masquerading as Dr. Hajra, etc. We were sitting on the verandah of the tourist bungalow and drinking coffee with camel's milk. Mukul was in the garden in front, playing happily, for he knew he was going back to Calcutta today. Having seen the Golden Fortress, he had lost all interest in Rajasthan.

Feluda turned to the real Dr. Hajra and asked, 'Was Bhabananda really guilty of fraud in Chicago? Were the stories in the papers true?'

'One hundred per cent,' said Hajra. 'There's no keeping track of all the misdeeds that Bhabananda and his assistant have been guilty of in different countries. And the Chicago affair was not as simple as you think. Along with his own fraudulent activities, he was also spreading false stories about me, creating infinite problems in my work. That was why I was finally forced to take steps against him. Of course, that was four years ago. I have no idea when the two of them came back to India. I myself have been back only the last three months. I had gone one day to Sudhir Babu's shop and heard about his son. That made me go and see the boy. The rest you know. When I decided to come to Rajasthan with Mukul, I hadn't the faintest idea that those two would come after me.'

'Well, who wouldn't want to kill two birds with one stone!' said Feluda. 'There was the hope of finding hidden treasure, and the sweet prospect of revenge . . . But are you sure you didn't see them in Calcutta?'

'Positive. The very first encounter was in the refreshment room at Bandikui Station. If I had not stayed one extra day in Howrah I would not have met them on that train. The two of them came up to me and sought to make friends.'

'And you didn't recognize them?'

'How could I? In Chicago, both of them were bearded replicas of Maharishi Mahesh Yogi!'

'And then?'

'Then they sat down and ate with us at the same table, made friends with Mukul by showing him magic tricks, and got on the same train in the same compartment as us. I had already decided to get off at Kishangarh and show Mukul the fort there. But I have no idea when the two of them got off and followed us under cover. They reached the fort shortly after we did. It is a rather deserted area. The two of them came like thieves, stayed out of sight and on .the look out, and then when the opportunity presented itself, they pushed me off the edge of the mountain. I rolled down for about a hundred feet until I was caught in a bramble bush, which saved any life. If I take off my shirt, you'll see I've got scratches all over my body. Anyway, I stayed for about an hour by that bush, without even trying to move. I wanted them to think that they had got rid of me, in which case they would feel free to depart with Mukul. By the time I made my way to the station, the eight o'clock train for Marwar had already left. And on that train had gone Mukul, all my belongings and those two Machiavellis. They had not even left me the means of identifying myself to other people.'

'But didn't Mukul have any objections to going off with them?'

Dr. Hajra smiled.

'Haven't you yet understood what Mukul is like? If he can happily leave his parents behind, then why should he make any distinctions between one unknown person and another? Bhabananda told him he would show him the Golden Fortress — and that was that.'

'Anyway, instead of giving up in despair, I felt doubly determined to carry on with my search. At least I had my wallet with me. I put my torn clothes into a bundle and transformed myself into a Rajasthani with my newly acquired outfit. But I wasn't used to wearing *nagra* shoes. That's how I got those blisters. The next day I got into your compartment on the train from Kishangarh. We also travelled on the same train from Marwar to Jodhpur.

There I got a room at the Raghunath Inn. I had one friend in town — Professor Trivedi. But I did not tell him anything straightaway. If there was too much fuss, then those two villains could decamp, or Mukul might get scared and do something unwise. I myself had already guessed that Jaisalmer was the place. So it was just a matter of waiting — for the moment when Bhabananda would start for Jaisalmer with Mukul. Until then, my job was to keep the two of them under surveillance.'

'So that was you, outside the Circuit House the other day?'

'Yes. And that created another problem. I realised that Mukul had managed to recognise me! Or that's what it seemed like from the way he came out of the gate and started walking towards me.'

'Afterwards you must have followed Bhabananda and taken the same train to Pokran?'

'Yes. And the funniest part was when I saw you from the train, trying to make it stop.'

'Hm. Bhabananda too must have seen that. And he must have therefore guessed that we would try to get the train from Ramdeora.'

Dr. Hajra continued with his story.

'Just before I got on the train I had called Trivedi and asked him to inform the Jaisalmer police. And well before that, I had telephoned Calcutta from his house, and had heard about you being here. I had also borrowed this suit from Trivedi to look like a gentleman again.'

'And when you arrived at Pokran — probably that was when you saw Bhabananda's assistant waiting with a taxi, wasn't it?'

'That's where the trouble began. I lost them. I had to wait ten long hours before catching the night train. I had no idea of course that you too were on that train. I saw you for the first time at this tourist bungalow. What I want to know is when you first started suspecting Bhabananda.'

Feluda answered with a smile, 'It would be a mistake to say that I suspected Bhabananda. The person I thought I suspected was Dr. Hajra. And that was not in Jodhpur, but in Bikaner. We found him lying gagged and trussed up in Devikunda. Immediately before that, I had picked up an Ace brand matchbox from the ground. I knew this was not sold in Rajasthan. So when I saw the gentleman in that state, I assumed that the matchbox belonged to the person responsible for the assault.'

'But then I discovered there was something fishy about the bonds. If you tie up a man both by the arms and legs, he will be helpless. But when only the arms have been tied in the back, any sensible person can fold his legs, pass his arms below, bring them forward and set himself free. I realised our friend had tied himself up. But even then, I continued to think of Dr. Hajra as the real culprit. The final revelation came this morning on the train — as I was staring at a letter written by Bhabananda on one of your letterheads.'

'How?'

'The letterhead had your name printed on top as Hajra with a J. And this man had signed the letter with a Z. Instantly I realised that our Hajra was not the real Hajra. But who was he then? Must be one of the people who had kidnapped Nilu in Calcutta. And the other kidnapper must have been Mandar Bose — who has an extra–long nail on his right hand and whose breath smells of cheroot smoke, as Nilu and I were both aware. In that case, who was the real Hajra, and where was he? There could be only one answer to that question. Hajra was the man who had blisters on his feet from wearing *nagra* shoes, who had shared our train compartment from Kishangarh, who had been lurking around the Circuit House and the fort at Bikaner, and who was limping with a stick at the tourist bungalow in Jaisalmer.'

'Sudhir Babu did a very smart thing when he consulted you,' said Dr. Hajra. 'I probably would not have been able to manage on my own. It was you who took care of Bhabananda's assistant. If only he can be caught and handcuffed, there will be nothing left undone.'

Feluda indicated Lalmohan Babu, saying, 'He contributed a lot towards suspicion being directed at Mandar Bose.'

Previously, Lalmohan Babu had made quite a few attempts to speak, but without success. Now he had his chance.

'Well Sir, what's going to happen to the hidden treasure now?'

'Why don't we let the peacocks go on guarding it?' said Dr. Hajra. 'You saw for yourself what can happen if you get on the wrong side of those birds!'

'Right now,' said Feluda, 'I think it is time for you to hand over your hidden treasure. Of course, the way your jacket is swollen at the waist, one can't call it hidden anymore.'

Lalmohan Babu looked rather downcast as he took out Mandar Bose's revolver and gave it to Feluda.

Feluda took it in his hands with a 'Thank You', and suddenly looked unexpectedly grim. He turned the revolver over several times. Finally, he muttered, almost to himself.

'Hats off, Mr. Trotter! You really managed to bluff Prodosh Mitter that time!'

'What is it? What's wrong?' We all clamoured in unison.

'This is a total hoax — made in Japan, it says — the kind of revolver magicians use on stage!'

Just before we all burst into laughter, Jatayu pulled the revolver out of Feluda's hand, saying with a broad grin, 'For my collection — and as a memento of our powerful adventure in Rajasthan!

'Thank you, Sir!'

THE BUCCANEER OF BOMBAY

A box of sweets in the hands of Lalmohan Ganguly, alias Jatayu, surprised me. Usually he carries nothing but an umbrella when he comes to visit us. True, he does bring a packet of books whenever one of his thrillers comes out — but that is only twice a year. Today there was a white cardboard box, the Rs. 25 size from the new sweet shop in Mirzapur Street, Kallol Mishtanna Bhandar, with a gold ribbon tied around it and 'Kallol Five–Mix Sweetmeats'was printed in blue letters on both sides of the box. If you opened the box you would see five compartments each with its own variety of sweets. And inevitably in the centre you would find Kallol's invention — the Diamonda — faceted like a diamond and decorated with silver foil.

Why was Lalmohan Babu carrying such a box? And why did he have this proud conqueror's smile on his face?

As soon as he had come in, put the box on a table and sat down, Feluda said, 'So you've just got the good news from Bombay?'

Lalmohan Babu's astonishment did not succeed in wiping the smile from his face. He only raised his eyebrows.

'How did you guess?'

'It's been an hour since the afternoon siren — and yet your watch still says three–fifteen. That can only mean that you forgot to look at it, in the first flush of joy. What's wrong — has the spring broken or did you just forget to wind it?'

Lalmohan Babu picked up his trailing blue shawl and flung it across his left shoulder in the fashion of a Roman toga.

'I'd asked for twenty–five,'he said, 'and, this morning the servant handed me a telegram as soon as I woke up. Here it is.'

Lalmohan Babu took out a pink telegram from his pocket and read it out to us.

'Producer willing to offer ten for *Buccaneer*, please cable consent.' I sent a reply, 'Happily selling *Buccaneer* for ten, take blessings.'

'Ten thousand!'Even a cool customer like Feluda was goggling. 'You have a sold a story for ten thousand.'

Jatayu smiled — a faint smile of satisfaction.

'The money hasn't come yet. I'll get it as soon as I go to Bombay.'

'You are going to Bombay?' Feluda's eyes widened again.

'Not just myself, the two of you also. At my expense. This story could not have been written without your help.'

This happens to be true, as I can explain.

It had been Jatayu's dream for many years, for one of his books to be made into a film. As Bengali films didn't make money, so he had set his heart on a Hindi film. He was determined to write a story appropriate for a Hindi blockbuster. He had a friend in Bombay's film circles — a man called Pulak Ghoshal. At one time this person used to live in Garpar, two houses down from Lalmohan Babu. He had worked as an associate director for three films made in the Tollygunge studios in Calcutta. Then, in a sudden fit of recklessness, he had gone off to Bombay. Apparently, he was now one of the top directors there.

When Lalmohan Babu had got stuck in the third chapter of this story, he had come to Feluda for help. Feluda had read the chapters and commented, 'Just as well you got stuck halfway. This would have been hard work for nothing. Bombay would never have taken this.'

Lalmohan Babu had scratched his head and said, 'Just tell me what they will take. I had thought of seeing a few current hits before writing this one. I queued up for tickets on two occasions. The first time my pocket was picked. The second time it took me an hour–and–fifteen minutes to reach the ticket counter, only to find there were no seats. Of course they were selling tickets at double prices outside. But somehow the fear of spending Rs. 12 only to get a headache made me give up.'

Finally, Feluda had said he would make up an outline for Lalmohan Babu. 'I hope you know, double roles are all the rage these days,' he had said.

But Lalmohan Babu had not even known what a double role was.

'Haven't you seen two leading characters in a film who look identical?' Feluda had asked.

'Oh you mean twins?'

'Well, they can be twins. Or they may not be related to each other at all, and still look the same. The same appearance, but one is a good man and the other a villain, or one is smart and capable while the other is a nincompoop. The latter is a commoner. You could improve on this by adding another element — two double roles instead of one. Hero number one is paired with villain number one, and hero number two with villain number two, the existence of the second pair will be kept secret in the beginning. Then . . .'

Lalmohan Babu had broken in here, 'Isn't that too complicated?'

Feluda had shaken his head. 'My dear Sir, you need material for three hours. These days there's a new rule — you can't have too many fights. So the story will have to be plotted differently. It should take an hour–and–a–half to build up the mystery, and another hour–and–a–half to unravel it.'

'So you think the double role will do the trick?'

'Why only that? There's lots more. Note them down.'

Lalmohan Babu had promptly taken out a red notebook and a gold pencil from his breast pocket.

'Listen — you must have smuggling, gold, diamonds, marijuana, hashish, whatever; five songs, one of which should be devotional; two dance numbers; two or three chase sequences — in at least one of which an expensive car should be seen rolling downhill; there must be one fire scene; the girlfriend of the hero must be the heroine, and the girlfriend of the villain has to be the vamp; you need a conscientious police officer; some flashback scenes for the hero; comic relief; fast action and change of scene so that the plot does not sag; if you can, shift the scene to the mountains or to the beach, so that your stars don't have to keep on shooting in the cramped atmosphere of a studio — Have you got it all down?'

Lalmohan Babu, who had been taking notes at a breakneck speed, nodded.

'And finally — this is a must — you have to have a happy ending. And if before that you can make the tears flow, then so much the better.'

This had been enough to make Lalmohan Babu's fingers ache. The next two months of struggling with the story had given him blisters on two fingers of his right hand. Fortunately, Feluda had no engagements outside Calcutta during the period. The farthest he had to go was to Barrackpore, to investigate the mysterious death of Kadar Sarkar. Lalmohan Babu used to come over regularly twice a week. In spite of all this, however, Jatayu's thirty–second thriller, *The Buccaneer of Bombay* was published just before the pujas. And the plot was such that no film made from that book would give you a headache. True, it had all the ingredients for a successful Hindi movie, but without the intolerable excesses of the breed.

Lalmohan Babu had already sent Pulak Ghoshal a copy of the manuscript. Ten days ago, a letter had arrived saying that the story had been approved, and that Pulak Babu wanted to start work very soon. He himself had written the screenplay. The Hindi dialogue was being written by Tribhuban Gupta, each one of whose lines was supposed to be like a dagger pointed at the heart of the audience, able to provoke the strongest reactions. Lalmohan Babu had responded to this letter by demanding twenty–five thousand rupees without even consulting Feluda. Today's telegram had come as the answer. I was sure Lalmohan Babu had realised that asking for twenty–five thousand had been too much.

Now, having taken a sip of his tea and expressed murmur of satisfaction with half–closed eyes, Lalmohan Babu said, 'Young Pulak has written that he is not making too many changes in the story: on the whole it is as I, or rather we — wrote — it.'

Feluda raised his hand.

'I'd be much happier if you didn't use the plural.'

'But–'

'Come on! Shakespeare himself borrowed his plots from other people. But did anyone ever hear him say, 'our Hamlet'?' Never. I may have contributed some of the ingredients. But the chef was you yourself. Can I claim to have your touch?'

Lalmohan Babu grinned from ear to ear with gratification.

'Thank you, Sir. As I was telling you, they've made only one minor change in the story.'

'What.'

'You won't believe it — the most amazing coincidence. I'm sure you'll say it was telepathy. You know I have this smuggler

Dhundhiram Dhurandhar — well, I mentioned a forty–three storey high–rise building as his place of residence. You've always told me to pay attention to details. So I provided a name for this building — Shivaji Castle. The action takes place in Bombay. So, I thought it would be appropriate to name the building after the greatest hero of the state of Maharashtra. Would you believe it — Pulak wrote back saying there really was a building with that name, and that the producer of this film happened to live there? Now what else is this if not telepathy?'

'Have they kept the kung–fu bit or not?' asked Feluda.

Ever since the three of us had gone to see *Enter The Dragon*, Lalmohan Babu had had the idea of having a kung–fu sequence in his story.

'Of course they have kept it,' he said. 'I had made a point of asking about that. They wrote back saying that a kung–fu expert was specially being brought from Madras. Supposed to have trained in Hong Kong.'

'When does the shooting start?'

'I've enquired in the letter I wrote today. Once we find that out, we can fix the dates for our trip. Our — I mean my — story is being filmed, so how can we not be there?'

I had had 'Diamonda' before. But somehow it had never tasted as good as it did today.

CHAPTER 2

The following Sunday brought Lalmohan Babu to our place again. Feluda had already decided to offer half the expenses of the Bombay trip since he had come into some money recently. It was not only income from his investigation. In the last three months he had translated two books from English — both of them travelogues written by two famous travellers of the nineteenth century — and he had received some advance payment for both of them. Even before this, Feluda had done some writing in his spare time. But this was the first time I'd seen him really get down to the business.

Lalmohan Babu, however, summarily dismissed Feluda's proposal.

'You must be out of your mind!' he said, 'You are my guide and godfather in the field of writing. This is only a token fee for that tutelage.'

With this, he produced two airplane tickets from his pocket and placed them on the table, saying, 'The flight is at ten forty–five a.m, on Tuesday. Reporting time is an hour before that, I'll go straight to Dum Dum and wait for you.'

'When does the shooting start?'

'Thursday. And straightaway with the climactic scene. Remember, that affair of the train, the car and the horses?'

Lalmohan Babu also had another bit of news.

'Something else happened last evening. A local film producer — he has an office in Dharamtala — got hold of my address from my publisher and showed up at my house. He also wants to film my *Buccaneer of Bombay*. Says there is no other option but to make Bengali films on the lines of the Hindi ones. He seemed very disappointed when he heard that I already sold my story. Though he did admit that he himself had never read my book — a nephew of his had spoken to him about it. He seemed quite astonished to hear that I had written that book without ever having been to Bombay. Of course, I wasn't going to tell him that this book would never have been written without Murray's *Guide to India* and Felu Mitter's guidance.'

'Was this man a Bengali?'

'Yes. His surname was Sanyal. He speaks with a slight West Indian accent — told me that he had grown up in Jabbalpur. He also smells strongly of some perfume. It nearly scorched my nose! This is the first time I have encountered a man using such strong perfume. Anyway, he gave me an address when he heard I was going away.' Said, 'If you have any problems, give him a call. This friend of mine is very helpful.'

Though Calcutta can get pretty cold in December, Bombay never cools down that much. We managed to pack everything we needed in two small suitcases. When I woke up on Tuesday morning, the fog was so thick that I could hardly make out Poltu's house opposite ours. Would the plane be able to take off? Strangely enough, by nine everything cleared and the sun shone brightly. Normally, there is more fog on V.I.P Road which leads to the airport, than in the city. But this morning even that was negligible.

There was still fifty minutes to go before take off when we reached the airport. Lalmohan Babu was already there. He had even got his boarding card which I saw peeping from his pocket.

'I hope you don't mind, Felu Babu.' said our friend. 'When I saw so many people standing in line, I was worried about getting myself a seat by the window. So I lost no time in checking in. I am in row H. Perhaps the two of you will get seats close to mine.'

'What's that you are carrying? Have you bought yourself a book?'

The brown paper packet had made me think that he was carrying copies of his own book to give to someone.

He said, 'Buy — certainly not. It was that fellow Sanyal — the one I mentioned the other day — he came and gave this to me about ten minutes ago.'

'A present?'

'No, Sir. This is going to be picked up by somebody at the Bombay airport. He has already been given my name and address.

This book is meant for some relative of Sanyal's.'

He smiled and added, 'Er — can't you smell adventure here?'

'That is rather difficult,' said Feluda, 'For the scent of Gulbahar from Bharat Chemicals has obscured all other scents.'

I too noticed the smell. This Mr. Sanyal used his perfume so liberally that even his package was redolent of it.

'Just so sir, ha, ha, ha,' agreed Jatayu. 'But I've also heard that people often pass dubious objects in this fashion.'

'Quite right, the checking counter even has a notice saying it is dangerous to accept anything to be delivered from a stranger. I suppose you can't really call this gentleman a stranger, not do I see grounds to suspect that this packet contains anything other than books.'

The three of us could not get seats together on the plane; Lalmohan Babu had the window seat three rows behind us. Nothing worth mentioning happened on the flight, except when Captain Datta announced on the microphone that we were flying over Nagpur. I turned my head, and suddenly there was Lalmohan Babu going towards the tail of the plane. Finally an airhostess stopped him and directed him the other way. At this, he walked all the way up to the pilot's door, opened it, entered the cockpit, came out instantly looking thoroughly foolish, and finally made his way into the toilet on the left. On his way back to his seat, he leaned over and whispered into my ear, 'Take a look at the man sitting next to me. Wouldn't be surprised if he was a hijacker.'

As I turned my head to have a look, I realized that Jatayu must be literally craving for adventure. There could be no other reason to think of such a harmless, chinless man as a hijacker.

Well before the plane landed at Santa Cruz airport, Lalmohan Babu had got the package of books out of his bags. As the three of us waited in the domestic lounge trying to locate our man, we heard someone say, 'Mr. Ganguly?' Turning to the right I saw a man in a red shirt accosting a gentleman who looked like a South Indian, and looking at him hopefully. The gentleman shook his head rather irritably and said no, and walked on. Lalmohan Babu, carrying his package, then went towards the man in the red shirt.

'I am Mr. Ganguly and this is from Mr. Sanyal,' said Jatayu

all in the same breath.

The man in the red shirt took the package, nodded by way of thanks and went off, while Lalmohan Babu shook his hands with relief at being freed of the obligation.

Our baggage took half–an–hour to turn up. It was one–twenty by then; by the time we got into the town it would be almost two o' clock. Pulak Ghoshal had already told us the number of his car, which turned out to be a saffron coloured Standard. The driver was well–dressed and seemed quite smart;· apart from Hindi he also knew some English. The prospect of having to drive three strangers around did not seem to be annoying him in the least. The way he saluted Lalmohan Babu almost made one think he was quite gratified at having this assignment. It was the driver who told us that we would be staying at the Shalimar Hotel, and that Pulak Babu would be coming to see us around five–thirty. The car was at our disposal; we were free to go wherever and whenever we pleased.

As was his habit, Feluda had read up on Bombay before coming here. He says if one does not do this before going to a new place, then the place can never become familiar. Cities, like human beings, show different aspects of themselves in their names, appearance, character and history. Feluda had not yet learnt much about the appearance and character of Bombay, but he knew this much — that the Shalimar Hotel was near Kemps Corner.

As soon as our car left the highway and drove into one of the main roads, Feluda spoke to the driver.

'See that taxi — MRP 3538 — follow it.'

'What's going on?' asked Lalmohan Babu.

'Just a little curiosity.' Feluda answered.

Our car overtook a motor–bike and two Ambassador cars, and came right up behind the Fiat taxi. Through the glass I could now see the red shirt of the occupant.

I felt a slight flutter inside. Nothing had happened, nor had I any idea why Feluda was chasing the taxi, but the simple fact that all this was so utterly unexpected made me smell mystery and adventure in the air. As for Lalmohan Babu he had by now come to the conclusion that it was no use expecting answers from Feluda by asking him about his doings. The answers would come in their own good time.

Our car drove along, keeping the taxi in sight, while we occupied ourselves observing the streets and the people of this new city. I must say I had never seen such huge posters of Hindi movies in any other city. Lalmohan Babu craned his neck to inspect some of these before saying, 'Everything seems to be mentioned except the writer of the story. Don't these people hire writers to give them the plots?'

'If you are hoping for renown as a writer then Bombay is not the place for you. Stories are not written here, they are manufactured — just the same way as other items in the market. Does anyone know who manufactured Lux Soap? People just may know the name of the company. You are being handsomely paid — so keep quiet. Forget about prestige.'

'Hm . . .' Lalmohan Babu seemed quite put out 'so what you're saying is that Bengal gives you prestige while Bombay gives you money?'

'Absolutely.' said Feluda.

The taxi we were following left behind the area Feluda said was called Mahalakshmi, and turned right into a road. Our driver said we would have go straight if we wanted to go to the Shalimar Hotel.

'Please turn right,' said Feluda.

A couple of minutes later, we saw the taxi disappearing into a gateway to our left. Feluda directed our driver to stop outside the gate. The three of us got out and immediately Lalmohan Babu made a noise like a hiccup.

The reason was obvious. We were standing in front of a huge tall building. At the second–floor level, enormous black letters proclaimed in English — Shivaji Castle.

CHAPTER 3

I was speechless with astonishment.

'This has to be the grand daddy of all telepathy,' said Lalmohan Babu.

Feluda was silent. He was not only observing the building but also its surroundings. To the left was a series of buildings, none of which would be less than twenty floors. The houses on the right were old ones, and not so high. Through the gaps, between them one could see the ocean.

Our driver had been observing our reactions with some surprise. Feluda told him to wait and walked straight in through the gates. Lalmohan Babu and I waited outside, feeling awkward.

Within three minutes, however, Feluda came out again.

'Please take us to Shalimar Hotel now.'

We started moving again. Feluda lit a cigarette before saying, 'Very likely that package of yours has gone to the seventeenth floor.'

'My dear Sir, this is pure magic,' said Lalmohan Babu. 'How could you figure out in just three minutes to which floor of that enormous building that man had gone?'

'You don't have to actually get to the seventeenth floor to find out whether someone has gone there. The lift has a panel on top showing the floor numbers. When I got to the lift, it had already started moving. The last number to be lit up was 17. Now do you get it?'

Lalmohan Babu sighed heavily. 'Yes indeed. What I can't get is how these simple explanations never occur to me.'

Within five minutes we were at the Shalimar. Feluda and I were given a double room on the fourth floor and Lalmohan Babu got a single room opposite ours on the same floor. Our room faced the street. Whenever you looked down from the window there was the ocean, visible between two tall buildings. That Bombay was a vibrantly alive city was evident even from this hotel room. We were all quite famished. So we washed and went down to the first–floor restaurant, Gulmarg. As soon as we had ordered the food, Lalmohan Babu asked the question which had been hovering on the tip of his tongue.

'So you too are beginning to smell adventure, are you Felu Babu?'

Feluda did not give a straight answer. Instead he asked, 'Did you happen to notice what the man did after he had taken the package from your hand?'

'Why, surely, he walked away!' said Lalmohan Babu.

'That's the trouble with you! You've only seen the obvious and ignored the subtler things. The man walked a few steps and took out some change from his pocket!'

'Telephone!' I exclaimed.

'Very good, Topshe. I think the man made a call from one of the public telephones in the airport. I saw him again when we were waiting for our baggage.'

'Where?'

'Right outside where we were waiting was the parking space for private cars. Remember?'

'Yes, yes,' I said. Lalmohan Babu kept quiet.

'That man got into a blue Ambassador. There was a driver. But the car refused to start even after five or ten minutes. The man got out of the car and shouted at the driver. I could not hear him — but it was quite clear from his manner and gestures. Finally the man gave up on the car and went away.'

'To take a cab!' said Lalmohan Babu.

'Exactly. Now what does that tell us?'

'That the man was busy — I mean that he was in a hurry.'

'Good. Eyes and brains — if both of these are alert, then one can deduce a lot. So you see, there was a very good reason why I wanted to follow that taxi.'

'What exactly do you make of this situation?' asked Lalmohan Babu sitting up straight, and resting both his elbows on the table.

'I haven't made anything of it yet,' said Feluda. 'There's something which strikes a false note.'

Around five, having had some rest, Lalmohan Babu came to our room. We had some tea sent up, and were having it when there was a tap on the door. The gentleman who entered could not have been a day more than thirty–five but his abundant wavy hair was heavily streaked with gray.

'There you are Laluda — is everything all right?'

Laluda! That anybody could call Lalmohan Babu by such a name had never occurred to me. This must be Pulak Ghoshal. Feluda had already told Lalmohan Babu to keep his (Feluda's) identity a secret on pain of death. So he was introduced to Pulak Babu simply as a friend of Lalmohan's.

Pulak Babu shook his head regretfully and said,'Just look at you, a friend of Laluda's, someone really close — and we are stuck for want of a hero. Can you speak Hindi?'

Feluda burst out laughing and said, 'No, I have absolutely no Hindi, and my acting ability is even less . . . but why should you be in want of a hero? I'd heard that you had already started shooting. Isn't Arjun Mehrotra doing the part?'

'That he is. But it is no longer the Arjun of the old days. He's now got a thousand mannerisms, I don't call these people heroes. I think they are no better than sneaking villains whatever they may be doing on the screen. And the producers here have spoilt them by truckling to them. Anyhow, I am inviting you for day after tomorrow. The shooting is taking place about seventy miles from here. The driver knows the place. Get ready early and come straight over. Mr. Gore, the producer, is not here now. He's travelling in Delhi, Madras and Calcutta for a week in connection with the picture. But he has asked me to see to it that you are looked after properly.'

'Where are you shooting?'asked Feluda.

'Between Khandala and Lonavala. It is a scene in a train. If I don't have enough passengers, I may put you in the train too.'

'By the way, we've already seen Shivaji Castle,'said Lalmohan Babu.

Pulak Babu frowned at this.

'How come? When?'

'Oh, just on our way here. Say about two o'clock.'

'Ah, then the incident must have happened after that.'

'What incident?'

'Murder.'

'Good heavens!' the three of us exclaimed almost in unison.

Somehow, those six letters put together make you shiver in spite of yourself.

'I heard about it just half–an–hour ago' said Pulak Babu. 'I have to visit that building quite regularly, you know. Mr. Gore also lives in Shivaji Castle — on floor twelve. You see why we had to change that name in your story. Of course, Mr. Gore is a most amiable gentleman. Did you happen to go inside?'

'I did,' said Feluda, 'upto the lift doors.'

'Good God! The murder was committed inside the lift itself. The body has not yet been identified. Looks like a hoodlum. It was around three when Tyagarajan, a resident of that building, rang for the lift which came down. As soon as the door opened and gentleman was about to step inside, he saw the body. The fellow had been stabbed in the stomach. Horrible!'

'Did anyone notice any persons using the lift around that time?' asked Feluda.

'There was nobody anywhere near the lift. But two chauffeurs waiting outside the building said they had seen five or six people entering about that time. One wore a red shirt, another wore brown and had a bag slung from his shoulder . . .'

Feluda raised his head and said, 'That second person was myself, so you don't have to say anymore.'

My heart leaped. How terrible — was Feluda going to get entangled with some murder case?

'Anyway, don't worry too much,' said Pulak Ghoshal reassuringly. 'All you've done is to say in your novel that a smuggler lives in Shivaji Castle. That's nothing to worry about — which apartment building in Bombay doesn't have a smuggler or two? After all the government doesn't track down too many of them. All they've done so far is to take the icing off the cake. It will be quite some time before they get to the bottom. The entire city lives on smuggling.'

Feluda was looking rather worried. But that expression disappeared with the appearance of a new character. As soon as the second knock sounded , Pulak Babu left his chair saying, 'This must be Victor,' and opened the door. A man of middle height, his body taut as a whip, came in.

'Laluda, let me introduce you. This is Victor Perumal. A

kung–fu expert trained in Hongkong.'

The gentleman gave us a charming smile and shook hands with all of us.

'He speaks some English,' said Pulak Babu. 'And Hindi of course, though he is a South Indian. He is not only a kung–fu instructor, he is also an incomparable stuntman. He is the one who is going to be made up like the hero's brother and jump on the running train from the horseback.'

Somehow I took to this gentleman immediately. There was a great deal of frankness in his smile. Being told that he was stuntsman only added a tinge of awe to my feelings towards him.

Victor Perumal told us that kung–fu was not the only thing he knew. 'I know mokka–iri also.'

Mokka–iri? What on earth was that? Even Feluda who knew so much, was stumped, Lalmohan Babu was useless because he hardly read anything except his own books!

Perumal told us that mokka–iri was a kind of combat technique which required you to walk on your hands with your feet in the air. This had apparently become the rage in Hongkong only over the last six months, though its origins were in Japan.

'Are you using this technique in the film too?' asked Lalmohan Babu rather anxiously.

Pulak Ghoshal shook his head and smiled. 'Its bad enough having to use kung–fu. Ever since the beginning of November, we have been training eleven people morning, noon and night. Your problems were over as soon as you wrote the book. But the real hassle is ours. Of course, the bit of shooting that you will see won't have any kung–fu. Only some good stunts . . . We'll make a first class movie out of your book Laluda. Don't worry about a thing.'

When Pulak Ghoshal left with Victor Perumal, Feluda got up and opened the window. Immediately the room was filled with the noise of the traffic. But since, we were on the fourth floor, it did not prevent us from carrying on a conversation. None of us were used to air–conditioning and we did not like it. True, a lot of noise did come in from outside, but so did fresh air.

Back from the window, Feluda sat down and said gravely, 'The scent of adventure is getting strong to the point of discomfort,

Lalmohan Babu. I wish you hadn't accepted the responsibility for delivering that packet. If I had been around I would have told you not to.'

'Yes but what else could I do?' Lalmohan Babu said apologetically. 'The gentleman even wanted to reserve the movie rights for my next book for him. How could I possibly refuse after that?'

'Yes, but generally when passengers go through security checks at the airport, the packages they carry are also opened. That wasn't done to you because you look so innocent. But who knows what would have been found if your package had been opened? And how can we be sure that there is no connection between that package and the murder?'

Lalmohan Babu cleared his throat and mumbled, 'Yes but what can a package of books . . .'

'It may not actually have been books. Did you know that kings and emperors in the old days carried poison in their rings? Could you call them just ordinary rings? They were just as much vials of poison as they were, rings . . . Anyway since you've managed to discharge your obligations perhaps you have nothing to fear.'

'You think so?' said Lalmohan Babu, smiling at last.

'Of course,' said Feluda. 'And remember, your problems are our problems too. The three of us are in this together. If anything happens to one, all three of us will topple.'

Lalmohan Babu leapt up from the bed, swung his left leg upward in proper kung-fu style, kicked the air, and said, 'Three cheers for the three musketeers, Hip hip . . .'

'Hurrah,' chorused Feluda and I.

CHAPTER 4

Around six that evening we left the hotel. All three of us believe that it is impossible to really see a new city unless you walk around. We had done it in Jodhpur, Kashi, Delhi and Gangtok Why not in Bombay?

To the right of the hotel, was the area known as Kemps Corner. There was a most impressive flyover there — a road constructed on huge pillars like a bridge. Traffic could go over and under that flyover. We crossed the road below, took Gibbs Road, and started walking south. Feluda pointed up the road climbing uphill, leading to the Hanging Gardens. This was the famous Malabar Hills.

We came to the sea after walking a mile or so. Somehow evading the rush–hour traffic, we crossed the street and stood by the waist–high stone parapet. The waves continuously broke against the other side of this parapet.

The road turned left and went directly east, formed a circular curve and finally ended south where the sky–scrapers could dimly be seen in the failing light of the afternoon sun. It was this bow–shaped road which was the famous Marine Drive.

'Whatever you may say about smugglers,' said Lalmohan Babu, 'what with the sea and the hill, Bombay is a super city.'

We started walking along the parapet towards Marine Drive. To our left were the cars, moving like a line of ants. After some time, Lalmohan Babu made another comment.

'I am sure there is no Municipal Development Authority here, as in Calcutta.'

'Why, because the roads are not full of potholes?'

'Yes. Even when we were coming into town from the airport, I noticed that we felt no bumps. Incredible!'

I had noticed a small crowd at one point beside the sea — just like the ones we see on Sundays around the Monument in

Calcutta. As we went closer, Feluda said that this place was called the Chowpatty. Apparently, there was a crowd here every day of the week as if a fair was on. There were rows of little shops. They looked like they were selling icecream, or *bhelpuri* or other junk food.

As we went right up to the crowds, I saw that I had made no mistake in thinking of it as a fair. And what a fair it was! Half of Bombay must have come there. Since Lalmohan Babu was soon becoming a rich man we had no compunctions about exploiting him. We took our bags of *bhelpuri* and made our way through the crowd and the bustle to sit on the sandy beach by the sea. Our watches said quarter–to–seven, but the sky was still pink. There were other people like us too who were sitting on the sand enjoying themselves. Lalmohan Babu finished eating, waved his hand and was about to recite a Sanskrit couplet, when he stopped suddenly. A newspaper, flying out of the hand of one of the people sitting on our left had landed on his face.

Lalmohan Babu had barely got hold of the paper and read out the title, *Evening News*, when Feluda snatched it away from him. 'How could you read the name without noticing the headline below?'

All of us bent over the paper. The headline said, 'Murder in Apartment Lift,' and immediately below was a picture of a victim. At least, it was not our man in the red shirt.

The news put the murder between two and two–thirty in the afternoon. The murderer had not been caught yet but the police were looking for him. The name of the murdered man was Mangalram Shethi. Apparently, the police had been on the trail for some time, since he was involved with smuggling. There were signs of a tussle within the lift. And among the clues discovered by the police was a bit of paper near the dead man's body. A name was written on that piece of paper.

A strange groan came out of Lalmohan Babu's mouth. I quickly put my arms around him, in case he fainted. And indeed, there was reason for him to faint. For, according to the *Evening News*, the piece of paper said, 'Mr. Ganguly, dark, short, bald, moustache.'

As soon as we had finished reading the news item, Lalmohan Babu almost clawed the newspaper out of Feluda's hands, tore it into shreds and scattered them in the wind.

'Why did you have to litter this beautiful, clean beach?' asked Feluda.

Then, as Lalmohan Babu was still unable to speak normally, Feluda said almost in a tone of rebuke, 'Do you think this entire city will jump to the conclusion that you are this man, as soon as they lay eyes on you?'

But even this was no consolation for Lalmohan Babu. He gulped and said, 'Yes, but– but– do you realize what this means? I mean, surely you can guess who committed the murder?'

Feluda remained quiet for a few seconds as he stared at Lalmohan Babu. Then he shook his head and said, 'Laluda, even after four years of associating with me, you haven't learnt to think cooly.'

'Why — the man in the red shirt . . .'

'What about the man? Even if you assume that he dropped the piece of paper in that lift, what does it prove? How can you be so sure that he committed the murder? Once he'd got the package from you, he needed to have nothing more to do with you — right? Which means that that piece of paper was no longer of use to him. So when he found that the piece of paper was still in his pocket as he entered the lift, he decided to throw it away. Why is it so difficult for you to accept that possibility?'

But even this could not soothe Lalmohan Babu's anxieties.

'I don't care what you say, since police have found my name and description next to the victim's body, that can only mean endless trouble for me. Yes, I can see it quite clearly. There's only one thing to do. I can't grow hair on my bald head, nor can I grow in height, nor change my complexion. That leaves the moustache. Whatever you may think, I am going to shave it off tomorrow.'

'Oh, and what about the hotel people? You think they haven't read the *Evening News*? Any report of murder is read by 90 percent of the readers. It is human nature. I think, if you shave that moustache, you will immediately draw attention, and with that, arouse suspicion.'

When the sky had changed from red to purple to almost ash, and Venus peeping through the clouds in the western sky was feebly trying to compete with the garland of a thousand lights to the east on Marine Drive — that was when we got up, shook the sand from our clothes, made our way through the crowd of shops and human beings, got to the road and took a taxi to the hotel.

As we went up to the reception desk to ask for our keys, I noticed that Lalmohan Babu extended his hand, but turned his face in the opposite direction. But even that did not help. For of the seven people — Indian and foreign — sitting in the lobby, three were reading the *Evening Standard*. And that paper too carried news of the murder and a picture of the corpse on the front page. It was most unlikely that the news did not contain any reference to short, bald, moustached, dark–skinned Mr. Ganguly.

CHAPTER 5

In the end Lalmohan Babu did not shave off his moustache.
When I asked him if he had slept well, he said that every time
he had dozed off, he had had the sensation that his room was
going up and down like a lift and inevitably he would wake up.

Pulak Babu had called us the night before to say that he
would pick us up at ten this morning and take us to watch the
shooting. So, having finished breakfast at eight, we got out,
strolled along Pedder Road, bought some *paan*, and came back
to the hotel by a quarter–to–nine. As soon as we entered we
became aware of an atmosphere of subdued excitement.

The reason was nothing more than the arrival of the police.
A man who looked like a police inspector was standing in front
of the reception desk. At a gesture from one of the hotel personnel,
he turned around and stared at Lalmohan Babu. Though the
inspector did not in the least look threatening, a sudden click,
made me realise that Lalmohan Babu's knees were knocking
against each other.

The inspector came forward with a smile. Feluda quietly pressed
Lalmohan Babu's shoulder to reassure him.

'Inspector Patwardhan. I am here from the C.I.D. Are you
Mr Ganguly?'

'Ye–yes,' said Lalmohan Babu.

Patwardhan looked at Feluda. 'And you two?'

Feluda took out one of his cards which said 'Private Investigator.'
Patwardhan read the words and looked enquiringly at him.

'Mitter. Are you the one who was involved with the case of
the stolen statues of Ellora?'

Feluda gave one of his lopsided smiles, and nodded.

'Glad to meet you, Sir,' said Patwardhan extending his hand.
'You did a very good job there.'

Being Feluda's friend certainly increased Lalmohan Babu's

status, but it didn't let him off the hook as far as the cross—examination went. The conversation took place in the hotel manager's office.

From what Patwardhan said, we learnt that there were lots of finger–prints on the corpse, but the murderer was still at large. The police, however, had got hold of the taxi driver and found out that a man wearing a red shirt had come to Shivaji Castle from the airport. The police felt that this man was the murderer, and the strip of paper had come from his pocket. Lalmohan Babu's words only confirmed Patwardhan's suspicions.

'I could guess he had gone to the airport to meet someone called Ganguly. We checked the names of all the passengers who arrived at Santa Cruz Airport between morning and afternoon yesterday, and found Mr. Ganguly's name on the list of Calcutta passengers. Then I checked every hotel in this area and found that Mr. L. Ganguly had checked into the Shalimar in the afternoon.'

What Patwardhan really wanted to know was the precise role played by Lalmohan Babu in this affair ; why his name and description happened to be on that piece of paper. When Lalmohan Babu recounted the episode of Mr. Sanyal, Patwardhan said 'Who is this Sanyal? How well do you know him?'

Lalmohan told him. Asked for Sanyal's address, he was forced to say he did not have it.

Finally, Inspector Patwardhan cautioned Lalmohan Babu just as Feluda had done. 'This is how harmless, innocent people are being used to pass smuggled goods these days. We've been informed that some very valuable gems have come into India from Kathmandu. We've even heard that the famous Naulakha necklace belonging to Nanasaheb is also among them.'

I had read about one Nanasaheb in my history books, the one who had fought against the British during the Sepoy Uprising. I wondered if Patwardhan was talking about the same person.

'I'm sure this particular package also carried contraband,' said Patwardhan. 'A member of the gang opposing the one that sent it from Calcutta had received information and must have been lurking around Shivaji Castle. That man must have attacked the fellow in the red shirt, and finally been murdered by him.'

Lalmohan Babu had assumed that since the police had found the paper containing his name and description, he would inevitably be sentenced to hanging, or a life sentence at the very least. To be let off only with a few words of advice brought a new glow to his face.

Though he had said ten, Pulak Babu did not show up until eleven. On hearing about the police interrogation, he said, 'I know. As soon as I saw the paper last night I felt terribly anxious. The name and description seemed to fit Laluda, and yet the whole affair was such a mystery to me.'

When he heard about the Sanyal incident he said, 'Sanyal who? Ahi Sanyal? Of medium height, deep–set eyes, cleft chin?'

'I didn't notice the chin. He had a beard, probably recently grown.'

'Well I'm talking about two years ago. Don't know if it's the same person. He was in Bombay for a while. Produced a film or two. As far I remember — they were all flops.'

'What kind of a man was he?'

'I really wouldn't know Laluda. But I never heard anything bad about him.'

'Then perhaps there's nothing wrong with that package.'

'You know Laluda, it's only because of all the smuggling that's going on these days. Otherwise, in the old days, all of us have taken packages from unknown people and reached them elsewhere. And there was never any trouble.'

In the same car we had used yesterday, the four of us drove to the Famous Studio in Mahalakshmi. As we got out, Pulak Babu said, 'We were having some problems with the Railways over using a train for our shooting tomorrow. As soon as he heard this, the producer took the evening flight from Calcutta and came here. Come, I'll introduce you.'

'Yes, but will tomorrow's shooting take place?' asked Lalmohan Babu anxiously.

'You bet it will. Don't worry.'

We entered a huge shed with a tin roof, much like a factory. This was where the shooting was done. Today, the kung–fu training was going on here. Several men, under the direction of Victor Perumal, were jumping on a huge mattress, throwing their legs up, and falling. Ten yards from the mattress a gentleman of about forty–five was sitting in a cane chair.

'Let me introduce you,' said Pulak Babu, 'This is our producer, Mr. Gore., Mr. Ganguly story–writer, Mr. Mitter, and — what's your name young man?'

'Tapeshranjan Mitter.'

Mr. Gore's cheeks were like apples, he had a shining bald patch right in the middle of his head, and his eyes were hazel. The paunch must be recent, because I could not imagine anyone deliberately wearing their clothes so tight. Pulak Babu disappeared after the introductions, for he had to make a lot of preparations for the following day's shooting.

'I'll be back at one–thirty, Laluda,' he said before leaving. 'All of you are having lunch with me.'

Gore welcomed us cordially, and had chairs brought for us. He himself sat next to Lalmohan Babu, saying in Bengali, 'I'm very glad you have come.'

'Why, you speak Bengali very, very well!'

Lalmohan Babu must have had his fee of Rs. 10,000 in mind to be so enthusiastic.

'Well, my father had a business in Canning Street. And I was a student at Don Bosco school for three years. Then my father died, and I came to live with my uncle in Bombay. I've been here all this time. This, however, is my first venture into films.'

Perhaps it was because Gore knew Bengali that Lalmohan Babu happily told him the whole story starting from Mr. Sanyal to the police interrogation.

Gore clucked in sympathy, saying, 'You can't trust anyone these days, Mr. Ganguly. You are an eminent writer. It's shameful to think of contraband goods being passed through you.'

Feluda now joined in the conversation.

'I hear you live in Shivaji Castle.'

'Yes, I've been there for the last two months. That horrible murder! I came on the evening flight. By the time I got home it was eleven. Even then there was a big crowd in the street. A murder in a high–rise building is bound to stir up a lot of trouble.'

'Er — do you know who lives on the seventeenth floor?'

'Seventeenth ... seventeenth ....' the gentlemen did not seem

to remember. 'Somebody I know lives on the eighth floor —
N.C. Mehta ; and there's Dr. Vajifdar on the second. My flat
is on the twelfth floor.'

Feluda did not ask any more questions. Mr. Gore also seemed
to want to leave. This, he told us, was a very complicated
production, something or the other was always going wrong.
Besides, tomorrow's shooting was going to be really on a grand
scale. A rented train would leave Matheran station and come to
the level–crossing between Khandala and Lonavala. Mr. Gore
would have to go to Matheran, since he would have to arrange
payment for the Railways. The train contained a first–class
compartment of the old days. Mr. Gore would get into it, and
come to watch the shooting.

'I'll be delighted if you come and have lunch with me. Are
you vegetarians?'

'No, No,' said Lalmohan Babu.

'What will you have, chicken or mutton?'

'We had chicken yesterday; let's have mutton tomorrow. What
do you say, Felu Babu?'

'Just as you wish,' said Feluda.

Feluda had been listening to everything Mr. Gore was saying,
but at intervals, I noticed, his eyes were straying to the kung–fu
training. One really had to marvel at the patience and perseverance
of Victor Perumal. Anyone could see he was determined to make
the thing perfect. A couple of the trainees were already very capable.

Perumal too had been looking at Feluda from time to time.
Probably the look of admiration in Feluda's eyes was providing
him with encouragement. As soon as Gore had left, Perumal
beckoned Feluda to come closer. Feluda threw away his cigarette
and strode up to Perumal.

'Come Mr. Mitter, have a go. It's not difficult.'

All the other trainees left the mattress and stood aside. Perumal
gave a tiny jump and lifted his right leg up to his head and
threw it out straight in front. If anyone had been standing in
the way of that leg, he would have been down on the ground.
Feluda got up on the mattress and jumped up and down several
times to limber up. Perumal, standing about four feet away said,
'Throw your leg at me.'

Of course, Perumal could not know that ever since we had
seen *Enter the Dragon*, Feluda had spent many mornings in our
sitting room practising kung–fu style movements. True, he had
been doing it only for fun – but he had learnt the trick of
throwing out his legs.

As soon as Perumal said one, two, three, Feluda's right leg
shot out horizontally at lightning speed, and immediately Perumal's
body was flung backwards on the mattress, even though I knew
that Feluda's leg had not touched him.

This went on for the next five minutes — kung–fu demonstration
by Victor Perumal and Prodosh Mitter. I kept on looking at
Perumal's trainees – people who had been undergoing such
rigorous practice for the last six weeks. What pleased me was
that instead of envy, their faces showed admiration. At the end
of five minutes, when the two combatants shook hands and patted
each other on the back, everyone spontaneously clapped their hands.

Around two, we entered the Copper Chimney restaurant in Worli, together with Pulak Babu and script–writer Tribhuvan Gupta, to have our lunch. There did not seem to be room for even one person — but Pulak Babu had reserved a table for us before hand.

'What will be the title of my film Pulak?' asked Lalmohan Babu.

I too had wondered about the name, but there had been no opportunities to ask questions. But I had guessed that the title *Buccaneer of Bombay* would not be retained for the film.

'My dear Laluda, you've no idea how much trouble we've had with the title. All the titles I could think of had either been used already, or were being registered by some other party. Ask Mr. Gupta here, how many sleepless nights he spent before coming up with a title. Finally, only three days ago it came — the high voltage spark.'

'High Voltage Spark? That's the title of this movie?' asked Jatayu in a very low voltage tone.

Pulak Babu laughed so loudly that heads at neighbouring tables turned our way.

'Have you gone out of your mind Laluda? How can one have a movie with a name like that? No, no. I was only talking about inspiration. The name will be *Jet Bahadur*.'

'What?'

'Jet Bahadur' It will be on the posters in the streets before you have left Bombay. You think about it — there could be no better title for the story you've given us. Action, speed, thrill — all that is conjured up by the word *Jet*. Add *Bahadur* to that — and the name and the casting will sell the movie.'

Lalmohan Babu's smile, almost about to reach high voltage dimensions, dimmed. Probably he was wondering why only the title and the cast were being mentioned. Did the story have no merit whatsover?

'Have you ever seen any of my films, Laluda?'asked Pulak Babu. 'The Lotus is showing *The Archer*. Why don't all of you go and see it this evening? I'll tell the manager — he will keep three good seats for you. It's a good film — just celebrated its silver jubilee.'

None of us had seen any films made by Pulak Babu. And Lalmohan Babu had plenty of reason for curiosity. So we all agreed to go. If you don't know people in Bombay, the evenings tend to drag. The car would be left with us — we could tell the driver to take us to the Lotus.

In the middle of lunch, one of the restaurant personnel came up to Pulak Babu and said something. That Pulak Babu was a frequent visitor here was evident from the grins on the faces of the waiters as we entered. Hit directors were clearly made much of in this city.

Pulak Babu immediately turned towards Lalmohan Babu, saying, 'There's a call for you, Laluda.'

It was fortunate that Lalmohan Babu had not yet inserted his spoonful of *pulao* into his mouth — otherwise he would definitely have choked. As it is, the start he gave resulted in some *pulao* spilling from the spoon and scattering all over the tablecloth.

'Mr. Gore wants you, said Pulak Babu. He may have some good news for you.'

Within a couple of minutes Lalmohan Babu had finished his conversation and was back at the table. Picking up his knife and fork once again, he said, 'The gentleman asked me to go to his house around four. Seems like I'll be coming into some money.'

Which meant that by this afternoon Lalmohan Babu would have ten thousand rupees in his pocket.

'The next lunch is on you,'said Feluda, 'And a Copper Chimney won't do — we'll need a golden one.'

By the time we had polished off our meal of *roomali roti, pulao, nargisi kofta* and *kulfi*, and come out of the restaurant, it was almost quarter-to-three. Pulak Babu and Mr. Gupta went off to the studio. Probably the script still needed some work. 'Every dialogue had to be sharp and pointed as a dagger — and that took time,' said Pulak Babu. Gupta smiled a little at this, his cheroot between his teeth. Though he had written so much dialogue he himself spoke very little.

We bought *paan* and got into our car.

'Shalimar?' asked the driver.

'It's unthinkable to come to Bombay and not see the Gateway of India,' said Feluda. 'Please take us to the Tajmahal Hotel' he told the driver.

'Very good, Sir.'

The driver had realised that we had no urgent business, all we wanted, was to see the city. So he happily drove us around Victoria Terminus, Flora Fountain, the television station, Prince of Wales Museum and finally arrived in front of the Gateway of India around three–thirty. We got out of the car.

Behind us was the Arabian Sea. I counted eleven ships, big and small. The road was enormously wide here. To our left, facing the Gateway, sat Shivaji on horseback. To our right was the world – famous Tajmahal Hotel. It would be silly not to go inside and take a look because the outside had already left us awestruck.

Inside the air–conditioned lobby, there was a mind–boggling variety of people. More than whites, it was the Arabs who dominated the scene. Why was this? I asked Feluda and he said that, since Beirut had become forbidden territory, the Arabs had all come to Bombay for their vacation. Thanks to petroleum, they had no lack of money.

We wandered around for five minutes before coming out and getting into the car. It was two–minutes–past–four, when we rang for the lift at Shivaji Castle.

We got to the twelfth floor, and came our of the lift. There were three doors in three directions. The middle one had Gore written on it. When we rang the doorbell, a uniformed servant came and opened the door.

'Please come in.'

Obviously, Mr. Gore had already told his servant to expect us.

On entering, we heard that gentlemen's voice before we saw him.

'Come in, come in.'

Then we saw him, coming down a narrow passage, a smile on his face.

'How was the lunch?'

'Very, very good,' said Jatayu.

The sitting room was amazing. Almost the whole ground floor of our house in Calcutta could fit inside this room. Through the row of glass windows on the west wall one could see the ocean. Individual bits of furniture in the room looked as though they would easily be worth two or three thousand rupees. Wall to wall carpeting, chandeliers, and paintings on the walls completed the decor. The expensive books in the book–shelves were so clean that they looked almost new.

Feluda and I sat side by side on a thickly upholstered sofa. Lalmohan Babu sat on a cushioned chair to our right. As soon as we sat down, a huge dog came and stood right in the middle of the room and began to survey the three of us. I saw Lalmohan Babu turning pale. Feluda put his hand out and snapped his fingers — immediately the dog went over to him. He told us later that this was a Great Dane.

'Duke, Duke.'

The dog left Feluda and went to the door. Mr. Gore, after seating us had left the room for a little while. Now he came in with an envelope in his hand, and sat down on the other side of Lalmohan Babu.

'I had planned to have everything ready before you came, but there were three long–distance calls.'

Mr. Gore held the envelope out to Lalmohan Babu, who steadied his trembling hand by sheer will power, took the envelope and pulled out a bundle of hundred rupee notes.

'Please count them,' said Gore.

'Count?'

'Of course. There should be a hundred notes there.'

By the time Lalmohan Babu finished counting, tea had been brought for us in a silver tea–set. From the taste it must have been the best Darjeeling tea.

'I still don't know anything about you,' said Mr. Gore looking at Feluda.

'I am Mr. Ganguly's friend — that's all.'

'No, Sir' said Gore, 'That's not enough. You are no ordinary person. Your eyes, your voice, your height, walk, body — nothing

is ordinary. If you don't want to tell me about yourself that's
fine. But you can't expect me to believe that your sole identity
is that of Mr. Ganguly's friend.'

Feluda smiled a little, took a sip of tea, and changed the subject.

'I see you have a lot of books.'

'Yes, but I don't read them. They are only for show. I've
ordered Taraporevala's book store to send me a copy of any
good book that comes out.'

'Well, a Bengali book also seems to have made its way in here.'

One had to marvel at Feluda's power of observation. From a
distance of fifteen yards he had noticed the Bengali title among
all those rows of books.

Mr. Gore burst our laughing.

'It's not just Bengali Mr. Mitter. There's Hindi, Marathi,
Gujarati. I have a man who knows Bengali,Hindi, and Gujarati.
He reads all the novels in those languages and makes synopsis
for me. I've even read Mr.Ganguly's book in outline. You see
Mr. Mitter, film–making requires . . . '

The telephone was ringing. Mr. Gore went towards the white
instrument resting on a three–legged table by the door.

'Hallo . . . Yes . . . hold on please. It's for you, Mr. Ganguly.'

The way Lalmohan Babu was being made to jump out of his
skin repeatedly made me wonder what it was doing to his heart.

'Is it Pulak Babu?' he asked, on his way to the telephone.

'No, Sir,' said Mr. Gore, 'I don't know this person.'

'Hullo.'

Feluda was looking at Lalmohan Babu out of the corner of his eye.

'Hullo. . . Hullo. . .'

Lalmohan Babu looked at us with a bewildered expression.
'Nobody's saying anything.'

'Must have got cut off,' said Mr. Gore.

But Lalmohan Babu shook his head, 'No, I'm getting other
sounds on the line.'

This time Feluda got up and took the receiver from Lalmohan
Babu's hand.

'Hullo . . . Hullo . . .'

Then he shook his head, saying, 'No, they've hung up.'

'Amazing,' said Lalmohan Babu. 'Who do you think it could be?'

'Don't worry about it, Mr. Ganguly,' said Mr. Gore. 'This happens all the time in Bombay.'

We followed Feluda's example and got up.

Perhaps it was the consciousness of having all that money in his pocket that made Lalmohan Babu take this mysterious incident quite lightly. His next words to Mr. Gore sounded quite casual.

'We are going to see Pulak Babu's film tonight at the Lotus.'

'Yes, indeed, you must. Pulak Babu is a very good director. And you can be rest assured that *Jet Bahadur* will be a smash hit at the box office.'

Mr. Gore escorted us to the door. 'Don't forget about tomorrow. I hope you have transport?'

We told him that Pulak Babu had arranged for a car from morning till night.

Outside, as he pressed the button for the lift, Feluda said, 'Did you see what real money is?'

'See? I've carried some of it away in my pocket.'

'Peanuts, my dear Sir, peanuts. Even a hundred thousand would be peanuts to these people. Did you notice that he did not make you sign a receipt for that money? That means you've got black money in your pocket. In other words, you've taken your first step towards darkness.'

With a clanging noise the lift came down from above and stopped in front of us.

'Whatever you may say, Felu Babu, if one has money in one's pocket — whether it is black or white . . .'

Feluda had opened the door to get into the lift and that is what silenced Jatayu. A whiff of strong perfume came from within the lift — the scent of Gulbahar. All three of us were familiar with this scent, particularly Lalmohan Babu.

My heart beating fast, I followed Feluda into the lift. But I could not help making a comment.

'There must be many people in India besides Mr. Sanyal, who use Gulbahar.'

Instead of answering, Feluda gravely pressed button number seventeen. We went up five more floors.

Like the other floors, the seventeenth also had three apartments. The door on the left said H.Heckroth. It was a German name,

Feluda told us. The right–hand door said N.C. Mansukhani. Definitely a Sindhi name. The middle door had no name.

'An empty flat,' said Lalmohan Babu.

'Not necessarily,' answered Feluda. 'Not everyone wants to put his name on the door. In fact, it's my belief that there is someone in the flat.'

Both of us stared at Feluda.

'A doorbell that has not been used would be covered with dust. But take a close look at this one. And then compare it with the other two.'

We went up close and saw that Feluda was right. The doorbell was clean and shiny with not a speck of visible dust.

'Are you going to ring ?' asked Lalmohan Babu, his voice trembling.

But Feluda did not do so. What he did instead, was far more astounding. He lay down flat on the floor and shoved his nose against the half–inch gap below the door. Then he inhaled deeply twice, got up and said, 'Smells of strong coffee.'

His next action was just as peculiar. Instead of using the lift, he started going down the stairs all the way from the seventeenth floor. And what he accomplished by pausing for half–a–minute on each floor and wandering around, was something he only knew.

By the time we had finished and were down on the ground floor, it was ten–past–five.

It was quite clear to us that we had come to Bombay and got embroiled in a most sinister.mystery.

'I hope you won't mind if I subject you to a little interrogation,' said Feluda addressing Lalmohan Babu.

We had come back from Shivaji Castle about ten minutes earlier. At the reception desk they had told us that half–an–hour ago — that is, when we were coming down the stairs of Shivaji Castle — there had been a telephone call for Lalmohan Babu. The caller had not left his name.

'It must be Pulak who's trying to get me,' said Lalmohan Babu. 'It can't be anyone but Pulak.' He then returned to the subject Feluda had brought up a few moments earlier and said: 'I've come out with flying colours from that police interrogation. Why should I object to yours?'

'Do you remember Mr. Sanyal's first name?'

'No, I never got around to asking him.'

'Well, try giving me an accurate description of the man. Not the kind of incomplete descriptions we find in your books.'

Lalmohan Babu cleared his throat, and frowned.

'Height. . . well. . . '

'Is that the first thing you notice about a person?'

'Well, if someone is really tall or really short. . . '

'Was this man very tall?'

'No, not really.'

'Very short?'

'No, not that either.'

'Then leave the height for later. Tell me about his face.'

'I met him in the evening. Please remember, the bulb in my sitting room is only 40 watts.'

'Never mind — just tell me.'

'He had a broad face. The eyes — well, he wore glasses ; he had a beard, a full, thick one; and a moustache, joined to the beard. . .'

'French cut?'

'Oh dear, no, probably not. It also went up to his sideburns.'

'Go on.'

'Salt and pepper hair. Parted on the right — no, no, on the left.'

'Teeth?'

'Clean. Didn't look like false teeth?'

'Voice?'

'Medium — that is, neither too deep nor too light.'

'Height?'

'Medium.'

'Didn't he give you an address? In Bombay? Told you to contact them if you had problems — said they would be helpful?'

'Good God! Of course! I quite forgot. Even when the police were asking all those questions I forgot to mention this.'

'That's all right. It's good enough if you tell me.'

'Let me see.'

Lalmohan Babu took out a piece of folded blue paper from his wallet, and gave it to Feluda. Feluda looked at it very carefully because Mr. Sanyal had written the address himself. Then he re–folded the paper and put it away in his own wallet, saying. . .

'Topshe, ask for this number — 253418.'

I gave the number to the hotel operator. Feluda then spoke in English.

'Hullo, can I speak to Mr. Desai?'

But there was no one called Mr. Desai at the number. The person who lived there was called Parekh, and he had been there for the last ten years.

'Lalmohan Babu,' said Feluda, putting the phone down, 'You can give up all hopes of selling your next story to Sanyal. The man sounds extremely fishy, and I'm convinced that the packet you carried was equally fishy.'

Lalmohan Babu scratched his head and sighed.

'To tell you the truth,'he said, 'For some odd reason I myself didn't think the man was quite straight.'

Feluda almost shouted at him.

'I can't stand that phrase of yours — for some odd reason. You have to know the reason and you must tell me. Try.'

Being told off by Feluda was nothing new for Lalmohan Babu. I also knew that he didn't mind because he himself had owned that Feluda's criticisms had improved his writing quite a bit.

Lalmohan Babu sat up straight.

'One, the fellow never looked me straight in the eye. Two, I couldn't see why he had to keep his voice so low. As if he had come for some secret consultation. Three. . .'

Unfortunately, even after much thought, Lalmohan Babu could not recall what the third reason was.

The movie was on at the Lotus at six–thirty, so we got out at six. By we, I mean myself and Lalmohan Babu. Feluda said he had work to do, and would stay back. His green notebook was already out of his bag, so I could guess what the work was.

We had to go back to Worli, for that was where the Lotus was. Lalmohan Babu was in a highly nervous state. *The Archer* would tell us exactly what kind of a director Pulak Babu was.

'If a man has made three hit films in a row, he can't be worthless, can he Tapesh?' said Lalmohan Babu.

What could I say? That was precisely what I had been saying to reassure myself.

Pulak Babu had not forgotten to tell the manager. Three seats in the royal circle had been kept for us. This was a re–run of the film, so many of the seats empty.

Well before the interval, it was evident that *The Archer* was nothing but a headache generator. Already in the darkness of the theatre, we had exchanged several looks. On the one hand I felt like laughing. On the other, wondering what *Jet Bahadur* was going to be like and what that would do to poor Jatayu, made me feel sorry for him. When the lights went on during the intermission, Lalmohan Babu sighed, saying, 'To think of a good Garpar boy wasting all these years turning out this sort of junk!' After a pause he turned to me and said, 'Every year, during the Puja holidays he used to get the neighbourhood boys together and put on a play ; and as far as I remember, he never managed to graduate from college. What else can you expect from him?'

As soon as the intermission was over, and the lights had been dimmed, the two of us sneaked out of the theatre. We were a little worried that Pulak Babu or somebody from his unit might be waiting outside. But we saw no one.

'If he asks me, I'll say it was a first rate film. You know Tapesh, if I didn't have those crisp new banknotes in my pocket, I could really be heart–broken.'

Our car was parked exactly opposite the cinema. Instead of going to it, Lalmohan Babu walked into a shop and bought a packet of spicy snacks, two packets of biscuits, six oranges and a bag of Parry's lozenges. Apparently he felt hungry from time to time sitting in his hotel room and these things would come in handy then.

We got into the car, with packages in both hands, and instantly I felt my head whirling.

The car reeked of Gulbahar. And it had not been there an hour–and–a–half ago.

'My head's spinning Tapesh,' said Lalmohan Babu. 'This is nothing but the work of an evil spirit. That fellow Sanyal must have been killed, and his ghost, wearing perfume, is haunting us.'

Not us — I thought to myself, only the car. But I did not say anything.

When we questioned the driver he said that he had been in the car most of the time. He had only stepped out for about five minutes which he had spent watching some programme in front of a television shop. Yes, he too was aware of the, perfume, but he was utterly baffled as to how the scent came to be there. It seemed absolutely incredible to him.

Back at the hotel we told Feluda about this. He said, 'This is how the plot thickens, Lalmohan Babu. Without this kind of thing happening, a mystery is not worth the name, and Felu Mitter's gray cells don't get stimulation.'

'But . . .'

'I know what you are going to ask, Lalmohan Babu. No, I haven't been able to solve this problem yet. Right now, I am only trying to figure out the nature of this web.'

'Looks like you did go out after all.' I suddenly made a very sleuth–like observation.

'Bravo Topshe. But I didn't step out of the hotel. I got this from the reception desk downstairs.'

There was an Indian Airlines timetable next to Feluda which had provoked my comment.

'I was finding out how many flights come to Calcutta from Kathmandu and when they arrive.'

The mention of Kathmandu reminded me of something I had been meaning to ask Feluda.

'That Nanasaheb Inspector Patwardhan was talking about — which Nanasaheb was he?'

'There's only one Nanasaheb known in Indian history.'

'The one who fought the British during the Sepoy Uprising?'

'Fought them, yes. But he also left the country to escape them. He went all the way to Kathmandu. With him he took a stock of fabulous jewels. Among these was a necklace of diamonds and pearls which was known as the Naulakha. Ultimately, Jang Bahadur of Nepal got custody of that necklace. In exchange, Jang Bahadur donated two villages to Nanasaheb's wife Kashi Bai.'

'Has this necklace been stolen from Nepal?'

'Seems like it, from what Patwardhan was saying.'

'Good God, have I been instrumental in passing that necklace?' asked Lalmohan Babu shrilly.

'Just think of it, said Feluda. 'Your name will be written in letters of diamond.'

'But . . . but . . . that necklace must have reached its destination by now. Whether it is taken out of the country or not is the lookout of the police. Why are you so concerned? Do you expect to catch these smugglers yourself?'

Just at that moment the telephone rang. And since it was closest to Lalmohan Babu, he picked it up.

'Hallo, yes, speaking.'

So the call was for him. Probably Pulak Babu. No, definitely not, Pulak Babu. That gentleman could say nothing which would make Lalmohan Babu's jaw drop like that, and make him hold the receiver away from his ear with a trembling hand.

Feluda took the receiver from Lalmohan Babu, but probably he heard nothing. He replaced the instrument and asked, 'Was that Sanyal?'

Lalmohan Babu seemed to be finding it difficult even to nod. Obviously, his muscles were not working properly.

'What did he say?' Feluda asked again.

'Said . . . ' Lalmohan Babu seemed to give himself a shake and gather courage, 'said if I opened my month, he'd slit my stomach.'

'Oh, good.'

'What . . .' Lalmohan Babu gaped foolishly at Feluda. Even to me, Feluda's relief at this moment seemed out of place.

'I wasn't getting too far with that Gulbahar perfume,' explained Feluda. 'It's too tenuous to be a proper clue. One couldn't even be sure if the man had come to Bombay himself, or if somebody else was using the Gulbahar. Now at least we can be sure.'

'But why threaten me?' Lalmohan Babu asked desperately.

'If I knew that then the game would be over, my dear Sir. You need patience in order to find the correct answer.'

Lalmohan Babu hardly ate at dinner–apparently he had no appetite. Feluda said that it did not matter, since the lunch at the Copper Chimney had been quite substantial. And it is a fact that Lalmohan Babu had eaten the most.

The day before, all three of us had walked out to get some *paan*. But today, it was impossible to get Lalmohan Babu to come out.

'Who's going to go into that crowd?' he said, 'I'm sure Sanyal's man is keeping a watch outside. The minute I step out he'll knife me.'

Finally it was Feluda who went out. Lalmohan Babu sat with me in our room and kept on saying, 'Oh, how I wish I hadn't accepted that package,' and finally, 'Why the hell did I have to start writing mystery thrillers?'

'I hope you won't be scared to sleep alone?' said Feluda after distributing the *paans*. When Lalmohan Babu kept quiet, Feluda reassured him, 'There's a little room off the corridor, right outside our room. You must have seen it? A hotel boy is always there. And some member or other of the hotel staff stays awake all night. This is no Shivaji Castle.'

The very mention of Shivaji Castle made Lalmohan Babu shiver. But finally around ten he gathered courage, said good night to us and went to his room.

Having to sit through half of Pulak Babu's film had exhausted me more than wandering around Bombay all day. Within ten minutes of Jatayu's departure I too went to bed. I knew quite well that Feluda would not sleep for a very long time. His notebook was lying on the bedside table. He had been writing in it at intervals throughout the day. Perhaps he was going to write more.

Once I am in bed at night, I have often tried to pinpoint the

exact moment when I fall asleep. But every time I have woken
up the next morning and realised that sleep had come upon me
unawares. It was the same this night. I was woken by the sound
of frequent knocks on the door and the shrill sound of the bell.
I got up and saw that Feluda's lamp was still on, and my watch,
lying beside my pillow, said quarter–to–one. As soon as Feluda
opened the door, Jatayu almost tumbled into his arms.

Lalmohan Babu was panting. But he did not seem to be
scared. Nor did his words indicate any fear.

'You won't believe what's been going on!'

'Come and sit down first,' said Feluda.

'Forget about sitting down — just look at the fabulous jewels
of Kathmandu which were being smuggled through me.'

What Lalmohan Babu was holding out towards Feluda was a
book. An English book, and quite a well–known one. I had seen
it in a shop on Lansdowne Road the other day — *The Life Divine
by Sri Aurobindo.*

Even Feluda was goggling.

'And not even a properly bound volume,' complained Lalmohan
Babu. 'After the first thirty pages, a lot of pages are stuck
together. What a dead loss if you don't look carefully before
buying. Did you ever think that the book–binders of Pondicherry
could do something so ham–fisted?'

'But then, what did you hand over that day to the man in
the red shirt?' asked Feluda.

'Would you believe it my own book — yes my own book! The
Buccaneer of Bombay! You see, I had sent Pulak only a copy of
the manuscript. So this time I thought I would give him a copy
of the book itself — with my blessings and my autograph. There
are three other copies in my bag, each wrapped in brown paper.
I know, I have devoted readers all over India. So I thought to
myself — here I am, going to Bombay, I may run into one of
them. So I brought several copies along, and it was one of those
that I — ha, ha.'

I had not seen Lalmohan Babu so happy for a long time.

Feluda took the book from him, looked it over and said, 'But
what about that threat from Sanyal over the phone? Is that
consistent with *The Life Divine*?'

But even this could not depress Lalmohan Babu.

'Who said it was Sanyal? Is it always possible to recognise a voice over the telephone? It could easily have been some unknown joker playing pranks. If a film like *The Archer* can become a hit in Bombay then anything is possible here.'

'And what about the smell of Gulbahar in the car?'

'I'm sure it's the driver. Have you noticed his hairstyle? The man is a fop. He was embarrased to be caught using perfume, and did not own up.'

'Well if that's all there is to it, you can now sleep in peace.'

'I most certainly will. I had a headache. That's why I opened my bag to look for an aspirin — and thus made this wonderful discovery. Anyway, since the mystery has been solved, why don't you concentrate on spiritual matters? I'll leave the book for you. Goodnight.'

Lalmohan Babu went off, and I went back to bed.

'Feluda, how do you think a person will feel when he finds he has got Jatayu's book instead of Sri Aurobindo's?'

'Furious.' said Feluda laying back with his head on the pillow. He did not switch off the reading lamp. And I almost laughed when I saw Feluda push his green notebook aside and turn the pages of *The Life Divine*. I am convinced that is the moment when I fell asleep.

CHAPTER 9

We were supposed to go near a level crossing between Khandala and Lonavala on the Bombay–Pune Road, to see the shooting. The last of the eleven climactic scenes in the film was going to be shot today. Not that everything could be done in a day. The entire cast and crew would have to be there four days in a row. We had decided that if we enjoyed the first day's shooting, we would also show up for the other days. The train would be made available on all five days exactly from one to two — that is, only for an hour. The horses belonging to the dacoit gang and the Lincoln Convertible for the hero would be there for the day.

In this scene, the villain takes the place of the engine driver and is driving the train, while the heroine and her uncle are lying trussed up in one of the compartments. The hero is in hot pursuit in his car. Meanwhile, his twin brother, who had been kidnapped by dacoits in infancy, and now was a dacoit himself, is coming with all his men to attack the train. Almost as soon as the hero drives up, the dacoit brother jumps from horseback on to the train. There is a fight in the engine and the villian driver is bumped off. Enter the hero and then . . . The rest you will see on the silver screen. We were told that three different finales would be filmed. After screening it would be decided which one was the best.

Pulak Babu had dropped in for a couple of minutes in the morning. Having checked that all preparations had been made for us to go to the shooting he said, 'Laluda, I can see you really liked my film *The Archer*.'

All morning Lalmohan Babu had been smiling to himself every time he remembered the previous night's discovery. It was this smile which Pulak Babu had noticed. Now, at Pulak Babu's comment, he laughed loudly and said, 'Oh yes — to think of a boy from Garpar doing this kind of thing!'

It would be late before we got back to the hotel. So Feluda told us to take our hand baggage with us. The oranges, biscuits and lozenges purchased the day before were distributed in the three bags. Lalmohan Babu's ten thousand rupees was handed over to the hotel manager for safe keeping and a receipt taken.

'After all,' said Lalmohan Babu, 'how can you be sure that a real dacoit or two is not hiding among the movie dacoits?'

Feluda went out once in the morning. He said his stock of cigarettes was low and it was quite possible that nothing would be available in the area where we were going for the shooting. Within ten minutes of his coming back, we started. Even today the smell of Gulbahar perfume lingered in the car.

Thane station was about twenty–five kilometres from Bombay. From there the road turns right and meets the National Highway leading to Pune. Eighty kilometres down this highway is Khandala. The weather was pleasant. Bits of cloud floated in the breeze, and the sun peeped through them to bathe Bombay in its gentle light. Pulak Babu had told us this was ideal weather for shooting. As for Lalmohan Babu, everything seemed to be giving him pleasure today. He kept on saying, 'This is as good as going abroad, my dear Sir! Have you noticed there are no passengers standing on the footboards of the buses? What civic sense these people have! Wonderful!'

It took us one hour to reach Thane. It was now quarter - past–nine. Since we still had some time to spare, we stopped the car in front of a tea shop and the three of us, as well as the driver, Swaruplal, had cardamom tea.

Shortly after leaving Thane, I noticed that we were driving beside the Western Ghats mountain range. The rail tracks were not running alongside any longer; after Thane they veered north in the direction of Kalyan. From Kalyan the tracks turned south and went to Pune via Matheran. Our level–crossing was midway between those two points.

Apart from Lalmohan Babu choking on an orange pip, nothing remarkable happened on our journey. I could not guess Feluda's state of mind by looking at his face. I had observed several times before that the fact of his looking grave did not necessarily mean he was worried.

One mile out of Khandala, around twelve–thirty, we saw what looked like a fair on one side of the road a little ahead of us. But why so many cars at a fair? As we went closer we saw something else apart from cars and people — horses. Now it was clear, the crowd was the crew and cast of *Jet Bahadur*. In all there must have been a hundred people, trunks and boxes, cameras, lights, reflectors, carpets — it was a most elaborate affair.

Our driver found a space between an Ambassador and a bus and parked the car. As soon as we got out, Pulak Babu came forward — he wore a white cap, and something like opera glasses suspended from his neck.

'Good morning. Is everything all right?'

The three of us nodded.

'Listen — Mr. Gore has sent word — he's in Matheran from where the train will come. He has to have some discussions with the railway bosses, perhaps arrange payment. So he may come here on the train itself, or he may drive down. You'll be informed as soon as the train arrives. But the important thing is, whether he comes or not, you people must get into the first–class compartment. All clear?'

'All clear,' said Feluda.

I had no idea that there were so many Bengalis working in the Bombay film industry. It was not surprising that some of them should recognize Feluda. As soon as he was introduced to cameraman Dashu Ghosh, the latter's eyelids crinkled.

'Mitter? Are you the detec–'

'That's right. But please keep it to youself,' said Feluda.

'But why? You are our pride. That whole affair of the statues of Ellora . . .'

Again Feluda stopped him, putting a finger on his lips.

Dashu Babu at last lowered his voice as he asked, 'Are you here on some investigation again?'

'No,' said Feluda, 'just on vacation with this friend of mine.'

Dashu Ghosh had spent the last twenty–one years in Bombay — in spite of that however he had kept in touch with Bengali fiction. He had even read a couple of books by Jatayu. Two other cameramen besides Dashu Ghosh were working on today's scene. But they were not Bengalis. Two of Pulak Babu's four assistants were Bangalis. But there were none among the actors. Aside from Arjun Mehrotra we also saw Micki who was dressed as the villain. Just Micki — he never used a surname. He was the top name among the rising 'villains' in Bombay. He had signed up for thirty–seven films, though twenty–nine of them were undergoing script changes to lessen the number of fights. Thank God, there were only four fighting scenes in *Jet Bahadur*. Otherwise Pulak Babu and Mr. Gore would also have been in a fix.

All of this we learnt from the production manager Sudarshan Das. He was from Orissa, and had been in Bombay for years. But he had decided to go back to Cuttack as soon as this film was completed, and direct his own film there.

Feluda, meanwhile, had strolled over to another group of people. The members of the dacoit gang were there, being madeup and getting dressed. I was quite taken aback to see Feluda having a friendly conversation with one of those dacoits. So I went up to them myself. But as soon as I heard this dacoit's voice I knew — it was the kung–fu expert, Victor Perumal. He had been made up to look like the hero's twin brother. His role today was to leap straight from horseback to the roof of the moving train. Then he would have to walk over the roofs of six compartments, get into the engine room and polish off the villain being played by Micki. Then would come the high–voltage encounter between the hero and his not–seen–for–twenty–years twin brother who had become a dacoit.

This whole grandiose affair seemed to have reduced Lalmohan Babu to silence. Actually he had a lot of reason to feel happy, since all of this was centred around his story.

'It's a peculiar feeling, Tapesh,' he said, 'to think that I have put so many people to so much trouble, expense and hard work, simply by writing a story. At times I have the illusion of being a really powerful person. Sometimes I even feel guilty. At the same time I can't help feeling that they have no real respect for an author. How many here have heard the name Jatayu?'

I tried to console him.

'I am sure they'll know,' I said, 'if the movie is a hit.'

'I hope so!' said Lalmohan Babu with a sigh.

Some of the dacoits who had finished their make–up were

already on horseback, practicing the chase. The horses had been rounded up under a huge banyan tree. I counted nine all together.

Within another minute the hero and the villain arrived in a huge white Lincoln convertible with shaded windows. The heroine did not have to come — the shots of her lying bound inside the train compartment could be taken inside the studio. Just as well. Given the excitement and hullabaloo created by the male stars as they got out of the car, the heroine's presence would have meant total chaos.

Sudarshan Babu had brought us some tea. As we were handing back our empty cups, a stentorian voice was heard over the loudspeakers. 'Train coming! Train coming! Everybody ready!'

It was exactly five–to–one as the engine with its eight bogies, chug–chugging down the tracks and belching black smoke, came to a halt near the level crossing. Even from a distance, I could make out that there was only one first–class compartment and it was as ancient as the engine. All the other compartments had been filled with passengers from Matheran. There were young and old people among them. As soon as the train stopped Pulak Babu became frantic in his activities. He kept running from one camera to another, from hero to villain, from assistant to assistant. Even Lalmohan Babu was forced to say, 'No, it's not money alone that makes a film.'

The hero's car was ready. At the steering sat Arjun Mehrotra, wearing dark glasses. Next to him was his personal make–up man and a couple of other young men — probably hangers–on. In front of Arjun was an open jeep with a three–legged stand for the camera which was ready for action. The band of dacoits, including Victor, had already gone ahead on horseback. At a signal from the moving train, they would come down from a particular hill at a particular point, and start galloping alongside the train. I saw Micki, the villain, walking towards the engine together with one of Pulak Babu's assistants.

We were not too sure what we should do, for there was no sign of Mr. Gore. We could not figure out if he had come on the train or not.

The crowd was thinning, and still nobody came towards us. Lalmohan Babu started fidgeting.

'Felu Babu, do you think they've forgotten about us?'

'There's only one first–class compartment,' said Feluda. 'As per instructions we are supposed to get into that one. But let's wait a few more minutes.'

Within a couple of minutes, there was a whistle from the train, and, simultaneously, hollering from Sudarshan Das.

'All of you, please come over, right now.'

Bags in hand, we made a dash for it. Sudarshan Babu came with us to the door of the first class compartment.

'I knew nothing about this before,' he said. 'Just now somebody came and told me. Mr. Gore is due in another half–an–hour. After the first shot the train will come back here.'

Inside the compartment we discovered a large flask of water on a bench and four white boxes bearing the name of Safari Restaurant. In other words, our lunch. One had to admire the gentleman's thoughtfulness in the midst of all this activity.

With the next whistle the train shuddered, and started moving. We got ready to look out of the window and observe the action outside. It was a totally new experience — so we all felt quite thrilled.

The train was gradually gathering speed. The road was on the right, and the three of us sat on the bench on that side. To the left would come the mountains, that was the dacoit's side. The right was the hero's.

After the train had gathered more speed, we could see the jeep with the camera coming on the right, followed by the hero's car. Now of course there was no one except the hero in that car. I could see that the camera was trained on him. Apart from the cameraman himself, there were three other people in the jeep. One of them was Pulak Babu's assistant. He carried a horn and was shouting instructions like 'Look right,' 'Look left,' to the hero.

Pulak Babu was with one of the two other cameras — inside one of the train compartments. The third camera was on the roof of the last compartment.

I was rather disappointed to see how tamely the hero was driving his car. But Feluda told me it would look like high speed on screen because the sequence was being flimed at low speed. Somehow, that had never occurred to me.

Soon after, the camera and the hero's car outstripped us and went ahead. The compartments being the old–fashioned kind, there were no bars on the windows. I wanted to put my head out to watch the action a little longer, but Feluda stopped me, saying,'Do you think you will like it if you go to see *Jet Bahadur* some day and see yourself leaning out of the train window?'

I restrained myself and had just got up to go and sit near the opposite window, when that smell came to my nostrils.

Feluda was no longer at my side. He was staring at the door of the bathroom and had gone to stand facing it, his right hand in his coat pocket.

'It's no use taking out your gun, Mr. Mitter, a revolver is already pointed at you.'

Now by the door the mountain side opened. A man holding a pistol pushed the door aside and entered, but did not come further inside. Had I seen him before? Yes — this was the man in the red shirt! But today he was dressed differently and there was ferociousness in his expression which had not been there that day at the airport. I was convinced that this man was a cold–blooded murderer. The revolver in his hand was aimed straight at Feluda.

Now the bathroom door which had been ajar, opened wide and the scent of Gulbahar flooded the compartment.

'San . . . San . . . '

Lalmohan Babu's entire body seemed to have shrunk into itself.

'Yes, indeed, it is Sanyal,' said the newcomer, 'and it's you that I have business with Mr. Ganguly. Surely you haven't left the package behind. Open your bag, take it out, and give it to me. I'm sure you don't need me to tell you what the consequences of not obliging will be.'

'Package . . .'

'You know what I am talking about. You must realize that I had not given you one of your own books for delivery, that day at Calcutta airport. Come on, take it out!'

'You're making a mistake. The package is with me, not with him.'

Everyone was having to raise his voice to be heard above the noise of the train. But Feluda's deep voice did not have to be raised to reach Sanyal even through that racket. Behind his glasses Sanyal's eyes gleamed.

'Have you really gained much by destroying all those pages of *The Life Divine*?'

Feluda's voice continued to be deep, his words measured.

'Nimmo,' said Sanyal in his rasping tones, looking at the ruffian standing in the doorway, 'If this man makes any trouble just finish him off . . . Keep your hands raised, Mr. Mitter.'

'Aren't you taking too much of a risk?' said Feluda. 'I know you can't afford to let us go even after you have got what you wanted. You will have to finish us anyway. But have you thought of what will happen to you once the train stops?'

'Very easy,' Sanyal bared his teeth. 'Nobody in this crowd knows me. Why should I not be able to blend in with all the passengers on the train? Your bodies will lie here, and I will go out and enter one of the other compartments. Very easy, isn't it?'

Repeated crises in Feluda's company had raised my courage. But there was no reason at this moment why, despite repeated attempts to gather courage, my whole body was turning to ice. That reason was nothing but Nimmo. It is only in books that you expect to encounter such a vicious, murderous countenance. There he was, leaning against the door, his fine, embroidered shirt ballooning at places because of the breeze coming in through the window, his right hand, despite swaying to the train's rhythm, aiming the gun unwaveringly at Feluda.

Sanyal advanced step by step. My nostrils were burning from that perfume of his. He was looking at Feluda's bag. I had no idea how Lalmohan Babu was feeling because he was now standing behind me. But despite the noise of the train I could hear his asthmatic wheezing.

The train was speeding along. That meant that the shooting had started all right. Did Mr. Gore know how disastrously he had let us down?

Sanyal sat down on the bench and pressed the catch of Feluda's bag. But it did not open. The bag was locked.

'Where are the keys? Where have you kept them?' Sanyal scowled in impatient rage. 'Where?'

'In my pocket,' said Feluda quietly.

'Which pocket?'

'Right.'

I knew that was the pocket where Feluda kept his revolver.

Sanyal stood up. He was heaving with fury. For a few moments he appeared nonpulssed Then . . . 'You — come here!' he roared at me.

Feluda also looked at me. From his exprexssion I gathered that he too was asking me to follow Sanyal's command.

As I started towards Feluda, another sound besides the noise of the train came to my ears — the sound of horses' hooves. Unnoticed by me, the mountains had appeared on our left. As I put my hand inside Feluda's pocket, I saw the band of dacoits coming down the mountain slope in a cloud of dust.

As I groped inside, I felt the key, right next to the revolver.

'Give it to him.'

I gave the key to Sanyal. Feluda's hands were still raised above his head.

Sanyal inserted the key in the lock and turned it. The catch opened. *The Life Divine* had been kept on top. Out came the book.

The hooves were sounding right next to the window. Not one horse but many — coming down the mountain slope at lightning speed and galloping parallel to the train.

Sanyal, holding the book, turned the pages and reached the spot where you could not turn any more. They were all stuck together. Now, instead of turning, Sanyal did something strange. He clawed in the middle and tore out those pages. Immediately, a square space was revealed. Some of the pages had been cut out in the centre to form that space.

But even as he took one look inside, Sanyal's expression was a sight to see. I don't know what he had expected, but all that the space contained was eight or nine cigarette stubs, a dozen burnt matchsticks, and a lot of cigarette ash.

'I hope you don't mind. I could not resist the temptation to use it as an ashtray.'

This time Sanyal raised his voice to such a pitch that I thought the whole train could hear him.

'How dare you! Where are the real goods?'

'What goods?'

'Scoundrel! Don't you know what I mean?'

'Of course I do. But I went to hear about it from you.'

'Where is it?'

'In my pocket.'

'Which one?'

'Left.'

The dacoits were right outside our window now, for we had reached the mountain range. Dust was coming in from outside.

'You there!'

I knew I was going to be ordered around again.

'What are you gaping at? Go and put your hand inside his pocket.'

Again I had to obey orders.

And what I took out this time was an object the like of which I had never laid hands on before. This amazing necklace made of diamonds and pearls was only fit for kings and emperors.

'Give it to me!'

Sanyal's eyes were gleaming again, but not with rage this time, only with lust and glee.

My hand went towards Sanyal, Feluda's hands were above his head. A groaning sound was coming from Lalmohan Babu. And the gang of dacoits . . .

B–a–n–g!

Our compartment seemed to tremble a little with that explosive sound, and immediately afterwards I saw Nimmo rolling about on the floor because a pair of legs had come in through the window and aimed a forceful kick at him. As a result, the revolver shot out of Nimmo's hand and shattered the glass of the ceiling lamp. Instantly, Feluda's hand came down at lightning speed and grasped his own revolver.

Now the compartment door on the mountain side opened once more by the person, dressed as a dacoit, who came in, was someone all three of us knew quite well.

'Thank you, Victor!' said Feluda.

Mr. Sanyal had dropped down on the seat. He was trembling, not with rage this time, but fear. For he knew there was no escape any longer, he was trapped.

Someone, meanwhile, must have guessed that something was wrong, and pulled the chain. For the train stopped exactly the way you expect it would if you pulled the chain.

Within seconds of the halt, we could hear a babble of noise outside. People were calling one person by name over and over.

'Victor! Victor! Where's Victor?'

This was Pulak Babu's voice. After all, it was Victor who had caused this confusion. He was supposed to have leaped down on the roof of the train, instead he had come straight inside our compartment.

Feluda opened the door, put his head outside and called Pulak Babu.

'Please come this way.'

That gentleman hurried forward and came inside. He looked very upset. I had heard that if a shot like this was spoilt it meant damages to the tune of thirty thousand rupees.

'What on earth is the matter, Victor? Are you out of your mind?'

'The one person who deserves the title of *Jet Bahadur* in your film, Pulak Babu, is Victor Perumal.'

'What is that supposed to mean?'

Pulak Babu stared at Feluda in astonishment. But there was a lot of irritation in his bewilderment even now.

'And for the role of the smuggler you should have chosen this gentleman instead of Parmesh Kapoor.'

'Why are you talking such nonsense? Who is this?' Pulak Babu asked looking at Sanyal.

By now, two cars had appeared on the road to our right — one was a police jeep, the other a police van. The jeep came to a halt beside our compartment, and Inspector Patwardhan got out.

At last Feluda answered Pulak Babu's question. He went over to Sanyal and stripped off his beard and moustache in two rapid movements. A couple more tugs and Sanyal's wig and glasses were off as Feluda said, 'I would have been even happier if I could have stripped off the scent of Gulbahar from your person, Mr. Gore. But that's one thing that even Felu Mitter can't manage.'

'Who told you the film would have to be ditched just because the producer has been arrested under M.I.S.A?'

It was Pulak Babu who asked the question. Not that Lalmohan Babu had said anything — he had just been sitting there brooding. And he did have reason to be worried about the future of *Jet Bahadur*.

'No one will be able to stop *Jet Bahadur*, Laluda,' went on Pulak Babu. 'Gore can go to hell, or to prison, or wherever he wants. He's not the only producer in Bombay. Chuni Pancholi has been after me for more than a year — you just wait, we'll start working under a new banner even before you leave Bombay.'

Today's shooting had of course come to a permanent halt at one–thirty. Gore and Nimmo had been handcuffed, and the Nanasaheb's Naulakha necklace was now in the custody of the police. Feluda had anticipated that something like this would happen. That was why he had stepped out in the morning on the pretext of buying cigarettes, and gone to see Inspector Patwardhan to arrange for the police to come. Apparently Gore had lived in Calcutta for twelve years at a stretch. Not just Don Bosco, he had also been a student at St. Xavier's so he knew Bengali quite well — though in Bombay he mostly spoke Hindi, Marathi and English.

We were sitting on the verandah of the rest house at Khandala. Lovely hilly location, and a distinct nip in the air. Many people came to Khandala from Bombay for their vacation. We had finished the *nan and mutton dopiaza* from Safari sometime ago. It was four– thirty now. So everyone was having tea and *pakoras*.

There were only the three of us at our table. Pulak Babu had just left us to join Arjun Mehrotra at his table. Mehrotra seemed to be in low spirits. One reason could well be that for today the only hero was Prodosh Mitter. Already many people had come to Feluda for his autograph — even Micki the villain.

The only other hero, beyond the shadow of a doubt, was Victor Perumal. Feluda had actually briefed Victor for this situation. 'When you reach the train on horseback, keep an eye on the first– class compartment,' he had instructed Victor. 'If you see signs of trouble, jump right inside.' Seeing Feluda standing with his hands raised was enough to tell Victor that trouble was afoot. But the amazing thing was he showed no signs of excitement after having performed in such a heroic manner. Already he had gathered his men together on the lawn in front of the resthouse, and had started practising his kung–fu.

'Yes . . . the problem is . . . '

Lalmohan Babu had opened his mouth at last.

But Feluda almost took the words out of his mouth saying, 'The problem is that you are still as much in the dark as you were before — aren't you?'

Jatayu smiled sheepishly and nodded.

'It won't be too difficult to enlighten you. But before that you must understand the man Gore. Then you will be able to make sense of all his actions.'

'The first thing to remember is that in reality he is a smuggler, though he was masquerading as a wealthy film producer. He was going to make a film based on your story. You've written that smugglers live in a place called Shivaji Castle. Understandably, Gore felt rattled. He wondered how much you knew about Shivaji Castle. For he himself was a smuggler who lived in Shivaji Castle. This is what he wanted to find out when he disguised himself as Sanyal and came to your house. Talking to you made him realise there was nothing to fear, because you were a harmless person and Shivaji Castle existed purely in your imagination. That was when he had the idea of passing the Naulakha necklace inside a book through your hands. Gore wanted to send this to one of his gang — someone who probably lived in Flat No. 2 on the seventeenth floor of Shivaji Castle itself. Even if you were caught, you would blame Sanyal, not Gore — right? Which means that Gore was keeping himself safe, by erecting Sanyal as the front man.'

'But then things did not work out as planned. Instead of a necklace worth five million, you handed over one of your own books, worth five rupees. It was that book which the fellow in the red shirt, alias Nimmo, was carrying as he was going up in the Shivaji Castle lift to the seventeenth floor. That was when someone belonging to Gore's rival gang attacked Nimmo to get hold of the book. Nimmo murdered this man, handed the package over to the right person, and took cover. Meanwhile, the news that there was no necklace inside the book forced Gore to come down to Bombay. He knew very well what had happened. There were two things he had to do. One, to recover the necklace; two, to finish us. His one hope was that we had not got to the bottom of *The Life Divine*, taken out the necklace and given it to the police.'

'As soon as he arrived, Gore realised that Sanyal would have to be resurrected. It was Sanyal who had sent the goods. So if Sanyal tried to recover it, no suspicion would fall on Gore.'

'But the Gulbahar . . .'

'I'm coming to that. The use of that perfume was an example of Gore's cunning. He had been prepared for this even from Calcutta. Sanyal meant Gulbahar, and Gulbahar meant Sanyal — this idea had become deep–rooted in your mind, hadn't it?'

'Yes — you can say that.'

'Good. Now try to remember. That day in his house, Gore left us for a few minutes in his sitting room and went out — pretending he was getting your money — right?'

'Right.'

'Well, would it have been too difficult to slip out and sprinkle a few drops of Gulbahar inside the lift? When I checked all the floors as we were going down, and found no traces of Gulbahar anywhere else, I realised that the smell existed only within the lift. Which meant that it had come, not from a person's body, but from a bottle. In the same way, it was equally easy to send someone to the Lotus cinema, some-one who would put his hand in through the car window and sprinkle a few drops of perfume.'

When Feluda explained, things seemed very simple. It was obvious that Lalmohan Babu had followed all this. So I was quite surprised to see that the smile did not reappear on his face. How was I to guess that only something said by Pulak Babu would restore the vanished smile.

We had finished tea, and were getting ready to return to town. The sun had set behind the mountains and it had suddenly become cold enough for us to shiver, when I saw Pulak Babu hastening towards us.

'Laluda, *Jet Bahadur* will be advertised on the posters on Friday —

but I need to know one thing before that.'

'What is it?'

'What would you prefer to use, your real name or the pseudonym?'

'It's the pseudonym that's real, my dear fellow,' said Lalmohan Babu with the broadest of smiles. 'And the spelling should be . . . J–a––t–a–y–u.'

MYSTERY AT GOLOK LODGE

'Who was Jayadratha?'

'Husband of Dushshala, Duryodhan's sister.'

'And Jarasandha?'

'King of Magadha.'

'Dhristadyumna?'

'Draupadi's elder brother.'

'Name the two conches that belonged to Arjuna and Yudhisthira.'

'Arjuna's was Devadatta, and Yudhisthira's Anantabijay.'

'Which missile, when released, makes the enemy lose their head completely?'

'Twashtra.'

'Very good.'

Thank God, that was over, and I had passed! Of late, the *Ramayana* and the *Mahabharata* had become what you might call staple reading for Feluda. I too had been reading them, and I did not mind one bit. After all, this was no bitter pill to swallow. On the contrary — it was an unending gourmet meal. Story after story after story. Feluda says a new adjective has become fashionable these days in the English language book trade — unputdownable. Which means, a book that you simply cannot put down once you have picked it up. Both the *Ramayana* and the *Mahabharata* are like that, unputdownable.

Right now, Feluda was engrossed in the second volume of Kaliprasanna Singha's translation of the *Mahabharata*. Mine was a simpler version, meant for younger readers. Lalmohan Babu says that he has memorised portions of Krittibasa's *Ramayana*. Apparently, his grandmother used to read aloud from the book; listening to her was enough for him to memorise a lot of it. Unfortunately, we do not have a copy of Krittibasa's *Ramayana* in the house. But I have been toying with the idea of getting hold of one and testing Lalmohan Babu's memory. For the time being though, our friend had gone into a self–imposed internment to finish his novel for the Puja annual, and we have not been seeing much of him.

Feluda looked up from his book at the sound of the doorbell. He had just come back on Friday, after having solved a murder case in Hijli. He probably wanted to take it easy for a while — which is why he did not show much eagerness at the sound of the bell. With the kind of fees he charged, one case a month was enough to see him through in comfort. As Lalmohan Babu was in the habit of saying, Feluda's lifestyle was 'one hundred per cent unostentatious.' I think I should mention here that a slight speech impediment often made Lalmohan Babu mix up his rolling rs– and soft rs– when saying the Bengali word for unostentatious. Feluda once advised him to practise a short tongue–twister full of r–s. Our friend stumbled four times at his very first attempt!'

Feluda says, 'Whenever a new character makes his or her entry, you should provide a reasonable description. If you don't do it, the reader is bound to imagine something. And later he will find enormous discrepancies between his image and yours.' So let me start out by saying that the man who now entered the room had a fair complexion, was five feet nine, and around fifty. His hair had gone gray around the ears. There was a mole in the middle of his chin, and he wore a gray safari suit. The way he cleared his throat on entering the room indicated a certain degree of hesitation. A right hand raised to his mouth as he cleared his throat made me feel he was rather westernized.

'Sorry, I couldn't make an appointment before coming to see you,' apologised the newcomer as he sat down on one corner of the couch. 'But all the telephone lines are dead in our neighbour-hood — the roads are being dug up, you know how it is.' Feluda nodded. We were all aware of the shambles the city was in because of the road repair work being carried out.

'My name is Subir Datta,' — the voice was good enough to be a T.V. newscaster's — 'Er, you are the private invest . . .'

'Yes.'

'I've come to consult you about my brother.'

Feluda remained silent. The *Mahabharata* lay closed on his lap, one finger stuck inside as a bookmark.

'But of course I must introduce myself first. I am a sales executive with Corbett & Orris. I think you know DineshChoudhury of Camac Street. He was my classmate in college.'

Dinesh Choudhury, I knew, was one of Feluda's clients.

'I see,'said Feluda gravely at his westernized best. Our visitor went straight to the topic of his brother.

'My brother Nihar Datta had once made quite a name for himself in the field of biochemistry. He had been doing research on viruses. Not here though — in the US Michigan University. One day, as he — was working in his lab, there was a huge explosion. My brother nearly lost his life — but one of the doctors at the hospital managed to save him. No one, however, could save his eyes.'

'Did he go blind then?'

'Yes, totally. He came back to India. He had married an American lady while living in the States. But she left him after the accident. My brother never remarried.'

'But that means he never finished his research either.'

'No, he didn't. I think it was that frustration which made him refuse to speak to anyone for nearly six months. We were almost sure he had gone round the bend. Finally, very slowly, he became his normal self again.'

'How is he now?'

'Oh, he still retains a lot of his enthusiasm for science — that is evident. He has engaged this young man — as an assistant or secretary — who was himself a student of biochemistry. One of his duties is to read out essays from scientific journals to my brother. Not that my brother is totally helpless. Every afternoon he takes a constitution on our roof all by himself, using a stick to guide his steps. Not only that, he can even walk out of the house and go up to the crossroads alone. Nor does he need any help to move from room to room in the house.'

'Does he have an income?'

'He had published one book on biochemistry in the US — that brings in something.'

'Tell me about the incident.'

'Excuse me?'

'I mean the reason for your coming here.'

'Oh, yes, of course.'

Subir Datta took out a cigar from his pocket, lit it and exhaled smoke.

'A burglar got into my brother's room last night,' he said.

'How did you find out?'

With this question, Feluda finally put his *Mahabharata* down on the table in front of him.

'My brother himself has no idea. And his servant too is not the brightest person around. But his secretary came this morning at nine, and guessed what had happened from the appearance of the room. Both drawers of the desk were half–open, some papers lay scattered on the floor, all the things on top of the desk were disarranged, and what is more, there were scratches around the keyhole of the steel safe. Obviously, someone had been trying to break into that.'

'Have there been other burglaries in your neighbourhood recently?'

'Yes. Two houses down from ours. We now have a couple of policemen doing the rounds in our area. By area I mean Ballygunge Park. Our own house is eighty years old, built by my grandfather. Our family used to be of *zamindars* in Khulna, you know. Grandfather moved to Calcutta in 1890, and set himself up as a manufacturer of chemical equipment. We had a huge shop in College Street. My father ran the business, too, for several years. But we closed down, about thirty years ago.'

'How many people live in your house?'

'Few, compared to the old days. Both my parents are dead. My wife also died in 1975. Both my daughters are married, and my elder son is in Germany. So the members of our household now are myself, my brother and my younger son. There are two servants and a cook. We live on the first floor. The ground floor has been split up into two flats and rented out.'

'Who are the tenants?'

'The flat in front is occupied by Mr. Dastur. He deals in electrical goods. Mr. Sukhwani lives in the back, he has an antique shop on Lindsay Street.'

'Didn't the burglar go into their rooms. They sound like affluent people.'

'Oh yes, they are affluent all right. The flats are rented out for Rs. 2,500 each. Sukhwani locks all his doors because he has so many valuables in his possession. But Dastur says he feels suffocated if all the doors are closed.'

'Do you know what the burglar was looking for in your brother's room?'

'Well, all the papers connected with my brother's incomplete research are kept in the safe, and I have no doubts about their value. But an ordinary burglar can hardly be expected to know all that. My guess is that the thief came in to steal money. You can well imagine how easy it is to steal from a blind man's room.'

'Yes,' agreed Feluda. 'I suppose, since he is blind there's no question of a bank account. Signing cheques, for him . . .'

'Quite right. Whatever money comes from the sale of the book is sent in my name. It is deposited in my account. I write a cheque to withdraw the amount and hand over the cash to my brother. All of that money also stays in the steel safe. I would say the total amount of cash in there will come to around Rs. 30,000.'

'What about the keys?'

'As far as I know, my brother keeps them under his pillow. I am sure you can understand — the main reason for my anxiety is my brother's blindness. He has to sleep with his door open at night. His servant Koumudi sleeps just outside the door, so that he can come in quickly at night if he's needed. But. if a burglar is really desperate and the servant doesn't wake up, then my brother will have no means of self–defence. And yet, he will not let us inform the police. He says all they know is how to cross–examine people, that they are a worthless, corrupt lot, etc. So I suggested your name, and he agreed. If you will at least come to our house once, then we can think of some preventive measures. What is more, the question of whether the burglar is an outsider or an insider . . .'

'Insider?'

Both Feluda and I were all ears.

Our visitor dropped ash from his cigar into the ashtray and lowered his voice as much as possible.

'My dear Sir, let me make one thing quite clear — I like to talk straight. I've decided to come to you, and I know that hiding facts will not be helpful to your work. First, I don't like either one of our tenants. Sukhwani has been here for the last three years. I know nothing about him myself. But I have heard from other people in the antique trade that he's not quite straight. The police have their eye on him.'

'And the other tenant?'

'Dastur came about four months back. My eldest son used to stay in that flat. But he has now settled abroad for good. He has a job with an engineering firm in Dusseldorf, and he's married a German girl. I've heard nothing bad about this Dastur, but he arouses suspicion by his excessive reserve. Also . . .'

He stopped. The rest of his statement he made with face downcast staring at the ashtray.

'My younger son, Shankar, is totally beyond reform.'

He relapsed into silence.

'How old is he?' asked Feluda.

'Twenty–three. He had his birthday last month, though I didn't lay eyes on him that day.'

'What does he do?'

'Drugs, gambling, petty crimes, hanging out with toughs — you name it! He has been arrested three times. Naturally, I have had to go and bail him out. As you may guess, our family still has a reputation, so it pays to mention our name. But I don't know how long that will last.

'Was your son home the day the burglar came?'

'He had come home for dinner — doesn't even do that everyday — but I haven't seen him since then.'

It was decided that we would visit Ballygunge Park in the afternoon. The case had not yet acquired enough dimension to be a proper case. But I knew that Feluda's imagination had been stirred by the story of the scientist blinded by explosion. He must be thinking of Dhritarashtra in *Mahabharata*.

It took Uncle Sidhu exactly three — and — a — half minutes, to dig out the news about a rising Bengali biochemist losing his sight because of an explosion in a Michigan University laboratory, from his twenty–second volume of paper clippings. And even out of that, two minutes were spent on telling Feluda off for not having showed up for so long. Though Uncle Sidhu is not really an Uncle, he is more to us than any relative by blood. Whenever Feluda needs to find out about the past, he goes to Uncle Sidhu instead of the National Library. That way he gets what he wants much faster and with much more fun.

As soon as Feluda mentioned the case, Uncle Sidhu frowned and said 'Nihar Datta? Researching with viruses? Lost his eyes in some explosion?'

Wow! what incredible memory! My father says he can remember anything if he hears it once. Feluda says he has a photographic memory: any interesting news item he reads or hears about gets imprinted on his brain forever.

'But the man wasn't alone.'

This was news to us.

'What do you mean — wasn't alone?' enquired Feluda.

'What I mean is, if I remember right . . .' Uncle Sidhu had moved to his bookshelf and was pulling out the relevant volume of paper–cuttings . . . 'He had a research partner — yes, here it is.'

Uncle Sidhu opened up Vol.22, and read the news item out to us. The accident had taken place in 1962. We discovered that Nihar Datta had a colleague working with him on this project — another Bengali biochemist, Suprakash Choudhury. The accident had done Choudhury no damage since he had been at the other end of the room. And it was this same Choudhury who had saved Nihar Datta's life. He had put out the flames and made arrangements for Nihar Datta to be sent to the hospital immediately.

'And what about Choudhury now?'

'That I don't know,' said Uncle Sidhu. 'It's not the kind of news I keep. People like this get into the newspapers when something remarkable happens in their lives — and that's the only reason I get to hear about them. I don't go out of my way to gather news. What's the use? How many people care about me that I should care about them? But one thing is for sure — if this Choudhury had done anything to create a ripple in the world of science, I would definitely have heard about it.'

Even an unobservant man would notice the signs of age on the house that was 7/1, Ballygunge Park. It was also quite obvious that if the owner of the house had had the means to cover up those signs, he would have done so. Clearly, the Datta family had seen better days. The garden was probably at the back of the house. In front, there stood a dead water fountain on a circular patch of grass. Two gravel-led driveways encircled the green patch and led to the porch. When Feluda enquired about the name 'Golok Lodge,' engraved on a mar-ble plaque by the gate, Subir Babu said that his grandfather's name had been Golok Bihari Datta. He was the one who had built this house.

It was still quite evident that as a private residence Golok Lodge had been quite something in its heyday. Three steps led up from the porch to the marble–paved landing, to the left of which was a flight of marble stairs leading to the first floor. Through one of the doors in front could be seen a corridor — apparently both the flats opened on to this passage from the right. To the left was a huge room which the Dattas had not rented out.

At one time, this room had seen many banquets and music and dance performances.

Right above this room was the first–floor living room, where we went in and sat down. Overhead was a chandelier wrapped in cloth, permanently out of commission. It was impossible to count all its branches. One wall had a huge mirror with a gilded frame, which Subir Babu said had been imported from Belgium. The thick carpet on the floor had come apart in chunks, to display the marble floor, chequered in white and black like a chess–board.

Subir Babu switched on a standing lamp and dispelled much of the darkness. Just as we were about to sit down on the couch, we heard a noise from the corridor outside — tap, tap, tap — the combined sound of a stick and a pair of sandals.

For one brief moment, the sound stopped outside the doorway —

and then the owner of the stick entered the room. All three of us stood up.

'I heard unfamiliar voices — the gentlemen must have come then?'

A deep voice, perfectly in keeping with the six–foot figure. His hair, gone completely gray, was somewhat dishevelled. He wore dark glasses, and was dressed in a fine cotton shirt and silk pyjamas. That the explosion had not only ruined his eyes, but had also left its mark on parts of his face was evident even in the diffused glow of lamplight.

Subir Babu moved forward to help his brother. 'Sit down Dada,' he said.

'Yes, I will. But please, ask the gentlemen to sit down first.'

'*Namaskar*,' said Feluda, 'My name is Prodosh Mitter. On my left is my cousin Tapesh.'

I said *namaskar* softly. After all, merely folding my hands in greeting would be wasted on a blind man.

'Ah, Mr. Mitter seems to be around my height, and the cousin will probably be five seven, or seven–and–a–half?'

'I'm five seven,' I blurted out.

Mentally, I had to take my hat off to the old gentleman for his accurate guess.

'Sit down,' said Nihar Datta, and sat down on the couch facing us without any help from his brother. 'Have you asked for some tea?'

'Yes,' replied Subir Datta.

As was his habit, Feluda came straight to the point without any unnecessary preamble.

'Didn't you have a partner working with you on this research project?'

The way Subir Babu started fidgeting made us feel that he too had been aware of this fact, and was feeling embarrassed at not having mentioned it to us.

'Not a partner,' said Nihar Datta, 'only an assistant, Suprakash Choudhury. He had been studying in the States. To call him my partner would be giving him too much credit. There was no way he could have carried on without me.'

'Have you any idea where he is now, or what he may be doing?'

'No.'

'Didn't he keep in touch with you after the accident?'

'No. I can tell you this much though — he did not have total commitment. He was interested in quite a few things apart from biochemistry.'

'Did the explosion occur because of carelessness?'

'To the best of my knowledge, I was never careless.'

Tea came. The whole room seemed to be throbbing with silence. I stole a quick look at Subir Babu. He also looked tense and perturbed. Feluda was staring steadily at the dark glasses.

There were savouries and sweets to go with the tea. I picked up one of the plates, but Feluda showed no interest in the food. He lit a Charminar and said, 'So, the research you had been conducting, is still unfinished.'

'I am sure I would have heard about it if anyone else had been working along those lines.'

'Are you sure that Suprakash Babu himself didn't do any further work on this?'

'All I know is that he did not have the ability to make any progress without consulting my notes. The papers connected with the final phase of my research were all kept in my personal locker. There was no way anyone from outside could get at them. And eventually, when I returned home, the papers came back with me. I still have them. I also know, if this research could have been successful, it would have brought the Nobel Prize within my reach. A cure for cancer would have been found.'

Feluda had picked up his tea cup. By this time I too had taken a sip from my own cup and I was quite sure that this tea was good enough to please even a fussy tea–drinker like Feluda. However, I was not allowed to see the expression of his face after he had had a sip. All the lights went out. Loadshedding.

'It's been happening exactly at this time over the last few days,' said Subir Babu as he got up. 'Koumudi!'

In the little daylight that still remained, Subir Babu made his way out of the room to look for the servant.

'The lights have gone out, have they?' said Nihar Datta. Then he added with a sigh, 'Not that it makes any difference to me.'

Exactly at this moment, the grandfather clock startled us all by sounding its chimes — it was six o' clock.

Subir Babu came back, followed by the servant Koumudi carrying a candle.

The candle, placed on the centre table, illuminated all our faces. Two wavering points of light could be seen reflected in Nihar Babu's dark glasses. The reflection of the candle flame.

Feluda took another sip of his tea and directed his question to the dark glasses.

'If your notes happen to fall into the hands of another biochemist, do you think it would be profitable for that person?'

'Certainly, if you consider the Nobel Prize to be profitable.'

'Do you think the burglar entered your room to steal your notes?'

'No, there's no reason to think so.'

'Another question. Who else knows about your notes?'

'I am sure many in the scientific community can deduce their existence. Aside from that, of course, the members of my household and my secretary Ranajit knows about them.'

'When you say members of your household, do you also include the residents of the two ground floor flats?'

'I have no idea what they know or don't know. They are businessmen. I can't imagine they would be particularly interested even if they knew about these matters. Though, maybe, that's not right. These days one can trade in anything, so why not research documents? Not all scientists are models of rectitude and high principles.'

Nihar Babu got up; so did we.

'Can I have a look at your room?' asked Feluda.

The old gentleman stopped near the door. 'Of course you can. Subir will show you around. I will be going up to the roof to take my evening walk now.'

All four of us came out to the corridor. The darkness had grown thicker. Candles lit within the rooms to the left and right of the corridor cast their faint light outside. Nihar Babu went forward to the steps leading to the roof tapping his stick. I could hear him say, 'I have already counted the steps. After the first seventeen you take a left turn to get to the stairs. Then you climb — seven plus eight–fifteen steps to the roof. Let me know if you need me again . . .'

An old–fashioned bed occupied a sizeable area in one portion of Nihar Babu's spacious room. Next to the bed stood a small round table. A covered glass of water had been kept on the table; ten or so tablets wrapped in foil lay next to the glass. Probably sleeping pills.

Beside this table was an armchair facing the window. The woven cane back showed dark patches from many years of use. I felt Nihar Babu spent most of his time in this chair.

Apart from all this, the room contained a work table — from which a candle emitted a dim glow — a steel chair, writing materials on the table, a rack for letters, an old typewriter and a collection of scientific journals.

Right next to the work table, left of the door, stood the iron safe.

As soon as he entered the room Feluda gave a quick look around and inspected the keyhole of the safe with the light from his pocket torch.

'They certainly tried their best to open this. There are scratches all around the keyhole.'

He then moved forward and picked up the tablets.

'Soneril . . . I had already guessed Nihar Babu must be taking strong sleeping pills. Otherwise he would have woken up.'

He turned to Koumudi who was standing just outside the doorway.

'How come you didn't wake up? What kind of a watchdog are you?'

Koumudi bent his head in shame.

'He's a notoriously heavy sleeper,' said Subir Babu. 'It's impossible to wake him up without shouting for him three or four times.'

We heard footsteps. A gentleman of about thirty now entered the room. He was thin, wore glasses and had curly hair. Subir

Babu's introduced him as Nihar Babu's secretary Ranajit Bandyopadhyay.

'Who won?'

It was Feluda, asking the secretary this unexpected question.
Ranajit Babu's bewilderment made Feluda smile.

'I can see the counterfoil of your ticket,' he said, 'in the breast
pocket of your see–through shirt. On top of that, your face looks
distinctly sunburnt. Surely, it's not too hard to imagine that
you've just come back from watching a League game?'

'The East Bengal team,' said Ranajit Babu with a grin. Even
Subir Babu's face wore a smile mixed with admiration.

'How long have you been working here?'

'Four years.'

'Has Nihar Babu ever said anything to you about the explosion?'

'I did ask him once,' replied Ranajit Babu. 'But he didn't
want to say very much. However, often, almost unconsciously,
he complains about the terrible consequences of losing his eyesight.'

'Anything else?'

Ranajit Babu thought a little before answering.

'One thing I have heard him say, that he is still alive simply
because he has some unfinished business. What that may be I
have never dared to ask. I think, he still has hopes of finishing
his research.'

'Well, he certainly won't be able to do it himself. Perhaps he
is hoping to find somebody else to do it. Isn't that likely?'

'Perhaps.'

'What are your working hours here?'

'I come at nine, and leave at six. Today, I had taken permission
to leave early so that I could watch the game. He didn't object.
But even if I do go out like this, I always look in on him in
the evening. Just in case . . .'

'Where are the keys for the safe?' Feluda asked abruptly. 'I'd
like to see the research papers and the money — what state
they are in.'

'There, under that pillow.'

Feluda moved forward and pulled out a keyring with five keys
from under the pillow. He then selected the right key and opened
the safe.

'Where's the money?'

'In that drawer,' Ranajit Babu pointed with his finger.

Feluda pulled the drawer open.

'Good God!' Ranajit Babu goggled in astonishment. Even in the candle light I could see the colour draining from his face.

All that the drawer contained was a roll of paper — which proved to be a horoscope on inspection — and some old letters in a Kashmiri wooden box. Nothing else.

'How can this be?' The words sounded like Ranajit Babu could hardly utter them. 'There were three rolls of hundred–rupee notes . . . altogether about thirty thousand . . .'

'Are the research papers kept in this other drawer?'

Ranajit Babu shook his head. Feluda opened the second drawer. It was absolutely empty.

Footsteps sounded outside — tap, tap, tap. Nihar Babu was coming downstairs.

'The research notes were all kept in a long envelope, embossed with the seal of Michigan University . . .' Ranajit Babu's voice sounded taut and dry.

'Were the money and the notes in here this morning?'

'I saw them myself,' said Subir Babu. 'The numbers of the hundred–rupee notes have been written down. My brother always insisted on that.'

'So,' said Feluda very gravely, 'the whole thing happened during the last fifteen minutes — that is, after the lights went off. When we were all sitting in the living room.'

Nihar Babu came in. We could see from his face that he had heard everything — from outside. We stood aside for him, and the old gentleman made his way to the armchair and sat down.

'Just think of it!' he said with a sigh, 'stolen from under the detective's nose.'

As we came out of Nihar Babu's room, Feluda asked Subir Babu, 'Apart from the front staircase, are there any other stairs that lead up to the first floor?'

'Yes,' said Subir Babu, 'the back staircase, used by the sweeper.'

'Do you have a power cut every day around this time?'

'Well, yes, at least for the last ten days it has been so. People have even started timing their watches by this. The power goes at six, comes back at ten.'

I tried to recall if there had been any other event as bizarre as this one. But nothing came to mind.

'Have any of your downstairs tenants got back?' Feluda asked as we came to the head of the staircase.

'We can find out,' said Subir Babu. 'They do usually come home around this time.'

The door facing the landing on the floor below was Mr. Dastur's. It was still locked, and we could see from outside that there were no lights in the room.

'If you want to get to Sukhwani's room you'll have to go by the back way,' said Subir Babu.

Round the eastern corner of the house, along the path bordering the flower garden, we went towards Sukhwani's room. A fluorescent lamp had been lit inside — one of those battery–powered lights that are so common these days.

The sound of our footsteps brought the gentleman outside. He could see the light from Feluda's torch, but he could not make out who we were. Subir Babu spoke to him in English.

'Can we come in for a few minutes?'

As soon as he recognized the voice, Sukhwani's expression changed.

'Certainly, certainly.'

On being introduced to Feluda, he positively babbled with excitement.

'You see Mr. Mitter — I have a roomful of valuable things. The very mention of burglary is enough to give me a heart attack. You can imagine what a state I was in when I heard this morning that there was a burglary last night.'

What Sukhwani said was true — I could never have imagined that so many valuable objects could be stuffed into one room. Statuettes made of stone, brass, and bronze — of various divinities — numbered nearly thirty. Plus, there were paintings, books, old maps, various containers, swords and shields, spittoons, hookahs, perfume bottles, and so many other things. Feluda said to me later, 'If only I had that kind of money, Topshe, I would at least have bought all the books and the prints!'

On being questioned, the gentleman said he had come home

only ten minutes before the loadshedding.

'Did anybody come this side during those ten minutes? There is a set of stairs leading to the first floor, right behind your room. Did you hear anything from that direction?'

The gentleman said he had gone into the bathroom as soon as he had come back.

'Besides, there's not much you can see in this darkness, can you? Just one thing though — are you suspecting someone from outside?'

'Why?'

'Well have you talked to Mr. Dastur?'

His whole manner indicated that as soon as we talked to Dastur we would realise that there could be no other suspect!

Before Feluda could say anything in response, he went on, 'He's a most peculiar character. I know I should not talk like this about my own neighbour, but I have been watching him for the last few days. At first, before I'd met the man, the sound of his snoring would come to my ears through his window. I'm convinced the noise even reached upstairs.'

The smile that lifted the corners of Subir Babu's mouth made me think that Sukhwani was not exaggerating too much.

'Then I met him one morning, when he came to borrow my typewriter. I just didn't like the avidity in his eyes, as he looked at the things in my room. Out of ordinary curiosity, I asked him what he did. He said he traded in electrical goods. Well, let me ask you this — if that's what he does, then how come he hasn't installed a battery–powered light and a fan in his room, with all these power cuts going on? The whole thing is suspicious.'

Sukhwani stopped, and we immediately took the opportunity to get up. Before leaving, Feluda said,'If you do see anything unnatural, please inform Mr. Datta. That will help us enormously.'

I had already heard the honking of a taxi as we were making our way from the eastern path to the front of the house. Now we saw a gentleman walking along the gravelled path towards the porch. Even in that dim light, I could make out that he was of medium height and plump. He wore a brown suit and sported a well–trimmed salt–and–pepper french–cut beard. His complexion looked fair. The brief case he was carrying seemed fairly new.

Subir Babu greeted him with a 'Good evening', as soon as he turned in our direction. The gentleman looked distinctly flustered. Clearly, he was not used to hearing 'Good morning' or 'Good evening' from anybody in this house.

'Good evening, Mr. Datta,' he responded.

A strange nasal voice. He started moving as soon as he had spoken but Feluda whispered to Subir Babu, 'Stop him!'

Subir Babu obeyed immediately.

'Er, Mr. Dastur.'

Dastur stopped. Together with Subir Babu, we approached him. As he heard about the incidents of the day from Subir Babu, Dastur's eyes goggled.

'You mean so much has happened in just these few minutes? Your brother must be terribly upset?'

Feluda had once told me that an abnormal state of mind can so change your voice as to make it almost unrecognizable. When Mr. Dastur spoke the last sentence in English, I noticed there was so much terror and amazement in his voice that the previous nasal quality was quite inaudible. It was almost like hearing another man speak.

'Did you see anybody leaving, as you entered the house?' Feluda asked him.

'No, no one at all,' replied Mr. Dastur. 'Of course, it is quite possible that I missed him in the darkness. Thank God, I have nothing valuable in my apartment.'

'Who's there?'

The question came from the landing on the first floor. It was Nihar Babu's voice. We had been standing near the porch steps as we talked. But now we went inside. As I looked up, I could see Nihar Babu's dark glasses gleaming even in the darkness.

'It's me, Mr. Datta,' Dastur said in English, looking upwards. 'Your brother's just been telling me about your loss. My sympathies.'

The dark glasses disappeared. And immediately after that we heard the receding sound of sandals and stick.

'Won't you come and sit down,' asked Mr. Dastur. 'It's nice to have company after a whole day at work.'

Feluda did not object. And I knew why. It is the first duty of a detective to get to know the people who live in a house where a crime has been committed.

After the opulence of Sukhwani's rooms, the bareness of Mr. Dastur's living room was certainly noticeable. The furniture consisted of one sofa, a couple of couches, a writing desk and a bookshelf. There was a low table in front of the sofa, but it was quite a small one. A candle had been placed on it. Feluda lit it with his lighter. I saw then that the walls sported nothing beyond a single calendar.

Our host had gone inside, probably to call his servant. When he returned, Feluda offered him a cigarette.

'No thanks, I gave up smoking for fear of cancer three years ago.'

'I hope you don't mind other people smoking. I see there's a half–finished cigarette lying in your ashtray.'

Feluda picked up the cigarette stub. 'It's my brand.'

In fact, even I can distinguish a Charminar stub from a distance.

'I have often thought of arranging for a battery to run a light and a fan the way Sukhwani has,' said Dastur. 'But as soon as I remember that ninety percent of Calcutta's people have to suffer from the heat and the darkness, I feel miserable. And so I . . .'

'But you deal with electrical goods in your business, don't you?'

'Electrical goods?'

'Yes, that's what Sukhwani said.'

'That man always makes the same mistake. It's electronic, not electrical. I've just set it up, over the last year.'

'All by yourself?'

'No, in partnership with a friend. I come from Bombay myself, but I have lived abroad for many years. I used to work with a computer manufacturing firm in Germany. My friend wrote from Calcutta asking me to come and join him. He's invested the money, I'm providing the expertise.'

'When did you come back to Calcutta?'

'Last November. I had to stay with my friend for three months. Then I heard about this flat, and moved in.'

The servant came in with cold drinks. Thums Up. Mr. Dastur had already found out who Feluda really was. He now lowered his voice and spoke confidentially.

'Mr. Mitter, it's true I don't have too many valuable objects in my room. But I've got to tell you one thing. My neighbour is definitely not an easy person to make out. All sorts of secret deals go on in his apartment. Unethical deals.'

'How do you know?'

'My bathroom is right next to his. There's a locked door between the two. And if you put your ear to the door, you can hear conversation going on in his bedroom.'

Feluda cleared his throat loudly.

'Isn't it just as unethical to eavesdrop on someone like that?'

But Mr. Dastur was not embarrassed at all. 'I wouldn't be doing it except for one thing. I noticed that when one of my letters fell into his hands by mistake, he steamed it open, and then resealed it before returning it to me. Naturally, I couldn't resist the temptation to get my own back. Basically, I am a simple fellow. But if he tries to harass me, I'm not going to let him off easily.'

We thanked him for the cold drinks, and took our leave. When we reached the gate, Feluda asked the watchman whether he had seen anyone entering or leaving in the last half–an–hour. He said he had seen no one other than Sukhwani and Dastur. That was not surprising. The boundary wall of 7/1, Ballygunge Park encircled the house on all sides. The house behind had been lying vacant for the past few months. An agile burglar could easily climb over that wall — all of us instinctively felt that this had been the work of an insider. At the same time, there was also the possibility that the insider had hired someone from outside to do the job.

We had no car. Subir Datta, of course, offered to give us a lift home in his. But Feluda said it would be no trouble for us to get hold of a taxi.

'It would be wise to inform the police,' he said.

I was totally unprepared for such a recommendation from Feluda. Even Subir Babu was surprised.

'Why do you say that?' he asked.

'Well, whatever your brother may think about the police, in terms of catching a runaway thief they have resources which a private investigator doesn't have. It would be particularly wise to let them in on this because such a large sum of money is involved. You said yourself the numbers on the notes have been noted down. That will help a lot.'

'Since we have called you in, and particularly since one accident has already taken place, I cannot think of not having your help,' said Subir Babu. 'Let the police come. But if you are also available, it will mean a lot to me and my brother. Of course, to tell you the truth, I myself can tell you who the thief is without any expert assistance.'

'You mean your son?'

Subir Babu sighed heavily, and nodded in assent. 'It can't be anybody but Shankar. He knows the lights go out in this neighbourhood at six. For a daring boy like him, it's nothing to clamber over that wall. Then to come up the back stairs, walk into his uncle's room, and open that safe — why, that's child's play for him.'

'Yes, but what's he going to do with Nihar Babu's research papers? Does he have access to scientific circles?'

'He doesn't need any access! He can extort money from his uncle in exchange for those papers. He knows very well how valuable those papers are to my brother.'

So many things had happened in such a short time that I felt quite dazed. That anything else could happen on that same night was totally beyond my imagination. But before I go into all that, I must tell you about the conversation that took place between me and Feluda when we got home.

I went into his room after dinner to find him stretched out on the bed, staring at the ceiling. He was munching a *paan* and smoking a Charminar. I could not keep to myself any longer the question which had been plaguing me even in Golok Lodge.

'Why were you trying so hard to let the case go?'

Feluda blew out two perfect smoke rings in succession.

'There are reasons, Topshe, there are reasons.'

'Is that the reason — what you said a little while ago — that it's easier for the police to get hold of an escaped burglar, particularly if he is carrying a large sum of money?'

'Do you think Subir Babu's son is the thief?'

'Who else? It's clearly the work of an insider. Dastur wasn't home. And it seems rather odd that Sukhwani would commit burglary, and then sit calmly at home. Even Ranajit Babu returned after the burglary. That leaves only the servants . . .'

'Yes but suppose the client himself has a hand in the matter?'

I gaped in astonishment at Feluda.

'Subir Babu!'

'Collect your wits and just think about the incidents immediately preceding the discovery of the theft.'

I closed my eyes and conjured up the picture of the four of us sitting in the living room. Tea was brought in. We were all drinking tea. Feluda holding his cup. The lights went out. Then — out . . .

A sudden flash of memory set my heart pounding with excitement.

'Feluda — Subir Babu went out of the room right after the power cut, to call the servant!'

'So! 'Just think of my position if it comes out that it was Subir Babu who had opened that safe. Nor is it improbable, particularly because that is one character about whom we know nothing. We don't have to disbelieve his story about calling the servant. But consider this .— if he has had big losses on the stock market or the race course, or if he has incurred huge debts, then is it surprising that he should have taken his brother's money?'

'But he voluntarily came to you! He's the one who appointed you.'

'If he is a criminal of a superior order, then it is not at all unlikely for him to do this to divert suspicion from himself.'

There was nothing more to be said after this.

Seeing Feluda pick up Kaliprasanna Singha's *Mahabharata*, and switch on his reading lamp, I got up from his bed.

As soon as I came into our living room I heard something outside. Motorbike. Not one, but many. They shattered the silence of our quiet neighbourhood and came to a halt just outside our house.

Immediately after that came the sound of the doorbell.

Times were not what they used to be. Besides, even if we did have an occasional late–night visitor, nobody came to our house on a motorbike.

So I did not move towards the front door. Instead, I lifted

the curtain and peeped into Feluda's room. He had put aside his book and had already got out of bed. 'Wait!' he admonished me. That meant — Don't open the door, I'll do it myself.

It did not take us five seconds to realize that the devil incarnate had entered as soon as the door had been opened. Subir Datta's son, Shankar Datta, entered the room, pushed the door shut with his back and looked at Feluda with glazed eyes as he proceeded to lash him with his tongue.

'Listen, mister, I don't know what my father has told you, but I can guess. Let me just tell you one little thing — nobody can put a private eye on to me and get away with it. I'm warning you, I am not all alone. We have a regular gang. And if you try to be too smart you'll pay for it. I'll make you wish you had never been born.'

As soon as he had delivered this piece of oratory, Shankar Datta made his exit as dramatically as he had entered.

Feluda had remained absolutely rigid through all this. It was only his extraordinary self–control that helped him remain impassive in the face of such indignity. He himself says that it requires greater strength of will to control one's anger than to to let it burst out in fury.

But even before the noise of the motorbikes had died away, Feluda, with lightning speed, had slipped on his shirt and shoved his wallet into his pocket.

'Come on Topshe, a taxi . . .'

In three minutes we had stopped a cruising taxi on Southern Avenue and got inside. We knew the motorbikes had gone north.

'Go down Lansdowne Road,' commanded Feluda. I had anticipated this, since the main road had been dug up and reduced to a mess.

It was a quarter–to–eleven. Southern Avenue was almost deserted. The taxi driver was a Bengali, his face looked familiar.

'Are you following someone, Sir?'

'Three motorbikes,' answered Feluda in a low voice.

We had not guessed badly. The motorbikes came into view as we reached the Elgin Road crossing. Shankar rode one himself, the other two had two riders each. We did not need to be told that these were notorious ruffians. Our taxi tailed them discreetly.

Down Lower Circular Road through Camac Street and into Park Street. The motorbikes took a left turn. Their serpentine zigzag motion indicated the daredevil, fun–seeking mood of their riders. Feluda sat well inside the taxi so that the street lights could not betray him. It was impossible to tell what plans were revolving his head.

After going some distance down Mirza Ghalib Street, the motorbikes turned left again. Marquis Street. The streets were getting narrower, the neighbourhood dark, the lights dim. To avoid arousing their suspicion our driver reduced speed and increased our distance from them on Feluda's orders. After two more turns we saw the motorbikes parked in front of a house.

'Drive on,' said Feluda.

Actually it was not a house. It was some kind of a hotel. New Corinthian Lodge was the name. New? It looked a hundred years old at the very least.

Feluda's work was done. I realized he had wanted to locate their base.

By the time we got home it was eleven forty. The metre showed nineteen rupees, seventy–five paise. Uncle Sidhu's arrival the next morning was totally unexpected. I knew he usually went out for a morning walk — but that was in the direction of the lake. Turning up at our place had to have a special significance.

'The volume was heavy. So I've copied the news out for you,' he said. 'Don't know if he is Suprakash — but here's a reference to someone called S.Choudhury, a biochemist.'

'The date?'

'1971. A Bengali happened to get caught by the police in the course of a raid on a pharmaceutical company in Mexico. His name was Mr. S. Choudhury. The company was trading in adulterated drugs that produced new and dreadful diseases. The biochemist was sent to prison. That's all the news there is. But since I have been thinking of someone called Suprakash, I did not immediately make the connection with S. Choudhury. Of course, whether it is the same S. Choudhury . . .'

'The same,' said Feluda gravely.

Uncle Sidhu got up. It was his day to have a haircut, the barber would be waiting for him. With a parting pat on the back for Feluda and having tweaked my ear, he tucked his *dhoti* more firmly into his waistband — and stepped outside.

Feluda had already opened his notebook and started scribbling. Three successive questions had been jotted down:

1) Why so many scratches around the keyhole?
2) What does 'who' mean?
3) What is the unfinished business?

Reading the questions naturally meant I too had to think about them. I too had seen those scratches around the keyhole of the safe last night by the light of Feluda's torch. Definitely, it was something to make one think. A steel surface would not show such markings without a forceful impact. And was Nihar Babu such a deep sleeper that he would sleep through the sound of that impact?

The question about 'who' did not make sense to me at first. Then I remembered. Nihar Babu had called out 'Who's there?' from the first floor landing when he had heard Dastur's voice. But I could not figure out why Feluda was worried about this.

Unfinished business — that too had been something that Nihar Babu had said. At least, according to Ranajit Babu. Didn't Feluda believe he had been referring to his research work?

Feluda was about to carry on with his scribbles, when the phone suddenly rang. The extension was in his room. Without getting out of bed, he stretched out his arm, and picked up the receiver.

'Hallo.'

A couple of 'hms', and a final 'I am coming right away,'— before he put the phone down. One sweep of the arm brought down a hanger with his shirt and trousers, before he said. 'Get ready. There's been a murder at Golok Lodge.'

My heart lurched violently.

'Who's been murdered?'

'Mr. Dastur.'

As we turned from the main road into Ballygunge Park, we could see the crowd and the police van in front of 7/1. Thank God, it was an upper class neighbourhood. Otherwise, the crowd would have been far bigger.

There was hardly anyone in Calcutta Police circles who did

not know Feluda. As soon as we entered Golok Lodge, Inspector Bakshi came up to him with a smile.

'So you've turned up, eh? The scent was strong enough then!'

Feluda responded with his lopsided grin.

'I've recently met Subir Babu. He rang me up and I decided to come over. I promise I won't interfere with your work. How did he die?'

'Hit on the head. Not once, but thrice. While he was sleeping. They are going to take away the body now for the post mortem analysis. Dr. Sarkar has already been once. He estimates it happened between two and three in the morning.'

'Have you managed to find out anything about the man?'

'It's all very mysterious. He'd started packing. Obviously, the man was planning to make a getaway.'

'Has any money been stolen?'.

'Doesn't seem like it. There are three hundred rupees in a wallet on the bedside table. I have a feeling that he never kept much cash around the house. And yet, there's no sign of anything like deposit books or cheque books. There was a gold watch beside the pillow. Of course, my men haven't yet been able to do a thorough search. They'll do it now. But there's no way you can guess this man's identity from what's been found so far.'

Subir Babu had just appeared and was standing near us. He now spoke to Mr. Bakshi.

'Sukhwani is carrying on like anything. Says he has an urgent appointment at Dalhousie Square. I've told him he won't be allowed to leave before he's been interrogated.'

'Quite right,' said Mr. Bakshi. 'But of course, you won't escape the third degree either, you know.' Mr. Bakshi smiled a little as he said the last bit. And Subir Babu nodded to show that he understood quite well.

'But it would be appreciated if you can spare my brother as much harassment as possible.'

'Naturally.'

'Can I see the room?' asked Feluda.

'Of course.'

Bakshi walked ahead with Feluda. I followed. Just before he entered the room, Feluda turned towards Subir Babu.

'By the way, your son came to my house yesterday.'

'When!' Subir Babu was palpably astonished.

Feluda briefly described the events of last night. 'Did he come home?' he asked.

'If he did, I wasn't aware of it.' said Subir Babu. 'But I haven't laid eyes on him this morning.'

'Well, at least we now know where your son hangs around,' said Mr. Bakshi. 'That hotel is definitely not a desirable place to be in. We've already raided it twice.'

The room we had seen the previous evening looked totally different today. It had been quite dark yesterday. This morning, sunlight came in through the eastern windows and touched the sofa and the floor. Somehow, it seemed strange to see the butt of last night's Charminar still lying in the ashtray. There were two policemen in the room; the police photographer, having done his job, was just putting away his equipment.

The murder had actually taken place in the bedroom next door. Feluda went in there with Bakshi. I went as far as the doorway and glanced at the bed to take a look at the body covered with a sheet. There was another policeman there, continuing the search. In an open suitcase on the floor, I saw some folded clothes. And right next to it stood the new briefcase Dastur had been carrying last night.

I spent a few more minutes in the living room looking at various objects. I knew very well that it was forbidden to touch anything — besides, both the policemen were staring at me.'

'C'mon Topshe.'

Feluda had come out of the bedroom.

'Are you going to be around some more?' queried Bakshi.

'I'll go and see the old gentleman once before leaving,' said Feluda. 'Let me know if you find anything interesting.'

Subir Babu had been waiting for us upstairs. We accompanied him to Nihar Babu's room.

He was stretched out in his lounging chair. Those same dark glasses, the stick laid on the bed beside him. Before this, I had always seen him carrying the stick — so I had never noticed that, it had a silver knob. The letters G.B.D., engraved among the decorations on the knob, made me realize that the stick had belonged to Nihar Babu's grandfather Golok Bihari Datta.

On being informed of our arrival, Nihar Babu's inclined neck straightened fractionally, as he said, 'Yes, I heard them. The sound of footsteps. Sound and touch — that's what I've been living with for the last twenty years. And memories . . .what could have happened, what didn't. People call it misfortune. But I know so well it has nothing to do with fortune. The other day you asked me whether the explosion had been the result of carelessness; I can tell you today, Mr. Mitter, the whole thing had been arranged to make a mockery of my life's work. As a detective, I'm sure you understand to what depths we can sink because of envy.'

The old man paused for a few minutes. 'So you are convinced that it was Suprakash Choudhury who was responsible for that explosion?' said Feluda.

'Do you agree that a Bengali can have no greater enemy than another Bengali?'

Feluda stared steadily at the dark glasses. Nihar Babu also seemed to be waiting for an answer.

'Have you ever articulated your suspicions, the way you did just now, to anybody else before this?' asked Feluda.

'No, I haven't. Never. It struck me as soon as I regained my senses in the hospital. But I never said it. What was the use? After all, my life had been ruined. If the person responsible for this were to be punished, would that restore my vision? Would it enable me to finish my work?'

'But what good did it do Choudhury to reduce you to permanent helplessness? Did he think he would finish the project single handedly, with the help of your documents, and thus make a name for himself?'

'It must have been been that. But he was wrong. I've already told you so. There's no way he could have advanced without my help.'

Both of us were sitting on the bed. I could tell, just by looking at him, that Feluda was in deep thought. Ranajit Babu had also come in during the conversation and was standing by the table. Subir Babu had gone out for some reason.

Feluda spoke. 'I don't know about that money. It might be

easier for the police to recover that. But I simply can't accept the fact that all your invaluable documents were stolen from the house while I happened to be present. I'm going to do my best to recover them.'

'You may do whatever you please.'

We did not stay much longer. The police were still going about their business. Mr. Bakshi told Feluda that he would call and let him know the outcome of the interrogation and search.

'And don't forget to tell me any news you may have about the New Corinthian Lodge,' Feluda reminded him.

We were back home by ten–thirty. From that moment, right up to lunch, Feluda gave vent to the myriad questions, suspicions, misgivings, doubts besieging his mind, by walking about, stopping short, stretching out, sitting up, keeping his eyes open or closing them, frowning, nodding, muttering, and sighing a whole gamut of sighs — short, medium and long. Once he fired a sudden question at me.

'Do you remember the layout of the ground floor of Golok Lodge?'

I thought for a while and said, 'Approximately, yes.'

'Can you tell me how one goes from Sukhwani's room to Dastur's?'

I thought some more. Then I said, 'As far as I remember, the passage which runs alongside both the flats has a door in the middle which is probably kept locked. If that door had been kept open, then you could have gone along the passage from one flat to the other.'

'Right you are. As things are, for Sukhwani to have entered Dastur's flat, he would have had to go around the garden, enter the passage opening out from the boundary wall, come to the front of the house and enter through the main door.'

'But is it likely that the collapsible iron gate in front of the main door will stay open in the middle of the night?'

'Certainly not.'

And he started pacing up and down again, as he talked.

'X,Y,Z . . . X,Y,Z . . . X equals the research papers, Y equals the money, and Z equals the murder. Now, the point is — are X,Y and Z interconnected or are the three separate . . .'

As soon as I had the chance, I blurted out, 'Feluda, I have

the feeling that Suprakash Choudhury disguised himself as Dastur and came to live as a tenant in Nihar Babu's house.'

To my amazement, I found that Feluda did not laugh away my idea. Instead, he slapped me on the back a couple of times before saying, 'Though I have thought about this possibility long before, I have to admit, you are displaying flashes of intelligence these days. But if Dastur was Suprakash then we have to assume that he wormed his way in there in the hopes of getting hold of those research notes. Which leads us to the next question — if he did indeed steal the envelope, then where has it gone? And how was it possible for him to steal it? The man never went upstairs.'

My brilliance was obviously scintillating. Of course — it was easy as pie! I said, 'Why should he have to go there himself? It is Shankar who must have stolen those papers and given them to him. He's probably been paid off for it too.'

'Excellent!' said Feluda. 'Now, finally, I can say you have become a worthy assistant. However, this does not solve the mystery of the murder.'

'Suppose Ranajit Babu had tumbled to the fact that Dastur was actually Suprakash. Ranajit Babu is aware of Nihar Babu's tragic story, and he is absolutely devoted to him. Couldn't he, in a fit of rage, have killed the man who ruined Nihar Babu's whole life?'

Feluda shook his head.

'Murder is not that simple, my dear Topshe. Ranajit's motive is not really strong enough. It's really unfortunate that the search in Dastur's room has not provided any clues. He was extraordinarily careful — our Dastur.'

'You know what I think, Feluda?'

Feluda stopped in his tracks and looked at me.

'If you had done the search, instead of the police, I'm sure you would have unearthed many clues,' I said.

'You think so?'

It was unthinkable that Feluda should be losing his self-confidence. And yet, that's precisely what I sensed from that comment. His next statement made my heart sink.

'I wonder if even Einstein would have been able to think straight in this heat and with these power cuts!'

Inspector Bakshi's call came at about two clock. Seventeen thousand rupees in American dollars and German marks had been discovered in a false heel compartment in one of Dastur's shoes. But there was not a scrap of paper or document to provide any information about the man. No new electronics shop had been unearthed, nor was there any news about Dastur's friend. There were hardly any letters. The only personal letter was from Argentina, from which it was evident that Dastur had spent time in South America.

The second piece of news Bakshi had was that the manager of the New Corinthian Lodge had identified Shankar from his photograph. Together with some friends Shankar had spent all of last night drinking and gambling in one of the hotel rooms. In the morning, they had paid their bill and left. According to Bakshi, getting hold of Shankar now was 'a matter of minutes.'

Feluda put the receiver down after listening to all this, and said, 'It would have been so convenient if our Shankar had paid his hotel bills with the stolen money. Anyway, at least this proves that he did not commit the murder, since he has an alibi for that time.'

I myself had learnt the meaning of the word alibi a long time back. But when I asked Feluda how to explain the meaning to those who were not aware of it, he said, 'Just use the definition given in the dictionary.' So, an alibi is 'a plea that when an alleged act took place one was elsewhere.' Shankar's alibi would be, 'I was gambling at the Corinthian Lodge when the murder took place in my house.'

Bakshi's phone call did not seem to have cured Feluda of his restlessness. Around three o'clock I noticed he was changing from pyjamas to trousers. He said he had to go out to get hold of some information. He came back at four–thirty. During the one–and–a–half–hours he was gone, I had nearly finished the *Mahabharata*.

It was exactly at that point in the book — when Draupadi, Nakula and Sahadeva had all dropped dead on the final road, and Arjuna was about to follow — that the phone rang. I answered. But it was for Feluda: Subir Babu from Golok Lodge wanted to speak to him.

Feluda picked up the receiver in his room; I went into the living room and glued my ear to the instrument there so that I could hear both parties speak.

'Hello.'

'Is that Mr. Mitter?'

'Yes, Mr. Datta.'

'We've discovered the sealed envelope containing my brother's papers.'

'Was it in Dastur's room?'

'Right. He had taped it to the underside of the bed. But the tape had come unstuck on one side and left the envelope dangling. Our servant, Bhagirath, found it.'

'Does your brother know?'

'Yes. But he seems to have given up on everything. He doesn't seem to be reacting to things any more. Nor has he left his chair all day today. I've asked our doctor to come over.'

'Is there any news of your son?'

'Yes. Their whole gang has been rounded up on G.T. Road.'

'What about the stolen money?'

'If he took that money, he's hidden it somewhere else. Of course Shankar adamantly refuses to admit the theft.'

'What are the police saying now about the murder?'

'They suspect Sukhwani. They've also found a new clue. A crumpled ball of paper lying outside Dastur's window.'

'What does it say?'

'A one line threat in English' — 'Are you aware of the consequences of excessive curiosity?'

'What does Sukhwani have to say?'

'He denies everything. Of course, there's no access from his room to Dastur's. But some hired thug could climb up the pipe into the first floor balcony, come downstairs, and easily commit the crime.'

'Hmm . . .OK, I'll be over.'

Feluda put the receiver down and muttered to himself, 'X and Y then are the same. The question now is, who's Z.'

He then turned to me and said 'Destination Golok Lodge. Get ready Topshe.'

CHAPTER 4

'Are you leaving?'

We met Ranajit Babu just as we entered the gates of Golok Lodge. The policemen outside made it evident that the house was still being watched.

'Yes Sir,' said Ranajit Babu. 'Nihar Babu told me that he wouldn't be needing me any more today.'

'How is he?'

'The doctor came to see him. He said that so many things happening at the same time had sent Nihar Babu into a slight state of shock. His blood pressure is fluctuating.'

'Is he able to talk?'

'Oh yes indeed,' said Ranajit Babu in reassurance.

'I'd like to see that envelope which has been found in Dastur's room. If you are not in too much of a hurry, do please come up one more time. I presume it must be in the safe?'

'Yes.'

'I promise I won't keep you too long. But I also know I won't be coming to this house too often.'

'But,' said Ranajit Babu with some hesitation, 'that envelope is sealed.'

'Maybe. But I'd still like to take it in my hands and examine it once.'

Ranajit Babu did not object any longer.

This evening, too, the house was plunged in darkness. The lights would not come back before ten — it was only quarter–past–six now. There were kerosene lamps burning on the first floor balcony and the landing. Nevertheless, darkness lurked in all the corners.

Ranajit Babu made us sit in the living room and went off to tell Subir Babu about our arrival. Before leaving, however, he told us that it would be impossible to show us the envelope if

Nihar Babu objected to taking it out of the safe.

'That goes without saying,' said Feluda.

Subir Babu looked tired. He said he had spent the whole day keeping the newspaper reporters at bay.

'However, one good thing out of all this is that people have started remembering my brother again.'

Within a minute or two Ranajit Babu appeared, holding a long, white envelope.

'It was probably because of you that Nihar Babu raised no objections,' he told Feluda. 'I don't think he would have let anybody else see it.'

'Amazing,' commented Feluda as he held the envelope under the lamp and inspected it from all angles. As far as I could make out, it seemed to be an ordinary long envelope, sealed with red lacquer on the reverse. In the top left hand corner of the right side was printed Department of Biochemistry, University of Michigan U.S.A. I could not understand what was so amazing about all this. Subir Babu and Ranajit Babu made no comment as they sat in the dark. They too probably felt the way I did.

Feluda came and sat down on the sofa. He was still staring at the envelope. Then he started talking to me, ignoring the two gentlemen. His manner was that of a schoolmaster. It was in this kind of a mood that Feluda had lectured me on many different subjects.

'You know, Topshe, these are amazing things — English typefaces. In Bengali we have about ten or twelve different typefaces. In English there are at least two thousand. I remember reading up on this in the course of an investigation. The letters have classifications and categories; each classification has a name of its own. This particular typeface, for instance, is called 'Garamond' — Feluda pointed to the printed address of the University and resumed his discourse.

'The Garamond typeface was invented in 16th century France. Then, gradually, it spread all over the world. England, Germany, Switzerland, America — not only was the typeface introduced in all these countries, factories started making their own moulds too. Recently, that's also being done in India. The funny thing, however, is that if you examine it carefully you'll see that the

Garamond typeface in one country always differs slightly from another. The structure of a few letters highlights this difference. The address on this envelope, for instance, should have been American Garamond. Instead, it has become an Indian Garamond. Maybe even a Calcutta Garamond.'

The room was filled with an oppressive silence. Feluda's eyes had shifted from the envelope to Ranajit Babu's face. I had seen pictures of the wax effigies of famous people in Madame Tussaud's museum in London; even though they are absolutely lifelike, the glass eyes betray their lifelessness. Though Ranajit Babu was a living man, his eyes had assumed the glazed look of the eyes of those wax effigies.

'Please excuse me, Ranajit Babu, but I am obliged to open this envelope.'

Ranajit Babu lifted his right hand in an obstructive gesture which stopped halfway.

A ripping sound — and Feluda had torn open one side of the envelope with two fingers. With another movement, those same two fingers extracted a bunch of fullscap papers from within the envelope.

Ruled fullscap paper.

There were only ruled lines on that paper, no writing. Just blank paper.

The glassy eyes were now closed, the head bent, the elbows on the knees, and the face hidden in the palms of both hands.

'Ranajit Babu,' said Feluda very gravely, 'When you came here last morning and put out that story about a burglar, you were deliberately hoaxing us, weren't you?'

All Ranajit Babu managed by way of an answer was a groan. Feluda continued, 'Actually, you badly needed to create the impression of a burglary in the night. You yourself were preparing to commit a theft, and you had to make sure that no suspicion fell on you. It's my belief that having conned everybody in the morning about a burglary having been committed, you opened the safe in the afternoon and got hold of two things — the thirty–three thousand rupees and Nihar Babu's notes. I also believe that this fake envelope was not ready yesterday; you got it printed overnight. Would you like to tell us why you suddenly felt it was necessary?'

At this, Ranajit Babu finally lifted his eyes towards Feluda. Then he started speaking in husky tones. 'Yesterday, in the afternoon when Nihar Babu heard Dastur's voice, he identified him as Suprakash Choudhury! He said to me, 'Greed has taken possession of that man again, after twenty years! He's the one who must have stolen my papers.' Then . . .'

'I see. Then you decided that was the opportunity of foisting the crime of burglary on Dastur. So it was you who fixed the envelope with cellotape under the bed after the police had gone —and in such a way that it would be clearly visible if one bent down, isn't that so?'

Ranajit Babu almost wailed.

'Please forgive me! I'll return everything. The money and the papers — I'll bring them back tomorrow, Mr. Mitter! I . . . I somehow couldn't help myself; it's the truth, I just couldn't resist the urge to have them.'

'Return them you must, of course. I hope you realize that otherwise I'll have to hand you over to the police.'

'I know,' said Ranajit Babu. 'But just one request. Please don't let Nihar Babu know any of this. He is very fond of me. He won't be able to bear the shock.'

'Very well. He won't know anything. I give you my word. But how could a brilliant student like you do something like this?'

Ranajit Babu stared helplessly at us. Feluda went on, 'I went to see your Professor Bagchi. My suspicions fell on you because of those scratch marks around the keyhole of the safe. An ordinary thief wouldn't take so much care. Particularly when there is a man inside the room and a servant sleeping outside the door. Anyhow, your professor told me what a bright future you have. Had you sat for your exams, he's convinced you would have done brilliantly. Did you quit your studies and take up this secretarial job as a short cut to the Nobel Prize?' Ranajit Babu was utterly speechless –– out of fear and shame and guilt. That Feluda, too, like me, was feeling sorry for him became evident from what he said after this.

'You can go home now if you want. We won't wait for tomorrow. Go and bring back the money and the papers today.

And — I have to make arrangements for a policeman to accompany you. It is not wise to wander around all by yourself with so much money.'

Ranajit Bandyopadhyay nodded like a docile little boy.

Whatever Subir Babu may have told us about his son, he must have felt thoroughly relieved to know that it was not his son who had stolen the money. At least that was what his voice and look conveyed.

'Will you come and see my brother once before you leave?' he asked Feluda.

'Of course, that is the most important thing I have to do.'

We followed Subir Babu into Nihar Babu's room.

'So you've come,' said Nihar Babu, still reclining partially in his chair.

'Yes, Sir,' said Feluda. 'Are you feeling relieved now that your papers have been recovered?'

'Actually they are of little value to me now,' said Nihar Babu in a low, tired voice. I had no idea that a man could become so pale just in the space of one day. Even yesterday the old gentleman had looked quite fit.

'Whatever you may think of their worth, the papers are of great value to us,' said Feluda. 'Particularly to many scientists worldwide.'

'I leave you to judge all that.'

'I want to ask you only one question. And I promise, I won't bother you any more after this.'

A faded smile lifted the corners of Nihar Babu's mouth. He said, 'Bother me — how can you possibly do that? I have gone way beyond all irritation.'

'Very well then. Last night I saw ten sleeping pills on your bedside table. It's the same today. Does that mean that you didn't take your sleeping pill last night?'

'No, I didn't. I will tonight, though.'

'Then we'll be off now.'

'Wait.'

Nihar Babu extended his right hand towards Feluda. Their hands met. The old gentleman gave Feluda's hand a vigorous shake and said, 'I know you'll understand. You have the vision.'

Even after we got home, Feluda remained grave and pensive. But I wasn't going to put up with all this mystery any longer. So, I cornered him. 'No more secrets you've got to tell me everything.'

In reply, Feluda went off into the *Ramayana*. Some of his tricks to prolong suspense are really too much for me.

'Six days after King Dasharatha banished his son Rama to the forests, he suddenly remembered that as a young prince he had been guilty of a terrible misdeed. And that was why he was suffering now from the loss of his son. Do you remember what that misdeed was?'

I had not read the *Ramayana* recently, but this was one thing I did remember.

'The son of a blind sage had been filling his pitcher from the river at night,' I said. 'Dasharatha heard the sound in the darkness and assumed it was an elephant drinking water. He let loose one of his sonar arrows and killed the boy.'

'Good. Dasharatha, therefore, had the ability of finding his target in the dark simply by hearing the sound. So did Nihar Babu.'

'Nihar Babu!' I nearly fell off my chair.

'Yes, Sir,' said Feluda. 'He did not take his sleeping pill because he wanted to stay up that night. When everybody was fast asleep, he went down the stairs barefoot, and entered Dastur–Suprakash's room. It was the same room where his nephew used to stay at one time. He was familiar with it. The weapon he was carrying in his hands was that stout silvermounted stick. He went up to the bed and aimed his deathly blows — not once but thrice.'

'But . . .but . . .'

I was still terribly bewildered. What on earth was Feluda saying? That old man was blind!

'Don't you remember one thing?' said Feluda impatiently. 'What did Sukhwani say about Dastur?'

It came back, like a flash of lightning.

'Dastur used to snore!'

'Exactly!' said Feluda. 'Which means that Nihar Babu had no trouble figuring out where the head touched the pillow and on what side the man slept. What more does a man need to know if his hearing is so sharp? And if one blow didn't do the job three certainly would.'

I remained dumbstruck for some time. Then I said fearfully, 'Was this the unfinished business Nihar Babu was talking about? Revenge?'

'Revenge,' echoed Feluda. 'The desire to kill. This is a motivation which can infuse even a blind man's body and mind with a tremendous surge of power. This was the motivation that had kept him alive all these years. Now, he is on his deathbed. And precisely because of that he's beyond the reach of the law.'

Nihar Ranjan Datta lingered for another seventeen days. Just before his death, he made a will, and bequeathed all his research papers as well as all his savings to his brilliant, young secretary, Ranajit Bandyopadhyay.

TROUBLE IN THE GRAVE YARD

One afternoon, exactly three days after the film made by Bombay's director Pulak Ghoshal based on thriller writer Jatayu's (alias Lalmohan Ganguly) book had its jubilee show at Paradise Cinema, a second-hand Mark II Ambassador honking in nerve-shattering musical tones stopped in front of our house. We were aware that Lalmohan Babu had been planning to buy a car, but we had no idea that it would happen so quickly. And not only had he bought a car, he had also acquired a driver; for Lalmohan Babu does not know how to drive. Nor does he ever intend to learn. He repeated it so often that Feluda had been forced to ask, 'And why not sir, why won't you learn?' Lalmohan Babu had said that he had started taking lessons once, about five years ago, using a friend's car. 'On the third day, a beautiful plot for a thriller came into my head. But just as I tried to switch from first to second gear, the car lurched so violently that I completely lost the thread of my story. That's a regret I've still not overcome.'

As the driver, dressed in white shirt and khaki trousers came out and held the door open, Lalmohan Babu trying to get out with a little hop, nearly tripped on his trailing *dhoti*. But even that could not wipe the smile from his face. There was no smile on Feluda's face though. Once the three of us had come inside and sat down, he said, 'Until you change that grotesque horn of yours and get a civilised one instead, that car is forbidden to enter Rajani Sen Road.'

Jatayu looked apologetic.

'I knew I was taking a big risk,' he said, 'But you know, when the salesman was demonstrating — somehow I couldn't resist the temptation. It's Japanese you know.'

'It's ear-splitting and nerve-racking,' said Feluda. 'I could never have believed that Hindi films would influence you so soon. And that colour — equally unbearable. Just like what you see in Madras films.'

Lalmohan Babu folded his hands and pleaded. 'Please Mr. Mitter! I'll change the horn tomorrow. But do please let me keep the colour. That green is so soothing.'

Feluda gave up, and was about to order some tea when Lalmohan Babu stopped him.

'Forget about tea. First we must go for a spin. I can't rest until I have taken you and master Tapesh for a ride in my car. Tell me now — where would you like to go?'

Feluda raised no objections. He thought for a while and said, 'Well, I have been thinking of taking Topshe to see Charnock's tomb.'

'Charnock? Job Charnock?'

'No'

'Then? Were there any other Charnocks?'

'I'm sure there were. But there was only one Charnock who was the founder of Calcutta.'

'But that's what I . . .'

'Yes, but his name should not be pronounced as J–a–w–b. It is J–o–b–e. The other word means employment, work. But job is a name. Why should you make the same mistake that so many other Bengalees make?'

I should mention here that Feluda's latest obsession is old Calcutta. He happened to be investigating a murder in Fancy Lane. The moment he discovered that Fancy was a corruption of the Bengali word *phansi* (meaning hanging), and that two hundred years ago Nandakumar had been hanged on that spot, he was hooked. There's no end to the books he has read, maps he has pored over, pictures he has seen during the last three months — all about old Calcutta. And I must add, that I too had learnt a lot in this time. Most of it from the two afternoons we had spent at the Victoria Memorial.

Feluda says that though Calcutta is a child compared to ancients like Delhi or Agra, it is not to be dismissed easily. True, we don't have the Taj Mahal or the Qutab Minar, nor do we have fortresses like the ones at Jodhpur or Jaisalmer, nor is there a Vishwanath *gali* as in Banaras.

'But just think of it Topshe — an Englishman sitting beside the Ganga, on the edge of a huge wasteland inhabited only by mosquitoes, snakes and frogs, thinks that he will set up business here. And lo and behold, the wilderness is cleared, houses are built, roads are laid out and lighted by rows of gas lights; horses and palanquins start travelling and before a hundred years pass, there grows up a city in that place that came to be known as the City of Palaces. The present disgraceful condition of that city is not the point. I am talking about history. We are now trying to wipe out our history by changing the names of our streets. But is that right? Or is it possible? I admit that the British did all this to pursue their own ends. But if they hadn't come, just think of what Felu Mitter would have been doing today!'

'Your Feluda — Prodosh Chandra Mitter and private investigator — bent over some ledger and making notes in some zamindar's estate where finger–prints would only signify the thumb–print signature of the illiterate.'

B.B. D. Bag — which was once called Dalhousie Square after the Dalhousie who had come here as Viceroy, gobbled up more and more of our territory and had also inaugurated the first railways and the first telegraph office in India — that was the location of the two–hundred–year–old tomb of Job Charnock. Though Lalmohan Babu said 'Thrilling,' I had a feeling that the comment was inspired more by the dark clouds in the sky and the deep rumble of thunder. After staring for a while at the marbel plaque on the tomb, he said, 'But this doesn't say Job — it's Jobus here. What does it mean?'

'Jobus is the latin version of Job,' said Feluda. 'Don't you see, the whole inscription is in Latin?'

'I don't know anything about Latin or Greek. All I can see is that it is not English. Why does it have D.O.M. written above the name?'

'D.O.M., is *Dominus Omnium Magister*. That is, God is the master of all. Let me point out one of the words below. *Marmore*. Just like the Bengali word *marmar*. They both mean the same thing — marble. What's even more funny is that the Bengali word is derived not from Sanskrit, but from Persian. There are so many words we have taken from Sanskrit, Persian or Arabic and we happily join them together to make new words. Just think of . . . '

But Feluda could not finish his lecture. Suddenly without warning, there came such a dust storm ('end of the world') said Jatayu) as I had never seen before. We ran for our dear lives and got into Lalmohan Babu's green Ambassador, and the driver, Haripada Babu, sped away towards Esplanade. For the first time I saw the Ochterlony Monument — or rather the Shahid Minar as it is now — completely obscured by dust. It was impossible to gauge the wind speed, for we had rolled up the windows. But we did happen to see one of the cane stands, that street vendors use to sell snacks, come spinning through the air from the direction of the Maidan, crash into the top of a double–decker bus in front of us, and fly off again in the direction of Curzon Park.

As we came near Park Street we saw that the trams could not run because a cedar tree had been uprooted and was lying across the tracks. Feluda had planned to show us the old cemetery of Park Street, but it would not be possible in this storm. Had we gone we might have been able to witness an incident which we read about in the papers next morning. During the disastrous storm of 24 June (wind velocity 145 kilometres per hour) a tree crashed down in the South Park Street cemetery and severely injured an elderly gentleman called Narendranath Biswas. He had been taken to the hospital. But what the papers did not tell us was what he had been doing that evening in that ancient graveyard.

CHAPTER 2

It rained all of next morning and almost half the afternoon.
Feluda had managed to get hold of an old map of Calcutta and
Howrah dated 1932. After a lunch consisting of kedgeree and
omlette, he put a *paan* in his mouth, lit a Charminar and unfolded
the map. We had to push back tables and chairs against the
wall to make a six–foot by six–foot space on the floor for the
map. We were bent over the map, looking at the streets of
Calcutta, and Feluda was saying, 'Don't look for Rajani Sen
Road, this place was a jungle in those days.' When Jatayu turned
up, he was not wearing his customary *dhoti* and *panjabi*. Instead,
he had on a pair of dark blue trousers and a yellow half–sleeved
shirt. 'Seventy–six trees are down after yesterday's storm,' he
announced as soon as he came in. 'And I have kept your request,
this horn will not remind you of Hindi films.'

We were in no hurry today, so we had tea before setting out.
Somehow, the news about seventy six trees being uprooted had
seemed incredible when we had read about it in the papers; but
from Park Street onwards I counted nineteen trees or branches
lying on the road. Three of them were on Southern Avenue alone.

When we arrived at the entrance to the cemetery (Feluda had
not let on that we were coming here until we were on Camac
Street) I looked at Jatayu and noticed that his natural cheerfulness
had diminished. When Feluda gave him an enquiring look, the
gentleman said, 'I once saw an Englishman being buried — in
1941 in Ranchi. When they finally lower the wooden coffin into
the grave and start throwing clods of earth it's a horrifying sound.'

'You are not likely to hear anything like that now,' said Feluda.
'No one has been buried in this cemetery for the last hundred–
and–twenty–five–years.'

As you enter, the watchman's house is to the right. Anybody
can come in during the day, so the watchman probably has very

little to do.

'But he does have to keep his eyes open,' said Feluda, 'in case people try to prise the marble plaques away from the tombs. Good Italian marble can fetch a pretty price in the market these days.'

'Here, you!'

The watchman came out of his room. We did not need to be told that he was from Bihar; he looked like he had just put the wad of chewing tobacco in his mouth.

'A Bengali gentleman was injured here yesterday, wasn't he? Hit on the head by a falling tree?'

'Yes, Sir.'

'Can we see that place?'

'Go straight down that path — right up to the end. Then turn left and you'll see it. The branches are still lying there.'

The three of us went along the paved path over which grass had started growing. On both sides were rows of tombs — some of them twelve to fourteen feet high. To our right was one that was as high as a three storey building. Feluda said that was probably the tomb of William Jones, which was the highest tomb in Calcutta.

On black or white marble plaques on each tomb was inscribed the dead person's name, date of birth and date of death and a few other words. Most of the tombs were like four cornered pillars, tapering upwards from a wide base. Lalmohan Babu said they looked like ghosts in *burkhas*. It was not such a bad description, though these ghosts could not move. They were more like guardian ghosts — guarding the person who was lying underground locked in the coffin. 'Try to remember the English word for these pillars Topshe — obelisk.' Lalmohan Babu muttered the word several times. I was looking right and left, murmuring the names on the plaques — Jackson, Watts, Wells, Larkins,Bibs, Oldhan . . . Sometimes there were several tombs side by side bearing the same name — obviously all from the same family. The earliest date I had noticed so far was 28 July 1779. Nine years before the French Revolution.

When we came to the end of the path I realised how large the cemetery was. The noise of the Park Street traffic was very faint here. Feluda told me later that there were more than two thousand tombs here. Lalmohan Babu pointed towards Lower Circular Road, to a block of flats adjacent to the cemetery, and said he would not live there for a million rupees.

The tree which was reported to have fallen was actually a huge branch of a mango tree. It had knocked down part of a tomb by falling over it. There were lots of other branches scattered all around.

We went towards the tomb.

Compared to the others, this was a short one — it barely reached Lalmohan Babu's shoulder. It was easy to see that the tomb had been in a precarious condition for some time. Even the side left undamaged by the branch was full of cracks and plaster had fallen away exposing the brick underneath. The white marble plaque had also been damaged by the blow; some of it still adhered to the tomb, the rest lay on the grass in ten or twelve pieces. Rain had made the whole place wet and muddy, but somehow there seemed a lot more mud here. 'Amazing,' commented Lalmohan Babu, 'the word God is still written on this tomb.'

'And not just God. Surely you can see part of the date given below.'

'Yes. One, eight, five — then it's broken off. Obviously this is the God who is the master of all.'

'You think so?'

Feluda's question made me look at him. He was frowning.

'You can't have observed the other tombs carefully,' he said, 'Just look at the one beside this.'

There was a large one next to this one. On the plaque was inscribed —

To the Memory of
Capt. P. Reilly, H.M. 44th Regt.
Who died 25th May 1923 aged 38 years.

'Observe that the date comes immediately below the name. Most of the plaques are like this. And have you noticed the word God on any other plaque?'

'So you are saying that God is the name of the dead man?'

'No, I don't think God can be anybody's name. But you can

see that there is a gap of about an inch to the left of G. Therefore, there was no other letter to the left which was part of this word. But we can't say the same about the d — whether there was a letter to the right of it — because that's where the marble has chipped. But it's my opinion that the man who is buried here had a surname whose first three letters were G – o – d; for instance, Godfrey or Goddard.'

'If we put the pieces of marble together side by side we can . . .'

As he spoke, Lalmohan Babu was advancing over the fallen branches and leaves to the tomb when suddenly he slid downwards, just as if he had stepped into a hole. But Feluda stretched out his long arms in the nick of time, grabbed him, pulled him up and helped him on to firm ground. What was it? How come there was a hole there? 'I knew something was wrong,' said Feluda. 'The branch from a mango tree is supposed to have fallen here, but there are leaves and branches from other trees here too.'

As it is Lalmohan Babu had been suffering from low spirits ever since entering the cemetery — now this had to happen. 'This is too much,' he grumbled as he dusted his trousers before going off to one side with his back to us. He was probably trying to get hold of himself.

'Topshe — move those branches, but be very careful.'

As Feluda and I cleared the area, steering clear of the hole, it became evident that there was a foot–deep canal right next to the grave. Feluda might have made out whether it had always been there or whether it had been dug recently, but I was at a loss.

Feluda now concentrated on the pieces of marble. The two of us collected eleven pieces and within ten minutes of playing with them as with a jigsaw puzzle, we arranged them in sequence on the grass. The result was this—

Sacred to the Memory of—
THOMAS — WIN
Obt. 24th April – 8, AET, 180 —

'Godwin' said Feluda. 'A memorial to Thomas Godwin. Obt. means *obitus*, that is death, and AET means *aetatis* or age. The thing to find out now —'

'Just look here, Sir!'

Jatayu's shout startled me. As we turned around he held up a square, flat, black object saying, 'Can we have dinner for three at the Blue Fox for thirty–seven rupees?'

'Why, what have you got there?'

Both of us went forward eagerly.

There was a wallet in Lalmohan Babu's left hand; in his right were three tens, one five and one two rupee note. Both the wallet and the money were in a pitiful state. Our friend seemed to have lost all his fears and wore rather a triumphant air. He knew he had unearthed a good clue for Feluda.

Feluda opened the wallet and took out everything there was in it. Four things emerged. The first was a bunch of visiting cards with N. M. Biswas written in English. There was no address, no phone number. Feluda said, 'Just look at these newspapers — they have turned Narendramohan into Narendranath.'

Secondly there were two paper cuttings. One was about the opening of this cemetery on South Park Street, the other contained news of the construction of the Ochterlony Monument. Which meant that both the cuttings dated back hundred and fifty to two hundred years. 'I wonder how Mr. Biswas managed to get hold of such ancient paper cuttings,' commented Feluda.

The third item was a receipt for twelve–fifty from Oxford Book Company on Park Street, and the fourth was a piece of white paper with a few lines in English written on it with a ball–point pen. I could not make head or tail of the writing, though the words Victoria Memorial were there.

'I know — there was an article on the Ochterlony Monument in the papers the other day,' said Lalmohan Babu suddenly, 'and as far as I can recall the author's name was Biswas. Yes — Biswas, Correct.'

'Which newspaper?' asked Feluda.

'Either *Lekhani* or *Bichitrapatra*. I can't remember exactly. I'll go home and check.'

Perhaps it was because he felt that Jatayu's memory was not all that dependable that Feluda refrained from saying anything more. Instead, he copied the writing on the piece of white paper into his notebook, returned the paper and the other items into the wallet and put the wallet inside his pocket. He then carefully inspected the vicinity of the tomb and discovered a couple of other objects which he also put in his pocket. One was a brown button from a jacket, the other a dog–eared racing book. 'Come along, let's talk to the watchman once more and then get out of here. It's clouding up again.'

'Are you going to return the wallet?' asked Lalmohan Babu.

'Of course. I'll find out tomorrow which hospital he is in, and go there.'

'What if the man has died?'

'We can't expropriate other people's property on that assumption. It's not ethical. Besides, thirty–seven rupees would not get us anything more than tea and sandwiches at the Blue Fox. So you can give up all hopes of dinner anyway.'

Once again we started walking down the path between the rows of tombs, but facing the other way this time. Feluda looked grave. He had already lit another Charminar. He had cut down a lot on his smoking, but any whiff of mystery made him light up almost without being aware of it.

When he suddenly stopped half–way, I could not understand why at first. Then as I followed his eyes, I saw something which made me stop in my tracks and also made my heartbeat falter for a moment.

A domed mausoleum, bearing the name of Miss Margaret Templeton on its plaque. And on an old brick lying on the grass in front of this tomb, was a half–smoked cigarette from which smoke spiralled upwards like a thin ribbon. The breeze must have stopped because of the impending rain. Otherwise, we would never have made out the smoke.

Feluda went forward, picked up the two–inch long cigarette and said, 'Gold Flake.' 'Let's go home,' said Jatayu. 'Shall we take a look around to see if the man is still here?' I said.

'If he was still hanging around, he would have kept the cigarette in his hand,' said Feluda. 'Or he would have dropped it and crushed it underfoot. He certainly would not leave it lying around in this half–smoked state. No, the man has escaped, and in a hurry.'

The watchman was not in his room. After waiting for two or three minutes we saw him emerging from behind some bushes and come towards us in a leisurely fashion. 'I've just finished off one of those rats,' he said.

So that's what he was doing behind the bushes. Feluda came straight to the point.

'The man who was injured by the tree — who discovered him first?'

The watchman said he had been the first person to do so. He had not been in the cemetery at the time when the tree fell. His shirt had been blown off to Park Street and he had gone chasing after it. But he had seen the man as soon as he came back. It was a familiar face, for the gentleman had visited the cemetery several times recently.

'Did anybody else come here yesterday?'

'I don't know, Sir. There was no one around when I ran out.'

'But someone could have been hiding behind one of these tombs —isn't that possible?'

The watchman did not deny it. I too felt that in all of Calcutta there was not a better place for playing hide and seek than this cemetery.

On seeing the state Biswas was in, the watchman had gone outside and informed a foreign gentleman who happened to be walking outside. From the description it sounded like one of the Fathers of St. Xavier's School. It was he who had called a taxi and made arrangements for Biswas to be taken to hospital.

'Did you see anyone come in here today — a little while ago?'

'Now?'

'Yes.'

No, the watchman had seen no one. He had not been near the gate. He had taken the dead rat for disposal behind the bushes. And after that he had had to relieve himself.

'Do you stay here at night also?'

'Yes, Sir. But there's no need to guard this place at night. Everyone is too afraid to come here. At one time a part of the Lower Circular Road wall had been broken. But these days nobody comes to the cemetery at night.'

'What's your name?'

'Baramdeo.'

'Here.'

'Thank you, Sir.'

Later, of course, we were well recompensed for the two rupee note that was being tucked into the watchman's palm.

CHAPTER 3

'Godwin . . .? Thomas Godwin . . .?'

Six waves appeared on Uncle Sidhu's forehead. To me Uncle Sidhu is an encyclopaedia. For Feluda he has a photographic memory. Both are correct. Anything he hears, anything he reads he will never forget if it is of interest to him. Feluda often has to come to him. As he has done today. Uncle Sidhu gets up very early in the morning and goes for a morning walk to the Lakes. After walking a couple of miles he returns home by six — thirty. Even rain never stops him; he'll go out with his umbrella. But once back home he is a fixture on the divan except when he gets up for a bath or for meals. He has a little desk in front, cluttered with books, magazines, newspapers. But he never writes. No letters, no bills, nothing. He only reads. He does not have a telephone. If he needs us, he sends word through his servant Janardan; we get the message within ten minutes. Uncle Sidhu never married; instead of a wife, he has made a home with his books. And he says so himself — home, wife, kids, family, doctor, teacher, brother, sister, mother, father — everything for him is books. It is Uncle Sidhu who is partly responsible for Feluda's current obsession with old Calcutta. But it is not just the history of Calcutta that Uncle Sidhu knows, it is the history of the world.

After two sips of his tea (without milk in it) Uncle Sidhu muttered the name a few more times. Then he said, 'The first person one remembers if you suddenly mention the name Godwin, is Shelley's father–in–law. But yes, there was a Godwin who came to India. What did you say was the year of his death?'

'1858.'

'And birth?'

'1788.'

'Hm. It could well be this Godwin. I think it was in 1848 or

may be in 1849, there was an article in *The Calcutta Review*.
Thomas's daughter. Her name was Shirley. No, no — Charlotte,
Charlotte Godwin. She wrote about her father. Yes, I remember
now. Good God! It was an amazing story, Felu! But Charlotte
did not write about his last years. So I know nothing about that
period. But his early adventures in India — they read like fiction!
You have been to Lucknow, haven't you?'

Feluda nodded. It was in Lucknow that Feluda first shone as
a detective over the affair of The Emperor's Ring.

'Then you must have heard of Sadat Ali?'

'Yes.'

'This was the time when Sadat Ali was the Nawab of Lucknow.
The glory of Delhi had been sadly reduced by then — all the
pomp and splendour was at Lucknow. Sadat had spent his youth
in Calcutta. He had hobnobbed with the British and picked up
some English. The other thing he had acquired was British
manners and etiquette. After the death of Asaf–ud–dowla, Wazir
Ali became the Nawab. Sadat was in Banaras then. He was
down in the dumps because he had been entertaining hopes of
getting the Nawabi throne after Asaf's death. Wazir, meanwhile,
proved to be a nincompoop. The British could not stomach him;
within four months they threw him out. You have to remember,
those were the days when the East India Company was a power
to reckon with in the state of Oudh. The Nawabs followed their
instructions to the letter. The British put Sadat on the throne
vacated by Wazir. Gratified, Sadat gave the British half the state
of Oudh.'

'In those days you would find an Englishman practically in
every lane and by–lane of Lucknow. The Nawab's army had
British officers and British traders, doctors, painters, even barbers
and school teachers; then there were some who had come only
for the money — hoping to make a fortune by ingratiating
themselves with the Nawab. Thomas Godwin belonged to this
last group. A young fellow from England — his home was in
Sussex, or Suffolk or Surrey, or one of those places. He had
heard about the doings of the Nawabs while in England, and
turned up in Lucknow. A handsome fellow with pleasing manners,
he managed to win over the Resident, Mr. Cherry, got a letter

of recommendation out of him, and showed up at the Nawab's court. Sadat asked him about his accomplishments. Thomas had already heard that the Nawab liked western cuisine, and he happened to be a gifted cook. So he said he was a chef, that he wanted to cook the Nawab a meal. The Nawab asked him to do so. And that was it — Godwin cooked such a feast that the Nawab immediately appointed him to the kitchen. From that time, wherever the Nawab went, Thomas Godwin went with him, along with the Muslim cook. Every time the Governor – General came to town, Sadat would invite him to breakfast. It was in his interests to keep the Governor–General happy. And the person Sadat relied on to do so was Thomas Godwin. Everytime a new dish was approved, Godwin received a reward. Have you any idea what a Nawabi reward was like? It was not just a ten–rupee note or a couple of guineas to be tucked into the palm. This was the Nawab of Lucknow — a mere wave of his hand could produce a treasure trove. So you can well imagine how Godwin's coffers swelled. Why otherwise would he stay on in the palace kitchen? He was no ordinary person.'

'Finally, he came out of the Nawab's domain. Came to our city of Calcutta. And the first thing he did was to marry an Englishwoman called Jane Maddock — the daughter of a Captain in the Company's regiment. Within three months of this event, he opened a restaurant on Chowringhee. And then — things turned not as they usually do. Good times don't last forever. Godwin was addicted to gambling. In his Lucknow days, he had gained and lost equally in cockfighting and other such games. Once settled in Calcutta, the old passion reared its head again . . . His daughter did not say anything more. As far as I recall, the article was published several months after Godwin's death. So it would have been difficult for his own daughter to throw much light on his vices. Particularly in that day and age. Anyway, you can go to the Asiatic Society and read the article. Naturally you will get many more details than I've been able to give you.'

It seemed to me, however, that Uncle Sidhu had given us the entire piece in Bengali.

Feluda and I sat quietly for some time after hearing this fascinating story of Thomas Godwin. It was Uncle Sidhu who was the one to speak again.

'But why are you making enquiries about Thomas Godwin? What's up?'

'I'll tell you,' said Feluda. 'But before that I need to know something else. Have you heard of anyone called Narendra Biswas — a man who writes articles on old Calcutta?'

'Which paper?'

'I don't know.'

'If he is writing for some little–known paper, I may not have noticed it. These days, I don't read anything except the standard publications.'

'But why this sudden question?'

Feluda recounted yesterday's adventures briefly and said, 'What puzzles me is this — if a man is hurt by a falling tree, why should his wallet jump ten yards away from his body?'

'Hm . . .'

Uncle Sidhu thought for a while.

'The wind velocity in yesterday's storm was ninety miles per hour,' he said, 'If we find that the wallet was in this man's breast–pocket then it's quite likely to have been flung outside as he ran to escape the storm. He could also have been hit by the tree while he was running.'

'In that case, where's the mystery?'

'The gentleman fell beside Godwin's tomb.'

'So what?'

'There's a hole beside it, almost looks like a ditch. I think somebody had started digging.'

Uncle Sidhu was goggling.

'Good God! Grave–digging! This is rather a grave piece of news. It is incredible! I know that newly–buried bodies are dug up and sold for the purposes of dissection. But a two–hundred – years–old body will have nothing left but a few bones. It has neither any archaeological value nor any resale value. Are you sure about the digging?'

'Not entirely. For the rain has washed away the signs of spade work. But still . . .'

Uncle Sidhu thought some more, then shook his head, saying, 'No, my dear Felu, I think this time you are on a wild goose chase. Obviously you have no other cases in hand, eh? So you are creating a mystery out of nothing, aren't you?'

Feluda smiled his lopsided smile and kept quiet. Uncle Sidhu continued, 'If only any of Godwin's descendants were around, one could at least make some enquiries. But I don't think they are here. Not all British families are like Barwell or Tytler, members of whose families have remained in India from the time of Clive to modern days.'

At last Feluda came out with the news he had kept secret for so long.

'After Thomas Godwin, someone or the other in their family for the next three generations has died in India — I happen to know this quite well.'

'What!' Uncle Sidhu was amazed. Only this morning, just before coming here, we had spent an–hour–and–a half in the Lower Circular Road cemetery. This was built after the Park Street one, and is still being used.

'I saw Charlotte Godwin's tomb there,' said Feluda. 'She died in 1886, at the age of 67.'

'You saw the name Godwin? That means she never got married. She was a very good writer, that lady.'

'Next to Charlotte is the tomb of her elder brother David, died 1874 –' Feluda had taken his notebook out of his pocket and was reading from it. 'He was the Head Assistant of Kyd Company in Kidderpore. Beside David are his son, Lieutenant Colonel Andrew Godwin and his wife Emma. Andrew died in 1882. Next to Andrew– Emma lies their son Charles. He was a doctor, died in 1920.'

'Bravo! One really has to admire your perseverance and curiosity!' Uncle Sidhu seemed really pleased. 'Now you have to find out if any of them are alive today, and in Calcutta. Did you see any Godwins in the telephone directory?'

'Only one. I called. But no connection with this family.'

'Well, keep looking. Someone may be around. Though I don't know how you will track him down. If you do — the grave – digging seems to me to be a false trail — at least you'll be able to get some more information about a colourful figure like Thomas Godwin. Good luck!'

CHAPTER 4

Back home, I waited till the afternoon before my patience finally
gave out, and I had to ask Feluda, 'What was scribbled on that
piece of white paper that came out of Narendra Biswas's wallet
yesterday?'

Feluda was supposed to go out later in the afternoon to return
Narendra Biswas's wallet. He had found out that the gentleman
was in Park Hospital.

Feluda opened his own notebook and held it out to me.

'If you can make sense out of this then I'll know you've as
good as got the Nobel Prize.'

On the ruled sheet of note paper was written–

B/S 141 SNB for WG Victoria & P.C. (44?)

Re Victoria's letters try MN, OU, AV, SJ, WN.

There goes the Nobel Prize, I said to myself. Even so, I said
to Feluda, 'It seems that the gentleman is interested in Queen
Victoria. But I can't understand the meaning of Victoria & P.C.'

'P.C. probably means Prince Consort, that is, Victoria's husband
Prince Albert.'

'But I can't make out anything else.'

From Feluda's expression, it did not seem like he had understood
much either. Uncle Sidhu's comment had also touched a chord
in my own mind — perhaps Feluda was trying to find a mystery
even where there was nothing mysterious. But even as I thought
so, I remembered the lighted cigarette we had seen yesterday,
and I felt a curiously empty feeling in my stomach. Who was
it that had run away from the cemetery because we happened
to be there? And why had he gone there that rainy evening?

We had planned to leave around four, to go and return
Narendra Biswas's wallet and it had been decided that Lalmohan
Babu would come and take us.

On time, we heard the sound of a car driving up to the house.

The gentleman came in, carrying a magazine.

'What did I tell you? Here's *Bichitrapatra*, and look, here's Narendra Biswas's article. There's also a picture of the Monument, though the printing is of poor quality.'

'But the name given here is also Narendranath, not Narendramohan. Is it someone else then?'

'If you ask me, it's those visiting cards that are wrong. They look like they've been printed by a third-rate press. Perhaps the gentleman didn't even bother to check the proof. Otherwise you would have to dismiss this entire thing as coincidence — those cuttings in the wallet, and this article. That's not possible.'

Feluda skimmed through the article, dropped the magazine on a side table and said, 'He writes well but there's nothing new in it. Now we have to find out whether the man who was injured by the tree is the same Biswas who wrote this.'

My father knew Dr. Shikdar at Park Hospital quite well. He had also come to our house several times, so Feluda knew him too. Within five minutes of Feluda sending in his card, we were summoned to the doctor's room.

'What's up? Some new case?'

Wherever Feluda happens to go, he has to listen to this, from anyone who knows him.

He smiled and said, 'I've come to return something to a patient of yours.'

'Which patient?'

'Mr. Biswas. Narendra Biswas. Day before yesterday —'

'Oh, him — but he's gone. Just left a couple of hours ago. His brother came with a car and took him home.'

'But the papers said —'

'Said what? That he was seriously injured? That's typical of newspapers. Do you think it's possible for a man to survive if an entire tree falls on his head? This was just a branch — an offshoot from a bigger one — that fell on him. It was more a case of shock than of injury. He's bruised his right wrist, we've put in a few stitches on his head — that's about it.'

'Well, can you tell us if this gentleman has some interest in old Calcutta?'

'Yes. That's him. Naturally I felt quite curious when I heard this man had been wandering around in a graveyard in the evening. So I questioned him — and he said he was doing research on old Calcutta. Good idea, I said, the farther one stays away from the new Calcutta the better it is.'

'Did the injury seem normal to you?'

'At last . . . this is more like a sleuth talking!'

Feluda could not hide his discomfiture.

'Well, I mean, did he tell you himself that the falling tree had . . .'

'Come on now, is there any scope for doubt about that branch having fallen? And this man happened to be there. So why should there be room for suspicion?'

'But did the man himself mention anything unnatural or suspicious?'

'Definitely not. He said he'd seen the tree falling but he could not estimate how far–flung its branches and off–shoots were. But yes, after he regained consciousness, he did say the word 'will' a couple of times. Now I have no idea if there is some mystery attached to this. I don't think so. For he only mentioned the 'will' that one time — never again.'

'Do you know the gentleman's full name?'

'Why, the same as in the papers, Narendranath Biswas.'

'Another question — please don't mind the trouble — do you remember what he was wearing?'

'Of course. Shirt and trousers. I even remember the colours — a white shirt and biscuit coloured trousers. Not Glaxo biscuits, cream crackers, ha! ha!'

Feluda had taken Narendra Biswas's address from Dr. Shikdar. We went straight from the nursing home to New Alipore.It's a real nuisance trying to find an address in New Alipore. But Jatayu's driver seemed to know the streets of Calcutta pretty well. We did not spend more than three minutes on locating the house.

It was a double–storey house, built fifteen to twenty years ago. On the street, outside the gates, stood a white Ambassador. There were two names on the gate. N. Biswas and G. Biswas. When we rang, a servant came and opened the door.

'Is Narendra Babu home?' asked Feluda.

'Yes, but he's sick.'

'Can't we see him just for a moment? It's rather urgent.'

'Whom do you want?'

The question came from behind the servant. A gentleman between forty and forty–five was coming towards us. A fair complexion, light brown eyes, clean–shaved face. He wore a half–sleeved shirt over his pyjamas, and a silk shawl was wrapped around him.

'I've come to return something belonging to Narendra Biswas,' said Feluda. 'His wallet, which fell out of his pocket in the Park Street cemetery.'

'Really? I'm his brother. Why don't you come inside. My brother is in bed, he's still got his bandages on. He can speak all right; but this was such a traumatic incident, you know . . .'

There was a bedroom behind the stairs leading to the first floor. That was where Narendra Babu was staying. he was a couple of shades darker than his brother, sported a thick moustache, and it was quite evident that the bandage covered a bald head.

He lowered *The Statesman* held in his left hand and bent his head in greeting. He was unable to use his right hand as it was bandaged. The brother left us and went out of the room. I heard him telling a servant to bring two more chairs into this room. There was only one chair in the room, beside the bed, in front of the desk.

Feluda took the wallet and held it out.

'Oh, thank you so much. So kind of you, to take the trouble . . .'

'Not at all,' Feluda was politeness incarnate. 'I just happened to be there, and this friend of mine picked it up. So . . .'

Narenedra Babu held the wallet open with his one free hand peered into the compartments once and looked questioningly at Feluda.

'Happened to be in the cemetery. . . ?'

'That's exactly what I was going to ask you,' smiled Feluda. 'You are probably doing some research on old Calcutta, aren't you?'

The gentleman sighed.

'I was, I was — but after this blow! Probably the Gods don't want me to meddle.'

'That article in *Bichitrapatra* —'

'Yes, that's mine. The one about the Monument. I've also

written a few others here and there. I retired from my job last year. One has to do something after all: I was a student of history. And even from my young days I've been interested in this subject. When I was in college, I once walked all the way from Bagbajar to Dum Dum, just to see Clive's house. Have you seen it? It was there till only the other day — a single–storey, bungalow–type house with the coat of arms of the East India Company on the facade.'

'Did you go to Presidency College?'

There was a table to the right of the bed, and a couple of feet above, hung a group photograph. Underneath was written, ' Presidency College Alumni Association,1953.'

'Not just myself,' said Narendra Biswas, 'my son, my brother, my father, grandfather — all of us are students of Presidency College. It's a family tradition, I feel ashamed to mention it now — but both Girindra and myself were gold medal winners.'

'But why feel ashamed?'

'Just look at us — what have we done with our lives? I went and got a job, and Girindra went into business. Who has ever heard of us?'

Feluda had walked over to look at the photograph. Now his eyes travelled downwards. There was a blue note–book on the table. It was open on the first page. One could see that nothing had been written after the first eight or nine lines.

'Is your name Narendranath or Narendramohan?'

'I beg your pardon?'

The gentleman had probably been daydreaming. When Feluda asked him once again, he smiled a little, seemed to be slightly taken aback, and said, 'As far as I know, it is Narendranath. Why, do you have some doubts?'

'Well, your visiting card says N. M. Biswas.'

'Oh, that: That's a printer's error. Every time I give somebody a card, I correct it with a pen. Of course I should have had some new cards printed. But I never got around to doing it. And to tell you the truth, I'm not likely to need visiting cards much, am I? Recently I had been meeting some of the curators and other big shots in museums and libraries, that's why I put some cards into my wallet. By the way, are you also thinking of writing about that cemetery? I hope not : I'll never be able to compete with a young rival like you.'

Feluda got up to leave, saying, 'No, I don't write — just knowing about things gives me pleasure. But I do have one request. If you happen to come across any references to the Godwin family in the course of your researches on Calcutta, please do me a favour and let me know.'

'The Godwin family?'

'Yes, Thomas Godwin's tomb is in the Park Street cemetery. In fact, the same tree that injured you also damaged Godwin's tomb.'

'Is that so?'

'Five other members of the Godwin family are buried in the Lower Circular Road cemetery.'

'Of course I'll let you know. But where? Your address?'

Feluda gave Narendra Babu one of his cards.

'Is this your profession? Sleuthing?' the gentleman seemed quite taken aback as he asked this question.

'Yes.'

'Well, I'd heard there were private detectives in Calcutta. But this is the first time I've laid eyes on one!'

'Why didn't you ask him about Victoria?' I asked Feluda as we drove towards Chowringhee. Lalmohan Babu was determined to take us to the Blue Fox today for tea and sandwiches. Who could have known about the dramatic turn events would take in the restaurant?

'Do you think the gentleman would have been pleased to hear that I had been prying into his wallet? And that bit of writing, even if it was not in code, was certainly in an abbreviated form. What if it was something he wanted to keep secret?'

'That's true.'

Lalmohan Babu was looking rather pensive. Feluda too had noticed that.

'Why have you got that dreamy look in your eyes?' he asked.

The gentleman sighed.

'I had thought up such a lovely plot for young Pulak. I'm sure it would have been another hit. But he has just written to tell me that there's no market for Hindi movies that are thrillers with lots of fighting. Apparently the new craze is for devotional pictures. Just think of it!'

'Well, what's your problem? Can't you summon up feelings that are devotional enough?'

Lalmohan Babu did not even bother to reply. Looking like anything but a devotee, he muttered 'hell!' several times and subsided into silence. But he wasn't really swearing because of Pulak Ghoshal's letter. We had just left the Birla Planetorium and were on Chowringhee. To our left, a huge mound of earth was obscuring the view of the maidan. For the last few days, Lalmohan Babu had taken to calling the subway under construction by the name of Hell Rail.

The car kept going over huge potholes, and Lalmohan Babu kept gritting his teeth.

'The springs are not as bad as you think,' he said. 'Let's drive down Red Road and you'll see what splendid shape the car is in.'

'You are complaining about metalled roads,' said Feluda. 'Two hundred years ago these were dirt roads. Think of that!'

'Yes, but they didn't have Ambassadors in those days, nor such huge crowds.'

'Well, crowds there were — but not of human beings. They were mostly adjutant birds.'

'Adjutant birds?'

'Four–and–a–half–feet tall. Used to pick at the refuse on the roads. Today we have crows and sparrows everywhere. In those days they had adjutant birds. Corpses would float down the Ganga, and the birds would happily perch on them and travel downstream.'

'Good God — this must have been a real jungle then! What a terrible thought!'

'And right in the middle of it all was the Governor General's residence, St. John's Church, the Park Street cemetery, the theatres on Theatre Road and so many houses belonging to the British. This area was known as the White Town — the natives were not to be found here. North Calcutta was the Black Town.'

'My dear Sir, you are making my blood boil.'

As soon as we turned into Park Street, well before we had reached the Blue Fox, Feluda asked the driver to stop.

'I have to look into the bookshop for a minute.'

Lalmohan Babu had no interest in the Oxford Book Company, because they never sold any of the thrillers. 'Thank God for our College Street bookstores and the Black Bookshops in Ballygunge,' he said.

Feluda went inside, looked around a bit, and went up to one of the counters. There were stacks of red and blue notebooks, files, diaries, engagement pads. Feluda picked up one of the blue notebooks and checked the price. Twelve–fifty. The one on Narendra Biswas's table was exactly like this.

'Yes?'

One of the salesmen had come up to Feluda.

'Do you happen to have 'Queen Victoria's collected letters?'

'Queen Victoria? No, Sir, But if you give us the name of the publisher, we can get it for you. If it is Macmillan or Oxford University Press, then we can check with their Calcutta office.'

Feluda thought a little. Then he said, 'Very well; I'll find out and get back to you.'

We came out on Park Street. The car had gone ahead and was parked in front of the Blue Fox. We started walking.

'Wait a minute' Feluda had taken his own note book out of his pocket. 'It's impossible to read when walking in a crowd.'

He glanced over the pages only for a few seconds and started walking again.

'Did you find something?' I asked.

'Let's go to the Blue Fox first and sit down,' he said.

As we sat down, we learnt that it was only because he was very taken with the name, Blue Fox, that Lalmohan Babu had brought us there. He himself had never been here before. Not only that, he had never even been to any other restaurant on Park Street.

'I live way down in Garpar,' he said, 'and my publishers are on College Street. Give me one good reason why I should come to this part of town.'

After ordering tea and sandwiches, Feluda took his notebook out again, and put it on the table. He then opened it on the relevant page and said, 'The first line is still shrouded in mystery. But I have deciphered the second. All of these are names of foreign publishers.'

'Which?' I asked.

'MM, OU, GAU. SJ and WN. They are Macmillan, Oxford University Press, George Allen and Unwin, Sidgwick and Jackson, Weidenfeld and Nicholson.'

'Bravo!' said Jatayu, 'How could you rattle off so many names without tripping once?'

'It's quite clear that this gentleman used to write or is still writing to these publishers, enquiring about Victoria's letters. But the irony is that it would have been far easier to go to the British Council or the National Library and read Victoria's letters.'

'Yes, rather like twisting your arm round your head to point to your nose' commented Jatayu.

Feluda returned his notebook to his pocket to make room for

the plates of sandwiches and lit a Charminar. Lalmohan Babu started drumming with his fingers on the table to the tune of some foreign sounding song, and said, 'Let's go off somewhere, out of town. Every time we go somewhere, you get a case, and I come up with a plot. Why don't you suggest a place? I want a place that is rugged. We don't need a flat terrain with a lush, lazy atmosphere. What we must find is . . .'

The arrival of the sandwiches put a stop to the discussions. All three of us were quite hungry. Lalmohan Babu took a huge bite out of two sandwiches held together, chewed a few times and suddenly stopped. Then, with eyes popping out, he muttered 'God be praised' a couple of times, so that bits of bread shot out of his mouth and fell on the table.

What had happened was this. Feluda and I had been facing the road, while Lalmohan Babu sat facing the rear of the restaurant. At the far end of the room was a low platform, obviously intended for the band that played there in the evenings. It was the signboard placed there that had reduced our Jatayu to this state. It contained the name of the band, and below the name it said: 'Guitar—Chris Godwin.'

Feluda put his sandwich back on the plate and snapped his fingers to call the waiter.

'Do you have music here at dinner time?'

'Yes Sir.'

'Can I speak to your manager for a moment?'

What Feluda wanted was to get hold of Chris Godwin's address, and he had a perfect excuse up his sleeve. As soon as the manager showed up, he said, 'We need a good band party for a wedding at Mr. Mansukhani's on Ballygunge Park Road. I've heard a lot about the band that plays here. Do you think they'll agree to play for a wedding?'

'Why not? It's their profession.'

'That Godwin whose name is on your board — he's probably the leader, isn't he? If you could give me his address . . .'

The manager wrote the address down on a slip of paper and gave it to Feluda. It said 14/1, Ripon Lane.

On any other day we would have spent much more time chatting over our tea and sandwiches. But Feluda was not hungry any longer; he did not have more than one sandwich. Lalmohan Babu gobbled up Feluda's two and his own three at extraordinary speed saying, 'Why waste food when we have to pay for it?'

One look at the exterior of 14/1, Ripon Lane was enough to depress my spirits — for I had not yet forgotten Sadat Ali's Nawabi days. But Feluda said there was nothing surpising about this place — four or five generations could see a family go way downhill. Not that any of the houses here were very small. All of them were three or four storey high. But they all had the most uninviting appearance. Lalmohan Babu was sure that every one of them was a haunted house.

Before entering, Feluda made some enquiries of the cigarette seller in the neighbourhood.

'Does someone called Godwin live in this house?'

'Godwin? The one who plays music?'

'Why, are there any others?'

'Yes, there's the old gentleman. Markis Godwin.'

'Where does he live?'

'First floor. Mr. Arkis is on the second floor.'

'Are they brothers — this Arkis and Markis?' asked Lalmohan Babu.

'No Sir, Mr. Arkis is Mr. Arkis. Markis is Mr. Markis Godwin's name. He is on the first floor. On the second . . .'

Feluda, by this time, had given up on the mystery of Arkis and Markis and gone inside 14/1. The two of us now followed him.

It was exactly as I had thought. The interior was no different from the exterior. The days are long in June, and there was still some daylight outside. But inside near the staircase, it was pitch dark. Feluda has this strange power — may be his eyes are different from other people's — he can see extremely well in the dark. Watching him as he sped up the stairs, Lalmohan Babu gripped the banister and started going up gingerly, saying, 'I've heard of cat burglars all right. But this is the first time I've seen a cat sleuth.'

The first floor was oppressively quiet. A faint sound of music came to us, probably someone playing the radio. There was a door facing the stairs, beyond that was a verandah. There was no electric light there, but faint daylight came in from outside

and illuminated the floor inlaid with coloured glass fragments.
The door that opened to our left showed an empty room —
there was no light burning there. We could make out another
room to the left of the verandah inside, for a streak of light
came from there and fell on one corner of the verandah. A black
cat lay curled up in that light and stared at us. A male voice
could be heard from the floor above. Once I also heard a hollow
cough.

'Let's go home,' said Jatayu 'This must be the Ripon Lane
cemetery.'

Feluda went towards the door leading to the verandah. 'Anybody
home?' he called out.

For a few seconds there was no response. Then came the
answer, 'Who's that?'

Feluda was hesitating when the voice spoke again, peremptorily
this time.

'Come inside. I can't come out.'

'Are you going in, or are you going home?'

But Feluda ignored Lalmohan Babu's question, crossed the
threshold and went inside. The two of us had to follow and we
slowly made our way inside.

'Come in,' came the command from the room on the left.

The three of us went in. A medium–sized sitting room. Facing the door was a sofa — the stuffing was showing through the cloth cover in several places. There was a white marble table in front of the sofa — though one could no longer call it white; that had been the original colour. To the left was an ancient black bookcase containing a dozen old books. On top of the bookcase were some dusty plastic flowers in a brass vase — but it was impossible to make out the colour of those flowers. There was a framed picture on the wall — but it could just as well be the picture of a horse or a train, so thick was the dust on the glass. The Philips radio which sat on the table beside the sofa must have been a model designed before Feluda was born. The amazing thing was that the radio still worked, for that was where the music had been coming from. Now a veined, pallid hand turned the knob and switched off the radio. The owner of the hand sat on one corner of the sofa, a cushion on his lap, his left leg on a footstool, and stared at us. One could see his British lineage from the colour of his skin and from the hazel tones of the few hairs which had not gone gray. I could not make out the colour of his eyes, for the bulb that was hanging from the roof could not have been more than twenty–five watts.

'I'm suffering from gout, so I can't move around.' said this Englishman. 'I have to take the help of my servant and that bastard absconds whenever he can.'

Feluda now went through the introductions.

If the old man was annoyed at our arrival, he showed no signs of it yet. Feluda went straight to business.

'I've only come to find out one thing. Are you a descendant of Thomas Godwin's — the one who came to India in the early part of the nineteenth century?'

The old man raised his head a little more. Now I could see

that the eyes were a pale blue. He stared at Feluda for a few seconds before saying, 'Now how the hell did you know about my great–great–grandfather?'

'So, I've guessed right then?'

'Not only that; I've even got something which belonged to Thomas Godwin himself. Or at least that's what my grandmother used to say. A hundred–and–fifty years — oh hell!'

'What's the matter?'

'That scoundrel Arakis — that charlatan! It was only last night that he borrowed it from me. Said he would return it tonight. They are going to have their meeting soon. It's Thursday today, isn't it? In a little while you'll hear them — strange noises overhead.'

Perhaps it was my confusion which made the room seem darker all of a sudden. Or may be it was evening already. No, I heard thunder. The sky had clouded over — hence the darkness.

Feluda was sitting in a broken armed chair in front of Mr. Godwin. To his left, sat Jatayu in a lounging chair. But he was not lounging comfortably; his fidgeting made me think there were bugs in the chair. I sat on his left in another chair. Feluda was staring fixedly at the Englishman. His expression said — I am here to listen to whatever you can tell me.

'It's an ivory casket,' said Mr. Godwin. 'There are some things in it too. Two old pipes, a silver snuff–box, a pair of glasses and a package wrapped in silk. It feels like books inside; but I've never opened the package. There were lots of other old things in our house, but that good–for–nothing son of mine has sold them off. He gave up studies, got into drugs — and that was when he started smuggling things out of the house. I've no idea why he hasn't taken the casket. Maybe he would have; but a sudden turn of luck made it unnecessary. He has formed his own band. That's what keeps him going now — if you can call this any kind of going. And how can I blame my son entirely? I have to take some responsibility too, don't I? I've heard that Tom Godwin became penniless because of his gambling. It's been the same with me . . .'

The old man paused. He was panting. Maybe because he had spoken for so long without a break. His face twisted, probably his gout troubling him! Then he started again.

'I went to England once, when I was a young man. My youngest uncle was in London, a cashier at the Midland Bank. But I couldn't stick it for more than three months. The cold was too much for me. The diet disagreed with me — I had grown used to rice and curry. So I came back to Calcutta. I got married. My wife died ten years ago. Now there's only Christopher. I hardly set eyes on him. He sits in the next room twanging away at his guitar. Seems to have a gift for it.'

A strange sound was now coming from above. Tap, Tap — tap, tap. It would start and stop and start again. The shadows in the room were swaying, for the light bulb hanging from the ceiling was swaying with the sound. Now it was not just Lalmohan Babu, I too was feeling scared. I had never come to a house like this, or a room like this one; nor had I heard such stories from a man like this one. But what was going on upstairs?

Mr. Godwin did not even look upwards as he said, 'The table's turning. Four frauds are sitting around it. They claim they are summoning the spirits of the dead — every time a spirit comes, the table starts rocking.'

'Who are these four?' asked Feluda.

'Arakis's group. A gang of spiritualists. Two Jews, two Parsees and Arakis himself. Wanted me to join them, but I wouldn't. One day I happened to mention Thomas Godwin to Arakis. He said he would arrange for me to communicate with him. I said — no, certainly not. I'll have to meet him anyway one of these days. Then the fellow came to me yesterday and said. . . ?'

The old man stopped. Tap, Tap, Tap. There went the table again.

'But why did he have to take the casket from you?' asked Feluda.

'I'm coming to that.' He said, — 'We'll bring Godwin's spirit without your help. But if you have anything belonging to him, please let me have it. It will be easier for the spirit to come if we put it on the table.' 'Well, from the sound of it, the spirit must have come.'

Tap, tap, tap. . . the table was rocking again.

'Do they do this in the dark?' Feluda asked.

'All charlatans work in the dark'— there was a jeering note in Godwin's voice.

'Can we go upstairs?'

Lalmohan Babu clutched the arm of his chair fiercely, to convey his objections as soon as he heard this. But Godwin's answer reassured him somewhat.

'They won't let you go in,' said Mr. Godwin. 'It's for members only. His servant stands guard. Of course if someone goes with intention of asking their help in summoning a spirit, it's a different matter. Twenty rupees in advance, and once the spirit has come and gone, another hundred.'

'I see . . .'

Feluda got up.

'Well Mr. Godwin, many thanks. Please don't mind us troubling you like this.'

'Goodnight.'

Mr. Godwin's emaciated hand went towards the radio again. What Feluda did as we came out on the landing startled me considerably. What it did to Lalmohan Babu was impossible to make out in the dark. Instead of going down Feluda made straight for the second floor.

'Here — have you forgotten which is up and which is down?' asked Jatayu in a panic.

'Just follow me. Don't be afraid,' came the answer.

As we reached the second floor, we were confronted by the servant guarding the door.

'Whom do you want?'

'I've only come to give you something my dear fellow.'

Feluda was holding a five–rupee note out to Mr. Arakis's servant. The fellow was utterly bewildered. Feluda brought his face close to his ear and said, 'Just tell me if the room your master is in is closed from all sides.'

The bribe worked. The room, the servant told us, was closed off from the verandah but there was a door from the bedroom which was open.

'You've nothing to fear — don't have to do a thing — just show us the bedroom. Otherwise, you'd be in trouble. We are from the police. This is the inspector.'

Lalmohan Babu promptly stood on tiptoe to add two inches to his height. There was a light in the landing. Feluda pushed forward the money a little more so that the note touched the servant's palm. The palm automatically closed on it.

'Come this way — but . . .'

'No buts! The police have their eyes on one of your master's cronies. That's why we have to go in. Nothing will happen to you or your master.'

'Come.'

The bedroom was dark, and so was the room on the other side of the open door. The three of us crept forward to the door.

No sound was coming from the seance room now. But shortly before we had heard the table turning three times. We could guess that the members of this spiritualist group were waiting with bated breath for the spirit of Thomas Godwin. Lalmohan Babu was breathing so fast and so hard, that I was afraid it would give us away to the people in the next room. Feluda must have gone even closer to the door by now. From somewhere I got a whiff of kerosene oil. Once I heard a cat mew. Probably the black tomcat we had seen downstairs.

'Thomas Godwin! Thomas Godwin!'

The name was called twice almost like a groan. Obviously, this was the proper way to address a spirit.

'Are you with us? Are you with us?'

Not a sound, not a movement. Half—a—minute went by. Then came the same anxious query.

'Thomas Godwin . . . Are you with us?'

'Ye – es! Ye – es!'

Now from my right also came a tapping noise. Not a table, but human limbs. Lalmohan Babu's knees.

'Yes! I have come! I am here!'

Though the voice said 'Here' it sounded faint and distant.

The leader of the seance asked again, 'Are you happy? Are you in peace?'

'No – o,' came the response.

'What is troubling you?'

For half—a—minute again there was silence. Then Arakis's group asked once more, 'What is troubling you?'

'I . . . I . . . I want my . . . I want my . . . casket !'

Immediately after this several strange things happened. A

fearful scream from the seance room — the kind that comes from extreme terror — and the very next moment a sharp tug at my arm, and a whisper in my ear — 'Come on Topshe.'

Arakis's servant seeing the three of us rushing out, was too bewildered to do anything. In a minute we had left Ripon Lane behind and were walking towards our car on Royd Street.

'This was some stunt!' said Lalmohan Babu, 'It would be a superhit in a film.'

The object which elicited this ecstatic from response Lalmohan Babu was nothing but the ivory casket given to Thomas Godwin by Sadat Ali. It was in Feluda's hands now.

It was the morning after. Feluda himself had asked me into his room. Last night, after Lalmohan Babu had dropped us, Feluda had bathed and finished dinner in half–an–hour, and locked himself in his room. As for me, I could hardly sleep at night. I knew now we were enmeshed in the web of an extraordinarily complicated mystery. Even the maze at Lucknow was a very poor second to this labyrinthine problem. I had no sense of any direction, Feluda was the only hope we had. But did Feluda himself know the way out of the maze?

Feluda was sitting on his bed, Thomas Godwin's casket in front of him, all the objects within now scattered on the bed. Two white pipes — I had never seen such pipes before; a silver snuff–box; a pair of gold spectacles, and four notebooks bound in red leather — on the cover of each was written the word 'Diary' in gold letters. The piece of silk in which the diaries had been wrapped was also lying on the bed, and next to it lay a blue ribbon. Feluda pushed one of the notebooks in my direction, saying, 'Be very careful, and turn the first page.'

'Good heavens! This is Charlotte Godwin's diary!'

'Yes, from 1858 to 1862. Beautiful writing, and a lucid style. I spent all night finishing these. It's incredible to think of such a priceless treasure lying in the black hole of Ripon Lane!'

I was still staring at the first page in amazement. I didn't dare turn any more pages because I could see how worn the paper was.

'Arakis must have opened this diary,' said Feluda.

'How can you tell?'

'If you are careless in turning the pages the paper crumbles at the top right–hand corner. Just look. . .'

Feluda demonstrated by turning a page carefully.

'And not only that,' he went on 'Look at this ribbon. Worn

away in patches — because it has been tied in knots for more
than a hundred years. But apart from those patches, notice how
the ribbon is twisted in a couple of other places. This is because
of the new knot. The person who untied this bundle, was not
careful enough to tie the knots in exactly the same spaces; had
he done so, it would have been difficult to catch him.'

'Why have you got black stains on your fingers?' I had noticed
these as soon as I came into the room.

'That's another clue,' said Feluda.

'I'll explain it later. But the stains are from that snuff–box.'

'Well, what did you learn from reading those diaries?' Curiosity
was almost stifling me.

'The last years of Tom Godwin,' said Feluda. 'A penniless,
peevish, old man. One son dead, only one other, David whom
he neither trusts nor feels strongly about. Godwin does not trust
anyone, not even his daughter Charlotte. But Charlotte still nurses
him, loves him with all her heart, and prays for his well– being.
Gambling has left Thomas Godwin a pauper; so Charlotte has
to run the house–hold on what she gets by her own work — by
sewing and knitting carpets which she sells to the English ladies
of Calcutta. All the valuable objects that Godwin received from
the Nawab of Lucknow have been sold, all except three things.
This casket, this snuff–box — which he had gifted to Charlotte
— and the third item, which was the very first thing Sadat gave
him as reward.'

'Did he leave that to Charlotte too?'

'No, that he gave to no one. Before his death he told his
daughter to put it beside him in the coffin and have it buried
with him. Charlotte followed her father's wishes and was at peace
with herself.'

'But what was the object?'

'In Charlotte's words — father's precious Perigal repeater.'

'What on earth's that?'

'Ah, this is where even Feluda Mitter is at his wit's end,
Topshe. The dictionary says that a repeater can be a gun or a
pistol, or even a watch. Perigal could be the name of a company.
Even Uncle Sidhu is not too sure. I went to see him before you
got up. I have to try Bikash Babu — in case he can throw some

light on it.'

There is a shop on Park Street called Park Auction House. A gentleman called Bikash Chakraborty works there. Feluda knows him quite well. He had had to go there several times in connection with a case. That's how they got to know each other.

'I went by just the other day, and there were lots of antique watches on display. My hunch is that this will turn out to be a watch, not a gun.'

Before Lalmohan Babu arrived, Feluda told me a lot of stories from Charlotte Godwin's diary. Charlotte had also mentioned a niece of hers. She refered to her as 'my dear clever niece.' Apparently this girl offended her grandfather for some reason. But before he died, Tom Godwin forgave her and gave her his blessings. Charlotte's brothers David and John were also mentioned in the diary. We had seen David's tomb in the Lower Circular Road cemetery. John went to Britain, and committed suicide. Charlotte never found out why.

Lalmohan Babu arrived and said. 'Until as late as last morning I was in a bit of a quandary. Should I start on a devotional story for Pulak Babu, or should I throw in my lot with you. But after last night, I have no more doubts. Thrill is better than devotion. Find anything in that casket?'

'I learnt from a hundred–and–twenty–five–year–old diary that we might find a Perigal repeater if we dig up Thomas Godwin's grave.'

'Peter who?'

'Never mind, let's get going. How much petrol have you got?'

'I filled her up with ten litres this morning.'

'Good, we have to get around a lot.'

As soon as he entered Park Auction House, Feluda frowned. 'Welcome Mr. Mitter! How wonderful to see you again. Are you on another case or something?'

Bikash Babu had come forward. A plump, shining face, mouth full of *paan*. Somehow he gave me the impression of being from North Calcutta.

'Well I can see you are doing good business all right,' said Feluda. 'Just the other day there were at least eight watches and clocks on display; how come you've sold them all?'

'Why, what kind do you want? Wall clock? Alarm clock?'

Feluda was looking around. Somehow Bikash Babu did not look like the kind of man who would know about watches with fancy names. In response to Feluda's question he said, 'I think a repeater is some kind of an alarm clock. But Perigal does not make sense. But don't worry, there's someone who can tell you all about watches and clocks. He's supposed to have two–hundred–and–fifty of them in his house. A watch–crazy man, you may say.'

'Whom do you mean?'

'Mr. Choudhury, Mahadeb Choudhury.'

'A Bengali?'

'Yes, but he seems to be from the Western parts of India. He only speaks halting Bengali. Mostly he speaks English. Very knowledgeable man. Used to live in Bombay at one time, has now settled in Calcutta. And ever since he arrived, he has been buying up whatever decent stuff he can find. Of course, he only goes for antiques. All those clocks you say you saw here — most of them are now in his house. And that man really knows a lot. Why don't you go and talk to him . He even put an ad in the papers — didn't you see it?'

'What ad?'

'Anyone who has any old watches or clocks for sale should go and see him.'

'The man sounds like a millionaire.'

'Oh yes — cloth mills, movie theatres, tea gardens, jute mills, racing horses, import–export — you name it, and he's got it.'

'Do you have his address?'

'Sure, Alipore Park in Calcutta. He's also bought a house by the Ganga in Panihati. His cloth mill is quite close to that house. He may be in Calcutta now, but don't go in the morning, afternoon is best. Right now, he'll be in his office . . . wait, let me write out the address for you.'

We came out of the Park Auction House with Mahadeb Choudhury's address.

'Why don't the two of you drop me at the National Library's Esplanade reading room,' said Feluda getting into the car, 'and go and take a look around the Park Street cemetery. See if there's anything to report.'

'Re–report?' Lalmohan Babu's voice was not quite steady.

'Yes, report. You don't have to do much. Just take a good look at the Godwin tomb and come back. It hasn't rained over the last two days. So you'll find the place quite dry. Once you've finished there come straight back to me — then we can get ourselves a bite to eat somewhere. It would be silly to go back home. There's a lot to be done; we even have to go to Ripon Lane once.'

Feluda had wrapped. Mr. Godwin's casket in brown paper and was carrying it under his arm.

'Of course there's nothing to fear during the day,' said Lalmohan Babu. 'It's only in the evening that one feels a bit – er . . . '

'Unless your mind is a hive of superstitions, there's never any reason to fear the supernatural.'

We were caught in a traffic jam on the way to Esplanade. As we waited, Lalmohan Babu asked Feluda. 'This watch you are looking for — would that be a pocket watch?'

'I don't really know, not yet.'

'Well, if you need a pocket watch, I have one.'

'Whose watch is it?'

'The same man who left me three of his belongings — the watch, a cane and a turban. My grandfather, the late Pyaricharan Ganguly. I've been meaning to give you this watch.'

Feluda was quite surprised.

'Why?'

'Well, I've been thinking of giving you a present for the last few days. After all, your contribution towards the success of my Hindi film was not insignificant. And that means, behind the acquisition of this car. Perhaps you'll discover that my watch is also a repeater or whatever it is you are looking for.'

'I'm afraid that's quite improbable. But I'm very grateful to you for offering it to me. I can promise you, I'll take good care of it. One can't really use a nineteenth–century watch. But I'll wind it every day. Does the watch function?'

'Perfectly.'

By the time we had dropped Feluda and arrived at the cemetery, it was nearly twelve. Once we had done our job here, we were going to pick up Feluda and go to Nizam's for mutton rolls. This was Feluda's idea, he was going to stand us a treat. But before that we would have to go over to Ripon Lane to return the casket.

There's not much traffic in Park Street around this time. So the cemetery seemed very quiet even in the afternoon. Once inside the gates we yelled for the watchman Baramdeo several times, but got no answer. Who knows where he was? Perhaps conducting the last rites of yet another rat!

We walked down the central path. No matter how much fun I made of Lalmohan Babu, and no matter how much Feluda lectured us about being superstitious, once you were inside this cemetery your courage was bound to drop. It would be one thing if it was just a collection of tombs. But all the trees, the shrubs, the patches of wilderness cluttered it in such a way that the place seemed even more eerie. However, there seemed no reason to carry on the way Lalmohan Babu was in broad daylight. As he advanced he would cast sidelong glances at the marble plaques, and continuously mutter something like a devotional chant. I concentrated hard to make out what it was he was muttering. It was certainly worth hearing.

'Please Mr. Palmer, please Mr. Hamilton, please Madam Smith — don't kill us, let's just finish our work in peace! You've given us a lot, taken a lot, taught us a lot and disciplined us a lot . . . Mr. Campbell, Mr. Adam and — oh dear I can't even pronounce your name dear Sir — please, I beg of you ever so humbly, please stay the way you are . . . dust to dust . . . to dust . . .'

I could not check myself any longer.

'What is all this about dust?'

'My dear Tapesh, we used to read about it in school. Dust thou art to dust thou returnest. All of them are dust.'

'Then what's there to be scared of?'

'Who knows — do the poets always tell you the truth?'

We had just turned left. The tree was still lying on the ground. The earth was dry. And there was a lot of it. A mound of earth around Thomas Godwin's tomb.

'Dust . . . dust . . . dust . . .'

Maybe it was an attempt to gather courage — Lalmohan Babu

went towards the tomb like a robot, muttering this one word. Then I heard him make some inarticulate noises, immediately after which he fell forward, teeth chattering, on the heap of earth, just like a felled tree.

Beyond his feet was the edge of the ditch, almost as deep as a man, and in that ditch there stuck out through the earth, a dead man's skull.

If Lalmohan Babu had not come to after the dozen or so times I shook him, I would have been in real trouble. I was an utter novice at this kind of thing. As he dusted his clothes, the gentleman said that writers have a tendency to pass out easily, particularly when frightened, because their imagination is so much more vivid than others. 'The superstition your cousin talked about is all rubbish. I don't have a drop of superstition in my blood.'

Neither one of us, however, wasted another minute there. We rushed off to Feluda. He had finished his work too. But even if he had not, news like this, I knew, would bring him hotfoot to the cemetery, leaving aside all other work. He inspected the tomb and the hundred–and–fifty–year–old skull peeking out. But even a thorough search all around did not yield anything more than a spade lying about ten feet from the tomb.

The watchman, however, had arrived in the meantime. Apparently, he had gone to the Lower Circular Road crossing where he had some urgent business with his nephew who had a *paan* shop there. He knew nothing about the grave–digging incident. He was convinced that it had all happened last night, and had been done by people who had scaled the walls to get in. With the watchman's help, Feluda filled the hole in fifteen minutes with earth and leaves. Before leaving, he told the watchman not to mention this to anyone.

From the cemetery we drove straight to 14/1 Ripon Lane.

But we had to halt on the stairs. A young man was coming down, a long leather case in his hand. A guitar case. He was perhaps around twenty–five. There is no need to describe him for you can see many like him on Park Street, particularly in the evenings. Chris Godwin was leaving now and probably would not be back till late, after playing at the Blue Fox.

The first floor was not as deathly quiet as it had been yesterday;

234 The Adventures of Feluda

a shouting match seemed to be going on in the sitting room. One voice was familiar; the other was probably that of the gentleman of the second floor. The first voice was raised in abuse, the second made plaintive protestations of innocence. Both seemed to be using the word 'casket' repeatedly.

Feluda went to the verandah and knocked on the door. Instantly, the response came like an explosion: 'Who's there?' The three of us stepped over the threshold. The new person had an yellowish complexion, freckled all over. He was bald, had a couple of gold–filled teeth and seemed to be between sixty and sixty–five. He had been standing with his back to us. Feluda went past him, unwrapped the package he had been carrying, and extended it to Mr. Godwin seated on the sofa.

'I couldn't resist the temptation of taking it yesterday. It's been invaluable for my research.'

Godwin, receiving the casket, was thunderstruck for a moment. Then he burst into loud laughter.

'So, you fooled them! You fooled them! Those fools — those wily cheats! the frauds!' — it was all anger and sarcasm now, and intended for the other man. 'So, Tom Godwin's spirit took away the casket, did he? Is this Tom Godwin's spirit? This gentleman? What do you think? Oh yes, this is the great Mr. Arakis, my second–floor neighbour, whose restless table ruins my evening every Thursday!'

Mr. Arakis had been staring stupidly at the casket; now he looked at Feluda, and just as stupidly he turned away, and started for the door. But he had to stop. Feluda had addressed him by name.

'Mr. Arakis!'

The man looked at Feluda, who said quietly, 'I think one of the items in this casket is still with you.'

'Certainly not!' roared Arakis. 'And how do you know? Marcus, you open that casket and see if everything there is all right.'

Finally we'd got to know Mr. Godwin's first name — and that was the end of the Arkis — Markis puzzle.

Marcus Godwin opened the casket, groped inside, and said rather hesitantly, 'Why Mr. Mitter everything seems to be here all right.'

'Will you take out that snuff–box? The one Charlotte has described in her diary as being studded with emeralds, rubies and sapphires?'

Mr. Godwin took the box out and turned it over in his hands.

'Can you see,' said Feluda, 'that it is a cheap new box which Mr. Arakis wanted to pass off as an antique by painting it black?'

Within five minutes, Mr. Arakis had brought the genuine snuff–box down from upstairs and Mr. Godwin made him swear by the lord that there would be no more table turning on Thursday evenings — or he would call the police. Arakis slunk out of the room like a thief.

'Thank you, Mr. Mitter,' said Marcus Godwin with a sigh of relief.

'Have you any idea how valuable Charlotte Godwin's diaries are?' Feluda asked.

'No, I didn't even know they were in that casket,' said Marcus Godwin. 'But I'll tell you one thing, Mr. Mitter — I have not the slightest curiosity about my forefathers. To tell you the truth, I have no curiosity left about anything any more. The only thing to do is to wait for the end. Apart from that cat, there's nobody I care for. I used to go over to someone's house in the evenings for a game of poker — but the gout has put a stop to that too.'

'Then it's no use asking you any questions?'

'What questions?'

'Your grandfather's father was David, the man whose tomb is in the Lower Circular Road cemetery.'

'Yes.'

'Did David have any brothers or sisters?'

'I don't remember. One of my ancestors did commit suicide. But I don't remember if he was David's brother.'

'David's son, your grandfather, was Andrew then?'

'Yes, he was in the army.'

'Charlotte Godwin mentions a niece. According to my calculations she would have been your grandfather's sister or. . . '

'My grandfather had no siblings.'

'Then cousin.'

'I can't tell you anything about them, Mr. Mitter. I have been losing my memory for quite some time. Besides, members of our families don't stay close to each other like yours. They all go their different ways. It is not like a Bengali joint family, you know.' We were having mutton rolls sitting at Nizam's in front of Society Cinema, when Feluda put a question to Lalmohan Babu.

'What do you make of that fellow Narendra Biswas?'

Lalmohan Babu finished chewing, swallowed and said, 'Seems quite all right. Nice look in his eyes.'

'Yes, I thought so too.'

'But you don't any longer?'

'Well, one can't condemn a person only on the basis of a single fault. But I do feel that gentleman has committed a dreadful crime.'

Both of us stopped eating.

'I discovered today that those two cuttings in his wallet were cut out with a blade from newspapers nearly two centuries old which have been carefully preserved in the National Library reading room. In my opinion, a man should go to prison for this.'

I tried to picture Narendra Babu in the reading room, breathlessly doing this dreadful thing behind the back of the library staff — but failed. It was so hard to look behind the facade of a person.

'You can also call this a disease,' Feluda continued, 'And people who can successfully get away with such immoral acts feel a strange, perverted pleasure. They think they are far more clever than other people and get much gratification out of that. Very sad.'

As he ordered *lassis* after the mutton roll, Feluda also asked for the bill. It was two–thirty by our watches. We had three more hours to kill before we could go to the watch–crazy Mr. Choudhury's house. I knew Feluda would not rest until he had got to the bottom of the Perigal repeater mystery.

'Tell me something — did those adjutant birds come and sit by the windows?'

There was a window overlooking the road beside us. A crow had been sitting there for some time cawing away. Lalmohan Babu was looking at the bird as he put the question.

'Probably not' said Feluda. 'But there are many old paintings that prove that the birds did come and sit on housetops or parapets.'

'Strange — I don't even know what those birds look like.'

'One way of finding out would be to go to the zoo. Otherwise we can go by Corporation Street. The Corporation emblem in front of the Municipal Building has an adjutant bird. I'll show it to you.'

'You still call it Corporation Street?' said Jatayu smiling.

'Oh, well — Surendra Banerjee. . . '

Feluda stopped. The look in his eyes changed. Out came the notebook and he looked at something. And immediately afterwards he started fidgeting because the bill had not arrived. Finally he called out, 'Waiter?' which was not like him at all. Having paid the bill and got into the car, he gave some directions to the driver Haripada Babu. As the car drove into Surendra Banerjee Road, Feluda was trying to make out the house numbers. One of the irksome things about Calcutta is that not all the houses are numbered, 'A little further Haripada Babu. . . Topshe, tell me as soon as you see No. 141.'

It came back to me — 141 S.N.B., Surendranath Banerjee. My heart started hammering.

'There it is — 141 !'

The car stopped. Bourne & Shepherd was written in front. So this was B.S.! We'd found it!

The two of us accompanied Feluda inside. We found we had to take the lift upstairs. As we emerged from the lift on the first floor we found ourselves in a room furnished with couches. One of the staff came towards us.

Feluda was hesitating because the question he had in mind was bound to sound rather silly.

'Er — excuse me — do you have any photographs of Victoria?'

'Victoria Memorial?'

'No, Queen Victoria?'

'Sorry, Sir, you'll only find photos of those who came to India. There's Edward VII — taken when he was the Prince of Wales — George V, the Delhi Darbar . . .'

'We can still get these here?'

'Not prints. But we have the negatives and we can make copies to order. All negatives since 1854 have been preserved.'

'Good heavens! 1854!'

'Bourne & Shepherd, Calcutta, happens to be the second oldest photograph shop in the world.'

'But that means there are thousands of negatives here.'

'Of course. I can show you if you like, Look at that one on the wall — taken from the top of the Monument in 1880.'

I had not noticed it before. A photograph one foot by five. Calcutta a hundred years ago, seen from the top of the Monument. Starting from Dalhousie and Esplanade and going as far north as the eye could see. The churches rose above all other buildings. Not a single high–rise building in sight. You could tell this was a peaceful city.

A look at the negative room made my head whirl. On all four walls were shelves rising from floor to ceiling, each shelf stacked with brown paper boxes. Each box had a label saying what kind of photographs it contained, and the dates.

Feluda wandered about observing the labels carefully for some time. Then he looked at his wristwatch, turned to us and said, 'Why don't you drive around for an hour or so. I have some work here.'

In the lift, Lalmohan Babu said, 'If your brother commands we must obey. That's one man I can't say no to! What a personality! Let's go to Frank Ross.'

We left the car on Surendra Banerjee Road and started walking down Chowringhee towards the Grand. I had no idea what medicine Lalmohan Babu was going to buy — nor did I need to know. Our main purpose was to kill time.

After making our way through the crowd without colliding with any one, Lalmohan Babu said, 'My dear Tapesh — have you any inkling of your cousin's plans?'

I had to tell him no, but I could guess that someone other than Feluda had been reading Charlotte Godwin's diaries, and that there was some connection between that and the hole dug in the cemetery.

'Did you know that even after being buried underground for two hundred years, the skeleton remains intact?' Jatayu asked me.

Feluda had once told me a story about Job Charnock's body — which I now told Lalmohan Babu. Two hundred years after Charnock's death one of the priests at St. John's Church suddenly began wondering if his tomb really housed his remains, or whether it was just an edifice erected in his memory. The suspicion became such an obsession that the priest finally got some people to dig up the grave. There was no sign of any remains even up to four feet underground. But two more feet down, a skeleton's arm suddenly came to light. The priest promptly had the hole covered up.

Just as Lalmohan Babu, standing in front of the counter at Frank Ross was saying 'One Forhans, family–size please,' I noticed a known face entering the shop. He did not recognise us immediately. Two or three times he looked at us before he smiled. It was Narendra Babu's brother Girindra Babu. He was carrying a huge box which said Hong Kong Dry–cleaners.

'I've come to get my brother's medicines,' he told us.

'How is Narendra Babu?' asked Jatayu.

'Better. By the way — apparently the other gentleman with you that day was the investigator Prodosh Mitter? My brother told me. I'd heard of him before. And I was wondering if. . .'

Girindra Babu frowned and seemed lost in reverie. Then he asked, 'When can one find him at home?'

'That's rather hard to say,' I said. 'But his number's listed in the directory. You can call before you come.'

'Hm . . . I have some. . . very well, I'll call him. Please tell Prodosh Babu I may need to consult him.'

We took a turn around New Market, walked along Moti Seal Street and came out on Surendra Banerjee Road. As we came up to Bourne and Shepherd, we found Feluda standing next to the car. His work had taken less time than he had anticipated. I told him about our meeting with Girindra Babu.

'Indeed?' he said. 'And what did that gentleman have to say?'

I knew it was never any use giving Feluda vague reports. So I gave him a detailed account of .our conversation, I even mentioned the box of laundry in his hand. Feluda heard me out in silence.

'How did your work go?' asked Lalmohan Babu.

'First class,' said Feluda. 'The place is a positive gold mine. I also managed a telephone call from there, and found that Mr. Choudhury has returned home. He's given us a firm appointment. The gentleman has a voice as smooth as velvet.'

I'd heard many chiming clocks before. But the kind of strange notes that came from one clock after another as we stepped into Mahadeb Choudhury's house was an utterly new experience for me.

'This seems like going through the gates of heaven, my dear Sir!' said Lalmohan Babu, 'Divine chiming — what an unbelievable receptionist!'

Of course we did not find our host as soon as we entered. Someone who seemed to be a staff member came and told us that Mr. Choudhury was busy and had asked us to wait a little. We were taken to a small office room. Even in this tiny chamber there were two fancy clocks — one on the wall and one on top of the bookshelf.

Now that the chiming of the clocks had stopped, the house seemed oppressive. It was a huge, modern house. You could see your face reflected in the marble floors below.

From time to time, a voice came to us from within the house. Feluda told us this was Mahadeb Choudhury's voice. I could not be too sure about any resemblance to velvet from where we sat. But I soon found out, that when raised, the voice had nothing in common with velvet.

Mahadeb Choudhury was shouting at someone. The three of us eavesdropped, almost breathlessly, and almost against our better instincts. The other person did not raise his voice, so we could not make out his words. The conversation was in English. There was Choudhury again — 'I never give an advance in matters like these. I only gave it to you because you really begged for it — and now you have the nerve to tell me you've spent that money! I don't believe a word you say. Nor can I see why such a small job should require so much money. Anyway, I'll give you some more — but I want the goods in two days flat. No more excuses — understand?'

Silence for a while. Then the sound of footsteps going towards the front door. Within another minute the employee came into our room.

'Please come with me.'

From the top of his head to the tip of his shoes — velvet smoothness marked Mr. Choudhury's appearance. He must have had the habit of shaving twice a day. How else could a man's face look so smooth at six o'clock in the evening? (Lalmohan Babu commented later that even a fly would have a hard time not to slide off that smooth cheek) And the enormous sitting room we were in was just as polished as Mr. Choudhury himself. It did not seem possible that there could be a speck of dust in any of the corners, or a single ant or cockroach.

Mr. Choudhury inhaled from a cigarette stuck in a gold holder, blew out smoke and directed his question to Feluda.

'Well, have you brought the clock?'

'Clock? What clock do you mean?' he asked.

'I thought you said you wanted to meet me in connection with a clock. I assume you are calling because you have seen my ad.'

'Please forgive me, Mr. Choudhury. But I haven't seen your ad. I need to find out certain facts, and they are probably connected with a clock. I heard somewhere that you are an expert on clocks. So. . . '

The velvet showed signs of crinkling. The gentleman moved in his chair with some irritation, saying, 'I don't have much time, Mr. Mitter. I shall be leaving town shortly. Please be brief.'

'I only want to know what a Perigal repeater is.'

The velvet suddenly turned to stone. The cigarette holder froze near the mouth. The pupils were absolutely still, the eyes staring unblinkingly at Feluda.

'How did you hear about it?'

'I read about it in a nineteenth–century English novel.'

I had noticed before too with what ease Feluda can lie when it helps his work.

'I looked up repeater in the dictionary and found that it can be a clock or a gun. But nobody seems to know anything about Perigal.'

Mahadeb Choudhury was still staring at Feluda. In his next

question there was a sharp edge under the smoothness of velvet.

'Do you always barge into the homes of strangers to find out the meaning of unknown words?'

'If it is necessary, yes.'

I thought the gentleman would now ask what the necessity in this case was. But instead, he continued to stare unwaveringly at Feluda, and his next words made my heart beat to the ticking of the clock sitting on the table at my right.

'You are a detective, aren't you?'

You had to admire Feluda's nerve. He might have paused all of five seconds to answer, but when he did speak, his voice too was velvet.

'I see you are well informed.'

'I have to be, Mr. Mitter. I employ people to gather information.'

'Perhaps you have forgotten my question. Or perhaps you don't have the answer. Or you may not want to tell me the answer, even if you know it. In that case, I'll take my leave. I don't want to waste your time unnecessarily.'

'Sit down, Mr. Mitter.'

Feluda had got up — which was why this command came. Lalmohan Babu looked like he was in no state to get up by himself. He would have to be helped up.

'Sit down, please.'

Feluda sat again.

'Repeater can mean a gun,' said Mahadeb Choudhury, 'But if you add the name Perigal to it, it becomes a timepiece. A pocket watch. Francis Perigal. Englishman. Towards the end of the eighteenth century, there were very few watchmakers in the world who were the equals of Francis Perigal. Two hundred years ago, it was England that produced the best watches, not Switzerland.'

'How much could a Perigal repeater cost today?'

'I don't think it would be within your means, Mr. Mitter.'

'I know.'

'But it is within mine.'

'I know that too.'

'Then why ask the price?'

'Curiosity.'

'Not to be satisfied.' .

Mr. Choudhury took a final puff from his cigarette, took it out of the holder, dropped it in the glass ash–tray beside him, and rose from the couch.

'Now that you've found out all you wanted to know,' said Choudhury, 'I think you should leave. And the only Perigal repeater which exists in Calcutta will come to me, not to you. Pyarelal!'

An employee appeared — the same one who had showed us into the office room. We got up. As we left the room, the velvet tones were heard again.

'I also have the other kind of repeater in my possession, Mr. Mitter but the sound it makes is not half as musical as the chimes of a clock.' 'It seems that this is the hero of your current adventure' said Jatayu.

We were returning from Alipore Park. The car windows had had to be rolled up because of the rain which had started as soon as we hit Judges Court Road.

Feluda did not answer Lalmohan Babu but sat looking out of the car window. Lalmohan Babu finds it impossible to keep quiet for any length of time. 'I know I should call him the villain rather than the hero,' he continued,' 'but you've always told us that everyone is a villain in a crime story as long as there is cause for suspicion — so I did not use that word. Though I must say that I still cannot figure out why I should suspect anyone. Is grave–digging a crime?'

Seeing that Feluda refused to answer any of his questions, Lalmohan Babu lost patience and said. 'My dear Sir, you look you've totally lost heart! Think of what that will do to us. As it is, that gentleman's manner and appearance are enough to give one the creeps. Then the chimes from all those clocks. On top of that, you're looking grim, it's raining outside, roads are full of potholes . . .'

'You're wrong, Mr. Ganguly. I haven't lost heart, not at all. Does one lose heart at finding a way through a tortuous maze? On the contrary.'

'You mean you've found the way?'

'Yes, I have. But I still don't know what lies at the end of the road. It is a road with many twists and turns. The end will come in sight only after we have progressed some more.' The drizzle continued even after we had returned home. Lalmohan Babu left us saying he would early next morning. 'This is one case Felu Babu, where I am your one hope. Just think of how much time you would waste if you had to use public transport!'

This afternoon, as we had sat at Nizam's, I had noticed Feluda scribbling in his notebook. When I went to his room in the evening after dinner, I found out what the scribbles were. Not that he had asked me to come; but I couldn't help feeling concerned about him. Ever since I had laid eyes on Mahadeb Choudhury and heard him speak, I had been feeling anxious. Somehow, every time I recalled that man's face, my heart beat faster. Hero or villain, whatever Lalmohan Babu might choose to call him, to me he was a terrifying figure. His appearance might have been velvety soft, but I knew that inside was the thorny wilderness of the Thar desert.

Feluda, however, did not seem to be suffering from any anxiety at all. He sat there, the notebook open in front of him, looking at a diagram with total absorption. As I entered he said, 'Look, here are all the branches,' and pushed the notebook in my direction. I have reproduced below what was written there.

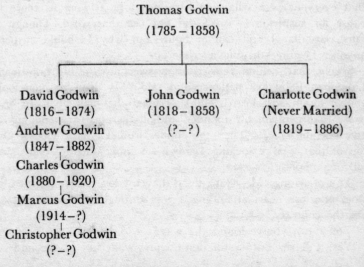

Thomas Godwin

(1785 – 1858)

David Godwin
(1816 – 1874)
Andrew Godwin
(1847 – 1882)
Charles Godwin
(1880 – 1920)
Marcus Godwin
(1914 – ?)
Christopher Godwin
(? – ?)

John Godwin
(1818 – 1858)
(? – ?)

Charlotte Godwin
(Never Married)
(1819 – 1886)

'Don't you think the right side looks rather empty?' said Feluda.

'But it's bound to, I said, Charlotte never married.'

'The problem is not Charlotte; it is this fellow John. That is the other branch of this family which is still hidden from us. Of course there's one thing which, so far, I have seen the wrong side up. It may cast some light on this matter when I get to see it right side up. That will be tomorrow morning.'

This was a typical Feluda riddle. And I knew that when he spoke in riddles he did so deliberately.

The rain had stopped in the course of our conversation. I was surprised to see Feluda suddenly get up in a hurry.

'Don't tell me you're going out?' I said.

'Yes Sir.'

'Where to?'

'On duty.'

'What duty?'

'Guard duty.'

I had not noticed before, that Feluda had brought out his hunting boots. Every time I see them, my spine tingles, because those boots are connected with every major case he has investigated. And nothing was more suitable for a midnight ramble in a graveyard.

'You're going to the cemetery,' I said huskily.

'Where else?'

'Alone?'

'Don't worry, I have a friend. My repeater.'

Feluda took his Colt .32 out of the wardrobe and put it in his pocket. I did not like the look of things at all.

'But what else do you expect will happen there?' I said. 'The grave has already been dug up. If the fellow has found the watch he's taken it with him.'

'No, the person or persons engaged in digging ran for their lives as soon as the skull became visible. Otherwise, they would not have left that spade there. They would either have taken it, or hidden it.'

This had never occurred to me.

I have no idea when Feluda got back. When I came downstairs his door was locked. It was a quarter–past–seven. I realised he was catching up on his sleep, after two sleepless nights.

He opened the door at nine. Spruce, shaven, no sign of exhaustion in his face or eyes. With a gesture of his thumb he let me know that nothing had happened the night before.

Jatayu arrived at nine–thirty.

'See if you like it.'

As promised, Jatayu had brought his grandfather's watch. A silver pocket watch with a silver chain.

'Splendid!' said Feluda taking the watch in his hands. 'Cooke–Kelvey had quite a reputation at one time.'

'Yes, but it's not that watch!' said Lalmohan Babu regretfully.' 'This, after all, is only a watch made in Calcutta.'

'But do you really mean to give this to me?'

'With my blessings and my compliments, I am three–and–a–half years older than you. So you should have no objections to receiving blessings from me!'

Feluda wrapped the watch in his handkerchief and went to the telephone. But before he could dial, the knocker on the front door sounded.

I opened the door and saw Girindra Babu. Though he had thrown out some hints yesterday, I could never have guessed that he would really turn up, and that too, so soon. We could see from his clothes that he was out on business — jacket, trousers, briefcase in hand.

'I dialled for ten minutes and couldn't get through. I hope you don't mind.' The gentleman seemed restless, nervous.

'There's nothing to mind. The telephone is as good as non–functional. What's up?'

Our guest sat on a chair instead of on the sofa. Jatayu and

I were on the divan and Feluda was on the sofa.

'I couldn't make up my mind where to go,' said Girindra Biswas mopping his forehead with a handkerchief. 'I don't have much faith in the police, to be quite frank. Since you happened to arrive on the scene anyway . . .'

'What's your problem?'

Girindra Babu cleared his throat. Then he said, 'My brother was not injured by a falling tree.'

The three of us were silent. Our guest too kept quiet after that statement.

'Then?' said Feluda at last.

'An attempt was made to murder him by hitting him on the head.'

Feluda calmly offered his packet of Charminar to the gentleman, who refused. Feluda then took one himself, saying, 'But your brother himself said it was a tree that hit him.'

'That's because my brother would die rather than accuse his son.'

'Son?'

'Yes, Proshanto, the older one. The younger one is in Britain.'

'What does this Proshanto do?'

'What does he not do? Every kind of nefarious activity. He's become like this over the last three or four years. My brother has made a will giving equal shares to the sons. My sister–in–law died in 1970. About a month ago, my brother got really annoyed at Proshanto's doings and threatened to disinherit him, and transfer his share to Sushanto.'

'Does Proshanto live in your house?'

'He certainly has the right. There's a room set aside for him. But he's never there. Hard to tell where he might be. He has a gang — the worst kind of thugs. It's my belief that he really would have killed my brother if that terrible storm hadn't started.'

'But what does your brother say about this?'

'He says it was the tree. Even after knowing everything, he still can't accept the fact that his son is responsible for the injury on his head. But whatever my brother might say, I'm telling you, if some steps are not taken, this boy — though he may be my own nephew — will make further attempts at murder.'

'If Narendra Babu makes a new will, then his son won't gain anything by murdering him, will he?'

'Financial gain is not always the only motive, Mr. Mitter. The boy could kill in a fit of rage. Don't people commit murder by way of revenge? Besides, my brother will never change his will. He has no sense of perspective. You have no idea how besotted a man can be with paternal love. These last few days I've been home. But today I have to go out of town for two or three days on business. That's why I have come to you. If you can think of . . .'

'Mr. Biswas,' said Feluda dropping almost an inch of ash into the ashtray. 'I regret to inform you that I have become involved in another investigation. Of course, steps should be taken for your brother's protection. But if he insists he was injured by a tree, that no one tried to kill him — then there's not a thing the police can do.'

Girindra Babu took his leave, having ruined our pleasure in the first sunny morning in days.

'Extraordinary!' said Feluda leaving the sofa and dialling a number.

'Hullo, Suhrid? This is Felu here . . .'

I knew that Suhrid Sengupta had been at college with Feluda.

'Listen — I once saw the centenary volume of the Presidency College magazine at your place — I think it was your brother's copy — published in '55, as far as I recall — do you still have it? . . . Oh good, leave it with your servant when you go out. I'll come around ten and pick it up.'

We finished our tea and set off. Feluda wanted to stop at three places — Narendra Biswas's, Bourne and Shepherd and the Park Street cemetery. I was somewhat surprised to hear him mention Narendra Babu. But Feluda said, 'Whatever I may have said to Girindra Babu, I can't dismiss his words idly. So I have to go once. You two need not come to my third stop now, but I think I'll take you along for tonight's guard duty. Not to feel the dead–of–night atmosphere in a graveyard is to be deprived of an extraordinary experience.'

Narendra Babu seemed much better physically. His aches and pains had almost disappeared, he said, and the bandages were due to come off any day — but there was something I did not like about the way he looked. Almost a withered, melancholic expression.

'I won't take up much of your time — I just want to ask you a couple of questions,' said Feluda.

The gentleman looked at Feluda distrustfully and said, 'Excuse me — but are you actually conducting a case? I'm asking because I know you are a detective.'

'You're quite right,' said Feluda, 'And it would help me enormously if you didn't try to hide the truth.'

The gentleman closed his eyes, the way people do in an attempt to tolerate pain. He seemed to have guessed that Feluda's cross–examination would be painful for him.

'Immediately after you regained consciousness in the hospital, you mentioned a will,' said Feluda.

Narendra Babu's eyes remained closed.

'Can you tell us why you mentioned the will?'

This time Narendra Biswas opened his eyes. His lips moved, trembled, and the words came.

'Surely I'm not bound to answer your questions?'

'Of course not.'

'Then I won't.'

Feluda was silent for a few moments. All of us were silent. Narendra Babu had turned away.

'Very well, I'll ask you something else,' said Feluda.

'But I have the right to decide whether or not to answer.'

'Most certainly.'

'Go ahead.'

'Who's Victoria?'

'Vic — toria?'

'Yes, I should confess I've done something unethical. I looked at the papers in your wallet. There was a slip inside saying. . . '

'Oh — ha! ha! ha!' the gentleman startled us by bursting into laughter. ' That is ancient history my dear Sir! I'd forgotten all about it. It happened when I was still working. We had an Anglo – Indian in our office — Norton — Jimmy Norton. Said he had a whole bundle of letters written by his grandmother. I never got to see those letters though. Apparently, this grandmother was in Bahrampur during the Mutiny — she must have been five or six years old then. The letters were written much later, but they contain an account of her childhood. You know how everybody seems to be writing about these things today. That's why I told Norton I'd give him the names of some foreign publishers. He himself had no experience on these lines. Wait a second — let me get that piece of paper.'

Narendra Babu extended his left arm, opened the drawer and took the slip out of his wallet.

'Yes, here it is — Bourne & Shepherd. What I had meant to tell him was to go over there and see if there was a picture of his grandmother's. And here are the initials of all the publishers. I never got around to giving him this slip. For Norton got jaundice. He was under treatment for about six weeks, and then he quit the job.'

Feluda got up.

'Very well, Mr. Biswas — but I can't help expressing regret over one thing.'

'What's that?'

'In future, do please refrain from tearing or cutting out pieces from books or newspapers in a library. This is my request. Goodbye.'

As we went out of the room, the gentleman could not bring himself even to look our way.

At Suhrid Sengupta's house on Beninandan Street, the servant brought Feluda a huge book. The centenary volume of the Presidency College magazine. Why Feluda should have pored over it all the way, and muttered 'Just think of it!' several times — was entirely beyond me.

He spent ten minutes at Bourne & Shepherd and came out carrying a large red envelope. One could see there were photographs inside.

'Whose pictures have you got there?' asked Lalmohan Babu.

'The Mutiny,' answered Feluda. Lalmohan Babu and I exchanged glances. Feluda had made it clear that the pictures were not meant for us, the public.

'I won't drag you inside the cemetery now. Just want to check if everything is all right.'

We had the car turned around and parked in front of the cemetery. As Feluda entered the gates, I saw the watchman Baramdeo saluting.

Within ten minutes Feluda was back, saying 'Okay' as he got into the car. It was decided that we would come back at ten–thirty in the evening.

My instincts told me we were very close to the final act of this drama.

CHAPTER 11

I have travelled to so many places with Feluda, on the trail of mysteries — Sikkim, Lucknow, Rajasthan, Simla, Banaras — and nowhere has there been any dearth of adventure. But I could never have dreamt that we would get enmeshed in such a chilling mystery right here, in the heart of Calcutta. Today's happenings in particular, we could never have anticipated. Black–letter day — Lalmohan Babu christened it — but later he changed it to black–letter–night.

'Have we ever been in such a fix before, my dear Tapesh?' he asked me.

And I have to admit, I couldn't think of any other occasion like this one.

Lalmohan Babu was habitually punctual; with the acquisition of a car, he was maintaining military punctuality. Normally he would rattle the knocker — but this evening he tapped on the door. The two of us had had dinner and were waiting for him. I too had put on my hunting boots. Mine had been bought last year, Feluda's were eleven years old. Probably they were not in very good shape — I had seen him mending the sole himself, in the afternoon. But now he was limping slightly — and I wished he had got hold of a cobbler to do the job properly. Surely he could not afford to limp on a night of danger like this one?

As soon as we heard the tapping we got up to go. Feluda had a brown leather satchel hanging from his shoulder, from which peeped the red envelope. I should mention here that all of us were wearing dark clothes tonight, according to Feluda's instructions. Lalmohan babu was wearing a black suit.

As soon as he entered, the gentleman said, 'Have you any idea about the heights reached by modern medicine? There's this new nerve–pill on the market — it even has two 'X' in the name — I took one after dinner as suggested by Dr. Bhaben. And

would you believe it, already my whole body feels electrified!
My dear Tapesh, we'll fight to the end, come what may, eh?'
What he was going to fight was something that Lalmohan Babu
knew as little about as I did.

Feluda had decided earlier that the car would have to be
parked at some distance from the cemetery gates.

'I wouldn't worry so much if the colour of the car matched
your suit.' Past St. Xavier's and a short distance from the Rawdon
Street crossing, Feluda told the driver to stop.

'Why don't you go ahead,' he said getting out of the car,'I'll
follow after I've given Haripada some instructions.'

We obeyed. I don't know what those instructions were. But
this I know that Haripada Babu, after having seen us in action
over the last few days, and having listened to our conversations,
was raring to go himself. His manner and expression showed
that clearly.

Within a few minutes Feluda had joined us. 'You're lucky Mr.
Ganguly,' he said, 'that you've found a driver like this one. One
can give him a responsible job and not have to worry about it.'

'What responsible job?'

'None, if there's no trouble here. But if there is, we have to
depend on him quite a bit.'

More than that Feluda would not tell us.

When we reached the iron gates we found them wide open.
When I asked Feluda about this in a whisper, he whispered
back that normally the gates were closed at this time, but today
he had made special arrangements. 'There are bits of broken
glass set on top of the wall — it would be difficult for us to
scale it. So I had to make alternative plans. But is that fellow
Baramdeo around?'

There was a dim light in the watchman's room, but it did
not look like anyone was there. We took a look around the place.
There was no one in sight. I could see Feluda frowning in the
pale light reaching us from Park Street. Obviously his arrangements
with the watchman had included the latter's presence here.

We went ahead. But not down that central path tonight. After
a few steps along that path, Feluda turned left. We started
making our way through the crowd of tombs. There was a strong

breeze tonight, patchy clouds were floating in the sky. The half–moon would peep through those clouds one moment and hide the next. In that fitful moonlight the names on the marble plaques flashed and disappeared from moment to moment. The same erratic light showed us that we were taking shelter under the overhang of the tomb of Samuel Cuthbert Thornhill. This was no tapering obelisk. This had a pedestal from which rose pillars topped by a dome. Three people could stay concealed here quite easily. No light reached this spot, but the advantage was that, if you looked through the gaps between the tombs, you could see a portion of the iron gates.

Assuming that there was no one besides ourselves in the cemetery now, Feluda spoke; but he did not raise his voice.

'Sprinkle a few drops of this all around, will you?'

He had taken a capped bottle from his satchel and was holding it out to Lalmohan Babu.

'S — sprinkle?'

'Carbolic acid. It will keep the snakes away. Just sprinkle it all round over a radius of four feet. That should be enough.'

Lalmohan Babu obeyed and was back in a minute, saying, 'Good, now we can rest in peace. Even a nerve–pill cannot remove the fear of snakes.'

'Have you lost your fear of spooks?'

'Totally.'

We could hear the frogs croaking and the crickets droning. One of those crickets must have made its home in the tomb next to ours. The darkness would periodically thicken, probably because some of the moving clouds were heavier than others. At those moments the tombs would all get lumped together and nothing but a mass of darkness would be visible. And then, as the moon emerged, and cast its light on one side of the sepulchres, they would recover separate identities again.

Feluda took a pack of Chiclets out of his pocket, gave us one each and put two into his mouth.

The sound of traffic was growing less and less. I started counting the seconds — one, two, three — and discovered that for half-a-minute we had heard no sound other than the frogs, the crickets and the rustle of leaves in the gusty breeze.

'Midnight,' said Lalmohan Babu in suppressed tones.

Why was he saying midnight? Just two minute ago I had put out my arm to catch the moonlight on my wristwatch and the time had been eleven twenty–five. When asked, he said, 'Oh I just said it! After all midnight has a special, you know . . . !'

'Special what?'

'Well — it's midnight in a cemetery after all! There's something about it. I've read about it somewhere.'

'You mean that's when the ghosts come out?'

Lalmohan Babu made noises which sounded like 'ex', concluded the last 'ex' with a prolonged hiss, and lapsed into silence. I heard a hardly audible scratch beside me and knew that Feluda had lit a match under cover of his palm. Still using his hand as cover, he lit a Charminar, took a puff, and let out smoke.

The clouds were gathering in the sky. No more sound of traffic. Not even the sound of the breeze. All stir, all sound seemed to have come to an end. Even the cricket close to us had piped down. I felt cold, my throat was dry. I licked my lips but could not wet them.

An owl screeched suddenly. From the sound of two slaps I gathered that Lalmohan Babu clapped his hands over his ears. Feluda slowly got up.

A car had come to a halt. It was impossible to gauge its distance so late at night. Then came the sound of car–doors closing. My hunch was that the sound had not come from the north, the Park Street side. It was from the west, Rawdon Street. On that side there was no gate, only the wall, but there were bits of jagged glass set on the top of that wall.

Even so, we continued to stare at the iron gates. Lalmohan Babu was about to speak. But Feluda put out his arm over my shoulder, pressed him on the shoulder and stopped him.

But nobody seemed to be coming in through the gates.

Maybe it was some other car which had stopped for some other reason. There were so many houses all around. Maybe someone had just come home from the night show. I hoped so; then there would be no reason to worry about this car.

Feluda, however, was still standing upright his back pressed against the wall. In front of him was one of the pillars. All around was darkness, black as pitch. It was impossible for anyone to see us.

But how were we to see them? What if they had come?

No, it was not necessary to see them. I realised that very soon. We did not need our eyes. The ears would serve.

There it was — the sound of digging. It went on for some time. We listened breathlessly. It stopped.

There was a light. In the distance. Reflected light falling on the grass between two obelisks in the distance.

The light was not steady — it swayed and moved. Light from a torch.

Then it was switched off.

'They've scaled the walls,' said Feluda through his teeth. 'We'll follow them.' I gathered he was waiting for the sound of the car again.

One more minute.

Then two, three, four minutes.

'Strange,' said Feluda.

Not a sound was coming from Park Street. Nothing from Rawdon Street either. The car which had come must still be waiting. What then?

Two more minutes went by. The clouds broke again and the moon came out. There was nobody there.

'Here, hold this.'

Feluda gave me his satchel and stepped down on to the grass. He went in the direction of the light. Nothing to fear — he had the Colt. 32 in his pocket. My instincts said very soon the roar of the gun would shatter the congealed silence of this cemetery to pieces. But he was limping! Slightly, but still limping. I wished to God he had not tried to mend his boots himself.

But where was the roar of the Colt?

'Mistake,' said Jatayu hoarsely, 'Your cousin has made a terrible mistake.'

I made a hissing sound with my tongue to stop him from speaking any more. Feluda had disappeared in the dark after the first few footsteps. I could not fathom what was going on among all those obelisks. Was that a sound from there? Surely not — my ears must be playing me tricks.

Midnight? What chimes were these? St. Paul's? The breeze came from that direction. If the wind was westernly we could hear the roaring of lions in the Alipore Zoo from our Ballygunge house.

There it was — the sound of the car at last!

The doors closed. The car started. Then came the sound of it speeding away.

I could not wait any longer. Not just fear this time, but acute anxiety.

Both of us got up. I was determined not to listen to Lalmohan Babu's mutterings this time; there was no time for that.

We went forward hastily. The tomb of Mary Ellis. We had to feel our way with our hands against the tombs. Jatayu was clutching my shirt from behind. The grass underfoot was still wet and cold.

The tombs of John Martin, Cynthia Colette, Captain Evans. Another obelisk. On the black marble plaque. . .

I had suddenly stepped on something — it got squashed with a soft noise. I moved my foot and looked downwards. There was enough moonlight to see. I picked up the object.

A packet of Charminars.

Not empty though. There were quite a few cigarettes inside. Feluda.

I remember nothing more — nothing except a hand pressing down on my mouth and a stifled scream from Lalmohan Babu.

CHAPTER 12

The first thing I thought as soon as I came to, was that I was on the beach at Puri. You could get this kind of breeze only near the sea. My ears were cold, my nose was cold, my hair was flying.

But where was the water? The sand? waves? This was not the roaring of waves; it was the noise of a moving car. We were speeding down an empty street through the darkness. I was on the back seat. There was myself in the middle, Lalmohan Babu on my right and a man I had never seen on my left. The driver in front wore a turban. There was another man sitting beside him. No one spoke.

As soon as I raised my head a little, the man beside the driver turned his head to look at me. He looked like a ruffian. But he didn't try to intimidate me. Why should he? He had no reason to fear us. We had no weapons. Our only weapon was with Feluda. And he was not in this car. I had no idea where he was.

But wasn't that his satchel?

Behind me on the shelf in front of the back window. The strap was hanging down to my cheek.

'Midnight,' said Jatayu suddenly. I looked sideways at him and saw that his eyes were still closed.

'Midnight . . . midnight . . .'

'Shut up!' said the man beside me threateningly.

We lapsed into a doze again, The sound of the car was fading . . .

The next time I opened my eyes I was almost sure I was inside a temple. No, not a temple — a church. For these were not our native brass bells. They sounded foreign.

But I discovered this was no temple. It was a sitting room. There was a chandelier overhead, but it had not been lit. There was very little light in the room — only one lamp. It was placed on a table beside a velvet upholstered sofa. I too was sitting on a velvet sofa. Not sitting really, half reclining. Next to me was Lalmohan Babu. His eyes were closed. To my right, on another sofa, sat Feluda. He looked grave. The right side of his forehead was swollen. To our left facing us, stood a man whom we knew as Pyarelal. In his hand was a revolver, a Colt .32. Definitely Feluda's.

Three other people stood looking at us. None of them were speaking. Probably the man who would do the talking had not arrived yet. For the largest sofa in front of us, the one upholstered in black velvet, was empty. It looked like it was waiting for someone. Most probably Mr. Choudhury. But this was no modern house in Alipore. This was an ancient building. The ceiling was twenty feet high, the beams were made of iron. A horse could walk in through those doors.

And there were other things too — clocks. Hanging clocks and standing clocks. One of them to my right was more than the height of a man. It was these clocks that had been chiming a little while back. Some of them were still going on. It was two in the morning.

I had met Feluda's eyes only once so far. It was the message in his eyes that had given me some confidence. His eyes said, 'Don't worry, I'm still here.'

'Good morning, Mr. Mitter!'

I had not noticed the gentleman because he had made his entrance through the door behind the lamp. He was still smooth as velvet, even more so than the last time we had seen him. There was no reason to be otherwise. For at this moment he was up, Feluda was down.

'What is in there Pyarelal? Have you done a proper search?'

The gentleman's eyes had come to rest on Feluda's satchel. I did not know how and when it had made its way back to Feluda.

Pyarelal reported that it contained nothing except books, notebooks and photographs. There had been a bottle, but that had been removed.

'Please don't mind my capturing you and bringing you here like this,' said Mr. Choudhury, addressing Feluda with an extra bit of polish in his tone. 'But I thought since you have such an interest in the Perigal repeater, it would give you a lot of pleasure to be present at the time when the object came into my possession. Balwant! Have they finished cleaning the watch?'

One of the servants nodded, saying that the watch was almost done, it would be brought in any minute.

'It has been lying in a grave for two hundred years,' said Mr. Choudhury. William did not tell me all this before. He just said he had a Perigal repeater. And then he has been dilly-dallying about bringing it. When I finally pressed him he confessed that it was buried underground, that's why it would take time to get it out. The thing has been lying next to a corpse. So I've told them not to bring it to me without cleaning it with brush and duster. I've even told them to rub it with Dettol.'

Feluda was staring levelly at Mr. Choudhury. It was impossible to read the feelings behind that face. They had used chloroform to knock us out but he had been hit on the head.

'How did you learn about this watch, Mr. Mitter?' asked Mahadeb Choudhury.

'From a nineteenth-century diary. It belonged to the daughter of the owner of the watch.'

'Diary? Not a letter?'

'No, a diary.'

Mr. Choudhury had taken out his packet of foreign cigarettes together with his gold lighter and gold cigarette holder.

'You mean you don't know William?' Choudhury was inserting the cigarette into the holder.

'I don't know anyone called William.'

With a flash, Choudhury's Dunhill lighter flared.

'So, it was reading that diary that made you want to possess that watch?'

'The desire for possession is your monopoly, Mr. Choudhury.'

An ominous shadow clouded the velvet presence. The cigarette holder was trembling slightly between the two fingers.

'You'd better watch your tongue, Mr. Mitter!'

'I never watch my tongue when it comes to the truth, Mr. Choudhury. My objective was to see that the watch remained in Godwin's grave as before. In the hands of people like you . . .'

But Feluda could not finish. A man came in and handed something to Mr. Choudhury on a silk handkerchief. The moment

Choudhury picked this object up, a groaning noise came from beside me.

'Mi . . . mi . . .'

Lalmohan Babu had regained his senses, and had noticed the object in Mr. Choudhury's hands. It was something he was very familiar with.

It is impossible for me to convey in writing the expression on Mr. Choudhury's face. It is Feluda who had once told me that the seven notes in an octave or the seven colours of a rainbow are all related to each other. But it was beyond my wildest imagination that there could be such an instant play of seven shades in one face. The abuse that came out of his mouth was unfit to hear, to utter, to write. Feluda, of course, was quite impervious to all this. I now realised that he had engineered this himself. He had done it when he spent those ten minutes in the cemetery yesterday afternoon. But had the real watch disappeared into thin air?

Like a madman, Mr. Choudhury flung the Cooke–Kelvey watch at the empty sofa to his right. And the very next moment he roared.

'Fetch William here! And give me that revolver!'

Pyarelal handed the revolver to Choudhury and left the room. After saying 'Scoundrel', 'Swindler' and a few other choice epithets, Choudhury rose from the sofa and started pacing up and down impatiently.

Now Pyarelal came in through the back door accompanied by another man. In the shadowy darkness I could make out his shoulder–length hair and the moustache drooping on both sides of his mouth. He wore trousers and shirt, and a cotton jacket.

'What kind of a watch have you brought me after all your grave – digging?' asked Mr. Choudhury in a thunderous voice. He had gone back to sit on the sofa, the revolver still in his hand, his eyes on Feluda.

'I brought what I found Mr. Choudhury,' said the newcomer in a plaintive voice. 'How can I get away with trying to hoodwink you — a great expert like you, Sir!'

'Did that letter contain a lie then?' asked Mahadeb Choudhury in a voice that rocked the room.

'How can I possibly tell? It was the one thing I was depending upon. Here is the letter — just take a look.'

The newcomer took out an old letter and handed it to Mr. Choudhury. The latter glanced over it and threw it on the sofa with a look of disgust. And that was when Feluda broke into laughter. Candid, hearty laughter. I had not seen him laugh like this for many days now.

'What's so amusing, Mr. Mitter?' barked Mahadeb Choudhury.

Feluda suppressed his laughter with some effort, and said, 'I couldn't help it, Mr. Choudhury — so much drama, and all for nothing.'

Mr. Choudhury, revolver in hand, left the sofa again and walked silently across the thick carpet to Feluda.

'Do you think the drama is over, Mr. Mitter? How can I be sure that you haven't got the real watch yourself? You've gone to the cemetery many times. Even tonight, you were there, ahead of William. Do you think I'll stop before I've taken that watch from you? You'll have to get it out yourself, from whatever hiding place you have put it in. And even if the watch does not exist — let's assume this letter does not tell the truth — how can you think I'll let you go? This habit of yours, of poking your nose into everything is much too inconvenient for me, Mr. Mitter. So why do you say the drama is over? It's just beginning.'

Now, at last, a very familiar note sounded in Feluda's voice. He always uses it at the moment of dramatic climax. Lalmohan Babu says it reminds him of Tibetan horns.

'You are quite wrong, Mr. Choudhury. The ball is now in my court, not yours. From this moment, I am the director, I am the one who will judge who is more to blame between the two of you — you, or the man who goes under the name of William . . .'

An upheaval in the room. With a gigantic leap, and having felled Pyarelal, who stood in his way, with a murderous fist, William was racing towards the front door. Choudhury's bullet missed him by a couple of feet and shattered to smithereens the dial of a clock standing to the left of the door. The damaged clock started chiming suddenly, startling all of us.

Two other men were chasing William; but they could not go very far. They were being obstructed by several armed men who now entered the sitting room together with William and the other two. The man in front was obviously a police inspector. With him were five other constables, and behind them, peering eagerly, was Lalmohan Babu's driver Haripada Datta.

'Bravo, Haripada Babu,' said Feluda.

'So you are Felu Mitter?' the Inspector was directing his question to the right person. 'Do tell me what's going on here. I know Mr. Choudhury all right — but who's this, the man who was making his escape?'

Before answering, Feluda took his revolver away from the dazed Mahadeb Choudhury, saying, 'Thank you, Mr. Choudhury, please take your seat now. It will then be easier for you to see the final act of this play. Besides, black velvet does suit you. And Mr. William . . .' Feluda's eyes had swerved that way. . . 'With your hair and moustache, you look exactly like your great–grandfather. Will you please be kind enough to take them off?'

As one of the policemen tugged, the wig and false moustache came away from William's face, and to my amazement I saw standing in William's place, Narendra Biswas's brother Girindra Biswas!

'Now, Mr. Biswas' said Feluda, 'tell us your full name.'

'Why, don't you know my name?'

'We now find you have two names. Together, they probably form your full name — isn't that so? William Girindranath Biswas. At least that is what the Presidency College list of gold medal winners says. And your brother's name is given as Michael Narendranath Biswas. Which means that the 'M' on that visiting card stands for Michael, right? It was because both of you preferred to use the Bengali names first that Narendra Babu had ' N.M.' printed on his visiting card, instead of 'M.N.' Am I right?'

Girindra Babu was silent. It was obvious that Feluda was right.

'By what name does your brother call you, Mr. Biswas?'

'Is that any of your business?'

'Very well, if you won't tell us, I will. Will. That's the name your brother uses for you. It was your name he mentioned twice after he regained consciousness in the hospital, wasn't it?'

Now Feluda pulled out a large photograph from the red envelope. 'Just take a look, Girindra Babu. Do you know any of these people? This photograph may not exist even in your house. But Bourne & Shepherd had it.'

The photograph was of a married couple. The kind that's called a wedding group. The resemblance between Girindra and the man in the photograph was astounding. The lady was English.

'Recognise them?' said Feluda. 'This man is Parbaticharan, or P.C. Biswas — your great–grandfather. You can tell by his clothes that he had converted to Christianity. And this lady is Thomas Godwin's granddaughter, the woman who wrote that letter — Victoria Godwin. There's also a photograph of her as an unmarried girl at Bourne & Shepherd. Victoria incurred her grandfather's displeasure by falling in love with a native Christian like your grandfather. But on his deathbed, Tom Godwin forgave Victoria. Within a year of that, Parbaticharan married Victoria. That means that Tom Godwin's name is connected with not one but two families in Calcutta — one in Ripon Lane, the other in New Alipore. And the amazing thing is that each family has in its possession a document that mentions Thomas's watch. Victoria's letter, and Thomas's daughter Charlotte's diary.'

What an extraordinary chain of events! Beats fiction hollow! Apparently a bundle of Victoria's letters had been lying for years in an old trunk in the Biswas house. But nobody had bothered to go through them. When he started digging up material for his articles on old Calcutta, Narendra Babu finally read them. That was how he had come to know about Thomas Godwin's watch and had told his brother about it.

Girindra Babu seemed on the verge of collapse after Feluda's interrogation. But it still was not time to let him off. Feluda asked suddenly, 'Are you in the habit of frequenting the races Mr. Biswas?'

Before he could answer, Mr. Choudhury barked, 'The fellow has taken advances from me and lost it, all at the races. And now he has dug up a Cooke–Kelvey watch from some grave and brought it here. Worthless fool!'

But Feluda paid no attention to Choudhury's outburst. He went on speaking to Girindra Babu.

'So, you've inherited one of the traits of Tom Godwin! And perhaps that's the reason why you took such a risk?'

The answer came sharply.

'I think you are forgetting, Mr. Mitter, that once a hundred years have passed, no particular individual has the right to any object inside a grave. That watch no longer belongs to Tom Godwin.'

'I know that, Mr. Biswas. The watch belongs to the government. It's not yours either. But the point is, that your crime does not stop with the theft of a watch. There's something else.'

'What crime?' Girindra Biswas was still staring pugnaciously at Feluda.

Feluda now took a tiny object out of his pocket.

'Let's see if this button really fell off your jacket — the one you brought back the other day from the Hong Kong laundry.'

Feluda went forward with the button.

'Look, it matches.'

'So what does that prove?' asked Girindra Babu. 'It fell off in that graveyard. I am not denying I went there.'

'And what if I say this is not your jacket, but your brother's — will you admit that?'

'What are you babbling about?'

'I'm not the one who's babbling, Mr. Biswas. It's you. You did that when you came to my house yesterday. And you are doing it now. This jacket belongs to your brother. This is what he was wearing on the day of the storm. He went to the cemetery and found Godwin's grave being dug up and you present. He tried to stop you. And you hit him on the head — with a stick or something. Narendra Babu lost his senses. You would probably have killed him, but for that sudden storm. You started running. A tree falling . . .'

'So you think my brother is a liar! He himself said that a branch from a tree hit him on the head. . .'

But it was not going to be easy to sidetrack Feluda, He went on — 'The branch broke off and fell on your back. You were not wearing a jacket that day. So, to hide your injuries, you took off your brother's jacket and put it on. One of the buttons tore off, and the wallet fell out of the pocket. From your own pocket the racing book . . .'

Girindra Babu tried to escape one more time, but did not

succeed. This time it was Feluda who grabbed him, tore off his jacket and showed us the bandage underneath the thin shirt.

'Your brother told many lies just to save you, Girindra Babu, because he was very, very fond of you.'

Feluda now put the Cooke–Kelvey watch and Victoria's letter inside his satchel, slung the satchel on his shoulder, and turned to the bemused Mr. Choudhury saying, 'I did not have the chance to hear what it sounds like when all your clocks chime in unison. But maybe someday I will.'

Jatayu needed to be called three times before he woke up. I had not realised till now that he had passed out again and had missed the real climax of the play.

'It's just not possible tò control such people, Topshe. Even the police can't do a thing. People like Mahadeb Choudhury are like Hitler. There's no counting the number of people they can buy off to serve their own purposes.'

The three of us were sitting on the steps leading to the Ganga at Panihati. It was about a five–minute walk from Choudhury's house. The eastern sky looked like the sun was due to rise any minute now. It is hard to say what would have happened to us if Haripada Babu had not followed his instructions to the letter. (We'd have been dumped in the river, said Lalmohan Babu.) What impressed me was the resourcefulness of the man who could follow us all the way here and inform the police. Lalmohan Babu took a sip from the cup of tea Haripada Babu had brought, and said, 'Hope you will now concede the advantages of owning a car?'

'Absolutely,' said Feluda. 'We've made excessive demands on your car over the last three days. Once we are back in town today, and I have visited two places, I promise not to make any demands for quite a few days.'

'Which two places?'

'One is Narendra Babu's house. We should tell him the whole story and return this letter to him.'

'And the second?'

'The South Park Street cemetery.'

'A — again?'

'Have you any idea how carefully I have had to walk, Topshe? That was why I could not give those men a real fight.'

Feluda took off the hunting boot on his left foot, inserted his hand within and took out the false sole he had contrived himself. Below that was a compartment in which, wrapped in cotton wool, lay an amazing object which, apart from its glass, had survived perfectly the rough and tumble of the night.

'Must return this to its rightful place, mustn't I?'

Suspended from Feluda's hand was the very first reward given by the Nawab of Lucknow, Sadat Ali, to Thomas Godwin, for his cooking — the repeater pocket watch crafted by one of the best watchmakers of England, Francis Perigal — a watch which even after two hundred years underground, was still capable of dazzling us with its beauty in the first light of the rising sun.

MORE ABOUT PENGUINS

For further information about books available from Penguins in India write to Penguin Books (India) Ltd, B4/246, Safdarjung Enclave, New Delhi 110 029.

In the UK: For a complete list of books available from Penguins in the United Kingdom write to Dept. EP, Penguin Books Ltd, Harmondsworth, Middlesex UB7 0DA.

In the U.S.A.: For a complete list of books available from Penguins in the United States write to Dept. DG, Penguin Books, 299 Murray Hill Parkway, East Rutherford, New Jersey 07073.

In Canada: For a complete list of books available from Penguins in Canada write to Penguin Books Canada Ltd, 2801 John Street, Markham, Ontario L3R 1B4.

In Australia: For a complete list of books available from Penguins in Australia write to the Marketing Department, Penguin Books Australia Ltd, P.O. Box 257, Ringwood, Victoria 3134.

In New Zealand: For a complete list of books available from Penguins in New Zealand write to the Marketing Department, Penguin Books (N.Z.) Ltd, Private Bag, Takapuna, Auckland 9.

A WRITER'S NIGHTMARE
R.K. Narayan

R.K. Narayan, perhaps India's best-known living writer, is better known as a novelist but his essays are as delightful and enchanting as his stories and novels. *A Writer's Nightmare* includes essays on subjects as diverse as weddings, higher mathematics, South Indian coffee, umbrellas, monkeys, the caste system—all sorts of topics, simple and not so simple, which reveal the very essence of India.

'(A book) to be dipped into and savoured'
— *Sunday*

THE DEVIL'S WIND: NANA
SAHEB'S STORY
Manohar Malgonkar

Nana Saheb was arguably India's greatest hero in the country's early battles against the British. This novel, by one of India's finest writers, brings alive the sequence of events that led the adopted son of the Maratha Peshwa Bajirao II to take on the British in the Great Revolt of 1857.

'A fascinating novel'—*The Sunday Times*

'A tragic and tremendous story'—*Pearl S. Buck*

'(Malgonkar writes) compellingly'—*Paul Scott*

A DEATH IN DELHI :
Modern Hindi Short Stories
Translated & Edited by
Gordon C. Roadarmel

A collection of brilliant new stories from the
writers who have revolutionized Hindi liter-
ature over the past forty years. The short
stories in this volume take up from where
Premchand (the greatest writer Hindi has
ever produced) and his immediate succes-
sors left off and offer the reader an excellent
and entertaining introduction to the diversi-
ty and richness that the modern short story
at its best can offer. Among the writers
represented are Nirmal Verma, Krishna
Baldev Vaid, Shekhar Joshi Phanishwar-
nath 'Renu', Gyanranjan and Mohan
Rakesh.

'By far the best collection of recent Hindi
short stories to have appeared in English'.
—*David Rubin*